ASSASSIN'S EDGE

BOOKS BY WARD LARSEN

The Perfect Assassin
Assassin's Game★
Assassin's Silence★
Assassin's Code★
Assassin's Run★
Assassin's Revenge★
Cutting Edge★
Assassin's Strike★
Assassin's Dawn★
Assassin's Edge★

★Published by Forge Books

ASSASSIN'S EDGE

WARD LARSEN

A TOM DOHERTY ASSOCIATES BOOK
New York

This is a work of fiction. All of the characters, organizations, and events portrayed in this novel are either products of the author's imagination or are used fictitiously.

ASSASSIN'S EDGE

Copyright © 2022 by Ward Larsen

A Forge Book
Published by Tom Doherty Associates
120 Broadway
New York, NY 10271

www.tor-forge.com

Forge® is a registered trademark of Macmillan Publishing Group, LLC.

The Library of Congress Cataloging-in-Publication Data is available upon request.

ISBN 978-1-250-79817-6 (hardcover)
ISBN 978-1-250-79818-3 (ebook)

Our books may be purchased in bulk for promotional, educational, or business use. Please contact your local bookseller or the Macmillan Corporate and Premium Sales Department at 1-800-221-7945, extension 5442, or by email at MacmillanSpecialMarkets@macmillan.com.

First Edition: 2022

Printed in the United States of America

0 9 8 7 6 5 4 3 2 1

To the memory of David Hagberg.
Author, patriot, friend.

ASSASSIN'S EDGE

ONE

On appearances, the two events could not have been more disconnected. In reality, they could not have been more intimately entwined.

Raven 44 cut smoothly through thin air, floating effortlessly in one of the earth's most hostile environments: the lonely sky above seventy degrees north latitude. As the big RC-135 skirted the northern border of Russia, the air outside registered sixty degrees below zero. At that temperature water goes instantly to ice, and fuel in the wings must be constantly heated. The jet's cabin, of course, was warm and dry, aeronautical engineers having long ago conquered such environmental adversities.

Other threats, however, were far less foreseeable.

"I've got an intermittent strobe bearing three-four-zero," announced Staff Sergeant Kyle Trask over the intercom. He was one of seven airborne systems operators manning workstations in the airplane's tunnel-like cabin.

"From the north, not landside?" asked Major Tom Meadows, the mission commander who oversaw the sensor suites.

"North," confirmed Trask. "Looks like it's coming from 401. Really high power, broad spectrum, comes and goes . . . haven't seen anything like it before."

The major rose from his own console, fighting stiffness from the long mission, and went to stand behind Trask. He studied the sergeant's display, which was a composite map of the surrounding area: a terrain relief of glacial coastline that hadn't changed in a million years, overlaid by airspace boundaries that hadn't existed when his grandfather was born. To Raven 44's left was the northern coast of Russia, the ice-rimmed frontier where the wilderness of Siberia met the Arctic Ocean. On the starboard side there were no land masses whatsoever, only sea and ice all the way to the North Pole. Thirty miles ahead, however, Meadows saw dashed lines representing restricted-use airspace. Aptly named Danger Area 401, it was a twelve-hundred-mile-long corridor that encompassed all the airspace from the sea's surface to outer space. DA 401 was used, on rare occasions, by the Russian military to conduct missile tests.

"Is it hot now?" Meadows asked.

"It is, sir. Went active a few hours ago."

"This is the first time I've seen it go live."

"I have a couple of times," Trask replied, "but it's pretty unusual." He had been running the northern surveillance tracks longer than Meadows.

DA 401 was exceptionally large, stretching hundreds of miles out to sea, and so it was rarely activated—doing so impinged on highly lucrative commercial airline overflights. Yet both men knew an advisory had been issued days earlier announcing its impending use. Indeed, this was probably why their mission had been moved up twelve hours: headquarters wanted to see what the Russians were up to.

Raven 44 was an RC-135W, a highly modified version of the venerable KC-135 tanker. The type had been in service with the Air Force since the dawn of the Cold War, and this particular jet had rolled off the production line in 1964—making it twenty years older than its oldest crewmember. Yet if the airframe was dated, its instrumentation was not. The jet had undergone extensive modifications ten years earlier to become the cutting edge platform known as Rivet Joint, and now the adopted child of the defunct Strategic Air Command was lurking along the borders of the old Soviet Union much as it always had.

Rivet Joint aircraft had a very specific mission: they trolled along the edges of hostile airspace—places like Russia, China, North Korea, and Iran—in the hope of capturing scraps of electronic intelligence, or ELINT. Radar emissions, telemetry data, communications intercepts. All were fair game, collected passively and recorded for later analysis. It wasn't as swashbuckling as dogfighting in fifth generation fighters, but in the bigger scheme of things the mission was no less vital to national security. And the intelligence gleaned made the F-22s and F-35s that much more lethal.

The crew was weary. It had been four hours since the last aerial refueling, twelve since they'd taken off from their home drome: Kadena Air Base in Japan. Long missions were typical for Rivet Joints, augmented crews standard. The coffeepots got a workout, as did the bunks in the rest area. Even so, with the crew nearing its second shift change, everyone was in circadian arrhythmia, their senses dull and caffeine no longer bridging the gap.

"What spectrum are we talking about?" Meadows asked, trying to ID the raw-data signal.

"S-band, roughly three gigahertz, but it's not in the library. Looks like they're painting us, although that's not unusual."

Meadows weighed how to handle it, and only one thing came to mind. He flicked a switch on his intercom and called the flight deck.

The chime on the intercom didn't exactly wake the aircraft commander, but it recaptured his thoughts, which had drifted to the barbeque he'd been planning for the weekend. Captain Bryan Crossfield tapped a switch to make the connection. "What's up?"

"Hey, Bryan," Meadows said from in back. "We're coming up on Area 401. Just wanted to make sure you were planning on staying clear?"

"Yeah, this course should keep us a good ten miles south of the active sector. Why?"

"We're getting some solid S-band from one o'clock. The library doesn't recognize the signal."

"Okay, thanks for the heads-up. We'll stay clear." Crossfield flicked off the intercom and addressed his copilot. "Sounds like they're testing a new one."

"Guess that's why we're here," said Lieutenant Rico Huerta as he gazed out the window on the right.

"How far to the end of our track?"

Huerta checked the flight management screen. "Nine minutes."

"Let's extend it." This was standard procedure. The Rivet Joint airframe was not ambidextrous—if they turned back east, the twenty-foot-long side-scan antenna on her starboard hip would no longer have a view of the test range. Unknown signals were always worth watching.

"We can't go more than about forty extra miles," said Huerta. "We're due at the last refueling track in less than an hour, and that's three hundred miles behind us."

"Fair enough. Let's just give them what we can so that—" Crossfield's words cut off abruptly.

"What?" the copilot asked, sensing his skipper's unease.

"Did you feel that?"

"No, what?"

"Like . . . I don't know, maybe a vibration."

"No, I—"

This time there was no mistaking it. Crossfield's hands instinctively seized the control column as the great airplane shuddered. Amber warnings lit on the main display, and then the ominous vibration seemed to stop.

"Fault on the weather radar and Sat-Com 2," said Huerta.

"That's the least of our worries. Maybe we picked up some ice on the engine fan blades when—"

A great *crack* stunned both pilots, and in a flash the side window near Huerta's shoulder spider-webbed, then failed. The decompression was explosive, rocking the airplane from nose to tail. All hell broke loose on the flight deck; the humid inside air crystallized to an icy fog, and papers and Styrofoam coffee cups flew through the breach. The cabin altitude, which had been at eight thousand feet, spiked to thirty-five thousand in seconds.

"*Masks!*" Crossfield shouted, reaching for his oxygen. He donned his O2 mask amid a riot of audible warnings and red lights. The autopilot kicked off, and the airplane began rolling into a dive—not a bad thing given their situation. "We need to get down to ten thousand feet!" he yelled as he pushed the control column forward.

The noise was overwhelming, and having removed his headset to put the oxygen mask on, Crossfield couldn't hear the intercom. What he did hear was shouting from the cabin behind. He glanced right and to his horror saw his copilot rag-dolling against the failed side window. There was blood on his face and he was clearly unconscious.

Crossfield shouted for help, but doubted anyone in back could hear him. He began running through the procedure for an emergency descent—a maximum speed dive to a lower altitude where supplemental oxygen would no longer be needed. With the nose continuing to drop, he tried to right the airplane, but found the controls sluggish. In the back of his mind he recalled one exception to the emergency descent procedure: if structural damage was suspected, a high-speed dive was ruled out.

Another great shudder from the airplane, like nothing he'd ever experienced. The jet seemed disconnected from his inputs, like a train no longer on the tracks. He fought the yoke desperately as the nose continued to bury. Rolling past ninety degrees—one wing pointed at the sea, the other toward the sky—the airspeed neared the redline. Just like that, the depressurization emergency became secondary to what was always priority one: *maintain aircraft control.*

Crossfield hit the stops on the control column, but the airplane kept rolling. Approaching an inverted attitude, but still flying, the airplane emitted a terrible groan. The controls went suddenly light in his grasp, as if the great beast was hesitating. In a near vertical dive now, the windscreen filled with sea—still miles away, but closing in fast. Crossfield's instincts told him—rightly, as it turned out—that the jet *had* suffered damage.

The airspeed was approaching Mach 1—never a good place to be in a sixty-year-old airframe that wasn't designed to go supersonic. For a moment his inputs seemed to find purchase, the flight controls beginning to respond. Then a second explosion, more disastrous than the first, sent everything tumbling.

Crossfield was thrown to the left, his lap belt the only thing keeping him from slamming against the side window. Whatever had happened, he knew it was catastrophic. They were screwed, falling out of the sky a thousand miles from nowhere. Amid the Christmas tree of warning lights on the panels in front of him, he picked out the hydraulic pressure gauges. All were pegged to zero. It meant he had no flight controls, along with a damaged airframe and an incapacitated copilot. With g-forces pinballing him around the cockpit, Crossfield did the only thing he could do—he kept fighting the listless controls and prayed for an idea . . . *any* idea.

Despite all his training, all his years of experience, nothing came to mind as the ice-clad Arctic Ocean filled the front windscreen.

TWO

The second critical event took place two thousand miles away. It involved not one of the world's most technologically advanced aircraft, but rather a melon stall in a market in Almaty, Kazakhstan.

In the stirring early morning, a slim young woman laced her way through the crowd. She was strikingly attractive yet had gone to great lengths to hide it. Her dress was long and shapeless, and a scarf cloaked her luminous raven hair. Her most arresting feature, a pair of olive eyes set above high cheek bones, was lost behind a pair of cheap sunglasses. Her ethnicity was vague, although in Kazakhstan such labels were often elusive. The country had long been a crossroads, a place where East met West, where traders intersected and gene pools mingled. While Asian features prevailed, faces bearing Slavic and Mediterranean traits were quite common. The dominant language was Russian, and the young woman spoke it with a local accent. This was no less than a tribute to her tenacity—when she'd arrived here, slightly over a year ago from warmer environs to the west, her Russian had been of the serviceable kind learned in a classroom. As with so much in her twenty-four years, the woman, whose name was Ayla, had set her mind to improving.

The market was active under a crisp blue sky, a chill rain having kept the crowds away in recent days. Ayla had been here twice before, on both occasions to prepare for today. This morning she ran a more intricate surveillance detection route than on her other visits, like an athlete warming up for a big game.

The agent had insisted she come alone. Ayla didn't like that part, yet there was little she could do about it—communications had been a one-way affair. It had all begun two weeks ago when a street urchin handed a message to a guard at the entrance of the Israeli embassy in Nur-Sultan. It was a suspicious contact by any measure, and made even more so by one particular demand: a request that the assigned case officer be female. Ayla was the only Mossad *katsa* in Kazakhstan fitting that description, and since the source seemed dubious to begin with, it landed on her desk with all the import of a discarded gum wrapper.

She'd followed the directions to a seemingly innocuous Gmail account, and there, deposited in a draft folder and left unsent, were instructions for a dead-drop pickup. As tradecraft went, the draft folder ploy was old school and marginally secure. Skeptical but intrigued, Ayla got approval from her supervisor to make the retrieval, and the next day, behind a loose brick in a churchyard wall, she found one USB memory stick. Back at the embassy she tried to see what was on it but was stymied by the stick's security. Sensing a dead end, she sent it via secure courier to headquarters and heard nothing for five days.

Finally, she was called in by her supervisor, who briefed her on the situation: the source, who'd begun as little more than a curiosity, had provided highly valuable information. After a second dead drop, Ayla got a call from a deputy director in Tel Aviv, whose instructions had been unequivocal: *We like what he's giving us. Do whatever is necessary to keep the flow going. This source will want something from us eventually. Until then, do nothing to compromise our good fortune.*

Despite her short time in the field, Ayla had already developed a distaste for directives from the soft-bottomed chairs of Glilot Junction. She also knew a great deal about Mossad's history, and understood that its greatest successes had come from risk-taking. *And anyway, I'm the one putting my rookie ass on the line.* Perhaps it was raw enthusiasm, being new to the game, or maybe the bulletproof assuredness of youth. Even more likely: the inherited obstinance of her father was taking hold. Whatever the reason, Ayla made up her mind. *I'm going to do whatever it takes to get eyes on this source.*

And what it took that morning, apparently, was a visit to a melon stall in Almaty.

The marketplace was open air, row after row of vendor stalls: fresh produce, dried meat, bread, spices. Those who couldn't afford rent set up on blankets in shaded corners. The traffic lanes that connected it all were thick with people—thick enough to make countersurveillance all but impossible. The previous dead drops had been in far quieter places—the first in a church courtyard on a rain-sodden Tuesday, the second on a walking path in the foothills of the Ile-Alatau Mountains. Both retrievals had gone flawlessly.

But this . . .

Instructions for today's rendezvous had been included on the second stick. At nine a.m. she was to go to a melon cart near a certain power pole, and the next memory device would be in the bottom of the back right-hand bin. Clearly, at some point before that, either the source, or possibly a courier, would arrive to make the drop.

Ayla was determined to see who it was.

She had arrived two hours early, just in time to watch the vendor in question, a weathered old man with a wrinkled forehead and gray beard, lift his crates onto an empty table. From a distance Ayla watched closely, rotating between vantage points she'd scouted the day before. So far, she'd seen nothing suspicious: a few customers who seemed typical, no one loitering near the corner bin, nothing but cash and coin going openly to the vendor. Mossad had already identified the merchant, a testament to the importance of what they'd been receiving. A team from the embassy, at

Mukhtar Auezov Street 8, had followed him for two days. Another had mined government records. Neither found anything to suggest he might be complicit. No revolutionary leanings, no connections to police or organized crime. No visits to other embassies. He was simply a sixty-four-year-old Kazakh who, by all accounts, had been hauling produce to the market for the better part of thirty years.

Concealed beneath the shadow of a tarp, Ayla checked the time. Five minutes to go.

The crowds were getting thicker. A young boy hawking prepaid phone cards darted from stall to stall like a hummingbird on espresso. The flower cart beside her was run by two querulous old women, and they were too engrossed in their harping to pay her any heed. Just to be sure, Ayla mimicked thumb-tapping her phone as if in a heated texting session, the pleasant scents of their roses and hyacinths going unappreciated.

From her staging point she had a clear view of the old man and his table a hundred feet away. At two minutes before nine, Ayla relented. She had seen no evidence whatsoever of a drop.

She set out at a metered pace, pausing occasionally to survey the area. When she arrived right on time, she was the only customer at the stall.

"Do you have sweet melons today?" she asked, because to say nothing would have been odd.

"These are the best," the old man replied, gesturing near where Ayla wanted to go.

She briefly held the old man's gaze, searching for recognition. Seeing nothing, she smiled and ran her long fingers over his fare. She squeezed a few, as she'd seen other women do, checking their softness or texture or whatever. The old Kazakh turned away as she reached the critical bin. She half lifted a melon as if testing its weight, then lowered it and let her fingers probe. She felt nothing. Ayla didn't panic. She tested a second melon, went through the same drill. Still nothing. This was a contingency she'd thought through ahead of time. She would search the other bins, but that would take time. Which meant getting the merchant on her side.

"I'll take this one to begin," she said, setting a melon aside without negotiating the price. She glanced at him, expecting a smile—and that was when everything went wrong.

The man seemed suddenly wary.

Feeling the first stab of caution, Ayla said, "Do you have any—"

"No," he said cutting her off. He put the melon she'd chosen back in a bin. "There is nothing here for you!" A harsh, clipped tone.

For this Ayla had no contingency, so she did the most natural thing that came to mind. She picked up an orange and turned it in the sun. She saw the man's eyes snag on something behind her. As much as she wanted to turn, Ayla kept her cool. She set down the orange, turned left, and walked away calmly. Steady and unhurried. In her peripheral vision she discerned two heavy shadows ten paces behind her.

She willed herself to ignore them.

Ayla had come to the market alone—the source was adamant about that—yet she wasn't without backup. Two members of her team were waiting in a car on a nearby street. She made a right turn, which took her in that direction. Ayla ventured a quick glance behind and saw them: two men, casually dressed and definitely following her.

Her support detail was two blocks away. They'd discussed setting up closer, but the chief of station had overruled it—he didn't want to risk irritating the source. It was clearly a mistake. Outside the market, Ayla picked up her pace on a charmless cobblestone sidewalk. Not running, but damn near it.

There were fewer people here, and Ayla realized she should have stayed in the market, let the team come to her. *Another mistake.* She pulled out her phone and discovered how hard it was to text while walking fast over cobblestones. She got off a one-word message: Aborting.

With the situation degrading quickly, Ayla tried to think clearly. She scanned ahead for options. A storefront fifty feet away had its door blocked open. Was there a back door if she turned inside? Perhaps an alley behind that would take her in the right direction? She should have known. The footsteps behind her quickened, and out of nowhere a sedan bounded over the curb ahead and cut her off.

No more pretenses.

She stopped and turned, saw the two men closing in. They looked at her with glares meant to intimidate. The one in the lead towered six inches above her own five-foot-seven frame and had to be twice her well-conditioned weight. The other was smaller and squat, a pugilist's face.

Ayla kept her composure, kept searching. To her right she noticed a damaged section of sidewalk near the gutter, and she was suddenly very glad she'd taken her Krav Maga training seriously.

As the bigger of the two men closed in, she looked at him questioningly, all doe eyes and slack posture. Then, the moment he was in range, she lashed out and kicked him in the balls. She made solid contact, and the man grunted and dropped to his knees, his hands cradling his crotch.

Ayla pretended to stumble to her right, dropping a hand as if to arrest her fall. As she did, she picked up the only improvised weapon within reach, a loose cobblestone the size of a beer stein. The second man rushed full force. Ayla feinted right, then moved left and spun, swinging the stone toward his head in a wicked forehand arc. It caught him a glancing blow and he reeled toward the car. But it was only half a victory. On contact she lost her grip on the stone, and the pugilist seized a handful of her dress—never the clothing of choice for close-quarters combat. It put Ayla off-balance, and together they careened into the car's fender.

Ayla was first to regain her balance, and she lashed out with a solid kick to his knee. He screamed as it buckled and started to go down, but he never lost the fistful of fabric. Ayla heard a car door open behind her, and before she could turn something hard struck her in the head.

She lurched away, dazed. Her vision went blurry and she felt her arms being seized on either side. She tried to swing an elbow, making marginal contact before a fist struck her on the temple. She thrashed and writhed, trying to twist her limbs free. Trying to fight. It was hopeless. There were too many of them—three, four?—all bigger and stronger.

Still, she never gave up, and it took another thirty seconds for them to wrestle her into the car's backseat. Once inside they pummeled her without mercy, her face and her body, and she was sure she broke a nose in return. They cursed in a language she didn't recognize. A massive blow to the head stunned Ayla, and the next thing she knew she was hopelessly immobilized on the floor, big hands and boots holding her down.

To her credit, she kept gathering information, all the way to the moment when the needle sank deep into her thigh. Only then, finally, did fear take its grip.

There were but a handful of witnesses to the donnybrook on the curb. A mailman down the street saw the end of the scuffle, and a nearsighted spinster knitting at the window of her second-floor flat caught a few flashes of motion. A teenager on his way to a music lesson saw the car bump onto the curb and watched a woman get accosted, but organized crime being what it was in Almaty, the boy instinctively turned and ran away with his violin clutched to his chest.

Only one person saw the row in its entirety.

He was sitting in a mostly empty coffee shop, across the street and on a slight diagonal. Dressed in simple work pants and a worn jacket, he was rooted to a stool at the window-side counter. A small tablet computer was in front of him, a lukewarm café Americano near his left hand—he'd been born right-handed, but an injury had forced him to adjust. Once a robust man, lean and athletic, he sat crookedly on the stool with one leg askew. He was thirty-eight years old, although on first impression most gave him ten more. The lines in his leathered face were deeper than they should have been, and flecks of white in his thinning hair were well ahead of schedule. His most remarkable feature was a pair of emerald-green eyes, although these, too, were faded beyond his years. At that moment, they were obscured by a pair of wire-frame glasses.

He'd spotted the woman as soon as she turned out of the market, two burly men trailing behind her like loosely joined boxcars. He had seen her before, but never this close, and even from across the street he was struck by how pretty she was. He had once appreciated beautiful women, even pursued them. That, however, was a thing of the past.

The car came out of nowhere, and he watched it veer onto the curb and cut her off. The girl's reaction was perfectly natural. He sat transfixed by the violence taking place not thirty meters away and was impressed—and not completely surprised—by the fight she put up. He glanced once around the nearly empty coffee shop to see if anyone else was watching. There were only three others, including the nose-studded barista, and none of them were in a position to see the melee.

He held his coffee and sat still, mesmerized, while the altercation played out in what seemed like slow motion. In fact, it was over in less than a minute. When the car finally backed into the street and spun away in a squeal of burning rubber, the man let go a long breath, no idea how long he'd been holding it.

He knew he had to leave—remaining here would be inordinately risky. He needed to get across town, to the safety of his room. If the police arrived quickly, he might be questioned, even compromised. Still, he had wanted to get one look at her: the woman who was risking her life for his information.

And so he had.

The agent, who Mossad now knew as Lazarus, never tried to call the police. Ten minutes earlier, he'd composed a hasty message and placed it in the draft folder. It was a warning that the drop had been compromised. Now, of course, the point was moot, and anyway, they never could have reacted quickly enough. Still, they would at least know he'd tried.

He folded the tablet closed, drained his cup, and slid carefully off his stool. On the sidewalk outside he turned left and set out at his usual slow pace into the chill morning. He walked with a distinct limp—the cold weather worsened the pain in his right hip. Lazarus looked up and down the street, listened for approaching sirens. So far, nothing. The poor woman, his primary link to Mossad, was probably a mile away by now. Swept up cleanly and professionally. He was sure Mossad would find a replacement—the information he'd been providing was first-rate. Teams of case officers would follow up, discover his too-late warning in the email account, and watch for new messages.

He was mentally composing the next one—he had no shortage of information to give—when the first sirens began rising in the distance. Lazarus tried to quicken his pace, but his hip protested. He cursed under his breath.

With one look over his shoulder, he turned left at the first corner and disappeared.

THREE

Reaction to the two events ran distant parallels.

The loss of Raven 44 launched through the power corridors of Washington, D.C., like an unguided rocket. It lit off at the Pentagon, shot toward the director of national intelligence, and apexed in the Oval Office.

President Elayne Cleveland was pulled from her morning intelligence briefing to be apprised of the fast-moving situation. The messengers were Secretary of Defense John Mattingly and Air Force deputy chief of staff for intelligence, surveillance, and reconnaissance, Lieutenant General Margaret Tran. After the doors were closed, the SecDef took the lead.

"One of our Rivet Joint aircraft has gone down in the Arctic, very near the Russian border. It was conducting a standard surveillance mission last night when it disappeared suddenly."

"Suddenly?" the president remarked. "Does that imply a hostile act?" Having long ago served as an intel officer in the Army Reserves, Cleveland was better versed than most politicians in the nuances of military vernacular.

"Based on what we know so far, it doesn't look that way. We were able to layer data from certain air and space sensors, and there's nothing to suggest a missile launch or an intercept by fighters. Rivet Joint aircraft also stream live sensor information over the course of their missions. Raven 44—that was the mishap airplane's call sign—was picking up some radar activity, but nothing high rate to suggest missile guidance."

"Well, that's good at least. What else do we know?"

"We're in the initial stages of planning a search, but the extremely remote location, combined with the impending weather conditions—there's a fierce Arctic storm on the way—will tie our hands for the next thirty-six to forty-eight hours."

"What about the Russians? Could they help with a search?"

The SecDef's answer was measured. "That is something we need to discuss." He yielded to Tran, a three-star general who'd risen through the Air Force's technical side—an outlier in the pilot-dominated upper ranks of the service. Tran had a PhD in engineering and a proven knack for translating technical breakthroughs to strategic implementation.

"Madam President, our intelligence networks are in overdrive trying to determine if the Russians have even noticed this crash. Based on radio traffic and communications intercepts, we see no sign of it. I will tell you straightaway that the fate of the crew, seventeen good airmen, remains foremost in everyone's mind."

"As it should be," the president seconded.

"Unfortunately, the initial reports are not promising. Our Rivet Joints have been upgraded with a system that streams snapshots of flight information in near real time. What it shows, unfortunately, is a dive that could not have been survivable. Because the RC-135 is a standoff platform, not meant to go behind enemy lines, it's not fitted with ejection seats or parachutes."

The president looked on grimly. "Are you telling me there's no chance of survivors?"

"I can't say that with absolute certainty. Yet there is further damning information. Two years ago, NSA began a program to pry into Russian air defense networks. They were surprisingly successful, and the northern-tier facilities proved especially vulnerable due to undersea cables that proved . . . accessible."

This was news to Cleveland. She tried to recall if it had been in any of her daily briefings but drew a blank. "You're saying we've hacked Russian air defense?"

"Not everywhere, but we get solid information from certain regional networks. Relating to Raven 44, NSA has forwarded their data for the last twenty-four hours. A radar station in Kotelny had a solid primary return on Raven 44. It documented her final plunge."

"Primary return?"

"That's the most basic kind of radar data, with no identifying information. The Russian operators would have seen Raven 44 as a blip on their scope. We fly surveillance routes regularly, and there's airline traffic as well, so they probably weren't watching too closely. If anyone saw the return disappear, they likely would have written it off as an anomaly. We studied that raw data closely and found more bad news. In the critical moments near the end, we were able to discern multiple targets. That suggests the aircraft broke apart in flight."

Cleveland looked at Tran, then Mattingly. She was beginning to see the decision she would be facing. "That *does* sound damning. All the same, we prioritize the crew, no matter how slim the chances."

"We agree, ma'am, yet there are complications. To begin, the wreckage we were able to track came to rest near Wrangel Island. That's Russian territory." From a portfolio General Tran extracted a satellite photo of the area. She put her finger on a trapezoid box overlapping a remote island. "We believe parts of the aircraft fell on the island itself, while others may have ended up in the sea nearby."

"Is this island populated?" the president asked.

"Minimally. There's a radar station, manned by a few technicians and a small unit of Russian Army regulars. No more than thirty men altogether, essentially there to keep the radar running. They venture out for occasional patrols in the summer, but this time of year everyone bunkers up. The island is also a designated wildlife preserve, and there's a small research station with three or four rangers in residence. Both these contingents live in prefabricated housing on the south shore of the island, forty miles from where the wreckage landed. Bottom line—unless the Russians realize what's happened, and it doesn't appear they have, nobody is going to stumble across this crash site. At least, not until summer."

Cleveland studied the overhead image. It reminded her of her days as a lieutenant in Army intel. "How certain are you about the location of this wreckage?"

"It's a rough estimate. We received a brief satellite ping from the flight data recorder immediately after the crash, but it disappeared. When an airplane goes down at sea, in deep water, the signal can be tricky to find. The hits we received are here." She pointed to a red dot labeled FDR in the sea near the island's northwest coast. "Plots for the rest of the wreckage field are less certain, mostly derived from the stolen radar data. It's a lot of guesswork, and our analysts are trying to tighten their estimates. We're coordinating some satellite passes that will hopefully give us better information."

"This emergency beacon—can the Russians see it as well?"

"No . . . at least we don't think so. Rivet Joints, owing to their highly classified systems, are equipped with a new black box that transmits discreetly. It was designed for this very situation. We've also been listening to Russian communications and watching nearby military bases for unusual activity. We're pretty sure they don't have any idea what's going on." General Tran looked expectantly at Mattingly.

Cleveland did the same, and said, *Pretty sure?* I'm hearing a lot of qualifiers in this briefing."

"Yes, ma'am, you are. We would be more definitive if we could."

"All right, give me options."

"First and foremost, we have to search for survivors. Unfortunately, our options are limited. We can't ask the Russians for help without admitting that one of our spy aircraft has gone down on their sovereign territory. That would give them first shot at the wreckage, which is a problem—this jet was carrying some highly classified technology."

"Aren't they going to find it eventually?"

"At some point, yes. But if we beat them to it, we can recover or destroy the most sensitive equipment. On the downside, if we try to organize a search ourselves it's going to take longer."

"How long?" the president asked.

"To begin, this time of year there's nearly solid ice coverage in the surrounding sea. The only practical surface ship would be an icebreaker, and we don't have many of those. The nearest right now is a Coast Guard ship operating in Alaskan waters, and she'd have to plow through hundreds of miles of ice—it would take three days to reach the scene. The other option is to use a submarine. One of our fast-attack subs, *New Mexico,* is much closer and she's equipped for the job—she's taking part in our annual

ICEX exercise as we speak. There are also two missile subs in the area, but they would have far less capability to respond. And of course, for national security reasons, we prefer to keep them silent. *New Mexico* could reach the crash site in about a day and a half."

"The weather is also a consideration," Tran added. "This storm is bearing down fast. It's going to shut down any rescue attempt for the next thirty-six hours."

"So even if we asked the Russians for help, they couldn't mount a search any sooner than we could?"

"Effectively, yes. After the storm passes, they would have far better resources for a large-scale response. But in terms of arriving on scene and standing up a search . . . everyone will be limited by the storm."

"If this turns out as we fear," Mattingly added, "and there are no survivors, our priority has to be securing the most sensitive wreckage—recover what we can, and then destroy anything too large or too difficult to retrieve."

Silence prevailed as Cleveland weighed it all. "All right," she finally said. "In that case, let's keep this to ourselves. Order *New Mexico* to respond, and make sure everyone knows that finding the crew is top priority."

Two nods in return.

Mattingly said, "I've also reached out to the CIA. As it turns out, they have a contingency plan for just this kind of scenario—recovering sensitive technology from foreign territory. SAC/SOG is putting together a mission as we speak." He was referring the spy agency's Special Operations Group.

"Anna Sorensen?" Cleveland asked.

"Yes, ma'am."

Had the circumstances been less somber, the president might have smiled. There was no one she'd rather have running such a delicate op than Deputy Director Sorensen. "All right," the president said, "do it. And if anything changes, I want to know right away."

As the U.S. secretary of defense was issuing orders regarding the crash of Raven 44, the more subtle disaster in Almaty worked its way through a large and busy building outside Tel Aviv. The dispatch from Israel's Kazakhstan embassy was quickly routed to Mossad director Raymond Nurin, who had left firm orders to be apprised of all developments involving the important new source known as Lazarus.

Nurin's tenure as head of the Office had been marked by both spectacular successes and stunning failures—the ratio was more or less in line with those of his predecessors, and par for the treacherous local course. Even so, when he was told about the message from Almaty, confessing that Lazarus's case officer had been snatched off the street in broad daylight, the director blinked. After the young man briefing him read the message a second time, confirming the name of the missing woman, Nurin issued an order he had never before given: an emergency, all-agency response.

Mossad's version of DEFCON 1.

On the headquarters end, it threw the agency into electronic searches and a desperate postmortem of a mission gone wrong. The more critical task, however, was getting boots on the ground in Kazakhstan. The embassy station there was minimally staffed, and so the only option was to send in reinforcements. Nurin was hardwired to caution when it came to committing assets on foreign soil—small operational failures had a way of snowballing. The situation in Almaty, however, was untenable. One of their own had been abducted. And that wasn't the worst of it—the matter of *who* the girl was loomed not large but titanic.

He called in his three most trusted advisors, and together they brainstormed a plan to dispatch fifteen operatives, some from Tel Aviv, others from neighboring stations, to aid in the search for the kidnapped case officer. In a moment nearing panic, Nurin told them to double that number, then added two. It would typically take weeks of preparation to insert such a force, but the director wanted it done within forty-eight hours.

That order given, he dismissed the team to put the plan in motion.

Alone behind his desk, Nurin looked at the nearby secure phone as if it were made of white-hot steel. He rehearsed in his mind a series of opening lines, but none seemed right. Some situations were simply beyond compassion. After telling his receptionist he didn't want to be disturbed, Nurin placed one of the most difficult calls he had ever made.

Within twenty-four hours, the two disasters were firmly on a collision course. Perhaps fittingly, they merged on a desolate mountain road near the Montana-Idaho border. A heavy SUV lumbered through thickening stands of pine. Of the three men inside, the two in front were well-armed and alert, the one in back grave-faced and exhausted.

The Land Rover negotiated a series of turns, ending on a private road that did not appear on Google Maps. After the third turn since leaving the highway, the vehicle paused before a broad cattle guard, and from the nearby fence line two men appeared. Both were carrying machine pistols and had earbuds implying a comm network.

After a few words and a close inspection, the Rover was allowed to proceed. The guards immediately blended back into a forest shot with shadows.

FOUR

The first thing Christine heard was the vehicle—the low rumble of a big engine, gravel crunching under wide tires. When one was far removed from civilization, such sounds stood out like fireworks on a clear winter night. She reluctantly put down the book she was reading—the latest investigations of Michael Connelly's Harry Bosch—and was rising from the couch when the secure comm system trilled.

Her alertness notched upward. She went to the kitchen counter and picked up a heavy plastic handset that belonged in a missile silo—she'd been told that was actually where it came from.

"What's up?" she asked, her eyes searching through the front window.

"Good morning, ma'am," replied a familiar voice—Thomas, head of the morning detail. "You have a visitor on the way up."

"A visitor?"

"He's approved."

Christine hesitated. In the last year, since taking up residence on the ranch, there had been only a handful of "approved" visitors. All but one related to the security team itself. The outlier had been Anna Sorensen, head of the CIA's Special Activities Center.

"Can you give me a name?" she asked.

"I actually wasn't told . . . but he was cleared specifically by Miss Sorensen. She said he's an old friend."

"Mine or my husband's?"

"Both."

Well, that narrows it down, she thought.

Hanging up the *Dr. Strangelove* phone, she went through the front door and stepped onto the weathered hardwood porch. Christine was immediately enveloped by fresh mountain air. Spring was a week away, winter losing its grip. The early sun was muted by thick mist, a dim orb behind a blanket of gray. She spotted the SUV a quarter mile away, topping the driveway on the low southern hill. A trail of dust rose behind it like a brown contrail.

The number of "old friends" she and David shared could be counted on one hand. Of those, she could think of only one who might be sent here by Anna Sorensen. Christine, David, and their son had been living on the ranch for a year under deep cover—the CIA's version of a witness protection program. Except the word "witness" didn't fit. Target was more like it.

The SUV pulled directly to the top of the gravel parking apron, and moments after stopping the rear passenger door opened. Christine instantly recognized the man who emerged. Early sixties, heavy build. Features weathered by time and sun, not to mention a life of artful deception.

Her first thought was, *I was right*. Her second—the question of *why* he was here—was far less satisfying. Anton Bloch was the former director of Mossad. He had recruited David into the agency straight out of university, ensnaring him through false pretenses. For ten years, before Christine first crossed paths with the man who would become her husband, Bloch had molded him into Israel's most lethal assassin. For that Christine would never forgive him. Just as she would never forget the moment, years later, when Bloch had taken a bullet to save her own life. It was an impossible contrast—as was so often the case in the world of mist and mirrors.

Watching him walk toward the porch, she thought Bloch looked older, more frail than the last time she'd seen him. How long had it been? Two years? Three?

He climbed the short set of steps and stood before her with the air of a supplicant facing a tribunal. "Hello, Christine."

"Hello, Anton," she replied guardedly. Their relationship was not one of hugs and *la bise,* but mutual respect prevailed.

He looked around the hills appreciatively. "You and your husband have a strong inclination to remoteness."

"We have our reasons . . . as you know better than anyone. I'm afraid David's not here at the moment."

"I know," the spymaster replied in his intractable baritone. "Actually, I was hoping to have a private word with you."

She raised one eyebrow and managed a wary smile. "Why not?"

Christine led Bloch into the house. She made coffee, as much for herself as for her guest. At ten in the morning she'd not yet had her bracer, and she had the distinct feeling she was going to need it.

Bloch stood by the farmhouse table in the dining room, watching her distractedly. She had always known him to be brusque and direct, a consequence, no doubt, of years spent running the Office. Having made countless life-and-death decisions, she'd assumed he was inoculated against doubt. Now, however, Christine saw nothing but hesitation. Even anxiousness. Bloch looked around the room nervously, like a priest in a brothel—a man desperate for distraction.

"Very rustic," he said.

"We like it. It was originally built in '08," she said, leaving the century in doubt. "We've made a few upgrades."

"I can only imagine David's contributions. Let me see: gun safe, safe room, firing range on the back forty? I'm surprised there wasn't a moat around the perimeter."

"Keep that to yourself—you might give him ideas." She handed over a mug of Death Wish coffee, and said, "Let's go out back."

He followed her through the back door onto an expansive terrace. The stonework was exquisitely done, intricate patterns and perfect joints on a split-level base, raised planters and benches around the main sitting area. It was all pleasing to the eye, yet Christine imagined Bloch would recognize more; clear areas, channels, walls near the home entrances. Subtle to be sure, but security was baked into the design. An offshoot at the back edge led to the project under way—a fire pit and sitting area with a view of the distant mountains.

"I see he still pursues his masonry obsession," Bloch said, his eyes panning over the perfectly mortared seams.

"You know David, he never does anything halfway. Sometimes I can't tell if it's a streak of artisanship or an exercise routine."

Bloch should have smiled. Instead, he said somberly, "Where exactly is he?"

She gestured toward the slope of a distant mountain. "Somewhere on the west ridge. He took Davy camping for a few nights. It's their new father-son thing."

He sipped his coffee distractedly.

Christine was getting impatient. "Anton . . . you didn't come here from Tel Aviv to tour our house."

He nearly responded, then faltered.

Christine's worry magnified. She thought herself familiar with Bloch's behaviors and mannerisms; indecision had never been among them.

"There has been an incident in Kazakhstan," he said. "One of our operatives has gone missing."

"When you say 'our' . . . I assume you're referring to Mossad?" Bloch had left the agency years ago, yet he retained a good relationship with his successor. A conspicuously *working* relationship.

The broad shoulders shrugged. "Certain bonds are not so easily severed."

"What does this have to do with David?" This was the loaded question, the one that generally had but one answer. Her husband had served Israel in a number of capacities, yet his specialty was distinctive: he killed people who deserved to be killed, and did it without leaving traces.

"The operative who's been taken was running a very valuable agent. As it turns out, one whose information is of great interest to America. We're desperate to find this missing case officer, and also to discover the identity of her agent."

Christine's eyes narrowed. As a physician, she was something of an expert at reading people under stress. What she saw on Bloch's face, in every crease and shadow, was closer to fear than worry. "I'm guessing Mossad is trying to locate this missing case officer?"

"Of course. But, in my opinion, they're not doing enough."

"What makes you say that?"

"I could tell you the steps they've *not* taken. I could tell you about budget cuts and personnel shortages, about delicate relations with certain involved countries. But the truth is rather more straightforward . . . the case officer who has gone missing is my daughter."

Christine stiffened. "*Ayla?* I didn't know she'd joined the service."

"I assure you, it was not my idea. She barely made it through university, although I'll grant that she has always had a knack for languages. Ayla approached one of my old deputies, the man who now runs recruiting. She said she was interested in a career with the Office and convinced him she had my blessing."

"But she didn't."

He sighed a father's sigh. "And so the deceptions begin. I tried to talk her out of it, but to no avail. Moira wouldn't speak to me for a week." Bloch looked at her with something near vulnerability. "If anything happens to her, my wife will never forgive me. Nor, I suspect, will I forgive myself. I should have seen this coming, should have prevented it."

Christine understood all too well. The previous year she'd found herself in a dire situation with Davy. She knew how it felt to have a child put at risk.

"Ayla and I have had our differences," he hedged. "Yet I must admit, the day she graduated from training . . . never have I felt such pride. If she had done it with my help, that would have been one thing. But to do it against my wishes, excel as she did . . ."

Christine didn't dwell on that thought, fearing an extrapolation to her own family. "Do you really think David can help?" she asked.

"I can think of no one better."

"So you're here for my blessing?"

"Miss Sorensen tells me the three of you have a delicate arrangement. She has provided this place and the attendant security. In return, David provides his services on occasion to her Special Activities Center. And you . . . you are the arbiter between the two. The ultimate approving authority."

"That's not quite the way I see it . . . but yes, David includes me in his decisions."

"Then I am here to ask your help."

"And maybe I owe you because you took a bullet for me?"

"I will be more shameless than that. I ask you as a parent."

It was the perfect answer. That he gave none of the details—where David would be asked to go, what dangers might be involved—was surely by design. Bloch might be tormented, but his instincts for manipulation remained intact. As always, the former director knew which strings to pull and which to leave slack.

"All right," she said. "If David agrees, I'm on board."

Bloch didn't bother with a pretense of surprise, yet when he spoke it was from the heart. "Thank you, Christine."

"I've been in your shoes. I know what it's like to feel that kind of worry. To feel helpless with your child at risk."

He nodded. "Is there a way to reach him?"

"You know David . . ." Christine got up and headed for the basement, the combination to the gun safe looping in her head.

FIVE

David Slaton watched his son turn a trout over the campfire, the long-handled grill basket wavering only slightly. He was getting the hang of it, keeping the filets at just the right height, giving them the occasional turn. The sweet smell was a memory in the making.

"When will it be done, Dad?" Davy asked.

"Almost there, buddy."

"Will it be as good as last night?"

"I hope so. But we can't rush it . . . you have to be patient."

He reached for his backpack, removed the plates and forks. They'd awakened with the sun, but cold morning air kept them in the tent for a time. Two rounds of Go Fish broke out, each of them winning once. After a beef jerky breakfast, they'd carried the fishing poles down the slope to the river, Davy leading the way, and found a perfect glade among the cottonwoods. The riverbanks were edged in frost, the water running fast and sparkling in the morning light. For an interval of time that defied any clock, they talked and watched the forest, and eventually pulled two big brook trout from the crystalline water.

Davy was starting to show an unusual ability to focus on tasks, and he almost never complained—not just any four-year-old would hike miles up a mountainside and spend two nights in near-freezing temperatures. Yesterday had gone by in a blur; gathering firewood, climbing trees, naming squirrels, skipping stones into the frigid river. The only casualty came when Davy slipped while crawling over a fallen tree and tore the pocket off his pants. He seemed to relish it all, and Slaton, in turn, felt a contentment like nothing he'd ever experienced. Watching his son learn, watching him grow.

He looked out across the chained peaks of the Northern Bitterroots. The early mist was fading, only pockets now in the deepest valleys. The view was turning majestic before their very eyes, the long shadows of morning giving way to contours of green and brown. The sun infused the great copper sky, its warmth beginning to cut the cold.

"Are we going home today?" Davy asked.

"I think we should. It's been two nights and Mom might be getting lonely."

"Yeah, I miss her."

"Me too."

"We should bring her next time."

Slaton thought it was a great idea. Better yet, he was glad Davy was already thinking about coming back. "Absolutely. Maybe you should invite her."

His son nodded, then pulled the trout closer and gave it an inspection. "I think it's done."

"Okay. Let's eat."

They split their catch on two plates, divided a can of beans that had been heating on the side. It was every bit as good as last night. They ate in silence watching a pair of hawks soar over a nearby hill, effortless as they rode the updrafts. Slaton pointed out a distant herd of elk grazing in a notch in the adjoining valley. Davy had no trouble picking them out—he'd been blessed with his father's sharp eyesight.

"I think next time we should go farther, maybe set up camp in that valley."

"Will the elk still be there?" Davy asked.

"It's possible, but they usually don't stay in one place for long. They never stop moving."

Davy was about to say something else when the sat-phone in Slaton's backpack chimed. He got up, dug it out, and checked the screen. It was a message from Christine: All is well, but we have a visitor. Need you to come back ASAP.

Slaton stared at the screen. *All is well . . .*

He forced himself to not overthink the situation. "It's a message from Mom. We need to head home."

A slight frown. "All right."

"I'll take down the tent and pack up. I need you to put the fire out . . . do it just like I showed you."

"Okay. But why do we clean up camp?"

The answer that nearly escaped was *So people won't know we've been here.* What he said was straight from Mom's playbook. "Because it's kind to others to leave nature as we found it."

SIX

"You're sure about this," Slaton said, studying his wife closely.

They were seated on one of the benches he'd built beside the patio.

After an hour's hike home, he'd been surprised to find Anton Bloch, of all people, waiting on his front porch. Christine had lured Davy inside with hot chocolate, giving Bloch time to explain the situation. As soon as he'd set eyes on Bloch, Slaton knew something was wrong. He looked weary, fragile—modifiers he'd never before applied to the legendary director. After struggling through greetings, Bloch had gotten right to the point. No sooner had he laid out the disappearance of his daughter than his Mossad-issued phone had gone off, and he'd diverted to the driveway to take an urgent call.

It gave Christine time for a one-on-one to explain her own thinking.

"It's his daughter, David. I've never seen Anton so . . . off his game."

"I agree," he said, watching Davy clamber over the playset he'd built near a pair of wintering Aspen. "But it's strange for you to be pushing me to go on a mission."

When the CIA came asking for his help, Christine generally insisted on a morally supportable case for his involvement. She implied that he committed to missions, at least in part, for the adrenaline rush of high-stakes ops—an "addiction" she'd once called it. Slaton never viewed it that way, but he understood why she might. And he knew better than to argue otherwise.

Today Christine had no reservations. "You and I know what it's like to have a child in danger. Anyway, we owe him. *I* owe him."

"There was a time when I would have argued otherwise . . . but yeah, I get it."

Neither of them could take their eyes off their son as he dangled one-handed from a monkey bar. Davy fell into the mulch, hitting hard. He lay still for a moment, and his parents watched with collective held breath. Like parents did. Davy bounced up and raced back to the ladder.

"Gives you a different perspective, doesn't it?" she said.

"Ayla is his only child. She's an adult now, living her life, making her own decisions—but I guess you never stop worrying about them."

"Anton says time is critical. He has a jet waiting in Missoula."

Slaton blew out a long breath. "Okay, I'll go pack a bag."

When he stood, Christine looked at him pensively. He was sure he knew what she was thinking. He also knew she wouldn't put it into words.

He leaned down and kissed her forehead. "Don't worry, I'll be careful."

Christine watched her husband disappear inside, then closed her eyes. David rarely misread her, but just then he had. *And how could he not?*

She resolved to let it go—for now.

Twenty minutes later the Land Rover was running back toward the main highway. Slaton waited patiently as Bloch finished a string of phone calls.

"There's been a change," Bloch finally said, ending the last call. "Instead of Almaty, we're going in a different direction."

"What direction is that?"

"North . . . Alaska, to begin."

Slaton showed no reaction. He knew missions could change quickly, although during his time with Mossad the detours had been more regional in nature. A car ride to Beirut switching to a trek through the Golan Heights. The idea that a private jet was now going to take him to Alaska instead of Kazakhstan . . . he supposed it was simply a matter of scale. The more practical problem was that he'd packed for the trip quickly; a few pants, shirts, a light jacket. All of it totally inappropriate for late winter in Alaska. Slaton had never been a fan of extreme cold, and he guessed Bloch was even less enthralled—for security reasons, former Mossad directors rarely traveled outside Israel, meaning his desert bones would run deep.

"Can you brief me in?" Slaton asked.

"I'll explain after we're airborne," Bloch replied. "Events are changing rapidly, and your new overseer has become involved."

"Anna Sorensen?"

"Yes."

"The Special Operations Group is going to help find your daughter?"

"There's a good deal more at play. As it turns out, the United States and Israel have found themselves with deeply converging interests." His phone went off again and he took the call.

Slaton went back to waiting, pushing deep into the plush seat. He felt the transition beginning. Campfires and monkey bars were behind him, more consequential challenges ahead. He thought back to his parting with Christine. Something had seemed amiss, although he couldn't say what. He shrugged it off and took one last look back at the fading Bitterroot Mountains. They had become intimately familiar, the meridians of his new life.

Slaton wondered when he would see them again.

The Falcon 900 could only be part of Mossad's hand-me-down air force. Slaton studied it on the brief crossing from the Rover and saw a paint job that was the aviation equivalent of a plain brown wrapper: dirty white, bordering on gray, with no discernable logo. The only identifying marks were those required by international law: a registration number and a tiny flag near the tail that wasn't Israeli. A Cypriot flash, if he wasn't mistaken. He noted extra antennae suggesting satellite communications and an HF radio. It struck him that he was becoming a connoisseur of such conveyances, although never as a matter of mere convenience. For Slaton, jets had become a tactical tool, the best way to take a fight to the enemy when distances were great and time critical. And in the ops he'd been drawing lately, time was *always* critical.

He followed Bloch up a short set of stairs into a cabin that was anything but opulent. Rough galley, serviceable fittings, a dozen seats in a variable configuration. It smelled like a limo after prom night, an image further advanced by a rack of mostly empty liquor bottles near the galley. On a given day, the airplane might deliver a dozen commandos to an overseas raid. On another it could whisk a defense minister to a secret tête-à-tête. And today? Today it was being used by a former director to collect his best assassin.

They were airborne quickly, and as the jet climbed northward through smooth air Bloch set up a laptop on a table between two worn club chairs. He seemed steadier now, back on solid operational ground. No time to dwell on what might be happening to his daughter. Slaton recognized this compartmentalization all too well—as long as you were busy there was no time for reflection. It was the idle moments—breaking for a meal or trying to fall asleep—when the demons of doubt had their way.

Slaton settled back in the wide chair. A tiny air vent overhead spewed cold air, along with a few shards of ice—as if the airplane knew where they were headed.

"I'll begin by explaining why I came for you," Bloch said, "although keep in mind, it was based on the situation as we knew it yesterday. Two years ago, Ayla took it upon herself to enter Mossad's academy. Needless to say, it was not my idea."

"I never knew. When you last mentioned her, you said she was going through a rebellious phase."

"That has been ongoing since she was twelve. School proved a constant challenge. Ayla is a smart girl, but applies herself selectively. Her mother and I battled this attitude for years, and effectively gave up during her third year in university. Curiously, as we pulled back, her performance improved."

Slaton filed this away as a parental lesson for the years ahead.

"Ayla came home the week after graduation from university and informed us of her decision to join Mossad. Moira was apoplectic. I tried to talk her out of it, but she was determined."

"Stubborn, is she? Can't imagine where that came from."

Bloch ignored the comment. "She excelled in training, then spent another six months fine-tuning her skills. After a brief stint in a headquarters planning cell, she took her first assignment in the field—our station in Almaty. She speaks decent Russian, which is a requisite for that posting.

Soon after she arrived, two months ago now, the station received an unsolicited message from a prospective source. On face value it appeared amateurish, the kind of contact bigger embassies get all the time, and that usually amounts to nothing. For unspecified reasons, the source requested a female contact. Ayla was given the assignment. She followed up, and managed to retrieve a memory stick from a dead drop. The information turned out to be quite interesting. It claimed the Russians were preparing to employ a new weapon. There was little technical detail, yet the source was quite specific regarding the target: a strike would occur in the Arctic against one of America's Rivet Joint aircraft."

"The ELINT platform—a modified tanker."

"Correct."

"Did you warn them?"

"We forwarded the message last week through the usual channels. Unfortunately, according to Director Nurin, our original communication implied a measure of skepticism about the reliability of the source."

"So the Americans didn't give it any credence?"

"I wouldn't go that far, but there was a definite lack of urgency. Such warnings can easily become lost in the machine. What is the term they use at the Pentagon? Analysis paralysis?"

Slaton had seen it all too often: a critical shard of intelligence not recognized until it was too late.

Bloch went on, "As this was all running its course, Lazarus—that's what the source calls himself—made a second drop, another memory device. That contained solid information as well, and included instructions for a third delivery. Yesterday Ayla went to make that pickup and something went wrong she was abducted."

"Did she not have backup?"

"There were two others on the team, but they made mistakes. Lazarus instructed Ayla to come alone, so they parked a few blocks away. Everyone was clearly complacent after the first two drops had gone so smoothly. All we know about the abduction is that four men bundled her into a car." Bloch hesitated mightily, then said, "Nurin called to give me the news. He assures me he's doing everything possible to get her back."

"I'm sure he is. Nurin has two daughters, doesn't he?"

Bloch nodded. "Yes, a bit younger, but it does give a frame of reference."

"Do you think Ayla was targeted because she's the daughter of a former director?"

"It would be reckless not to consider the possibility," said a man who was never reckless.

Bloch's angst was coming through again. Slaton imagined the long flight to Montana must have seemed interminable. He surmised, "You couldn't sit home and wait."

"Can you imagine it? Me pacing around the house under Moira's accusing eye, watching the phone for what could be days, weeks . . . a life-time. It's not something I could tolerate."

"So you came to recruit me."

"It seemed the most direct action at my disposal. That was where things stood when I reached your house, but now this series of phone calls has pro-vided some new direction. At virtually the same time Ayla was being ab-ducted, a Rivet Joint aircraft disappeared off the northern coast of Russia."

Slaton straightened slightly in his seat. "So this warning from your agent, Lazarus, turned out to be dead-on."

"Apparently so. I spoke with Miss Sorensen, and she said the Ameri-cans don't yet know what brought the airplane down."

Bloch reached up and steered an air vent toward his face. The unbut-toned collar of his shirt rippled in the microbreeze.

"All right," Slaton said. "What's the near-term plan?"

"Clearly these events are linked. Nurin is sending a small army of op-eratives into Kazakhstan to support a search for Ayla. I had intended to include you in that effort until news came of the downed airplane. After considerable discussion, Miss Sorensen and I agree that the best way to find out who is behind Ayla's abduction, and what their motive is, is to dis-cover what brought this aircraft down. That's where you can do the most good for the moment."

"Do you think the Russians are involved?"

"President Petrov has long been active in Kazakhstan, and he is always boasting about new weapons. Still, he is not a fool. Poking the Americans in the eye like this—it seems exceedingly provocative, even by his stan-dards."

"What's in Alaska?"

"A staging point. The Americans are launching a mission to reach the crash site—it's on an isolated island, Russian territory. The chance of survivors can't be ruled out, and aside from that, they want to recover classified equipment and look for evidence of what brought this airplane down. I would like one person on that mission who knows about Lazarus's involvement."

"What about the Russians? Are they responding?"

"They don't yet seem aware of the crash, but the Americans are watch-ing closely. This expedition is being run by the Special Activities Center—Sorensen will provide details when we arrive."

Slaton nodded. "Sounds like a reasonable approach. Mossad can cover the situation Almaty, but there's a definite link between the two. I think you're right to attack both sides."

"But will it be enough?" Bloch said, his voice near a whisper.

Before Slaton's very eyes, Bloch descended into a tunnel of darkness—one that he himself had visited. The former director diverted his gaze to an oval window rimmed in ice crystals. Bright light streamed in, capturing the strain on his features, highlighting every worry line.

Bloch said, "Minutes before Ayla was taken, Lazarus sent a warning that the meeting was compromised. It was received too late to intervene."

Slaton responded with what needed to be said. "I think we both know what's happened, Anton. Ayla was targeted."

Bloch nodded, and the hollow voice returned. "She is everything to us, David. The idea that she is at risk because of what I once was . . ."

Slaton didn't bother with a *This isn't your fault* speech. Because it was . . . or as much as it could be.

Bloch's head dipped, and his eyes came back inside. "Now you have my confession . . . which proves how disoriented I am right now."

"We'll find her," Slaton said, hoping there was conviction in his words.

SEVEN

The Falcon 900 delivered the former spymaster and his assassin not to the busy Anchorage International Airport, or nearby Joint Base Elmendorf-Richardson, but instead to a less frequented airfield far to the southwest.

Two hundred and fifty miles from Alaska's largest population center, the U.S. Coast Guard's Air Station Kodiak stands fast and alone as if in another world. In the summer months the island is a second-tier tourist destination, catering to hunters and hikers seeking unvarnished Alaska wilderness. In the winter it is something else altogether. Wind howls in from the Bering Sea with unchecked ferocity, and the residents who don't snowbird south are forced to bunker up in thick-walled homes. The only part of the island that keeps to business as usual are the resident military facilities.

The tri-jet taxied to a quiet corner of the airfield and its engines spun down wearily. Through an oval side window Slaton saw a ramp full of Coast Guard aircraft: mostly C-130s and helicopters. A small passenger terminal shivered in the distance, snowbound and hollow as if hibernating for the season.

One of the pilots came back to the cabin, opened the entry door, and then immediately retreated to the cockpit. There was no friendly flight attendant to issue "Buh-byes," so Slaton led the way. He shrugged on his light jacket—it still smelled like a campfire—stepped outside, and was immediately smacked in the face by an Alaskan winter. The wind blew snow across the tarmac in undulating ribbons, mocking the clear late afternoon sky. His jacket felt paper-thin against a temperature that had to be in the teens.

A Toyota Land Cruiser with snow tires sat parked nearby, lights on and engine running. Even though Slaton was the first to deplane, Bloch, whose jacket was even lighter, beat him to the SUV. They bundled inside in a flurry of snow and exhaled vapor.

The Toyota's only occupant was in the driver's seat, a thirtysomething man wearing camo fatigues and a parka. His broad grin was nearly lost in a mutinous blond beard, and his crinkled blue eyes were framed by long dishwater hair. His uniform, if that's what it was, bore no insignia of any kind.

"Welcome to paradise!" said their host. "I'm Dave Killian—most call me Tracer. I'll be your guide during your stay at Ice Station Zebra."

Slaton and Bloch introduced themselves, deliberately avoiding any organizational affiliation—if Tracer was meant to know, he'd have been told.

"Our campus is just outside town," said their host. "It's a school from which I am a proud graduate, and now some misguided soul has seen fit to make me an instructor."

"The SEAL facility?" Slaton asked.

"Well done, sir. Officially it's referred to as our Cold Weather Training Detachment. If the water off San Diego isn't enough to induce hypothermia, this place will do the trick. But then, I understand you're not here for training. A contingent from another unnamed agency arrived a few hours ago, and we've been tasked to outfit a few of you for winter ops." He cast a disparaging look at his charges. "I can tell you right now, those clothes are *not* gonna cut it."

Tracer steered toward a guarded gate, and once they were through, he began navigating through town. The harbor in the distance was packed: the local fishing fleet tied down for the season, every boat and dock covered in a foot of snow. The buildings in town were square-edged and practical, painted in tones that blended with the curbside slush. It struck Slaton as a place where no architectural liberties were taken, no lumber wasted or stone squandered in the name of style.

Ten minutes later, the stubborn toehold of civilization that was Kodiak gave way to an ice-encrusted wilderness.

The training detachment facility reflected the town: bare bones. There was a main cluster of buildings, and outside that a few storage sheds orbited like haphazard moons. It was all basic and no-nonsense, faceless structures with black-stenciled numbers. Yet there was an efficiency, a discipline about the place that spoke to the mission. It wasn't dollars or equipment or buildings that made this place special—it was the mindset, the commitment of those inside.

Tracer parked in front of the most prominent structure, a two-story concrete-block façade straight out of the Navy design bureau. At five in the evening the northern twilight was minimal, and on the perimeter everything blended into the dusky forest like a sea into a fog bank. In stark contrast, the detachment headquarters building was lit like a carnival.

Slaton had noted a fence around the facility's boundary, two guards at the entrance gate, but otherwise security seemed light. It made sense, he supposed. A remote island in Alaska, miles from the nearest town. A detachment run and occupied by Navy SEALs who no doubt kept an extensive armory. He doubted there was a more secure site in all fifty states. For those who lived on base, it was the ultimate in gated communities.

On entering the headquarters building, Bloch and Slaton were asked to leave their phones at the administration desk. Tracer led them down a hall and badged them through a cypher lock into what looked like a command post. There were at least ten people inside, all of them busy. Slaton immediately picked out one familiar face: Anna Sorensen.

She was an attractive blonde, trim and focused, and at the moment looked like an island of calm in a sea of chaos. If Slaton discerned anything new—it had been six months since he'd seen her—it might have been a wariness in her gaze. He'd always thought Bloch had copyrighted the look, but apparently it was intrinsic to the job. As chief of the CIA's clandestine operations, Sorensen faced decisions on a daily basis that few could comprehend. Soul-crushing choices that could be shared with no one outside the agency.

She was presently leaning over a table, in deep conversation with a mountain of a man Slaton had never met. Based on what Bloch had told him about the mission, however, he was quite sure he knew who it was. He was soon proved right. Sorensen looked up as he and Bloch approached.

"David!" she said, gravity losing its grip on her expression.

Slaton had worked a number of difficult ops under Sorensen's watch, and the fact that she could still smile at the sight of him spoke of their outcome. "Anton," she added, offering up handshakes. "Good to see you both."

"It's good to see you," Bloch said reflexively.

Sorensen stepped to one side, and said, "I'd like you to meet Jammer Davis."

When the big guy stood straight, he looked even bigger. Probably six four, NFL-wide, a face with good-looking, regular features that had taken some hits—Slaton recalled Sorensen telling him that he played rugby. He'd never met Davis in person, but they'd worked in parallel on a mission a few years back, operating on different sides of the world. He was a former Air Force pilot, and an aircraft accident investigtor—which made perfect sense given the situation. On a more personal level, Slaton knew that Davis and Sorensen were an on-again, off-again item. He shook Davis's hand, wondering what Sorensen had said, in turn, about him. If there was unease, Slaton didn't sense it.

"Good to finally meet you," Davis said.

"You as well. Apparently we worked together at a distance a few years back."

"It wasn't easy, as I recall, but we got the job done."

Slaton was about to respond when Sorensen interrupted. "You guys can reminisce later—we've got work to do." She addressed Bloch, "I'm guessing you filled David in on the basics?"

"As I understood them, yes."

"Okay, things are changing fast, so I'll give you an update." She walked over to a map that had been stuck to the plaster wall with pushpins and duct tape—a hint, Slaton reckoned, of where things were headed.

She pointed to a red box centered around Wrangel Island. "As expected, the weather in the crash area is deteriorating. *New Mexico* is enroute and should be the first on scene. We still have no sign of survivors. The equipment on Raven 44 included two handheld survival radios that link via satellite. So far neither has been activated. The emergency locator beacon from the flight data recorder is giving a weak signal—we're picking it up intermittently near the northwest corner of the island. Since Jammer is our resident expert, I'll let him cover the rest."

"I'll start with the worst of it," Davis began. "The radar data does not bode well. It looks like this airplane broke apart in flight. If that's the case, the chance of survivors is virtually nil. All the same, we can't be certain without getting eyes on the scene."

"What could cause a breakup like that?" Slaton asked.

"At this point it's only speculation, but I'd start by considering the airplane. This jet was upgraded as a Rivet Joint ten years ago. That's a major overhaul. Every inch of the airframe is reconditioned from nose to tail. That said, the aircraft came off the assembly line in 1964. Something could have been missed, fatigue cracks or damage from its previous service. Outside that, catastrophic engine failure can do extensive damage, or possibly a fuel tank explosion. You also have to consider the weather. Thunderstorms, wind shear, severe turbulence—any of them can bring down an airplane in a worst-case scenario. I took a preliminary look, and as far as I can see there was no severe weather in the area at the time of the accident. All of these factors are provable if we can get a good look at the wreckage and find the black boxes—but that, of course, requires access and time."

"And we might not have either," Slaton said.

"Limited at best."

Slaton appreciated Davis's approach. He saw no pulled punches, no ulterior motives.

"With that in mind," Sorensen picked up, "our priorities are clear. The first task is to determine if there are survivors. Hopefully, *New Mexico* can give us an answer. If the news is good, we'll move heaven and earth to render aid."

"And if not?" Bloch inquired, his pessimism honed by years of running a spy agency.

"Then we move on to the secondary mission—figuring out why this airplane went down. Raven 44 was being illuminated by an unidentified radar right before it crashed, but we've seen nothing to suggest a missile launch. Bottom line, we need to get Jammer to the crash site."

Davis said, "The first order of business is to pinpoint the wreckage. We have a wide range of satellite assets at our disposal, everything from DOD birds to NOAA climate mappers. Combining that with what we learn from *New Mexico,* we should get a pretty good picture of where the pieces are. The challenge then becomes reaching it before the Russians do."

"Which brings up an important point," Sorensen said. "During all this maneuvering, we'll be looking over our shoulder. We want to get a look at this crash, but if the Russians get wind of what we're doing, it'll force us to our last resort—destroying the most sensitive portions of wreckage to keep them from being compromised."

Slaton checked the wall clock. "How long do we have to pull all this together?"

"You're out that door in five hours," she said, pointing to the entrance.

Slaton frowned.

"It's rushed, I know, but waiting is not an option."

"Logistics for getting there?"

She moved to another map that depicted Alaska, the Bering Strait, and the Chukchi Sea. Global warming or not, Slaton knew that the ocean on the top of the world—depicted in blue on the map—would most likely be white this time of year.

Sorensen's long-boned, unmanicured finger went to the map, a peculiar touch of élan for a spy chief briefing a blunt-force mission. She tracked a line drawn from Kodiak to a point on the extreme northern coast of Alaska. "At one a.m. local, roughly six hours from now, two V-22 Ospreys will depart from the airport here on Kodiak. A third Osprey will serve as a spare, following the primaries to our staging point." She tapped on a coastal village just north of the Bering Strait, effectively the farthest northwest airfield in Alaska. Slaton decided the name, Point Hope, could not have been more fitting.

"After refueling in Point Hope," she continued, "two aircraft will launch northwest toward Wrangel. It's roughly a three-hundred-mile trip, and the Ospreys will arc slightly to the north to stay below radar coverage as best they can. NSA is exploring the possibility of screwing with Russian air defense networks in that sector, but they can't give any guarantees. Understand, you *will* be penetrating Russian airspace without clearance and undertaking a mission on Russian soil. If the Ospreys are spotted on ingress, there's a good chance we'll get wind of it via radio chatter or comm intercepts."

"From another Rivet Joint?" Slaton asked.

"Yes, a sister ship from the same squadron as the one that crashed. They're already en route and will be on station before you arrive. They have orders to stand off well outside Russian airspace, but together with space-based assets we'll have excellent coverage. Needless to say, the Raven squadron had no shortage of volunteers for this mission."

Sorensen's eyes fell on Slaton and Davis. "Since portions of the wreckage may be submerged, it's possible there will be some cold-water diving involved. I know you're both trained divers, but are you up for it?"

The two exchanged a look, and Davis said, "It's been awhile since I put on a dry suit. Are you sure they have one that will fit me?"

Tracer, who'd been silent on the periphery, said, "We don't get a lot of six-foot-four SEALs coming through the pipeline, but cold-water training is what we do—I'll find you something. If there's time, I'll throw in an abbreviated refresher course for you both."

Slaton said, "What if we have to destroy wreckage?"

Sorensen said, "That's on me. I've got a team from SAC/SOG who will take care of it—two EOD specialists."

"Who else is coming to this party?"

"One combat medic and a comm specialist, also SOG. I've recruited Tracer and two of his instructors from the detachment here—aside from cold weather expertise, they're all-around good guys to have on board. Including you and Jammer, that's a total of nine."

"Not much of an army for invading Russia."

"We're not going in with guns blazing. This is all about stealth. We have two options for extraction. Primary is for you to come out on *New Mexico,* with a contingency of sending the Ospreys back. You'll be hauling a fair amount of equipment going in, but by keeping the unit small we can exfil personnel only using a single Osprey if necessary."

Someone called Sorensen's name, and she cut off her briefing to check a stream of new intel.

Slaton slid a glance toward Davis and guessed they were thinking the same thing. He said in a hushed voice, "Fly across the Arctic in winter, violate Russian territory. Maybe go for a dive under the ice and blow a few things up."

Davis allowed a muted laugh. "Yeah . . . what could go wrong?"

Evening in Alaska was morning in Nur-Sultan, Kazakhstan. Astana Park lay fixed in the center of the city and, in spite of the March chill, was its usual busy self. At the edge of the river stood a frigid sand beach, and the umbrellas of summer had been replaced by overturned rowboats. As if to compensate for being the world's largest landlocked country, Kazakhstan's parks were often near the water. This particular expanse was rumored to have once been a favorite of Genghis Khan. His Mongol hordes had foreshadowed a long line of invaders, most recently the Soviets, yet today, with eight hundred years of subjugation behind it, the city finally seemed to be breathing again.

The park's sidewalks were busy, and few people took notice of a lone man limping along the main waterside path. He was dressed warmly, a fur-trimmed hat pulled down over his ears. He seemed in no hurry to cross the Ishim River footbridge, and on the far side he turned right, following the embankment to the east. It was there, close to the water's edge, that he finally drew attention, although not from any human. He pulled a large bag of bread crumbs from his pocket and began tossing them by the handful toward the water. A raft of ducks were the first to notice, paddling hard to keep up, and then a small flock of seagulls grew interested. The question of why there were gulls so far from the sea was a curiosity, but little more. Lakes, landfills, rivers. The birds had their reasons.

What the gulls lacked in numbers, they made up for with aggressiveness. They snatched and pilfered from one another, crying incessantly, and swirled in what could only be called a frenzy. Feeding the flock continuously, the man turned away from the river and dragged his charges into the city, a kind of avian Pied Piper. He kept it up for five minutes, all the way to Mukhtar Auezov Street 8.

There, on his left shoulder, he encountered a high wall topped by concertina wire. The wall completely ringed the building behind it, as well as a parking lot and a narrow open space configured as a sitting area and garden. None of that interested the man as he shambled along the sidewalk. His objective lay fifty feet ahead—the compound's lone entrance where two guards stood alertly in front of a heavy barrier.

Lazarus glanced up and saw only a few gulls still with him. *The thinnest and hungriest of the flock,* he thought. *I know how you feel, my friends.*

He kept up a meager flow of crumbs as he neared the guard post. One of the men was watching him, but more with annoyance than concern. Lazarus subtly tugged down his fur cap, and kept his face canted away from the entrance—the cameras there were the only ones on this section of Mukhtar Auezov Street. Steps away from the gate, he dug deep into his bag and let fly. He tossed what was left of the crumbs high into the air, and on an angle that sent them raining toward the irritated guard. In the periphery he saw the man step back as bread crumbs skittered toward his feet. He might have said an unkind word, but Lazarus could barely hear over the gulls' riotous squawking. He never stopped moving.

Mission complete, he turned right at the next corner and disappeared every bit as quickly as his straggling flock of associates.

EIGHT

The Montreux Convention was put into effect in 1936 by the League of Nations, and to this day remains one of the most obscure and oft-ignored treaties ever put to paper. As was often the case with international agreements, fine print that made sense to negotiators nearly a century ago had been overtaken by technology and shifting balances of power. What carried forward, in twenty-nine Articles, four annexes, and one protocol, was a bog of legal ambiguity.

The convention's original intent was to govern naval operations on the Black Sea, effectively limiting the passage of military vessels through the dual Turkish Straits—the Bosporus and the Dardanelles. The size of ships permitted to pass and the duration of their stay in the Black Sea were strictly limited, with exceptions made for nations with littoral borders along those shores. Enforcement proved problematic and had hit a low point in recent years. After seizing Crimea in 2014, Russia increasingly regarded the treaty with a jaded eye, challenging its own transition limits and complaining that others were regularly in breach. It didn't help that the twin straits themselves were governed by Turkey: ostensibly a member of NATO, but a nation whose allegiance to the West was transitory.

Against that backdrop, it seemed perfectly fitting that as the U.S. Navy guided missile destroyer *Ross* cut a swath through the darkened Black Sea, she did so shrouded in an impenetrable marine fog layer. She had sailed the previous night from the Romanian port of Constanta and was now fourteen days into her second Black Sea cruise. *Ross* was only the third U.S. Navy vessel to transit the Bosporus and enter the Black Sea since the beginning of the year. The previous year had brought four such patrols, all characterized by Sixth Fleet command as "routine maritime security operations." The Russian foreign ministry, not surprisingly, had responded with a far less charitable description, characterizing the Navy's visits as "blatant acts of maritime aggression."

Aggression or not, *Ross* made her point exactly as her sister ships had: a supersized Stars and Stripes flew proudly amidships.

"Helm, ten degrees right rudder," *Ross*'s captain, Commander Robert Highstreet, said from his seat on the bridge. The command was repeated and the compass began swinging.

"Anything on radar?" Highstreet asked. They'd been cutting through fog all night, but visibility was worsening and a heavily used sea-lane lay roughly twenty miles ahead. In the predawn murk, they would have to watch the scope closely to avoid traffic.

"I'm getting an occasional strobe to starboard, but no targets ahead," answered the operator.

"What kind of strobe?"

"I think it's military radar. Either test work or somebody screwing with us."

Highstreet considered it. "More likely the latter. The Russians know we're here and they don't like it."

"Yes, sir."

"Let's screw with them right back. Helm, make the new heading zero-four-zero."

"Aye, sir."

They were presently five miles outside the twelve-mile territorial limit. Under better conditions, lights on the southern coast of Crimea might be visible off the port beam. Highstreet had been occasionally jinking closer to shore, teasing the Russians, who were certainly tracking their every move. Still, he had to be careful, his orders from Fleet being unequivocal: they were never to "bust the dashed line." Five miles, in his opinion, was plenty to work with, and the compass soon settled on the new heading.

Highstreet had assumed command of *Ross* one year ago, a mandatory step in the career of any surface warfare officer who aspired for promotion. During his time at the Naval Academy he'd envisioned this day, a third-generation captain in the United States Navy, following his father and grandfather. That his own command had come slightly below the zone he carried with no small amount of pride.

He got out of his seat and ventured outside. On the port wing he was hit by a cool breeze, and he pulled the collar of his jacket higher as he studied the horizon. The night had been pitch-black, the Sea living up to its name. He could barely see the water, no breakers to define its surface, and the visibility was so poor he struggled to make out their own bow. With no moon or stars, no lights from shore, the blackness felt stifling. Even *Ross's* own subdued lights were beaten into submission by the fog. He'd seen such conditions before, and he knew they often continued for weeks at a stretch in these waters. Whatever morale boost the crew had gotten from shore leave in Romania would dampen quickly in the abyss that was March on the Black Sea.

"Captain!"

Highstreet edged back inside. The ensign behind the main nav display was looking at him anxiously.

"What's up?"

"I show a position jump."

"A *what*?" Highstreet went and stood next to him.

"Our position on the map—it just shifted almost twenty miles."

The captain looked down and saw a significantly different picture than he'd seen minutes earlier. "What the hell? Nav, did you cross-check the GPS data to—"

Highstreet was cut off by the sound of a collision warning. He checked the screen and saw a flashing red return less than a hundred yards ahead.

"Helm, all back emergency! Left full rudder!"

Everyone on the bridge braced as the twin propellers reversed pitch and began biting into the sea.

"Sir!" shouted the lookout on his right. "Ship dead ahead!"

Highstreet looked up and saw it—a dark shape looming over the bow like a mountain. It was far bigger than *Ross* and he saw stacks of shipping containers piled high. *Ross* shuddered under the pull of her great twin propellers. She was slowing rapidly . . . but not fast enough.

"Sound general quarters!"

The order went out over the loudspeaker, and across the ship crewmen rushed to close watertight doors. But they had only seconds.

The massive ship rose out of the gloom, the spray of her deck lights hovering like so many moons. Highstreet could tell the container ship was also trying to maneuver, and in the last instant he realized his turn minutes earlier had probably negated their evasive move—two people trying to pass on a sidewalk but moving laughably in the same direction.

Highstreet watched helplessly, the sickening inevitability clear. On his order, the officer of the deck again took to the loudspeaker, "All hands brace for impact!"

Highstreet gripped a rail and held tight. Everyone on the bridge was thrown violently to the deck as *Ross*'s bow scythed squarely into the beam of the massive freighter.

NINE

Tracer took Slaton and Davis to an adjacent building to be fitted for gear. He began with real winter clothing: synthetic base layer, winter camo jacket and pants, wool socks, boots, gloves, beanies, and goggles.

He gave them each a loaded backpack, and after itemizing the contents, Tracer said, "That's basically your survival gear. Either of you want a weapon?"

Davis said, "I'll make do with the ice axe."

Slaton suppressed a smile, and said, "SCAR-H?"

"I can do that." Tracer disappeared into a nearby room and emerged with an FN SCAR-H. It was one of the assault rifles issued to SEAL units, and he was given the standard version, a middling blend of close-quarters functionality and long-range accuracy with a twenty-round magazine.

"Okay," Tracer said, "next comes the dive gear. We're not sure if that'll be necessary, but the plan is to bring three sets: the two of you and myself."

It took nearly an hour to get geared up, fitted, and briefed on the peculiarities of the SEAL-spec rig. "We have more exotic stuff," Tracer said at the end, "but there's not enough time to check you out. This will get you down to a hundred feet, maybe one-twenty in a pinch with limited bottom time."

"Any deeper than that," Slaton said, "and I'm happy to leave it for an underwater drone."

Tracer gave both men a refresher on dry suits. Unlike a standard wet suit, which trapped a warm layer of water next to the skin, full dry suits were the only option for diving in extremely cold water. They were also bulky, annoyingly buoyant, and difficult to work in.

As they loaded it all into the back of the Land Cruiser, straining the ample cargo bay, Slaton was beginning to see Sorensen's wisdom in keeping the contingent small. Between the mission and dealing with an Arctic winter, they were going to be hauling a lot of gear.

"We're also taking two snowmobiles," Tracer added. "It's the only way to get around on Wrangel this time of year. They tell me *New Mexico* is already carrying two—they were taking part in a winter exercise before getting diverted to Wrangel. Lucky for us, *New Mexico* is also fitted with a lockout chamber."

"A what?" Davis asked.

"It's a compartment that can be flooded, a way to deploy and recover divers. It's the only way to go, especially in bad weather."

"Or if you don't want anybody to see you jumping in," Slaton added.

"Yep."

When they finished loading, Tracer, who would act as operational commander of the mission, assembled the entire team in the brown-slush parking lot. Slaton and Davis were introduced to Sorensen's EOD team. Both were former Navy SEALs who had transferred into SOG. Ben "Super" Kuperman was a ten-year frogman with multiple deployments downrange. George Sharp was an EOD instructor before landing at the CIA. The two wiry explosives experts had clearly worked together before, evident by a constant stream of gallows humor that would have left the Grim Reaper doubled over in stitches.

Last to be introduced were the comm specialist and combat medic, and Tracer's two recruits. In Slaton's view, every one of them seemed solid. They eyed him in return with clear curiosity, causing him to suspect his reputation had preceded him. The legend of an Israeli assassin who spanned the world like a shadow, and who reappeared regularly after rumors of his demise, had long been talked about in Special Ops circles. To have an Israeli before them now who might or might not be that ghost was rocket fuel for speculation.

Slaton said nothing to confirm or deny the suspicions. Either would only complicate matters, and everyone needed to focus on the task at hand.

Tracer announced that a meal would be served in the main building—the last hot chow they would likely get for days—before giving everyone twenty minutes for personal prep. As they walked back to the main building, Davis pointed out a recent repair in the nearby perimeter fence. "You have a security breach?" he asked Tracer.

"Actually, yeah. But not the kind you worry about in most places. A bear tore through the fence to get to the dumpster."

"They a problem here?"

"When they want to be. There's one Kodiak bear per square mile on this island. That works out to one for every three people. You won't see any this time of year, though. Males won't start coming out for a month or so."

"I hear they're big," Slaton said.

"Around fifteen hundred pounds, which makes them bigger than grizzlies. Ten feet tall when they stand. There's only one bear subspecies on earth that's bigger."

"Dare I ask?" said Davis.

Tracer laughed. "Polar bear. As it turns out, Wrangel Island has one of the densest populations of those on earth. And they don't hibernate."

"Of course."

"Wouldn't worry about it," Slaton said. "The way I see it . . . those bears are going to be the least of our worries."

Arkady Nabiyev pushed his ancient wheelbarrow from the tiny shed to the far side of the yard. His chore today was to prepare the small rose garden for spring. It was time to turn the soil and clip back for new growth. Having worked inside the walled compound for nine years, he had developed an attachment to the garden. The grounds surrounding the Israeli embassy in Kazakhstan were not large, and certainly not his own, yet he kept them with pride.

He set the wheelbarrow down at the edge of the rose garden and took to his task methodically, clipping stems and churning soil. Arkady had been at it for ten minutes when he noticed something on the ground near a wintering Duc de Cambridge: a tiny shard of red plastic the size of his thumb.

He picked it up and turned it in his hand—a mistake, he would later be told, but not one he could have been expected to foresee—and then snapped it open from the tiny pivot point. He had never in his life owned a computer, yet he knew what it was. His son had used such devices in school, and his nephew once used something similar to show him family photos on a laptop.

Arkady glanced at the embassy's distant entrance. He knew perfectly well where he worked, and by extension, he understood the device might be meaningful to his employer. The question of what to do with it floated for a moment, but was quickly resolved. Some of his Muslim friends had issues with the Jews, but those here at the embassy had always treated him well.

He went to the main entrance and asked to see the facility manager. Arkady was not allowed inside the consulate without an escort, and as the full-time gardener he rarely needed such access. The shed held his tools, and a small covered table gave him a place to eat lunch. When the weather was bad, often the case in the winter, he simply took the day off. That he did so at full pay did not go unappreciated.

It took ten minutes for the manager to arrive. He smiled, although in a way that suggested to Arkady that he ought to be brief. The man was probably expecting questions about what annuals to plant in the spring, or perhaps a request for a bit of cash to purchase a new spade. When Arkady held up the plastic flash drive, the look on the manager's face shifted.

"I found it in the rose garden," Arkady said.

The man took it, and after a brief inspection, he squinted and asked, "On the east side, near the wall?"

"Yes."

After a brief hesitation, the Israeli said, "Come inside, Arkady. I may have a few more questions . . ."

For two reasons President Cleveland took the news about *Ross* badly. First was that it arrived at five fifteen a.m. after her morning shower. Second was that it was delivered not by any element of the national command authority, but inadvertently by her valet as he set out the presidential morning tea.

The valet turned on the morning news, as was his custom, and the footage was a nightmare. The aftermath of a maritime collision on the Black Sea was presented in a choppy, unstabilized video: the foundering destroyer *Ross*, listing badly to port and with gray smoke billowing from a gash in her hull. A sodden American flag amidships hung into the sea like a wet beach towel. The camera shifted, and in the distance a massive container ship sat becalmed with a great dent on her starboard waterline. The air and water around *Ross* were besieged by rescue vessels—fishing boats, ferries, and a helicopter bearing Ukrainian markings—circling like so many vultures around a mortally wounded animal.

President Cleveland dressed quickly and rushed to the basement.

The White House Situation Room had recently undergone renovations. Communications had been upgraded and high-definition monitors installed, assuring secure links for the nation's leadership to any command post or frontline military unit in the world. Unfortunately, technology did nothing to resolve the lack of sheer square footage. Being situated in the White House basement, the room's hardened walls were constraining, and its low ceilings magnified the lack of space. When attended by a full complement of staff, the SR was nothing short of claustrophobic. For that reason, Cleveland limited the size of meetings whenever possible.

She walked in that morning to find a skeleton crew, the overnight watch team at the end of its shift. Everyone stood when the president entered: four duty officers, one communications specialist, and an intel analyst. Three were active-duty military, attached to the NSC from the Pentagon, while the others were permanent party NSC staff.

"Why wasn't I notified of this?" the president demanded, pointing to a screen on the far wall displaying the ongoing news coverage.

When no one spoke up, the duty officer in charge realized he was holding the short straw. "We've been following it closely, Madam President, but information is just now arriving. We were planning to cover the *Ross* incident during the morning briefing."

"Where exactly did this happen?"

"*Ross* went down in the Black Sea, south of Crimea."

Cleveland stared incredulously at the messenger, a vaguely familiar Navy officer whose name tag said JACKSON. "Went *down*? As in sunk?"

"I'm afraid so—the news footage is a couple of hours old. It all happened very quickly. *Ross* collided with a larger ship."

The president looked accusingly at the rest of the team, then locked back on the man in charge. In an unfortunate twist of fate, he happened to hold the rank of a Navy captain. "And how could this happen?"

The captain's hesitation might have been taken for embarrassment. In truth, he'd spent his entire career in Navy intelligence, with virtually no time at sea, and had been asking himself the same question. *How does a United States Navy destroyer run into another ship and sink in less than an hour?* "We have no details on the collision, ma'am. The good news is that there were a number of other ships in the area and they've been taking on survivors. I can tell you there were three hundred and twelve crewmen on board *Ross*. On last word, two hundred ninety-eight are accounted for."

Cleveland was suddenly consumed by an uneasy feeling. Only two days ago she'd been getting briefed on a disaster involving an Air Force reconnaissance aircraft: seventeen crewmembers presumably lost. Part of her wanted to be grateful that today's disaster had better prospects for the crew; grateful that she didn't have to approve another risk-laden rescue mission. What filled her head instead was *What are the chances of two disasters in two days?*

"I want everyone here in one hour for a full NSC meeting," she ordered.

"Yes, ma'am. I'll send out the alert."

Cleveland headed for the door, and on her way out she glanced back once at a room that was about to get very crowded.

TEN

Slaton was in the equipment room packing the last of his gear when Sorensen appeared. She rounded a rack of diving rebreathers and stood watching him. "The Ospreys arrived right on schedule."

"Good to hear. How's the weather on Wrangel?"

"Getting worse, but the forecast is for gradual improvement beginning in a few hours. *New Mexico* should be able to give us an update before we launch on the insertion."

Slaton wedged snowshoes into the oversized rucksack he'd been given.

"I wanted to have a word before you leave," she said.

He zipped the duffel closed and gave her his full attention. He'd worked with Sorensen enough to have a loose read on her moods, yet right then he was drawing a blank. "What's up?"

"To begin, I owe you an explanation as to why you're not running this op. I know how much experience you have when it comes to—"

"No," he broke in. "I wouldn't have wanted to run it. Tracer is solid, and we're using guys from his team. They've worked together, trained together, and the four guys from your section have similar backgrounds and training. Putting me in charge would only have complicated things. I'm only guest help, here because this crash is tied to another mission—finding Anton's daughter and getting her back."

She nodded thoughtfully. "Thanks for understanding."

"What else?"

A hesitation. "Aside from you, there's one other outlier on this expedition."

"Jammer."

She nodded.

"I think he was a great choice. We're dealing with an air crash, so we need someone with his expertise."

When Sorensen didn't respond, Slaton thought he understood. He went closer and held her with a level gaze. "Are we venturing onto delicate ground, Miss Deputy Director?"

"I wish it was otherwise, but yes. I've asked for Jammer's help before, but never on a mission that put him in harm's way. In those ops there ended up being problems, but they were either unexpected or . . . of his own making."

"I don't see any need to worry—we're just looking for a downed airplane."

Sorensen looked obviously at two assault rifles cradled in a nearby Pelican case.

"Look, Anna . . . can I offer a little advice?"

"Sure."

"When I served in Mossad, it was a lot like the organization you run now—a small community that's tight and familiar. You build relationships over time, get to know people and care about them. But invariably, the commander has to send his unit into dangerous places to do dangerous things. It's the nature of the business. At a time like this, with everyone loading up, it's natural to have reservations. I'd think less of you if you *didn't* have them. But an hour from now, when those Ospreys take off, everything turns to business. I'm sure Tracer and the others see it the same way. No room for doubts or distractions. I've also spent time in command centers, watching ops like this play out, so here's my advice—you owe it to everyone to adopt the same mindset. Focus completely on the task at hand. That's the best you can do for any of us."

"You're right . . . and I will. The thing is, I guess I don't see Jammer as being in your league. He's a flyer, a top-notch investigator, but when it comes to tactical ground operations . . ."

Slaton cinched up a strap on his duffel. "From what I've seen, he looks pretty capable."

"He can hold his own in a bar fight, I'll give him that."

"A bar fight? Sounds like a good story."

"Ugh . . . never mind."

He shouldered his ruck, shrugged it high on his back. "I take it the two of you are an item again?"

She nodded. "For better or for worse."

"And you want me to look out for him."

"Is it wrong of me to ask?"

He thought about that. "Not for me to judge. For what it's worth, I'll have his back. But to be square with you, Anna—I'll be looking out for the others every bit as much."

Lazarus watched intently as steeply rising terrain filled the windshield of his car. He was approaching the back range of the Altai Mountains, where the Kazakh steppe lifted to meet the sky. Russia was twenty miles north, China twenty south. Forty miles east would put him in Mongolia. The Altai had sourced all those borders, the natural battlement between Central Asia and the Far East. Which made it the perfect setting for today's business.

He wriggled in his seat, a routine adjustment to alleviate the chronic pain. The drive from Nur-Sultan was arduous, although having made it a number of times now he was beginning to enjoy it. He liked being out of the city, free of its people and noise and hyperactive traffic. It hadn't always been that way. Lazarus had grown up in an urban setting, thriving among people and civilization. Then his life had been altered forever, and in a way that prevented him from ever going home.

The road was in good shape, better than the last time he'd made the journey—in January three inches of fresh snow had taxed his little Lada. Now, even if the mountains remained thick with snow, the roads were clear.

He stopped after three hours at a roadside restaurant that had become a regular waypoint. He ordered an omelet with toast and coffee, and ate in silence. There was one other couple in the place, a man and a woman who were roughly his age. With empty plates in front of them, they lingered over a pot of tea. Neither seemed to notice him as they chatted warmly, fingers occasionally brushing over the table. Like the cities and crowds, one more thing he'd forsaken.

Today's meeting had been on the calendar for weeks, and all three principals would be waiting. The timing was not by chance: the first two strikes were complete, and it was time to evaluate the effects. Had the weapons worked as planned? Were the parties reacting as expected?

On the question of reactions, the answer was a resounding yes. One attack had generated a global news event. The other was being held closely by the Americans, but word would soon escape. Best of all, the question of who was responsible for it all remained a mystery.

As for the technology, both strikes were resounding successes, and had utilized different systems. This was not Lazarus's area of responsibility. The weapons came from the men he would meet today. Men whose lives had been spent, and fortunes made, in their respective corners of the defense industry. One had overseen a defense electronics conglomerate, another a government research lab. The third man had run a key weapons manufacturing plant.

Lazarus was the outlier of the group: he was a mere contractor whose job, in effect, was to maintain the mystery. The logistics chain he'd built was functional, yet completely obscure: corporations, warehouses, shipyards, personnel. A web of complexity that had been nearly a year in the making. By all accounts, he had succeeded spectacularly, yet things were about to get more challenging. The first two attacks had been surprises. Now the targets were forewarned and would be rightfully be wary.

He ordered a second cup of coffee for the road and set back out toward the looming mountains, the saw-toothed peaks now shrouded in mist. He soon reached the familiar turnoff, a nameless road that wandered aimlessly north. The road was paved but in terrible shape, and quickly became enveloped in forest. He'd seen but a handful of vehicles since leaving the city, and after making the final turn he encountered only a single tractor. The impossibly weathered farmer waved as he passed.

Lazarus didn't wave back.

He cracked open his window, and sweet evergreen air filled the car. He felt drawn to the Altai, and he suspected he knew why: it was the most divergent backdrop imaginable to supplant the one that haunted him. Endless open spaces without walls or floors. Only harmless farmers who waved amiably. And best of all, seasons. Stifling summers and frigid winters to replace the dank, eternal sameness. Seven of each had been wiped from his life. Lazarus barely remembered what had come before. Worse yet, he'd lost any hope for what might follow.

His dark musings ended abruptly.

All at once, the forest fell away, and on a sun-splashed hill the lodge appeared.

ELEVEN

How the tiny nation of Sri Lanka had lost sovereignty over the port of Hambantota was a mystery to its citizens, a red flag to its neighbors, and a source of astonishing profit for a handful of crooked politicians.

It had all begun fifteen years ago when, desperate to become a cog in the world's economic engine, the Sri Lankan government entered talks with China. The Chinese made a persuasive case that Hambantota, a second-tier, bare-bones harbor, could be transformed into a prosperous maritime hub. They ignored previous doubt-riddled feasibility studies and made it all sound easy. China would supply technical assistance, cheap labor, and even lend money at a time when traditional banks were pulling back.

After the deposits of a few well-targeted "consulting fees," key legislators came around and approved the project with great fanfare. Progress, however, was slow, and debt levels quickly rose. When the port finally opened, years behind schedule, the troubles of the Hambantota Port Development Project seemed only to heighten. In spite of being adjacent to some of the world's busiest shipping lanes, the port logged fewer than fifty arrivals in its first year—one ship for every hundred that sailed from nearby Colombo.

It was an all too familiar story. Too many delays, too little oversight, and contractors steeped in bribery and graft. Forty million dollars was paid in one instance to remove a single submerged boulder from the port's main channel. Within three years of opening, the inevitable endgame played out: in 2017, Sri Lanka ceded control of the debt-riddled project, relinquishing the port itself, along with fifteen thousand surrounding acres, to China for a term of ninety-nine years. It was as anticlimactic as it was predictable—and one more notch carved in China's Belt and Road Initiative.

China immediately set to improving its newest Port to Nowhere. A favorable fee schedule was set for Chinese conglomerates, and a steady stream of freighters materialized virtually overnight. Quiet deals were made with regional shipping companies, some of whose reputations were less than sterling. Warehouses began to rise, and inspections were kept to a minimum. From a financial standpoint, the port turned a corner under Chinese administration. It would never be the regional hub promised, yet it nearly broke even on an operating basis—if the books could be believed. More relevantly, Hambantota became effectively annexed, one more shiny jewel in the necklace of China's long-term ambition.

Among the port's murkier new entrants was a company with no pedigree whatsoever in shipping. It employed no local longshoremen, and not one of its employees spoke Sinhala or Tamil. The warehouse it rented went largely unused, to the point that some suggested the tall, corrugated-metal structure, which abutted a quiet pier, served as more of a visual screen than storage space.

Over the previous six months, only two ships had docked at the remote Pier 6, each for roughly ten weeks with a short overlap. They came, by all appearances, for some manner of technical refit. Crates and equipment appeared in the middle of the night, and the work was undertaken on a punishing schedule. Dockworkers on nearby piers noted the glow of welder's torches as the superstructure of each vessel was modified, although most would admit this was an inference: large tents had been erected over the sections of the ships where the work was being done. According to security guards, of which there were many, and none of whom were Sri Lankan, the tarps were there to keep the equatorial sun off the men doing the work.

The locals who watched the proceedings argued about what was really going on. Some thought the ships were being modified for smuggling operations, while others imagined luxury features being added for private owners. A few deemed the ships some new class of pirate vessel. None of the theories were ever confirmed, and so the dispute was never settled.

A fair result, really, since each held a bit of the truth.

It was the height of the day, amid unusually torpid midafternoon heat, when the third ship owned by EDG Industries idled slowly toward Pier 6. Like the two before her, she was not a military design. There were no deck guns or missile tubes, no racks of depth charges. Her lines weren't designed for speed or to minimize radar reflections. Indeed, her bulbous hull and superstructure gave more the aura of an oversized tugboat. Tears of rust wept from her joints, and the weary bilge pumps ran incessantly. Her name was *Poyarka,* and if anyone was to research her background—few ever had—they would learn that she had once served as a hydrographic survey ship for the Polish government. The question of why a country with limited coastline, and even less aspiration for global maritime engagement, had any need to survey the Seven Seas was long ago swept into the dustbin of Cold War trivia.

Her keel had been laid in a restless Gdansk shipyard in 1982, ninety-five meters of blue-water discovery. For over a decade she'd plied the near shores of the Baltic, occasionally measuring and mapping, but more often than not finding herself in the vicinity of passing NATO warships. Ultimately, budget cuts and the fall of Communism had scuttled her usefulness. *Poyarka* had lain oxidizing ever since, until the day, two years ago, when she was sold at a steep discount to an obscure private buyer.

Without so much as an inspection, two further transfers were completed, until the ship's title ended up in the vault of a newly formed Liberian-based concern. After decades of neglect, the ship was given basic repairs to become seaworthy, and began limping haphazardly through a string of global ports—a new oil cooler here, an electrical upgrade there—until she finally reached the harbor where her main retrofit was to take place. Finally, late last year, a revitalized *Poyarka* was sold yet again and registered with EDG Industries. Her Liberian operator liquidated the next day. Altogether, it left a chain of provenance as misty as the Baltic fog banks the ship had once plied—a string of shell companies that no longer existed, erased by owners who were themselves enigmas.

As she slipped smoothly into Pier 6, mooring lines were thrown shoreside by her crew. Much like the ship, they were a bare-bones contingent, cast-off journeymen sourced from around the world. All had been hired during the previous six months, while *Poyarka* had been berthed in a cold-water port as baseline work was completed and sea trials run.

Curiously, for all the changes *Poyarka* had undergone since her rebirth, the "operational type" block on her registry papers remained unchanged: hydrographic survey. This could have been disproved on close examination. The primary sensors beneath her hull, used for precision sonar readings, had been removed in the retrofit. Also gone were certain antennae topside, now electronic relics, that had decades earlier been adept at collecting intelligence on passing NATO warships. Aside from these subtractions, her new owners had made one obvious addition: on the foredeck, ahead of the bridge, a great dome that could have housed a small swimming pool. From a distance the dome gave the appearance of a giant golf ball whose bottom was sunk into the steel deck. The geodesic shell gave the old ship an oddly asynchronous appearance, like a rural barn topped by a sophisticated satellite array.

As soon as *Poyarka* was moored, a small army of technicians flooded aboard. A few disappeared beneath the dome, while others made their way to the newly installed Deck 3 control room. Mechanics arrived to tune the old diesel engine, and also double-check a new backup generator.

To a man, they beavered away against a hard deadline.

Poyarka was to set sail again the very next day, and on a voyage that would be her last.

TWELVE

Slaton and Davis rode to the Kodiak airport in a Navy-issue sedan, Tracer behind the wheel. The Land Rover, bursting with gear, had been taken ahead for loading by one of Tracer's men. After so many hours of equipment issue and briefings, Slaton felt like he was part of a mobilizing military unit—which, in effect, he was.

They arrived at the airfield slightly after midnight local time, and after passing through a guarded gate, Tracer steered to the military side of the joint-use field. The darkness was beaten away by rows of brilliant overhead lights that gave the aura of a martial-themed stadium. On center stage: three V-22 Ospreys.

The spare aircraft sat in the background, still and serene, while the two primary Ospreys were in the final stages of being loaded. Their aft-mounted ramps tongued down to the tarmac as loading crews secured the final tie-downs. Not for the first time, Slaton was impressed by Sorensen's organizational acumen. Orchestrating a complex mission on short notice was no small feat, and she definitely had the knack—aided, of course, by a government that spent more on its military each year than the next ten nations combined.

Slaton studied the aircraft with interest. The Osprey was one of the few Western-manufactured transports he'd never flown on. Half airplane, half helicopter, it looked awkward and ungainly: a shoe box fuselage with a straight wing, outriggered by a pair of large tilt-rotor engines. Parked on the ramp, the great propellers were angled skyward at a forty-five-degree angle—not vertical flight, not horizontal, but something in between. Which summed up the aircraft perfectly.

"Ever been on an Osprey?" Davis asked as they climbed out of the car.

"Never had the pleasure," Slaton replied.

"They've been around awhile. Pretty reliable now, although they had some problems in the beginning."

"That's not very encouraging . . . I mean, coming from an aircraft accident investigator."

"Don't worry, I'm getting on board with you. The concept is a good one. It can hover for takeoff and landing like a helicopter, but during flight the props rotate forward for better speed and range. The way our mission is drawn up, there's no other aircraft that could make it happen."

Tracer got out of the car and pointed to the nearest Osprey. "That's my ride—we'll be lugging the snowmobiles. Your bird is carrying the rest of the gear."

The three men split, Davis and Slaton veering toward the second Osprey.

They were met at the ramp by the loadmaster, a crusty master sergeant with a salt-and-pepper crew cut. "Welcome aboard," he growled in a cigar-smoker's voice. "I'll give you fair warning—Ospreys ain't pressurized, and the cabin heat sucks. I'd strongly recommend you keep those winter jackets on." He jabbed a greasy thumb toward the starboard side to indicate their seating assignments—the world's most surly flight attendant.

Slaton walked up the ramp, and once inside he was hit by the ambiance shared by every military transport on earth: the harsh tang of spilled oil and hydraulic fluid. The interior was a mechanic's nightmare, every inch of sidewall and ceiling strung with miles of wires, cables, and hydraulic lines. Pallets of gear were lashed down in the middle of the cargo bay, and along either side Slaton recognized another standard feature: fold-down webbed seats that looked excruciatingly uncomfortable. Between that and the noise of the two big engines, he decided sleep would be out of the question.

Twenty minutes later the doors shut and everyone was strapped in. The Osprey shook to life like a giant blender, and Slaton sensed motion as they taxied toward the runway. There was a burst of acceleration, followed by a surprisingly smooth transition to flight.

"Four hours to Point Hope," Davis said.

Slaton looked across the aisle and saw two of Tracer's men, eyes shut but certainly not sleeping. He recognized this for what it was: imposed calm, that personal zone soldiers put themselves in when engagement was imminent. On the face of things, there was no reason to expect hostilities. If all went well, they were looking at little more than a transportation exercise: aircraft and submarines and snowshoes, maybe a cold-water dive thrown in. The problem, as always, involved contingencies. These were made clear by what loomed in front of Slaton. Comm gear, medical supplies, weapons. And of course, men whose lives were committed to using it all with good effect.

He closed his eyes and made his own personal escape; his mind filled with a vision of the Bitterroot Mountains on a glorious winter morning. Meadows ablaze in sunlit frost; misted valleys under cobalt skies. Slaton was deep in that emotional attic when a sudden clatter ruined his trance. His eyes shot open and he saw the Air Force loadmaster picking up a dropped wrench. The man grunted and walked aft.

Slaton glanced to his right, and with mild astonishment saw Jammer Davis sleeping like a NyQuilled baby.

The satellite had departed Earth six months earlier, a billion-dollar arrow, spewing fire and smoke, shot from Vandenberg Air Force Base in

California. The National Reconnaissance Office referred to the mission's payload, with a straight bureaucratic face, as USA-432.

The launch was veiled in secrecy, as were all previous departures involving the new class of satellites, code named Amethyst, that comprised the NRO's Future Imagery Architecture program.

Avoiding the tragedies that so often befell such technological marvels—it was, after all, rocket science—USA-432 had climbed faultlessly to its designated celestial station and gotten to work. The satellite skimmed ceaselessly above the atmosphere in low-earth orbit—slightly over a thousand kilometers—to capture finely detailed two-and three-dimensional images using the motion of the satellite, rather than a scanning antenna, to contrast targeted areas.

Hours earlier, on a regular swoop over Russia's polar region, its sensors were trained on coordinates it had never before overseen: the windswept hills of Wrangel Island. Because USA-432 mapped with radar, its images were unaffected by darkness or cloud cover. With enhanced resolution, the satellite could typically distinguish a particular car in a parking lot. Perhaps even tell you whether or not the sunroof was open. And if so, how much change was in the cup holder.

The survey of Wrangel Island that morning began with certain advantages. Teams of analysts from a sister agency, NSA, had been poring over the heisted data from Russia's air defense networks, and after hours of filtering and plotting they nailed down key details of Raven 44's last moments. At roughly fourteen thousand feet in its terminal dive, the airframe had broken into four distinct sections. Two of these landed on the northwestern edge of Wrangel Island, including the largest section, likely the main fuselage, while the remaining two echoes ended in the nearby sea. With that head start, NRO technicians focused USA-432's sensors on the island's northwest shores.

They easily picked out the debris field, each major section of wreckage less than a quarter mile from its predicted location. Precision mapping confirmed one segment to be the right wing, with one engine still intact. The second, as hoped, was the bulk of the main fuselage, from the nose cone to the tail bulkhead. The condition of this segment was poor, the hull crushed and accordioned. Because it also encompassed the cockpit and crew workstations, any remaining hope for survivors was effectively dashed.

The submerged sections of wreckage proved more elusive. Satellite-based radar could not penetrate the sea surface, meaning USA-432 had no hope of seeing what lay beneath. Locating that debris would require a different approach, and one that was not yet available—the submarine *New Mexico*.

All this information flowed upward, ending on the provisional desk of Anna Sorensen, who'd set up a makeshift command post in Kodiak. She wasted no time in applying the results to the mission now under way.

On one hand she was encouraged: the equipment and personnel en route were appropriate, fitting the scene confirmed by the overheads. The near-confirmation that there were no survivors was the somber counterweight.

The biggest variable, which was completely out of Sorensen's control, was updated when she took a call from a U.S. Navy Seventh Fleet meteorologist.

"I've got a revision on the weather forecast for your mission . . . it's not good."

THIRTEEN

The lodge was on top of a gentle hill and cut in the image of a Swiss chalet: steeply gabled roof, external beams, brown weatherboard. The land immediately surrounding the main house had been cut back a hundred yards in every direction, acres of tea-brown grass flattened by winter. On the largest level plot, a short walk from the main house, two sleek helicopters sat shivering in the mountain air.

Lazarus guided the Lada toward the expansive main parking apron, pulling to a stop next to an S-Class Mercedes that belonged on a showroom floor. The contrast of his Lada to the shiny sedan was inescapable. It had been that way since the beginning, Lazarus demonstrating restraint, the others engaged in ceaseless competitions of wealth. He wasn't envious in the least, recognizing it for what it was—an unwinnable contest. There was always a faster Ferrari, a bigger private jet. Money had never been his motivation. They paid him well enough, and he squirreled most of it away in tax havens on the odd chance he survived. It was always better to have hope. He told them he kept driving the Lada because he didn't want to draw attention. It was true, in part. Yet what the little car meant to him, his employers could never understand.

Security was heavy, a dozen men around the lodge and certainly more out of sight. His hosts took care of that as well. They were much alike, the three, cut from the same bolt of cloth. Nationality, ethnicity, patronage. They'd never offered their names, not their real ones, which wasn't unusual in his line of work. In a collective sense, they referred to themselves as The Trident. How they referred to him he had gathered in whispers: he was "the cripple."

He got out of the Lada and stretched his aching joints. A familiar security chief, nearly bald and with a cinder-block head, appeared and pointed around the side of the house. Lazarus followed his direction, and after turning the corner he saw his three employers gathered around one of the choppers. The aircraft appeared to be a new acquisition, and the owner, the researcher, appeared to be extolling its merits to the others. Lazarus couldn't say for certain because the man was speaking his native language. By necessity, they transitioned to English when he was present.

When they saw him hobbling over, the conversation ended abruptly. Greetings were exchanged, although with little sincerity. The men of The

Trident were not Lazarus's friends. Not in any sense of the word. Yet they *were* indispensable to his destiny.

As he was to theirs.

The meeting convened in a voluminous room with a roaring fire. Bearskin rugs checkered the floor, and the deeply upholstered furnishings belonged in a ski chalet. The three members of The Trident sat side by side in high-backed chairs, a tribunal of sorts. Lazarus faced them alone.

For the best part of an hour they discussed the outcomes, as far as they knew them, of the first two strikes. The consensus opinion: both systems had worked well. After that, it was time to discuss strategy.

"President Petrov has been quiet," the center man prompted.

From the right, "Somewhat. He reveled in gloating over the fiasco in the Black Sea—one of his navy frigates rescued twenty American sailors from *Ross*. The crash in the Arctic, however, has gone unmentioned. Still, there is one complication—according to our intelligence, some of the wreckage appears to have landed on Wrangel Island. We should have brought the airplane down farther at sea. There are indications the Americans have launched a mission to recover certain components, although this could work in our favor."

"Or put us at risk of discovery."

"Impossible. Even if they learned the method, it could never be traced to us. The system we used was classified at the highest level."

A brief silence ran, and Lazarus suspected the others were thinking what he was: *don't underestimate the Americans.*

The center locked his eyes on him. "Tell us how the next strike progresses."

Straightening in his chair, Lazarus said, "*Poyarka* sets sail tomorrow. I will meet soon with my personnel deputy who has been overseeing her departure. So far, he reports no problems. Her run to the operating area should take three days." He covered the itinerary and tactical plan in detail.

"And the target?"

"En route and expected to arrive on schedule—or as close to 'on schedule' as ever."

Muted laughter from The Trident.

The left seat said, "I am told installation of the device went well. There were minor software issues, yet nothing that should affect the mission."

"Have you resolved how to deal with the crew after the attack?" the center asked, his eyes boring into Lazarus.

"I coordinated with *Poyarka*'s captain, and he has promised to take care of it."

Three stares, no words.

The rest of the meeting held no surprises, and at the end they invited

Lazarus to join them for dinner. It was all he could do to force a smile, and say, "Why not?"

Lazarus remained for dinner, but not a minute longer. He had spent the night at the lodge once before and viewed it as wasted time. The conversation had been dreary, talk of yachts and mistresses and gambling. The drinking had bordered on the obscene. When they brought in the girls at midnight, he'd claimed he was feeling ill and excused himself. He had never stayed the night since. He had caught a bit of banter about it on a subsequent visit. One of them thought he was religious, while another was convinced he was a homosexual. Lazarus let them have their opinions then and did nothing to dissuade them now.

The Lada started up smartly, the little engine purring. He steered down the long driveway and back into the tree line. The relief was palpable as he returned to his preferred setting, the forest and solitude.

While he drove, Lazarus applied what he'd learned. The logistics of the operation were extensive, yet so far he'd kept everything together. There were further attacks planned, although most were stuck on the drawing board. Only one was locked and loaded. Tomorrow he would meet with Bagdani and get the latest on *Poyarka*. If the mission went as smoothly as the first two, it would be time to take a step back. Time to wait and watch. On one end of the spectrum, The Trident might decide to accelerate the next strikes. And on the other? They could simply sit back as World War III played out before their eyes.

Darkness took hold as the woods deepened, the Lada's feeble headlights straining to find the way. Lazarus found his thoughts drifting to the girl in Almaty. He wondered how she was being treated by her captors. Was she being fed? Beaten? Abused?

The thoughts proved consuming, impossible to push away. They ratcheted in his head all the way back to Almaty.

FOURTEEN

Above the Russian Far East, Wrangel Island sits high and alone on the ice-clad Arctic Ocean. Split perfectly by the 180-degree meridian, the International Dateline shifts eastward around the island as if to keep Alaska at bay.

It might have been otherwise.

After numerous sightings in the mid-1800s by whalers and explorers, Calvin Hooper's expedition was the first to lay claim to the island, planting a United States flag in 1881. Thirty years later, a Russian icebreaker set ashore under the banner of the czar's empire. In 1921, Canada put down its own marker to prevent a feared Japanese foothold. All these trouble-laden ventures had one thing in common: owing to the ice, they were never able to establish a continuous presence. In effect, the Arctic won. Ultimately, through a combination of geographic proximity and revolutionary persistence, it was Russia's claim that finally stuck.

The interior of Wrangel Island is a string of low mountains, yet it holds no glaciers. The foreboding, barren terrain rides the coastal plains to sheer cliffs in some areas, rocky beaches in others. Snow falls roughly half the days each year, and the island is regularly bound by polar pack ice. Wrangle's claim to fame came five thousand years ago when it held the last remaining population of woolly mammoths. The reason for the herd's survival was clear to paleontologists: until that time, the hunter-gatherers known as sapiens had avoided extreme climates. Today, however, in an era of natural-resource grabs and opening northern sea-lanes, Wrangel's days of isolation were fast coming to an end.

Two miles off the island's northern shore, concealed beneath the pack ice, the fast-attack submarine *New Mexico* crawled ahead at minimum speed. Her commanding officer, Commander Tristan Zimmerman, watched the displays closely. Forty hours ago, his boat had been 210 miles northeast, taking part in the Navy's annual Ice Exercise, or ICEX. That training was abruptly curtailed by a priority message—one that had sent them, quite unexpectedly, into Russian territorial waters.

"Comm, do we have a new FLAP yet?" the captain asked.

"Not yet, sir," replied the young man at the communications station.

In the service's endless sea of acronyms, FLAP stood for Fractures, Leads, and Polynya Analysis. It was a satellite-derived forecast of gaps in the polar ice coverage. Fractures were visible cracks in the ice, and a lead was one big enough to accommodate a submarine. *Polynya* was a Russian term—an allowance to that country's pioneering work in polar operations—that referred to open-water voids caused by warm upwelling currents. Taken together, the FLAP report was a rough map of where the ice sheet might be breached. It came with the credibility of any weatherman's forecast—a decent reference, but no guarantees. Yesterday's report, the most current, was not promising for the waters immediately northwest of Wrangel Island.

"Nav?" Zimmerman prompted.

The man at a nearby station answered, "Best option bearing one-seven-zero."

Lieutenant Commander Craig Dooley, the executive officer, who was tracking temperature and pressure measurements, said, "XO concurs."

Two hundred yards farther on, the captain said, "All right, let's hold here. Bring up the video."

Ever so slowly, *New Mexico* slid to a dead stop. She was ninety feet below the surface, her keel two hundred above the rocky bottom. The undersea slope on the island's northwest coast varied greatly, and Zimmerman had chosen a section where the gradient was steep, hoping for an upwelling current to thin the ice above.

"Video coming," said Dooley.

An upward-facing exterior camera was turned on, and the panorama was striking: ghostly, gray-shaded images of the ice above. The low-light video was designed for just such penetrations.

"I don't know," said Dooley. "Not much variance."

"No," Zimmerman agreed. "But based on temp alone I think we're good."

"I'd agree," seconded the exec.

Zimmerman had long encouraged his crew, from top to bottom, to speak up with reasoned dissent. Hearing none, he gave the order, and *New Mexico* was configured for penetration. Periscopes and masts were retracted, the dive planes rotated to a vertical position. All eyes went to the depth gauge, watching the slow rise.

The first contact came five feet below the surface. Zimmerman recalled his first punch through the polar cap—everyone did. It reminded him of a slow-motion car wreck, the interminable grinding and crunching of steel on ice, vibrations as chunks broke free. Finally, things stabilized.

"There, that was easy," Dooley said with faux lightheartedness.

"Okay," the captain said. "Let's see what we've got."

Minutes later Zimmerman was on the observation platform, Dooley at his side. "Damn!" he said, squinting into an obscure night sky.

Snow swept across the ice shelf in curtains, driven by a furious wind, and freezing drizzle peppered his face. The captain turned his head away from the maelstrom, realizing he should have worn his hooded jacket. He'd brought binoculars out of habit, but they were entirely useless. At five a.m.

in the Arctic, in the middle of a raging winter storm—he could barely see the bow, let alone the shoreline half a mile distant.

"Visibility is down to nothing."

Dooley said, "According to the forecast, it's going to stay that way all day. Do you think it's safe to put a team ashore for a search?"

"Safe is a relative term. I wouldn't do it on a training exercise, but you saw our orders. This is the real deal, and thankfully, we've got the gear for it."

The objectives of their original training mission, ICEX, had been to establish a temporary outpost on an ice floe, mark landing zones for helicopters, and perform short-range, land-based reconnaissance. In essence, precisely what they were about to do for real on Russian soil.

"True," Dooley agreed, "we couldn't do it without the snowmobiles. It would help if we knew where to look for this wreckage."

As if on cue, a petty officer poked his head out of the hatch. "Captain, new message from Fleet. It's marked urgent."

Point Hope scythed into the Chukchi Sea like an Arabian scimitar, its modest runway fixed near the tip of the blade. Slaton was seated behind the pilots on a folding jump seat, having been invited to watch as they made their final approach in the Osprey. The weather was ominously quiet, a gentle breeze and clear skies under the scant light of dawn. For the last twenty minutes, Alaska had been presented in all the glory of winter twilight: shadows on shadows, an Ice Age panorama of endless hills in shades of gray.

Where land met sea was the place called Point Hope. The runway was barely discernable: from thirty miles away, a tiny thread of gray. The adjacent town was little more than a fistful of amber jewels, and beyond that the boundless sea swept away, dark and foreboding in the half-light.

The aircraft commander, Major Ty Westlake, said, "This airport doesn't get many arrivals in the winter. A few cargo flights, the occasional medevac. Most of the airplanes that do come in have skis instead of wheels."

Slaton studied the village. "Not exactly a metropolis."

"I've been here once before," said Westlake. "Most of the towns this far north are temporary, basically camps for workers set up by oil companies. This one's legit, a real Native American village. It's been continuously inhabited for over two thousand years."

"I guess they like their solitude."

"Apparently." He jabbed a thumb toward his copilot, a captain named Paulson, who was working a secondary radio. "My partner's talking to one of the locals, the guy who runs the weather station."

Paulson finished and gave his report. "Winds are calm, five degrees Fahrenheit. Current MU reading is point-two-seven."

"What's MU?" Slaton asked.

"Runway condition," the skipper explained. "They measure it with a pickup truck and what looks like a bicycle tire. It's surprisingly accurate. Anything below point-two is pretty much an ice rink. Point-two-seven is at the edge of our operational envelope, but I think we can manage."

"Couldn't you just hover to land?"

"It's a tradeoff. With all the gear in back we're heavy, which lends itself to a powered landing. Hover also creates a big downwash, and with so much snow on the ground we'd probably put ourselves in whiteout conditions right before touchdown. We've got a runway, so we'll use it."

Slaton nodded. It made sense, and once again he had the impression he was dealing with professionals. The question of how they were going to put down on Wrangel Island, without a runway or weather reports, he decided was better left unasked.

"How long will we be on the ground?"

"Orders are for minimum turn time. Assuming the fuel trucks are standing by, that's about thirty minutes. But we need to get a situation update before launching and take a real close look at the weather. I'd say an hour is more realistic."

Westlake flew a curvilinear path to line up with the runway. The runway lights were turned up to maximum intensity, defining the borders of the paved surface. Without them, making out the runway would have been nearly impossible—despite the good visibility, the snow-encrusted concrete was indistinguishable from the surrounding tundra.

With three miles to go, the skipper said, "Better go strap in."

Slaton went aft and took his seat. As the aircraft slowed, the noise level rose, vibrations from the big props rattling the airframe. He said to the others, "Almost there. Expect about an hour on the ground. We'll get some fresh intel and maybe some food. If the weather in the target area is acceptable, the plan is to go." He looked across the aisle and got nods from Tracer's guys. Davis, sitting next to him, was just stirring.

Slaton shook his head, and thought, *One of these days, I'm going to learn how to do that.*

FIFTEEN

Commander Zimmerman hovered over an electronic chart, the northwest quadrant of Wrangle Island depicted in precise topographical detail. Before him was the team about to go ashore.

"We're twelve hundred yards offshore," he said. "The ice should be solid all the way in, so the sleds are a go. Command has identified two coordinate sets where they think we'll find wreckage. One is here." He tapped a reference mark roughly a mile distant, tucked in a saddle between two low hills. "The second is a few hundred yards farther, in the center of the next cove. That's the first section you need to access—it's been identified as the main fuselage. Your orders are to locate the wreckage, report back, and investigate for as long as the weather permits."

"Is there any chance of survivors?" asked the lieutenant leading the expedition.

"From what I've been told, given the nature of the crash and the conditions outside, the chances are effectively nil. We've been tasked to recover remains if feasible."

A somber nod.

Zimmerman addressed the petty officer at the comm station. "Latest weather?"

"Wind is down to twenty knots, Captain. Forecast to continue decreasing, but slowly. Frozen mixed precipitation on and off, but nothing extreme."

"Any news on our inbound Ospreys?"

"Just checked," said the exec, Dooley. "They're airborne, scheduled to arrive in roughly two hours. We've been ordered to scope out an appropriate landing zone ashore. The Ospreys are too heavy to risk putting down on the ice like a helo."

"Are we still playing host?"

"We are—the Ospreys are drop and go. We can expect nine individuals of indeterminant service affiliation."

"Gotta be Spec Ops," the captain surmised.

"No doubt. And they're coming equipped to dive on the submerged wreckage."

"Seriously?"

Dooley only shrugged.

Zimmerman looked around the table. Five faces looked back expectantly. The burden of what they were doing—launching a minor invasion onto Russian soil—was beginning to sink in.

"All right," he said, "let's get it done."

Bloch and Sorensen managed a few fitful hours of sleep—both knew the remainder of the day would be busy. By seven that morning they were back at work. They'd been given carte blanche to set up shop at the Kodiak SEAL detachment and chose a corner of the command post near the comm workstation. Because the outpost was a training detachment, the hardware for secure comm was bare bones, yet they were able to link to their respective operations centers in Langley and Tel Aviv.

The two spymasters convened for a bit of information sharing in a side conference room that was decorated, if the term could be used, with the official photos of current Navy leadership.

Sorensen began. "We've got a pretty good idea of where the wreckage ended up. I forwarded the coordinates to *New Mexico*—they're on scene and about to begin a search. We've also been studying some data on the crash. Rivet Joint aircraft are wired to uplink certain signal intercepts during missions. After analyzing the end game of Raven 44, we're convinced the airplane was getting painted by a radar from the north right before the crash sequence began."

"The north?" Bloch commented.

"You see the problem—the Russian coastline would have been south. There is some restricted airspace in that direction, Danger Area 401. It's a missile test range, Russia's biggest, but it isn't used very often."

"Are you suggesting some kind of accidental missile launch?"

"No. Our people have analyzed the signal closely, and it's a low-rate search radar—not at all what a missile would use for terminal homing. Somebody was watching Raven 44, tracking it from a distance. The curious thing is . . . this radar didn't fit the electronic profile of any known Russian system."

"Who then?"

"Don't know. The analysts are quite sure it was a ground-based system, which means we're looking at a ship and not an airplane. We've been going over satellite logs, searching for ships in the area, but there's not much to go on. We don't have much coverage in those parts, especially this time of year—it's virtually impassable to surface ships due to ice. At the moment, we're also competing for assets. The Navy has a crisis of its own—one of their guided missile destroyers, *Ross*, collided with a container ship in the Black Sea and sank."

"A collision," Bloch remarked. "How unfortunate."

"And untimely. Our second military disaster in two days."

"Do you have any details?"

"A few. Nine crewmen were lost, but the rest survived, including her commanding officer. His initial report suggests the ship was suffering navigation problems just prior to the collision. Visibility was poor, and there was conflicting position data."

"That sounds confusing."

"To say the least." Sorensen leaned back in her chair and looked up at the secretary of the Navy on the wall. The glowering expression in his official photo was ruined—someone had added an extravagant grease-pencil mustache. She was glad the CIA wasn't into the whole photo-on-the-wall thing—special operators, by nature, didn't handle authority well, and she shuddered to think how her own picture might be defiled. "Has there been any progress in finding Ayla?" she asked.

"Director Nurin assures me everything possible is being done . . . exactly what I would say if the tables were turned. Local teams from the embassy are searching around the clock. A few witnesses have turned up, but so far they've provided nothing useful. Our cyber teams are trying to identify the car used in the abduction."

"Are the Kazakhs helping?"

"They say the right things, but as I'm sure you know, loyalties are fleeting in that part of the world."

"I'll send word to the director—our consulate in Almaty might be able to help."

"Any assistance would be appreciated." He looked at a blank television monitor mounted in the room's corner. "Tell me, the loss of this ship in the Black Sea . . . I assume it is public knowledge?"

"All over the news."

"And the loss of Raven 44? Has that been made public?"

"The Air Force has tried to keep a lid on it. The next of kin have been quietly notified that the jet is missing—which technically is the truth."

"Having served in the military, I can assure you the rumor mill on base will be buzzing."

"No doubt. Last I heard, DOD was working on a vague press release to declare the plane missing. Once that hits the wires, the Russians are going to get very curious."

"Which threatens our mission to Kodiak."

"No two ways about it. Our window for getting answers is shrinking fast."

Six thousand miles from Kodiak, behind a coffee-stained plastic table in a conference room, Bloch's successor sat watching a video of a swirling flock of seagulls.

It was all but a cliché that failures in the intelligence world came in unimaginable forms. Critical messages were sent to wrong numbers. Bribes got paid to the wrong cop. An assassination team might shoot a waiter instead of a terrorist. As Raymond Nurin sat watching security camera footage, taken early that morning along the south perimeter wall of the Israeli embassy in Kazakhstan, he did so with the ill feeling that a new standard of incompetence was being set.

"Here he comes," said Beni Katz, Mossad's chief of operational security.

Nurin watched a man in a blue jacket approach on the sidewalk near the main compound entrance. He reached his gloved left hand into a plastic bag and began throwing what looked like bread crumbs in the air. A group of a dozen gulls, which appeared to be following him, swarmed to pluck up the morsels.

"Here," Katz said, slowing the playback.

The camera's resolution was excellent—it was, after all, monitoring an access point to a highly vulnerable foreign mission. As the man neared the side gate, he threw a handful of crumbs toward the entrance. He didn't bother to watch where they fell, yet most ended up in the gravel near the guard post. The surly guard looked on disapprovingly. One or two of the crumbs were plucked out of midair by the gulls.

Katz froze on a particular frame, zoomed in, and tapped the screen. "You can see it here."

Nurin did. One "crumb," larger, more colorful, and shaped differently from the others, flew high in the air toward the guard shack—until an enterprising gull plucked it from midair.

The video ran in slow motion, and as the gull flew over the wall Nurin saw another bird try to snatch away the object. In a flurry of flapping wings and snapping beaks, the red stick fell to the earth somewhere behind the wall.

Nurin buried his face in his hands, no longer able to watch.

Katz stopped the video. "The gardener found it near the rose bushes. Thankfully, he turned it in."

"Lazarus," Nurin said.

"Yes."

"Do we know what's on the device?"

"We do. Lazarus is running scared. He says he saw his case officer get abducted near the market in Almaty. He was afraid to use the email folder and decided this was the best way to reestablish contact—a drop at the embassy gate. The bread crumbs were his idea of tradecraft, a way of not walking directly to the gate to hand the stick to the guard. He probably never saw the bird snatch it."

Nurin held steady.

"He's given us a new email address, so we expect he'll use the same tactic. We've been watching, but so far there's nothing in the draft folder. Lazarus is convinced he's been compromised. He says he's going into hiding." Katz looked despondently at the birds on the screen. "Obviously we need a more secure means of communication, but as it stands . . . we can only wait. Oh, and there was one other bit of information."

Nurin looked at him, his expression pleading, *Tell me this can't get any worse.*

"He mentioned a second threat against an American asset. He said it would involve a U.S. Navy ship on the Black Sea."

"And this would have been—"

"Less than one hour before the destroyer *Ross* sank. It seems we've stumbled on to the best intelligence source we've had in a decade. Unfortunately, he is to spying what Inspector Clouseau is to detective work."

Nurin's head drooped as if in prayer. "Seagulls," he said despairingly. "God forgive us the amateur."

SIXTEEN

The expedition from *New Mexico* to the shore of Wrangel Island launched without a hitch. A team of four men doubled up on two snowmobiles, each of which pulled a utility sled. One sled was packed with communications gear and survival equipment, while the other, grimly, carried a stack of body bags.

The weather had improved slightly, making the conditions merely awful. The clock claimed it was early morning, but the deep Arctic night held fast. Twenty knots of wind, combined with temperatures well below zero, required careful precautions. Exposed skin was immediately subject to frostbite and breathing was painful. The ship's medic told the men going ashore to limit their exposure to no more than two hours.

Fortunately, it was realistic: They'd been given updated, finely tuned coordinates for the plots of wreckage by the National Reconnaissance Office. Also in their favor was that the terrain was perfectly flat to begin—a solid ice pack over the bay—and only gentle hills once ashore.

It took twenty minutes to reach the most important section of debris. The lieutenant in charge was the first to discern it in the Arctic twilight: half-covered in snow, a barely recognizable tube of metal the length of a tractor trailer. He brought the snowmobiles to a stop in the lee of a nearby hill and everyone dismounted.

The initial inspection took ten minutes, after which the lieutenant, who had never seen such a sight, made a radio call to *New Mexico*. His voice cracked only slightly. "We've found the main wreckage field and confirm there are no survivors. This thing is in really bad shape."

Commander Zimmerman replied, "All right, stand by while I run it up the chain."

A flurry of satellite messages ran between *New Mexico* and command authorities, and after five minutes the captain came back with new orders. "Have two of your men stay there, recover remains as best they can. I want you and one other to make your way to the second site."

The lieutenant did as instructed and ten minutes later called back. "It's just like they said, Captain—the other section is the right wing. Just a bunch of mangled metal and one engine still attached."

"All right. Take pictures from every angle, especially the engine. Then scout out an LZ for the inbound Ospreys that meets the requirements we discussed."

The lieutenant had gotten detailed instructions before leaving the ship: the landing zone had to be relatively flat, on solid ground, and at least two hundred meters long with no high hills on either end. Brownie points would be given if it was oriented into the wind. "I saw a couple of possibilities on the way in," the lieutenant said.

"Once that's done, go back and help the others with the recovery. Everyone needs to be back on board in five-zero minutes. I don't want anyone going hypothermic on me."

"Copy all, Captain."

As *New Mexico*'s expeditionary team was going about its grim chore, analysts deep in the National Reconnaissance Office continued poring over satellite images. They focused on a composite product taken from scientific birds operated by NASA and NOAA. Of particular interest was data taken from ICESat-2, NASA's orbiting project to map and measure seasonal variations in the polar ice caps.

While the mission of ICESat-2 was straightforward, and strictly scientific, NRO had long maintained that data was not to be wasted. This point of view was seconded by the directors of the scientific agencies, who saw it as a selling point on Capitol Hill: data sharing for defense purposes always added backing. So, while ICESat-2 was funded and operated by NASA, NRO regularly received caches of raw data. With its vast capability for analysis, and a deep understanding of photo-surveillance, no imagery would be wasted in times of need.

A special NRO working group was assembled overnight, the objective being to identify anomalies in the Arctic ice pack, in the vicinity of Wrangel Island, that had appeared in the previous seventy-two hours. Within twelve hours they succeeded on two fronts.

First was the discovery of three small breaches in the ice within a mile of the island. All had appeared suddenly, and two simultaneously. The two that appeared concurrently were each the size of a swimming pool, and careful analysis showed no hydrographic or environmental reason for their creation. It seemed, as alluded to in their briefing, that something had "fallen out of the sky." The working group was told to ignore the third breach, but surveillance analysts being what they were, they took up the challenge and easily identified its source: a Virginia-class submarine punched through the ice sheet.

The second bit of intelligence gleaned from the effort, and the one that would prove far more telling, was stumbled upon quite by accident. In making its request for the search, the CIA had neglected to provide boundaries other than "in the vicinity of Wrangel Island." Wanting to be thorough, the team leader had programmed a search radius of one hundred nautical miles—far greater than what the CIA would have requested had they thought to impose a constraint.

Because of it, early that afternoon, at the beginning of the late shift, a curious analyst noted an elongated breach whose source was obvious: a lone icebreaker pounding ahead at full steam. Based on the clear trail the ship was leaving, and the speed at which it was traveling, it was simplicity itself to determine where it had been and when it had been there. Icebreakers were not uncommon in Arctic waters, yet this vessel's proximity to Wrangel, along with its course and position, caused the find to be passed up the chain.

When the information reached the CIA, specialists there agreed it was suspicious. The agency input the best images of the icebreaker through its own internal paces, and soon a cascade of connections began.

For years the CIA had been building a digital library of the world's ships, tens of thousands of profiles catalogued by type of vessel, tonnage, ownership strings, as well as detailed images taken from satellite and maritime reconnaissance. Every large ship was invariably unique in some way: structure, fittings, lifeboat positioning, antennas, rust patterns on hulls, even damage from minor loading accidents. As a result, there were but a handful of vessels on earth exceeding four thousand gross tons that could not be identified from a few high-res overheads.

As a relatively small vessel, the ship in question might have fallen through the cracks had its mission not been specifically targeted for added attention. With fast-warming oceans, the northern sea routes were expanding every year, and icebreakers were getting special interest from intelligence services: one more battleground in the ever-shifting sands of geopolitics.

The ship was identified quickly: Her name was *Sibir*. She had been commissioned thirty years ago in Latvia and until recently had been operated by the government of Kazakhstan. A diesel-electric boat, *Sibir* was rated to penetrate ice up to four feet thick—more than sufficient for plying the relatively warm Caspian Sea, where she'd gotten her start, at the height of winter. Six months ago, the Kazakhs had put her up for sale, and she'd been purchased by a private owner. After the sale finalized, she was tracked to a shipyard in Sri Lanka where she underwent unspecified retrofits. From there, CIA followed *Sibir* through port calls in Taiwan and, more surprisingly, North Korea.

The questions of who owned her, and for what purpose, remained impenetrable. More vexing yet: Why was she now plowing through the ice-clad waters north of Siberia? Researchers at CIA trained their vast processing power on the mystery and soon uncovered an even more disturbing link. At the port in Sri Lanka where *Sibir* had spent her fall months, she'd briefly been docked bow-to-stern with another ship. Her name was *Atlas*, and she was owned by the same shadowed consortium—EDG Industries.

Further investigation of *Atlas* brought the most astounding revelation: she was pinpointed, the previous day, as having been less than twenty miles south of the destroyer *Ross* when she sank in the Black Sea.

SEVENTEEN

The flight segment from Point Hope to Wrangel Island was far shorter than the first leg. It took the Ospreys two hours to reach the point of no return: the border of Russian airspace.

Slaton and Davis were hunched behind the pilots on the tiny flight deck, everyone waiting for the final green light. The copilot, Captain Paulson, was flying while Major Westlake coordinated on the radio.

When he was done, the skipper said, "We're good to go. No sign of Russian air defense activity. We also got word that *New Mexico* is on site. They found the shoreside sections of wreckage—one wing and the fuselage. There were no survivors, and the crew are doing their best to recover remains. They scoped out an LZ for us not far away. The weather is lousy, but slowly improving. It's going to be dodgy, but hopefully we can make it in."

Westlake took control of the aircraft and then passed the coordinates of the landing zone to the copilot, who began inputting them into the navigation system.

"Any updates for us?" Slaton asked.

"No changes. We're dropping you off with your equipment, then we head back to Point Hope. We'll be on call for an emergency extract, but it would take us five hours to refuel and get back—best case. They want you to retrieve as much of the Air Force's classified equipment as you can, along with the two black boxes, then destroy what's left. *New Mexico* will be your ride out."

Davis asked, "Have they located any of the submerged wreckage? One of those plots has to be the tail, and that's where the black boxes will be."

"Didn't mention it," said Westlake. "But there was one other point of emphasis. So far, there's no sign the Russians have caught wind of our operation. That said, headquarters doesn't want you to spend any more time than necessary on the ground. Get in, grab what you can, blow up the rest."

Slaton gave Davis a sideways glance, and said, "Wish we had those orders in writing."

"I wish we had *any* orders in writing," he replied.

"Initial point in five minutes," the major said. "On the ground in fifteen. You better go talk to the loadie. He's going to need your help getting the equipment off. If we actually manage to land, I don't want to spend any more time on the ground than necessary."

Slaton and Davis returned to the cargo bay and were hit by a wall of cold. The Osprey's feeble heating system was losing the battle against the extreme temperatures outside. And it was about to get a lot colder.

Two hundred miles southwest, in Eastern Military District air defense headquarters, outside the Siberian town of Pevek, Colonel Dmitri Burinov hurried down the hall to his chief engineer's office. He was not a happy man.

As the sector commander, Burinov was charged with finding the reason behind an outage at the Ushakovskiy radar station on Wrangel Island. A team of technicians there had been working for hours to get their Sopka-2 radar back online. The system broke down regularly, mostly due to the extreme conditions on the island. When it wasn't the ice, it was poor design, lack of spare parts, short circuits, or the island's regular power outages—the outpost's generators were held together, quite literally, by shoestrings and baling wire.

He was dreading the report he would have to write explaining the malfunction, and contemplating who to blame, when his mobile phone vibrated in his pocket. He pulled it out expecting to see a call from his wife or daughter. The number that showed registered in his contacts as Ludmilla—his aunt from Kiev who'd died two years ago.

Burinov stopped in the hallway, his anger rising, and he took the call.

"What are you thinking? I told you to never call me at work! You—"

"Shut up and listen!" said a voice Burinov didn't recognize in accented Russian.

He'd been expecting Katrina, his mistress for the last eighteen months. She was half his age, financially strapped, and completely dependent on his largess. And now apparently, the stupid bitch had lost track of her phone. "Whoever this is," Burinov growled, "you have no idea who you are talking to. Clearly you—"

"I am talking to Colonel Dmitri Burinov, who will soon be court-martialed if he does not do precisely as I say."

Burinov was stunned to silence, his mind racing.

"I am about to give you information that will either end your career or advance it—the choice is yours. Your radar equipment on Wrangel Island is presently having difficulties, is it not?"

This was posed as a question, yet Burinov was not so unsettled that he would give out operational information over the phone to a stranger. "Go on," he said.

"The station is down because the Americans are interfering with your signal while they invade Wrangel Island."

"What are you talking about? *Invade?*"

"You should confirm it with your sister sector. Call Far East command and request temporary overlap coverage. You will see American aircraft. There is also a submarine in Pestsovaya Bay."

Burinov's caution ramped up exponentially. He could do the overlap easily enough. It was a standard backup procedure, although one he had so far avoided—it would mean admitting to headquarters that his own sector was having trouble. But how could *this stranger* know such a thing?

"Who is this?" the colonel demanded. "And how could you know about—"

The call ended. A furious Burinov called the number back, his sausage fingers thumping the phone's screen. After five rings, Katrina answered. She sounded sleepy. "What it is, darling?"

"Who is using your phone?" he demanded. He envisioned her sitting up in bed, straightened by his tone, a pout on her full lips and her long hair askew.

"What are you talking about, Pasha? My phone is right here."

"And no one is with you?"

"How could you say such a thing? My love for you is—"

Burinov cut the connection. Even Katrina, stupid as she was, would not be party to such deception. It had to be some kind of digital trickery. This realization forced him to a choice. Ignore the matter entirely, or call and ask for help. He tapped his fingers idly on the handset, but only for a moment. He diverted to the control room and picked up the sector coordination landline. The risk was simply too great.

He soon was talking to his counterpart in Sector Four. "Yes, Colonel Mazov. This is Burinov at Three. My equipment has gone down on Wrangel. I'm sure it's only a minor problem . . . you know how the weather can be there. My technicians are working on the problem, but I would like you to overlap that area for a short time."

Mazov said he would be glad to—Burinov could almost see the man smiling, and he imagined how he would play it up at the weekly staff meeting.

Then Burinov remembered the caller's words: *information that will either end your career or advance it—the choice is yours.* He added, "Something else, Mazov. Right before the feed went down, I saw a suspicious return north of Wrangel. I thought for a moment it might be an invasion." He chuckled halfheartedly. "It is probably only an anomaly, but I mention it because the return caught my eye. Perhaps you should look into it . . ."

With that, Burinov's part was complete. He had reacted precisely as the man who'd commandeered his mistress's phone expected. In the mountain lodge deep in the Altai Mountains, the researcher, who'd drawn the chore because he was the best Russian speaker of the bunch, returned to the sitting room.

To the two men waiting, who were sharing a pot of hot cocoa, he said simply, "It is done."

EIGHTEEN

The turbulence was getting worse. Strapped into the webbed seat, Slaton's lap belt strained and his shoulders pressed into the Osprey's sidewall. The cabin heater seemed to have failed, and the temperature was below zero—Slaton knew because his water bottle had frozen solid.

"Is it always this bumpy in the Arctic?" he asked Davis, who was sitting next to him.

"They have storms here like anywhere. I just hope the visibility is good enough to land—it would suck to come all this way and have to turn around."

The pallets of gear groaned against their tie-downs as the airplane jolted through gusts. The landing lights snapped on, evident by a milky reflection through the side viewing ports. Both men leaned forward and peered through the passageway that led to the flight deck. The front window was partially in view, and with the landing lights on, the snow came at them like a galaxy of onrushing stars.

"Should we go up front and ask for an update?" Slaton said.

"Better we don't bother them. I'm sure they know what they're doing."

In the Osprey's cockpit, Paulson looked at his aircraft commander, and asked, "You sure you know what you're doing, boss?"

"Not really." His hands a blur as he fought the controls, Westlake looked like a pastry chef whipping a bowl of merengue. Every move seemed too late, out of synch with what the airplane was doing.

"Just help me keep sight of Felon 01," he said, referring to the lead airplane. The other Osprey was barely visible through the mist and snow, little more than a shadow and a set of navigation lights two hundred feet ahead. They normally would have turned off all exterior lights for a tactical mission, but the weather made the lights a necessity—and highlighting themselves was hardly an issue given the uninhabited terrain below. When the call signs, Felon 01 and 02, had been assigned, they seemed to fit the mission perfectly—come in like burglars, under the radar, for a smash-and-grab heist. As it turned out, the pilots barely used it—they hadn't talked to an air traffic controller since leaving Alaska.

"Distance to the LZ?" Westlake asked, not wanting to take his eyes off the lead aircraft.

"One point two miles. Altitude one thousand feet and descending."

"Is that baro or radar altitude?"

"Barometric."

"Are we still feet wet?"

The lieutenant checked his map display, saw they were still over water, frozen as it might be. "We are . . . I show half a mile to the shoreline. No significant terrain on the run-in course."

"Hallelujah for that."

"Weather radar shows heavy precip near the LZ. It's going to be tight getting in."

Westlake saw the lights of the lead aircraft flicker, then disappear in dense clouds. He was about to make a radio call saying he'd lost visual when the lead aircraft reappeared. "Why did I not just keep my college job?" he fussed, working the controls furiously.

"What was that?"

"Greeter at Walmart. They don't have to deal with shit like this."

Paulson actually grinned.

Westlake struggled to keep Felon 01 in sight all the way down, and nearing the landing zone, he got a visual on the ground. "Looks pretty frozen down there—it'll be slick when we set down."

A gust of wind rocked the airplane, and the controls hit the stop as Westlake righted things.

"One hundred feet radar," the copilot called out, referencing their height above ground from the radar altimeter. "Fifty feet. That thick precip is right in front of us."

They both saw the lead Osprey touch down, then disappear, lost in the private cloud of its own downwash.

At thirty feet the landing lights began illuminating the flat, almost featureless snowbound terrain. At ten feet their own downwash began kicking up snow. Then everything disappeared in a wall of white.

It wasn't so much a landing as a controlled crash. Felon 02 hit hard and bounced, but Westlake handled it well, holding the aircraft steady in a gyre of competing forces. The second touchdown was actually smooth, and the Osprey settled on its wheels with a groan that could have been taken for relief.

Westlake looked over at Paulson—his typically steady copilot had gone ashen—and said, "Welcome to Russia."

Zamir Bagdani stood on the wing of *Poyarka*'s bridge, a dying cigarette held tenuously between two fingers. On the deck below, he saw the final preparations being made. Every technical problem had been solved, or so the chief engineer assured him. At this point the chores being carried out were the same as on any ship about to set sail. Provisions carted over the gangway, crewmen with duffels headed for bunk rooms.

Bagdani was not the ship's master—he knew little about the sea—but rather considered himself something closer to an admiral. The strategic commander of a tiny fleet, *Poyarka* serving as flagship. In keeping with that image, like any good admiral, he fretted over what might go wrong in the coming days.

He flicked the cigarette butt spinning into the harbor, checked his watch, and allowed ten more minutes. He would soon have to leave to catch his flight—his scheduled meeting with Lazarus loomed. He didn't like meetings in general—a relic of his cautionary formative years—and even less so with men he didn't trust.

Once more, he found himself in that all-too-familiar role: an indelicate man in a delicate situation. An ethnic Albanian, Bagdani was big and rough-edged, a cruiserweight boxer past his prime. Thick muscles were overlaid by layers of flab, yet his block head and crooked nose endured, testament to a hard life. His story began like a million others during the lost decade of the Yugoslav Wars. Bagdani's earliest memories were of a hardscrabble upbringing. Abandoned as a child, he'd spent his formative years being shunted between orphanages. A series of escapes put him on the hard streets of Tirana, and it was there, at the determinative age of fifteen, that his instincts for commerce were first realized.

Young Zamir discovered he had a knack for reading people, for recognizing their wants and weaknesses. Be it drugs, handguns, or women, he was adept at brokering deals and extracting his cut. A series of short stints in prison narrowed his prospects, ruling out any notions of education or a responsible job.

When he was eighteen, still on the streets and spiraling downward, and with the Yugoslav Wars at their worst, a chance encounter altered Bagdani's life: He witnessed an altercation in a portside bar. On one side were four locals who reminded him of himself, perhaps ten years older. After watching them engage two foreigners over a spilled beer, Bagdani doubted they would live ten more. The locals were left broken and bleeding, while the men they'd attacked barely worked up a sweat. Intrigued, Bagdani offered to buy the men a drink and asked where they'd learned to fight. Three drinks later they were still telling stories. Two after that, Bagdani had made up his mind. It was time to abandon Tirana, with its dubious prospects, and take the path these men had: he would join the French Foreign Legion.

The process took nearly a year, but his persistence paid off, and after four months of training, Bagdani was shipped out to Africa. He was a hard man, accustomed to privation, yet in a service comprised of the planet's most desperate castoffs, he was nothing special. He went on patrols when ordered to do so, but never volunteered. He was surprised by the fervor of the Islamist fighters, and after a close call one night that left two bullets embedded in his body armor, he decided life on the front lines was not to his liking. Bagdani began angling for a transfer from the killing side of the Legion to its softer underbelly, the regimental Compagnie d'Appui.

Support and logistics, the lifeblood of any army.

It was there that he found his true calling. From the rear echelon he watched the movement of money, the transfer of material, and on a scale he'd never before imagined. Food, weapons, vehicles. Cash for payroll and local contractors. He drove trucks brimming with supplies into the field and was tasked to deliver suitcases full of U.S. dollars. It was a larcenist's dream. Like any good felon, Bagdani started out cautiously, watching and waiting, staying beneath his commander's radar. In time he was given more autonomy, a faithless dog on a lengthening leash. He began with small gifts: a rifle to a militia quartermaster, bribes to a few guards. He made contacts in Mali and Ghana, loaned trucks to NGOs for shipments of morphine.

His first cuts were thin, yet the techniques were no more than an escalation of what he'd been doing his entire life: small margins taken to connect suppliers with willing buyers. He diverted shipments of rice and wheat to villages that paid a small kickback. He managed deliveries of medical supplies to favor particular end users.

His business expanded when a minor shipment of small arms fell into his lap. The crates of rifles, supposedly lost in transit, were tracked down by Corporal Bagdani and sold at a steep discount to a rebel militia—the very group that the tip of the Legion's spear was fighting. Bagdani felt neither guilt nor pleasure in taking what France was providing and selling it to their enemies. In the moral mudhole of sub-Saharan Africa, such was the way of life.

The Legion, however, like any military organization, was not without its cross checks. When an audit discovered missing crates of ammunition, Bagdani blamed shoddy paperwork. A captain bucking for promotion began digging deeper and found evidence of further transgressions. For the second time, Bagdani recognized the limitations of his position. The Legion had given him opportunity, but once suspicion was raised his prospects faltered. With a reenlistment decision looming, and a deepening investigation, he destroyed incriminating records, obfuscated others, and paid off a handful of witnesses. It bought him just enough time to leave the service under a cloud of suspicion, but with no formal charges brought.

Bagdani disappeared virtually overnight, but in fact, he didn't go far.

He recognized the value of the contacts he'd made in Africa. Within two months he made his first deal, brokering a transfer of rifles between a crooked minister in Burkina Faso and rebels in Ivory Coast. Inside three years, Bagdani established himself as one of the preeminent arms merchants in Africa. He graduated to more advanced equipment, seeing the higher profit margins. Kalashnikovs led to surface-to-air missiles, which led to light attack aircraft. Leveraging old connections in the Legion, he branched out and began recruiting men to go with the materiel. With conflicts blazing across the continent, the developed world had been sending trainers to Africa for decades: special operators, technicians, highly experienced NCOs. Men who were happy to double their pay by going private.

This became Bagdani's niche: not simply thugs who would point a rifle, but technically proficient warriors who could use the latest equipment. His profits exploded. Drone operators, attack pilots, explosives experts, Special Forces instructors—Bagdani could fill virtually any military specialty. He expanded into the Middle East, and eventually Asia, his reputation growing. Within ten years, the one-time urchin from Tirana was at the pinnacle: a headhunter who could recruit men and women, if the price was right, with the skills to bring any weapon to bear.

Now he looked down at the culmination of it all, concealed beneath the half dome on *Poyarka*'s foredeck. He knew little about how the device worked, yet they'd told him what it could do. After working nonstop for weeks, the weapon was ready, as was the crew he'd procured. The operators had arrived and were going through their paces, planning for onboard contingencies. He'd been told the one thing they didn't have to worry about was countermeasures—against this weapon, there was no defense.

Poyarka would sail soon with its skeleton crew—ten men of six different nationalities. Joining the technicians who would handle the strike were a vagabond captain, two engineers to keep the propellers turning, and five deckhands rounded things out, two of these doing double duty in the mess hall.

Bagdani himself, of course, would not be aboard. If anything went wrong, only the men on the ship could be held accountable. A band of castoffs from around the world who knew nothing of the greater strategy. Most were ordinary seamen, and only the captain and the two operators knew the ship's mission: *Poyarka* was carrying a weapon that defied comprehension.

For Bagdani, it was a dangerous game. Yet if he could bring everything together, come out unscathed—it might be a happy ending to a difficult life's journey.

He checked his watch again. It was time to leave for his outbound flight.

He didn't want to keep Lazarus waiting.

NINETEEN

The temperature in Wrangel made Kodiak seem like an equatorial paradise. Slaton walked down the Osprey's loading ramp in full winter gear. It wasn't nearly enough. The wind cut like a blade, whipping unhindered off the ice-covered sea and finding every gap in his outer shell.

Davis was right behind him, head down. He shouted to be heard over the wind and the exhaust of the Ospreys' auxiliary power units. "What the hell was I thinking when I signed up for this?"

Slaton had to agree. "For the first time in my life I wish I was in Kazakhstan."

"Kazakhstan?"

"That's what I signed on for—long story."

A new sound overrode the din, a snowmobile approaching, its headlights reaching out of the gloom. They'd been briefed they would be met by crewmen from *New Mexico*. Briefing or not, Slaton's hand went to the stock of the SCAR-H hanging on his chest.

The machine ground to a stop behind the second Osprey, and recognizing the familiar winter gear, Slaton's grip eased. A Navy lieutenant named Richards introduced himself to Tracer, Slaton, and Davis.

"Glad the LZ worked out," Richards said.

Tracer responded, "The LZ is fine—the problem was the weather. We almost didn't make it in."

"Conditions were better an hour ago. If nothing else, it'll keep the Russkies from seeing what we're up to."

"Where is *New Mexico*?" Slaton asked.

The lieutenant pointed out to sea. "About fifteen hundred meters away. We located both landside sections of wreckage, but unfortunately there were no survivors. We've been working on collecting remains."

Davis said, "It's the fuselage and one wing, right?"

"Yeah, basically."

"I need to see both, but let's start with the fuselage."

The lieutenant presented a handheld GPS device. "You can keep this. I've marked both sites, along with *New Mexico*'s position. The ice is solid all the way out, so no worries on transport. I was told you guys brought your own rides?"

"Two two-seaters," Tracer said. "Not enough to haul everyone, but we maxed out on weight."

The plan was set minutes later. A lead element, including Davis and Slaton, would press ahead on the snowmobiles to begin a survey. Tracer would follow with the rest of the team on foot, while *New Mexico*'s crewmen continued their solemn recovery work.

That settled, everyone went to the tilt-rotors and began to unload.

The Ospreys departed thirty minutes later, thundering into the wind-whipped sky and disappearing almost immediately into low clouds and swirling snow.

Davis mounted the lead snowmobile, equipment strapped down on the seat behind him. Slaton drove the second with Kuperman, one of the EOD men, riding shotgun behind him—quite literally, as it turned out, a Benelli 12-gauge hanging on one shoulder. They made good time, and when they reached the first site fifteen minutes later the visibility had improved. It was eight in the morning local time, but given the high latitude, and time of year, first light barely registered. The sun would not be "up" for over an hour, and over the course of the day it would never be more than a dim orb bowling across the horizon.

The first section of wreckage came into view as they rounded a hill. Davis stopped a hundred yards short and shut off his machine.

"Anything wrong?" Slaton asked, pulling to a stop beside him.

"No. I just like to have a first look from a distance. Sometimes you can see things in the big picture that aren't obvious up close. You guys go ahead. I'll be there in a minute."

Slaton didn't argue and set back out, leaving Davis to his survey.

Davis dismounted and studied the greater scene. The fuselage was partially intact, nearly a hundred feet of high-grade metal pancaked to the wet ground. The gray tubular shape was intact only in a few spots, and the hull had broken into three distinct sections. The forward twenty feet contained the cockpit and a few forward stations. That section terminated, Davis was sure, at some kind of structural bulkhead. Behind the breach were two larger sections of roughly equal size, lying disjointed like a broken length of pipe.

For all the apparent randomness, most of what Davis saw he expected. Yet there were points of interest. He noted some evidence of fire, black marks near the wingbox, yet there had been no raging inferno. He'd been told Raven 44 was nearing a scheduled aerial refueling before going down. That meant the jet would have been relatively low on fuel, most of what remained being in the wing tanks. Since the wings had separated, there was little left to burn on impact. Any hotspots that did light off would have fizzled quickly in the frigid, wet conditions.

Davis noted gouges in the frozen ground close to the wreckage. This told him the fuselage had struck with a nearly flat impact. He looked in every direction, as far as the visibility allowed, and searched for stray bits of debris. Very little, it appeared, had caromed outside the primary accident footprint. He pulled out a compact high-res camera to take a few pictures, which forced him to remove his gloves. The frigid air was merciless, colder than the world had a right to be. As soon as he was done, he pocketed the camera and tugged his gloves back on. Davis studied the scene for a long moment, like a portrait artist memorizing a face, then cranked up the snowmobile.

It was time for a closer look.

Colonel Mazov at Sector Four wasn't initially sure what to make of Burinov's call. Clearly the colonel from the adjacent area was having technical difficulties—they all suffered outages now and again in their outdated systems. Still, Mazov was bothered by Burinov's comment that he might have spotted something north of Wrangel.

There was no choice but to look, and once his operators reoriented their scan, they *did* see something—ten miles beyond the island's northern coast, a pair of primary returns heading east. Speed two hundred and eighty knots, five hundred feet above the sea. At such low altitude, they might have escaped Wrangel's radar even if it *had* been working—the equipment there was tuned to identify high-flying targets, and terrain on the island blocked low altitude returns in the north. Mazov's sector, however, was on a different azimuth, and situated on high ground near the sea. Terrain was never a problem.

The colonel watched the two blips for less than a minute before the significance of it all dawned on him. Irrespective of who they were, or what they were doing, the aircraft were about to depart Russian airspace. His options were limited. He could launch interceptors from the nearby Mys Shmidta Air Base, new MiGs that could easily catch up with the targets. Unfortunately, no matter how fast they flew, by the time the MiGs caught up with the bogeys they would be firmly in international airspace. Even more problematic, and the reason he hesitated, was that the weather remained miserable. Fighters could find and track the targets with radar, but there was no chance of getting a visual identification or taking pictures in such thick cloud cover.

Mazov stewed as he watched the screen. The fact that there were two returns, flying in close proximity, suggested he was looking at a military formation. He also found the targets' airspeed notable: too slow to be jet traffic, but too fast for helicopters. The only thing that made sense, in his experience, was some kind of turboprop. During the summer such aircraft made supply flights to Wrangel from the mainland, yet this time of year there were few—and those aircraft *never* flew in formation.

In the end, Mazov did what any self-interested Russian field grade officer would do: He punted the entire matter up to higher headquarters. Someone there could stick their neck out and make the call.

TWENTY

Colonel Mazov was right—a decision was made at headquarters, although not the one he would have imagined.

While a team of Americans was sorting through wreckage on the northwest corner of Wrangel Island, a group of soldiers on the opposite shore received orders for their own mission. The base on the southern coast of the island was called Ushakovskiy. It had been established three years earlier as a long-range radar station and, together with the seasonal park ranger outpost, was the lone toehold of civilization on Wrangel. The base was staffed by a contingent of thirty individuals, drawn from various units of Russia's Twenty-Ninth Army. Half the soldiers were technicians assigned to maintain the moody Sopka-2 radar, while the others were a mix of cooks, mechanics, and quartermasters.

The end result was that the unit's security detail was a cobbled-together force of twelve men whose primary duties lay elsewhere. On that frigid morning, all stood grumbling and stomping their feet outside the prefab barracks while awaiting their orders. Most had been rousted out of warm bunks, although a few early risers had been diverted from the dining hall. The only hint of their mission so far involved what stood outside the equipment barn: six fully fueled snowmobiles. It was the only viable method of transportation during March on Wrangel, and it implied they were going out into the teeth of a mean storm.

Finally, the new lieutenant emerged from the main building to explain their orders. Today's objective, he said, was to span the length of the island, weather be damned, and search for signs of a team of foreigners on the northwest shore. The grumbling deepened. Not even the crazy biologists trekked to Wrangel's north shore in winter, and while the unit occasionally practiced such patrols in better weather, the idea of an invasion seemed preposterous. The rumor began circulating that it was an exercise of some kind, meaning they would be going through the motions merely to help their colonel in Chita make general.

Resigned to their collective misery, the squad began loading the snowmobiles. There were two radios, and each man carried a standard-issue AK-74 assault rifle along with enough survival gear to last three days in the wild—not that anyone expected to stay that long. Of the twelve men, eight were conscripts performing their mandatory year of military service, while the other four were career army. Their leader was a lieutenant three months out of basic officer training, and only one man, the senior sergeant, had seen combat, an unhappy two years in Syria. By any measure it was a rear-echelon force, not built for combat operations, but rather to keep a remote radar station running. Yet for all these shortcomings, the squad did have two distinct advantages. First was that they possessed deep local area knowledge. The second was that they were Russian, which meant the hardships of operating in a subzero climate came as second nature.

Sensing the ill mood of his men, the lieutenant decided a quick speech was in order before setting out. "I know the weather is shit," he said. "Passage to the northern coast will take between two and three hours. Assuming we find it empty as ever, I assure you we will not waste time. With any luck we should be back in time for a late lunch."

As soon as the lieutenant turned away, eyes rolled and curses were muttered. Still, his words had hit their mark. A return to the station, creaky and drafty as it was, along with the image of a hot meal, was fixed in everyone's mind.

The snowmobiles rumbled to life, and in a flurry of noise and fumes, the detail set out in single-file formation toward the gentlest passage through the central hills. A thirty-five-mile journey across the spine of a frozen and windswept wilderness.

Sorensen combed through the Kodiak detachment building searching for Bloch. She found him behind one of the last doors she tried, sitting alone in a dimly lit room and, if she wasn't mistaken, praying.

"Sorry," she said. "I didn't mean to interrupt."

He spun around in the frayed government-issue swivel chair. "It's all right. Is there news?"

"There is," she said, then added quickly, "although nothing specific on Ayla." She looked up and down the hall. The place seemed oddly quiet for midday, but then it occurred to her that most of the unit was either on Wrangel Island or at home sleeping off yesterday's midnight mobilization. "How about a cup of coffee?"

"Have you tasted what they make here?"

"No . . . but thanks for grounding my expectations."

They diverted to the empty break room, where Sorensen braved the high-octane dregs of a long-ago brewed pot. Bloch opted for tea.

"NRO made a couple of good finds," she said, taking her first sip and wincing. "To begin, they spotted two breaks in the ice near Wrangle, roughly three miles apart. We think it's where the remaining sections of wreckage probably landed."

"Will it be possible to retrieve the black boxes?" he inquired, understanding this was the most critical evidence.

"Unknown. One of the sites is near the island. Our maps of the undersea topography aren't great that close to shore, but we think the water might be shallow enough for a dive. Unfortunately, we don't know if it's the tail section, where the recorders are, or the missing wing."

"Has there been any word from the scene?"

"Only that our team arrived. We should be getting an update soon. NRO also found something else of interest—something that relates to the bigger picture. They captured images of an icebreaker leaving the area. It's speculative, but this ship could have been in the vicinity of Raven 44 when it went down."

"Are you back to the missile theory?"

"We're not discounting anything."

"Is it a naval vessel?"

"That's the strange part. We were able to identify the ship—don't ask how—as a midsized icebreaker named *Sibir*. Until recently she was owned and operated by Kazakhstan."

Bloch abruptly pulled his tea away mid-sip. *"Kazakhstan?"*

"It's not so surprising—the Caspian Sea *does* ice over in winter. Last year *Sibir* was sold to a private party with very obscure ownership. We were able to track her to a shipyard in Sri Lanka—the entire port was co-opted by China, part of the Belt and Road Initiative. She spent three months there getting some kind of retrofit. But here's the real kicker: during that time there was another ship berthed with her, owned by the same company, and *that* vessel was very close to *Ross* when she sank off Crimea two days ago."

Bloch straightened notably. "I will not even attempt the word *coincidence*."

"Exactly. Langley has gone into overdrive researching this company."

"Can I share this with the Office?" he asked. "We might be able to add something."

"I think you should. I'll have someone put together detailed files."

"Until then," he said, dropping his empty cup into the trash, "I think I will go to back to that quiet room and finish what I started."

Minutes later, the former Mossad director who had led Israel through so many dark days, the persuader who had convinced prime ministers to sign kill orders, the father who had seen his daughter kidnapped, locked himself in a small room and prayed to God for whatever hope could be had.

TWENTY-ONE

The acrid scent of jet fuel hung on the air, and Slaton was happy to have a fleece gaiter over his nose and mouth. He watched Davis park his snowmobile twenty yards short of the wrecked fuselage. He'd left his own farther back in an abundance of caution. He had taken part in the investigations of terrorist attacks, so he was familiar with the forensic protocols of bombings and mass shootings. Those of an air crash, however, might be different.

"So, got it figured out yet?" he asked as soon as the engine went silent.

"Hardly," Davis replied, dismounting. "But I did notice a few things."

"Such as?"

"Mostly stuff I suspected before we got here—what we talked about back in Kodiak. The very fact that the wreckage is strewn about, big sections that are miles apart, confirms the airplane broke up inflight. That's a rare event, and only a few things will cause it."

"Missile?" Slaton ventured.

"A possibility, especially since the jet was skirting the edge of hostile territory. Fortunately, missile strikes are fairly easy to identify."

Slaton looked up and down the crumpled fuselage. It had been here for days now and was half covered by snow and ice. "What does a missile hit look like? All I see is mangled metal."

"There's a science to it. To begin, you have to understand that anti-aircraft missiles aren't designed to actually strike their target. They get very, very close, but at the last instant the warhead explodes to send a disc of shrapnel into a very fast-moving machine with relatively thin skin. From an engineering standpoint, it gives you a higher chance of catastrophic damage."

"Lovely."

"Yeah, I've always thought weapons designers have to be some of the most conflicted people on the planet. The other thing to know about missiles is that there are two basic kinds—radar guided and heat-seekers. Radar missiles tend to home in on sharp angles, like the corners where the wings join the fuselage. Heaters lock on warm spots."

"Engines?"

"Almost always. Which means you begin by checking those places for damage patterns, clusters of holes in the metal skin that have failed inward."

"Sort of like hitting a cone of bird shot at five hundred miles an hour."

Davis gave a half smile. "Not a bad way to think about it. But then, I shouldn't be surprised you'd put it in ballistic terms."

"Besides missiles, what else might cause an inflight breakup?"

"If this had happened anywhere else, I might consider a midair collision. Problem is, the airspace here is some of the most remote in the world . . . the odds are about the same as being hit by a meteor."

Slaton took on an inquisitive look.

"I'm not even going there," Davis said. "The most likely scenario is actually pretty dull—this airplane is sixty years old. Structural fatigue, flight control anomalies, vapor in an empty fuel tank catching a spark from a frayed wire. All those things can take an airplane down, and they can be proved—*if* you have enough time and access to the wreckage."

"But we don't have much of either."

"A few hours at best. Which means *this* is going to be really important." Davis extracted a high-end digital camera.

They made their way to the largest section of fuselage, both men trying not to step on anything that looked man-made.

"You can help me out here," Davis said. He pointed to a portion of charred skin. "Right here we've got fire damage. You can see where the soot marks trail up from the source. That's a postcrash fire. An airborne fire looks different—it leaves soot trailing back in the wind stream. Check the other side and let me know if you see anything like that. Also keep an eye out for patterns of shrapnel like we talked about."

Slaton circled to the opposite side and began checking. He stepped over bent metal and deep scars in the frozen earth. Portions of the fuselage looked almost new, while others had crumpled beyond recognition. He heard the camera clicking as they both made their way forward. Minutes later they merged near the remnants of the cockpit.

"All the burn marks looked the same," Slaton said. "Ground fires. And no blast damage that I could see."

"Same here." Davis moved on and began surveying the exterior of the cockpit. The aircraft's once-aerodynamic lines had been ruined in the crash; however, this section was in better shape than the rest. Davis stopped at the very front and stared at the nose cone. He didn't move for a long time.

"See something?" Slaton asked.

A hesitation. "I'm not sure. Never seen anything like this." He took a knee in his winter suit and studied the nose cone. "This is the radome—it houses the weather radar antenna at the very front."

Davis started taking pictures.

"What got your attention?"

He pointed to series of concentric wrinkles in the surface. "I've never seen damage like this."

"Is that metal?"

"No, that would screw up the radar signal. It's composite, fiberglass layers over a foam core." He stood and began studying the cockpit windows, then paused a second time on the aircraft's right side.

"Another problem?"

"Big one this time. We've got a missing window." He pointed to the battered frame. "There are six windows that wrap around the flight deck, plus a couple of smaller eyebrow windows above. It looks like the aft window on the right side blew out. All the others are shattered, but that's impact damage. This one's completely gone, and the shards on the edges of the frame are angled outward."

"So it blew out? Like in a depressurization?"

"Looks that way."

"Could that be what brought it down?"

More pictures, including close-ups of the window frame. "In and of itself . . . doubtful. It'd be an attention-getter, for sure, but nothing that would cause a crash. The crew would have been surprised as hell, but they'd have reacted. They would have put on their oxygen masks and descended to a lower altitude. It's loud, tough to communicate, but that's a scenario all pilots train for. The airplane flies just fine, and it certainly doesn't break apart in midair."

Davis took a hard look at the other windows, pushed on one with the palm of his hand. "Something about these others doesn't look right either. Cockpit windows typically have three layers, but these all look . . . I don't know, like they've delaminated or something." His eyes went back to the nose cone, "I'd like to bring out a piece of this radome." He tried to pry off a section by hand but had no luck. Davis circled around the remains and entered the cockpit, passing through the bent passageway where the flight deck door had been. Mercifully, the pilots' bodies had already been removed. He came back outside with a wicked-looking ax in hand—six-inch blade on one side, a puncturing awl on the other.

"Where did that come from?"

"Crash ax. Every big airplane has one on the flight deck—theoretically, in case you need to tear through a panel to fight a fire." Davis leaned over the biggest section of the radome, ran his fingers over the suspicious grooving like a butcher contemplating a side of beef. Then, without further measure, he went full Paul Bunyan on the nose cone, eventually hacking off a section the size of a doormat.

He'd no sooner freed his trophy when Kuperman appeared and pointed to a spot in the distance. "Hey guys, heads-up."

Slaton followed his gesture to a nearby hill and saw a massive polar bear watching warily, its great shoulders arched as if preparing to break into a run. Not sure which direction it had in mind, Slaton found one hand going to the SCAR hanging across his chest. It was the kind of moment that made one thankful for twenty-round magazines . . . and spare magazines.

The great beast stood down and meandered away, its white coat blending perfectly with the frozen earth.

"Guess he was just curious," Davis said. "But man, those suckers are big."

When the bear disappeared behind a hill, Kuperman waved them over. "Come check out what I found."

Kuperman led toward the shoreline, clambering over an expansive field of smooth stones. Near the high-tide line, he diverted to an outcropping of boulders and stopped on the lee side. "What do you reckon this is?"

They all stared at what looked like an abandoned rowboat, a twenty-foot-long hardwood skeleton whose planking had fallen outward like petals from a dying flower. Within that outline was a great pile of derelict gear frosted in snow: coiled lines, planks, oars, and the tattered remains of what looked like an oilskin coat. As far as Slaton could tell, there were no bones inside the coat.

"Looks ancient," Slaton said.

"I'll bet it's been here fifty years," Davis seconded.

"Probably more like a hundred," countered Kuperman. "I researched this place before we came. Wrangel was never properly settled, but a lot of ships pulled ashore. They were whalers mostly, going back a couple hundred years."

To Slaton it made sense. Wrangel was a place for pioneers and, owing to its isolation, always would be. He was about to comment when the handheld radio in his jacket pocket squawked. He took it out, responded, then mostly listened for thirty seconds.

Davis and Kuperman heard only one side of the conversation. "How long ago?" followed by, "How solid is this?" Finally, "Okay, sounds like a plan."

Slaton repocketed the brick.

"Problem?" Davis asked.

"Maybe. That was Tracer, and he just got a heads-up from Langley. Apparently NSA intercepted a message sent to the radar station on the south side of the island. It was an order to investigate a possible intrusion in our area."

"Damn," Davis said. "Our clock just got shorter."

"Exactly." Slaton glanced up at the battleship-gray sky. "The weather is improving, but that might not be in our favor. Tracer is assuming the worst, that we could get company soon. He's setting up a perimeter to keep watch."

"How long do we have?" Davis asked.

"Assuming they're on sleds like we are, which seems likely, and if NSA's timeline is accurate—probably a couple of hours. If they do show up, we need to be long gone. Hopefully they'll be so distracted by the wreckage, they won't notice our tracks until *New Mexico* is under the ice. The last thing we need is an international incident."

"In that case, no more investigating," Davis said. "We've got to concentrate on recovery. I was given a list of boxes in the E and E bay that the Air Force wants back."

"E and E?" Slaton asked.

"Equipment and electronics—the belly compartment where all the high-dollar computers are racked."

"But not the black boxes."

"Unfortunately, no. The flight data and voice recorders are in the tail section—which right now is somewhere under the polar ice cap." Davis addressed Kuperman. "You'd better come with me. I might need help prying out the hardware. After that, I'll show you what to blow up."

The EOD man's wind-chapped lips cracked into a smile.

TWENTY-TWO

Israel has long had an inclination for naming critical intelligence divisions numerically. The section responsible for signals intercepts and code decryption, technically a branch of military intelligence, is Unit 8200. The clear implication is that there are at least 8199 *other* intelligence units engaged in vital missions. Few were so easily misled, yet the ploy was a distraction from one certainty: Unit 8200 was among the largest and most effective forces in Israel's arsenal.

The unit's address was more virtual than physical, being spread over a number of highly secure facilities—which was perfectly in accord with the fuzzy guardrails of the digital battlefield. The information collected was funneled upward on a steep curve to the nation's military and intelligence decision makers. And never had it been more vital than that night.

"We're making progress," said Ari Berman, Unit 8200's bespectacled chief, from a soft leather chair in Nurin's office.

The directorial brow furrowed. Nurin was weary, but not so far gone that he didn't recognize verbal bromides when he heard them. He wanted breakthroughs, not "progress." It was nearly midnight at the Glilot Junction campus, and as was too often the case, the staccato pace of the day's events had crushed any hope of a normal circadian rhythm.

"Specifically?" he pressed.

"We located every camera within three blocks of the street where our *katsa* was abducted. A handful turned out to be accessible, and we are quite certain we've identified the car."

"Well, that's something," Nurin allowed.

As it turned out, the lead was a fizzle. Berman went on to explain that the car had disappeared and there were few avenues for tracking it: most CCTV in the country involved primitive closed network systems, and traffic cameras were virtually nonexistent. The Kazakh government was anything but net-centric, and without nodes of access, digital vulnerabilities were few and far between. By Berman's own admission, Unit 8200, for all its prowess, had hit a cyber wall.

After five minutes Nurin dismissed Berman but told him to keep trying. Once he was alone, the director leaned back in his chair and contemplated the insides of his eyelids.

If Ayla was going to be found, he knew, it would be from spycraft in its elemental form. Local informants pressed. Bartenders given heavy tips. Banal questions put to old women sweeping front steps. He was thankful he'd gotten that ball rolling: his tiny army of Mossad operatives would soon arrive in Almaty. Nurin took solace in the thought that this was how Bloch himself would have handled it.

He only hoped it was enough.

The twelve-man squad from the radar station at Ushakovskiy knew they were getting close. The convoy of snowmobiles stopped a mile short of their search area, and the lieutenant and first sergeant forged ahead to a nearby hill. The rest of the men dismounted and stood shuffling their feet against the frigid morning air.

The lieutenant followed his sergeant up the hill, ice crunching under their boots. He looked back at his men once, saw them watching closely. Most of the boys had little experience beyond basic training, yet the sergeant was different. He had been to Syria and, according to his file, nearly made it through airborne training. By his own admission, he'd busted out of that school after his third violation for drinking on duty. The fallout had been harsh, and he was given two choices for a follow-on assignment: senior NCO on Wrangel Island, or a bunk in a Siberian work camp.

Whether he'd sobered up remained an open question, but there was no denying the sergeant's tactical acumen, nor, after a year on station, his intimate knowledge of the island. To his credit, the lieutenant had been paying attention on the day in his own training when it was suggested, by a crusty old NCO, that junior officers should always listen to crusty old NCOs. He'd mostly adhered to that advice, including ten minutes ago when the sergeant had suggested they cut their engines before reaching their objective to scout out the best approach.

The sergeant stopped climbing just short of the hill's crest. He set his feet in a firm stance and pulled out a chart, holding it so they could both see.

"This is where we are," he said, pointing to a spot where the elevation lines bunched tightly. "To reach the area we've been ordered to search, here, there are two obvious corridors." He dragged his gloved finger across two valleys. "If you ask me, both are too predictable, too easy to watch. If there is indeed someone in these coves, better to surprise them. I recommend flanking left, an approach along the western shore. The cover is far better."

The lieutenant studied the map. "Won't that take longer?"

"Actually, no. It is farther, true, but if we take these direct routes, I would strongly suggest leaving the machines here, covering the rest of the way on foot. If we arc left, given the terrain and the direction of the wind, we can drive almost on top of the area before anyone would hear us."

The lieutenant could think of no counterarguments.

The two men came down from the hill like priests ready to issue God's word. The lieutenant explained the plan, and everyone mounted up once again. It took fifteen minutes to maneuver to the coast, and five more to reach a point near the coves. Another short hike ensued, and from a wind-whipped promontory, with his left shoulder to the sea, the lieutenant looked down into a valley and saw three men circling the wreckage of a large airplane.

He glanced at his weathered sergeant, a great doughy man with blond hair and alabaster skin, and saw him smiling broadly. He was clearly satisfied his instincts had prevailed. The lieutenant, too, was happy. Yet he was also unsure about what to do next, so he looked expectantly at his senior NCO, hoping he had a plan for this as well.

As it turned out, he did.

TWENTY-THREE

"Visual west! Multiple Tangos!" The words shot through the comm net like a warning flare.

Slaton dropped the electronic box he was carrying and took a knee near a large boulder. He scanned the gloom with the SCAR shouldered and ready. Kuperman was nearby. He'd certainly heard the warning, but he was keeping to his task, furiously running wires and connecting detonators throughout the wreckage.

"Where?" Tracer's voice. He was with the main group in the next valley.

"West side, fifty meters from reference point Alpha!" replied one of his men.

"All right, stay low and prepare to egress. Do *not* fire unless fired upon!"

"I've almost got everything wired!" Kuperman reported over the net. "Need three more mikes!"

"Expedite!" Tracer said, a superfluous order under the circumstances. He'd no sooner said it than the first burst of incoming fire shattered the morning air.

The frozen earth around Kuperman erupted, tiny explosions of ice and dirt. He dove behind the section of fuselage where he was working, and in the next instant Slaton saw him roll in the dirt and grab his thigh.

"We're taking fire!" Slaton said, adjusting his position behind the rock.

These were the critical seconds in any engagement—surviving first contact. He ventured a look and saw two clusters of muzzle flashes—both on high-ground knolls, fifty meters apart. Given the angles of fire and where it was being directed, Slaton doubted he himself had been seen. He discerned two moving targets, and with a good line of sight he settled into a prone firing position. Slaton referenced his scope and fired. The lead man went down, and Slaton immediately shifted to the second target. He sent two closely spaced rounds from ninety yards. At least one hit.

The incoming fire paused. *Hits are always the best suppression.*

He rolled to his feet and dashed low toward Kuperman. Davis was nowhere in sight, and since he was unarmed, Slaton assumed he'd taken cover.

He threw himself behind the fuselage, and the first thing he noticed was a dozen new through-and-through holes in the thin skin of the wrecked jet. He sank lower where the metal had pancaked to multiple layers. Kuperman was half inside what had been a belly compartment on the airplane, still hard at work. His right leg was bleeding, but Slaton saw no overt sign of arterial involvement.

"You okay?"

"Not exactly, but I'll get by. Almost done here."

Slaton keyed his mic and explained the situation to Tracer, who came back with, "We're inbound, thirty seconds out. Can you give me a position on the Tangos?"

"High ground to the southwest. We're pretty much pinned down, haven't seen Jammer. Super took a hit but he's pushing through—almost done prepping."

Slaton heard gunfire from the east, then shouting in the knolls. Backup was arriving.

Tracer again on the radio, "We've got a good look. I see seven from my position and we're engaging. They may flush to your right so be ready."

Slaton low-crawled through snow and ice to the end of the wreckage section. There he set up prone a second time. He waited and watched. More inbound fire from the hostiles, but increasingly sporadic and wild. Panic setting in. The visibility was better than when they'd arrived, and Slaton had a good look angle and a manageable range for the SCAR. He scanned through his optic, then pulled away in favor of a wider field of view with his naked eye.

He caught a flash of movement ghosting through the mist, shapes traversing a swale to the south. Quickly he resighted on a running target, wagged a Kentucky-windage lead, and fired. The form spun writhing into deep snow. Two others, after seeing the point man fall, went low and tried to zigzag through shin-deep drifts. Four shots later both were down.

Slaton kept scanning, saw no other threats. More fire erupted to his left. Different weapons, familiar reports. Tracer and his team moving and killing. Slaton had no idea how big a force they were fighting, or if they had reinforcements. All they could do was fight back and then get the hell out.

Slaton was still searching, his eyes straining into the gloom, when he heard a noise behind and to his right. The sound was as distinctive as it was alarming: a rifle sling rattling on its swivels.

He spun switchblade-fast, bending at the hips to arc his weapon around. A huge, fair-skinned man was ten yards away, near the edge of the wrecked cockpit. He was in decent cover and had the barrel of his rifle level but seemed to be fumbling with something. Slaton was an instant away from firing an unsighted group when something flew in from the right. The blond man went rigid, eyes bulging, arms locking out. Slaton watched in amazement as he dropped his rifle and staggered fully into view.

Slaton tried to make sense of the scene: the man had been run through by what looked like an eight-foot spear with a wickedly flanged head. The Russian's eyes rolled back, and he fell hard into the slush and went still.

"*What the . . .*" He kept his weapon poised as he got to his feet, searching for other threats.

"Friendly," said a familiar deep voice from behind the wreckage. Davis emerged casually, the crash ax hanging loose in his left hand. He held it up to Slaton, and said, "I had two weapons to choose from. The other one seemed more appropriate for the situation."

Slaton stared at the dead man. "Is that what I think it is?" he asked, gesturing to the shaft impaling the oversized Russian.

"When the shooting started, I took cover behind that old whaling boat. Saw this beneath the oars and figured it might be useful."

"A harpoon."

"Yeah, well . . . first time for everything."

Firefights end in one of two ways: either an abrupt cessation, implying a decisive outcome, or in a gradual tapering off as two forces disengage. On that morning the silence came with the swiftness of a guillotine. One final crackle of fire, then nothing but voices shouting commands.

Slaton heard Tracer coordinating on the comm net, ensuring the area was secure. Kuperman seemed in good shape, evidenced by the fact that he was still on task. The wreckage was wired to blow in five locations, each home to sensitive hardware that couldn't be retrieved. When he was done, the EOD man limped toward Slaton and Davis. He looked at each in turn, then did a double take on the great Russian lying dead in the snow, a wide pool of red spreading beneath him. "Seriously? Is that a—"

"Yeah, it is," Davis said with growing irritation.

Tracer issued an all clear, then ordered everyone to rally at the sleds. Kuperman departed with his remote trigger in hand, everything primed and ready to blow. Davis abandoned the crash ax in favor of all the avionics he could carry.

Slaton was the last to leave. With one last look at the Russian, he fell in behind Davis and muttered to himself, "And I was supposed to take care of *him*."

Once everyone had gathered, Tracer gave a sitrep. "We tallied twelve adversaries, all Russian Army. We also found six two-seat snowsleds a few hundred meters back. Eight enemy morts, two wounded, and two surrendered. We can't take prisoners for about a hundred reasons, so I gave the order to disarm the survivors and turn them loose. We also confiscated their radios, but there's no way to know if they called in our position before the engagement started. We rendered aid to the two wounded, and both were transportable. I imagine they'll be loading up right about now.

"On our end, Super took a graze to the leg—that's the only damage I'm aware of. Our plan now is to load up what Jammer salvaged, blow the wreckage, and hightail to *New Mexico* for egress. I've already given them a heads-up, and they'll be ready to sail when we arrive. Comments or questions?"

Slaton asked, "Estimate for how long it will take those four to get back to base?"

"I found the map they were using and it had a route marked. No way they can make it back in less than two hours. But again, it's possible they made radio calls when they first saw us. Either way, sometime in the next few hours I'd expect this corner of the island to be swarming with Russians."

"We still need the black boxes from the submerged tail section," Davis said.

Tracer frowned. "Yeah, well . . . we'll figure that out after we're warm and dry."

The tightly sequenced explosions rocked the still morning. Dozens of terns scattered from the hills, and the concussive wave induced a minor avalanche of a cliffside ice sheet.

The fuselage of Raven 44, already accordioned by one tragedy, succumbed to the final indignation of having its remains pulverized by five large C-4 charges. The midships E & E bay bore the brunt of the damage, circuit boards and wiring raining a hundred yards in every direction. So, too, the side-mounted radar antenna and communications control heads in the cockpit, all obliterated in milliseconds.

Only Kuperman, Slaton, Davis, and Kuperman's partner, George Sharp, were present to witness the devastation, the rest of the team having set off toward *New Mexico*. The blasts resounded off the hills before fading uncertainly into a heavy, snow-laden sky. Afterward, the four men stood shoulder to shoulder in surreal silence.

Davis, standing next to Slaton, said, "This feels weird."

"How's that?"

"I've investigated a lot of crashes, but this is the first time I've ever intentionally destroyed evidence."

"Yeah, I see your point. Hopefully we recovered enough to get some answers."

"The best source is still the two recorders. I hope we get a chance to go after them."

Slaton considered that, how it might affect the broader mission. He thought about Ayla Bloch, and who her father was. He looked out across a hill covered with bodies. Someone, somewhere, had made a poor decision. A squad of Russian Army regulars had been thrown into a buzz saw. They'd no doubt been sent here because they were the only unit on the island, yet they had no idea what kind of force they would come up against: a unit of nearly the same size, but composed of some of the best special operators in the world. When it came to engagements, Slaton never liked a fair fight. He wanted every advantage, and today, excluding the element of surprise, they'd had it.

The repercussions were unknowable. A U.S. Air Force spy plane had gone down under suspicious circumstances, followed by a clandestine operation to recover vital wreckage. A response by Russia had ended in a firefight and a rout. Try as he might, Slaton couldn't envision it all as some random series of events. He sensed motive, a greater conspiracy.

"You're right," he found himself saying. "We need to find those boxes. We need all the answers we can get."

Sudden motion snagged his gaze—a polar bear darting up a hill in the distance, no doubt spooked by the explosions. Slaton suspected the beast would return soon, the scent of fresh kill and late-winter hunger overriding caution. Survival instincts kicking in.

The team turned toward the snowmobiles, cranked them to life, and were soon thundering away toward *New Mexico* in swirls of thrown snow.

TWENTY-FOUR

Director Nurin's plan to increase manpower in Almaty was carried out with the urgency one would expect from a spy agency trying to rescue one of its own.

Thirty-two Mossad operatives, drawn from various locations, were dispatched for insertion into Kazakhstan. Mossad's documents specialists worked overtime to provide so many legends in so little time, but in the end they came through. Most of the identities issued were legitimate passports from other countries, some derived by thievery, others supplied by expatriate collaborators, also known as *sayanim*.

They traveled either solo or in pairs, and by a variety of means—a shotgun approach that guaranteed both successes and failures. For the most part borders were crossed via legitimate corridors: airports, highways, and even one ferry across the Caspian were utilized. Of the thirty-two men and women sent, only five failed to enter the country undetected. Of these, two pairs were detained for questioning—not because their documents were questioned, but because they were too quick to initiate a bribe. In the end, their money was taken and they were summarily dumped on the next flights back from where they'd come: two to Tashkent, and two to Istanbul.

The other misfire, a woman trying to cross in a rental car over a remote road from Kyrgyzstan, was accosted by bandits near the border. A man stepped into the road with an ancient AK-47 demanding that she stop, while his partner waved a pistol and approached the driver's-side window. From the bandits' point of view, it seemed an easy shakedown. The Mossad operative, a veteran of places like Syria and Gaza, did not so much as bat an eye. After initially slowing, she gunned the engine and ran down the rifleman, sending him twenty feet into a ditch. When she reversed and tried to chase down his partner, he ran into the forest like a startled deer. Her extensive experience proved doubly vital when she realized that, despite the victory, the man who had gotten away might alert the authorities. Knowing she could not allow herself to be questioned, she returned to Bishkek, turned in a slightly dented rental car, and boarded the next outbound flight to Berlin.

Finally, two operatives, after successfully entering the country, failed to reach Almaty when their train broke down in a remote region near the Uzbekistan border. The rail line's representative could give no estimate for continuation, and when the local police began arranging accommodations for the passengers in town, the stranded pair quietly hired a car and made their way back to Tel Aviv.

Overall, the insertion was an admirable success. Within a day and a half of the order being given, twenty-five of Mossad's best operatives were entrenched in safe houses in and around Almaty. From there, each of them began a mission that director Nurin had characterized poignantly in his marching orders: to perform the search they would want if they were the one who had been abducted.

Sorensen's heart skipped a beat when she read the opening line of the report from *New Mexico*: *Mission aborted early, engaged by opposing force. Demolition complete. One casualty.*

Her fears didn't abate until the end of paragraph three: *Casualty minor, treated. PO3 Kuperman.*

"News?" Bloch asked, siding up to her in the makeshift operations room.

Sorensen didn't respond until she'd gone through the report a second time. "Trouble. The Russians *did* send out a unit from the radar station. A squad of army regulars—they engaged our team and it didn't go well for them." She read out the enemy casualty count. "One minor injury on our side."

"That doesn't feel like a victory," he said.

"No, more like we just kicked a hornet's nest. Our team let the survivors go, but took away their comm gear. Sometime in the next hour or two, Russian high command is going to hear what happened."

"How do you think they will react?"

"No telling. I'm sure they'll start by sending a much larger force to investigate. The casualties will be confirmed, and they'll get a look at what's left of Raven 44."

"At least *New Mexico* will be gone."

"That depends. I'd like to try for those black boxes, but if we leave her in the area to search, she might be vulnerable."

"It's not my area of expertise, but even the Russian Navy must have limitations this time of year."

Sorensen worked through it. "They can't send surface ships. Their icebreakers could reach Wrangle, but they have no capability to search for a submarine. Russia's best option would be to use their own submarines." She grabbed a pen and paper and began scribbling notes. "I need to set up a secure call with Navy command, find out whether *New Mexico* is at risk if she stays in Russian waters."

"That will take time."

"Probably an hour, at least," she said.

"And if you were to include all the concerned agencies . . ."

Sorensen's eyes narrowed as she began to see his lead. "It might take even *longer* to sort out."

Bloch shrugged his wide shoulders. "Much could be accomplished in such a window."

"I think you've faced this kind of problem before."

"And I think you will be facing them for a very long time."

Chicken gumbo. Never in his life had Slaton been so thankful for a bowl of hot soup. After spending nearly half a day in subzero conditions on the Osprey, then hours more exposed to the elements on Wrangel Island, he was frozen to the core.

He was seated in *New Mexico*'s mess hall, the rest of the team around him. Davis seemed equally grateful as he hunched over his third bowl of the chef's finest. All spaces on submarines were compact, and Jammer looked like a linebacker at a grade school cafeteria table.

Once back on board, they'd spent twenty minutes with the ship's CO composing an interim operational report. After that, Commander Zimmerman had mercifully sent them for sustenance.

Slaton had been on submarines before, but always the Dolphin-class variety used by the Israeli Navy. Those boats rarely ventured from regional waters, and while they had limited capability for weapons delivery, they'd proven themselves time and again as a means of inserting teams of commandos onto the shores of Lebanon, Syria, and Egypt.

Much to Davis's annoyance, the story of his taking out a Russian army sergeant with a harpoon had all the hallmarks of an instant legend. The fact that the victim, who'd been about to engage Slaton, was very large and possibly an albino only sealed Davis's fate: a new call sign was born.

"Hey, Ahab," said Kuperman, whose wound had been treated. "Pass the bread, would you?"

Davis glared at him, a not inconsequential expression. His rugby-beaten features and sheer size were enough to give anyone pause. In the uncharacteristic role of peacemaker, Slaton pushed the bread basket across the table.

New Mexico had submerged as soon as the team and equipment were back on board. The captain, however, had yet to set a course. Davis had tried to convince him that their mission, malleable as it was, was only half-complete—they still needed to retrieve the black boxes. In light of the engagement landside, however, Zimmerman understandably wanted to make for international waters and disappear before the Russian Navy came swarming.

Neither man got their wish, at least not yet, as the decision went into a holding pattern while higher authorities made the call.

"Thanks for what you did back there," Slaton said quietly to Davis.

"You would have had him," he replied. "Truth is, I didn't have much choice. Anna made me promise to look after you."

Slaton looked up, saw a wry smile. He decided to change the subject. "Did you look over the charts?" Sorensen had forwarded coordinate sets where the two remaining sections of wreckage mostly likely lie.

"One looks doable," Davis said. "The other is deeper and on a steep slope—that section might already have slipped down into thousands of feet of water. The plots are only a couple of miles apart, but we're pressed for time."

"So we go for the shallower of the two. Fifty-fifty chance."

"Pretty much. The skipper told me they can probably find it using a remotely operated vehicle—they've got one on board, launches through a torpedo tube and has side-scan sonar, top-of-the-line technology. If it turns out to be the wing and not the tail, we won't bother with a dive."

"And if it *is* the tail . . . how tough would a recovery be?"

Davis used a hunk of bread to mop the bottom of his bowl. "There are two boxes—the flight data recorder and the cockpit voice recorder. They're both inside a panel at the base of the tail, where it joins the body of the airplane. It's easy access for normal maintenance—maybe a dozen screws, pop off a panel, and you're in. But after a crash you never know. Things get bent, broken, thrown clear."

"Not very encouraging."

"That's reality. To get at the boxes we'd need tools—I've only done it underwater once before, and on a different kind of airplane. On top of that, we'd be working in bulky dry suits, and effectively in the dark."

"Aren't the boxes damaged when they get submerged?"

"Sometimes, but they're designed for extreme conditions. Even if they flood, we can probably salvage the data."

"How many divers?" Slaton asked.

"At least two, but three would be better."

"You, me, and Tracer?"

"We all brought gear. I would do the surgery, you manage the tools. Tracer acts as divemaster, keeps track of our depth and time—that's his specialty. We'd also need every light we can get. Above the Arctic Circle, in winter—it'll be pitch-black out there."

"Not to mention chilly. I hope those suits are as good as advertised."

New Mexico's executive officer entered the mess. He visually picked out Davis and Slaton, and said, "Captain wants to see you both. We've got new orders."

TWENTY-FIVE

Turkmenistan Airlines Flight 12 arrived early that morning in Almaty, the regularly scheduled feeder service from Ashgabat.

Bagdani had gotten three hours' sleep in Ashgabat, an entirely forgettable experience by his fast-rising standards. Nights spent on straw mats under open skies in Africa were all but a memory. The Four Seasons was now his preferred brand, yet since the capital of Turkmenistan was not so blessed, he'd made do with a three-star chain hotel at the airport.

He cleared customs easily and was met on the curb by the usual driver, a taciturn Kazakh whose only words were, "Twenty minutes."

Bagdani took a seat in back, having been through the drill before. Lazarus was constantly on the move, so the meetings were always in a different place. He clearly trusted the driver who was, as far as Bagdani knew, his only local employee. Lazarus kept no guards, no physical security, relying completely on the protections of movement and anonymity. So far, it seemed to be working.

Bagdani operated under a different set of rules. He traveled occasionally in the course of his head-hunting, but only when absolutely necessary. The bulk of his days were spent in the fortress that was his safe space. That was his plan when today's meeting ended; recede into his private battlement to watch the next mission run its course.

As the driver set out, Bagdani rehearsed his briefing. *Poyarka*'s departure was imminent, her final preparations complete. The technicians had performed a number of tests, but whether the weapon would actually work was anybody's guess. It seemed that with each strike, the systems were becoming more elaborate, even futuristic. From what he'd been told, the weapon on *Poyarka* was unique, an experimental test bed killed during its development. The project wasn't cancelled because the device was defective, but rather because it had been overtaken by a similar system, and funding for both was not available. This created a dilemma for its manufacturer: what to do with a one-off weapon, of incalculable potential, that would never be put into production. The answer, apparently, involved a forty-year-old Polish hydrographic survey ship and a castaway crew of mercenaries.

Bagdani considered the men he'd recruited for the voyage. Some were little different from those he'd hired during his days in Africa—not killers, but ruffians and malcontents, men who were paid well for hard work and who knew how to keep their mouths shut. A few had stains on their records, which made his job only that much easier. Lost security clearances, arrest records, gambling habits. If there was a weakness, Bagdani found it, fueled it, and used it as his vise. Failing that, he entrapped his recruits the old-fashioned way: by finding the right price.

As the twenty minutes neared its end, he looked outside and saw the neighborhood trending downward, great tenement blockhouses crumbling at the edges. Bagdani tried to keep track of the street names he saw, a rough map forming in his head. It was a lesson he'd learned long ago in the Legion, and one that had served him well over the years: *if you learn the way in, you can find your way out.*

The car drew to a stop in front of a hulking residential building.

The driver said, "Room 386."

Without so much as an acknowledgement, Bagdani stepped onto the curb, went inside, and minutes later was knocking on yet another strange door.

Slaton and Davis were nearing the control room when they heard Commander Zimmerman's voice. "I am not liking this! I feel like we've been chopped!"

Davis leaned toward Slaton and at a whisper explained the slang. "Change of operational control."

They rounded the corner together and Zimmerman immediately lasered onto them. "Your head spook wants us to stay and find this missing tail section. Seventh Fleet is punting, so for the moment I have no alternate guidance."

"Sounds like indecision up high," Davis ventured.

"Given what happened on the island, I'd say very high. I can't imagine the president isn't involved."

"Any word of a Russian response yet?" Slaton inquired.

"Stone silence, so far."

"Then let's do it," Davis said. "In the time it takes them to make up their minds, we can have the job done."

Zimmerman glared. "Which is probably just what your boss has in mind. The thing is, I'm the one responsible for this ship and her crew."

Davis's eyes narrowed, and his voice went to a deeper tone, his words carefully spaced. "You also have a responsibility to protect your country's national interests. An airplane went down, and seventeen good men and women died. We need to find out *why* so that it doesn't happen again."

Zimmerman stood fixed, unyielding. He finally said, "How long would you need?"

"From the time you put us on top of the wreckage, no more than an hour."

The captain looked at his XO, who didn't appear eager to insert an opinion. "All right," Zimmerman said. "We'll head for the shallower of the two plots and deploy the ROV. If we can find this wreckage, and don't get any superseding orders in the meantime . . . I'll give you your hour."

It took fifteen minutes for *New Mexico* to reach the shallower of the two coordinate sets. As she crawled silently through the frigid sea less than a mile off Wrangel's northwest coast, traces of sweat and bilgewater rode the air. *New Mexico* was a modern submarine, but no amount of air-scrubbing or filtering could wipe out the essence of what she was: a machine of war.

The search ROV, nicknamed Seeker, was a tethered unit that deployed through a torpedo tube and maintained contact with the operator via a two-hundred-meter umbilical. Its primary sensor was a side-scan sonar system that was excellent for mapping undersea terrain.

New Mexico eased to a stop within spitting distance of the targeted area—in oceanic terms, roughly a hundred meters—and Seeker was deployed. All attention then went to the man who would be, in the next few minutes, the most important on the boat: a redheaded E-4 who'd set up in the sonar shack with a laptop and a joystick. Appearing younger than his twenty-four years, he looked like a high schooler prepping for an epic gaming session. Space in the sonar shack was tight, but Captain Zimmerman and his exec, Dooley, shouldered in. Slaton, Davis, and Tracer maneuvered to get line of sight to the screen from the perimeter.

Not forgotten was the senior sonarman at the adjoining station. He'd been listening intently for any sign of approaching ships, and so far had nothing to report. Passive sonar in the Arctic was a mixed proposition. There would be no commercial shipping traffic here this time of year, yet operating under the ice cap was always problematic. The movement of the ice itself, particularly during a storm, created a ceaseless veil of background noise that could mask the sound of other submarines. And the tenuousness of their position was lost on no one: *New Mexico* was still in Russian waters, and if she wasn't the target of a search yet, that was going to change soon.

The laptop screen came alive as Seeker motored forward, and within minutes high resolution images began streaming. The sensor employed sonar, although higher frequencies than the ship's own listening arrays. The result was an astoundingly sharp relief of the ocean floor. The bottom sloped gradually upward toward the island, and rocky but mostly featureless contours were clear. Soon it approached the coordinates provided by Sorensen—which turned out to be dead-on.

"We've got something," said the redhead. "Definitely a man-made object, about the right size. I show the return ninety meters from the bow on a two-two-zero bearing. Roughly eighty feet of water."

"Eighty feet," Tracer remarked. "That's good."

Slaton was hopeful, but not convinced, recalling the derelict whaling boat they'd discovered on shore. The ocean's floors were littered with "man-made" debris.

Seeker edged closer, took an oblique angle, and the picture sharpened. "There we are," said the operator.

A detailed image appeared on the screen and Slaton's spirits sank. It didn't take an aircraft accident investigator to see that the shape was all wrong. Not the right angles of a tail section, but a single linear surface. "It's the other wing."

Everyone stood mesmerized as the ghosted green-and-white outline sharpened. The battered wing had come to rest upside down, its two engine pylons clearly discernable—the engines themselves were missing but had to be nearby. None of it helped their cause.

"Looks like we lost our coin flip," the captain said. "Too bad." There was no response, and he looked over his shoulder to see Slaton and Davis staring at him. Zimmerman's gaze narrowed, sensing what was coming.

"We've come this far," Davis said. "It's only two miles from here."

"The other section is in deeper water," Zimmerman argued.

"We don't know how deep," Slaton countered. "It might be manageable."

An extended silence fell. To Slaton, in these surroundings, it was the hush he would have imagined if a destroyer were hunting them from above. All eyes were on the captain—including, notably, those of his crew.

Zimmerman heaved a long sigh. "I am *highly* doubtful, but if that's the only way to get you guys off my ass, then so be it. We'll pass right by the spot on our way out anyway, so it can't hurt to take a look." He gave the order to recall Seeker, then addressed Tracer. "What's your limit on depth for a dive?"

"One hundred and twenty feet," Tracer said, then hedged with, "maybe a little more with limited bottom time."

Slaton recognized this as an expansion of what he'd said back in Kodiak, albeit a small one.

"From what I've seen on the charts, that's about what we'll be looking at," Davis said, "unless the tail section rode the slope into deeper water."

Zimmerman looked at them each in turn. Without further comment, he ordered the helmsman to set the new course as soon as Seeker was back on board.

TWENTY-SIX

Of the three ships owned by EDG Industries, the national command authorities of the United States were presently tracking two. The easiest to find and follow was *Atlas,* the vessel known to have been shadowing *Ross* right before her collision. She was at that moment steaming south from the Suez Canal and into the Red Sea.

Owing to the region's endless conflicts, when it came to surveillance on shipping in the Middle East, American intelligence agencies enjoyed comprehensive coverage. *Atlas* was being watched in near real time, and the U.S. Navy's interest was particularly high. Based on interviews with *Ross*'s CO and crew, it was clear that the destroyer's navigation suite had suffered multiple electronic anomalies, including a significant position shift, in the minutes prior to the collision. Also, for reasons not yet determined, cross-checks built into the triple-redundant system had failed to warn of the error.

A search was under way for the ship's voyage data recorder, which functioned much like an aircraft black box, but it had not yet been located. Even so, Navy investigators knew the odds against so many independent failures were astronomical. Which only further cemented suspicion on *Atlas.* She'd been quickly located exiting the choke point of the Bosporus Strait and had been watched continuously ever since. As she was tracked using a web of surveillance assets, it wasn't lost on anyone that *Atlas* was making nearly twenty knots—which had to be close to her top speed.

The ship's history had been researched extensively in the last day. *Atlas* had been christened fifty years ago in Bremerhaven and spent decades as a pelagic trawler, combing the North Atlantic for cod and haddock. When her Portuguese corporate owner went bankrupt, she was sold to the Hellenic Navy for a pittance. The Greeks converted the ship to a "fleet service vessel," a droll and amorphous title meant to mask her true mission— spying on the Turkish Navy. The two nations had been sparring over the Aegean Sea since the Byzantine Empire, and it became *Atlas*'s mission to troll those contested waters like a bomb-sniffing dog, searching for scraps of electronic intelligence.

She did her bit for the Greeks for twenty years, after which she was decommissioned. *Atlas* had been dry-docked for four years, awaiting either a buyer or the scrapyard, when an entity called EDG Industries proffered an unsolicited bid. The ever-cash-strapped Greek government accepted the offer with the ink barely dry, and with no thought given to what a private consortium would want with a derelict spy ship. The deal went through in record time—the buyers required no survey, and the Greeks had long ago stripped the vessel of all classified electronics. What remained, however, was not without value. *Atlas* was mechanically sound, having been refitted with new diesels a year before her decommissioning. She was also uniquely equipped with large secondary generators and an electrical system with upgraded capacity. Intriguing as all that was, however, it did little to explain why she was cutting through the Red Sea that day at full steam. Nor did it give clues as to where she might be headed.

The second ship being watched was the icebreaker *Sibir*. Since being identified in the Arctic Ocean, she had proved harder to track. The most recent contact showed her steaming through the Bering Sea, the volatile body of water that separated Alaska and the Kamchatka Peninsula, on a southerly course. She appeared to be leaving the ice cap behind for warmer waters and was making good speed as the Northern Pacific opened up on her bow. Surveillance was more challenging in that region due to limited satellite coverage, yet the chore was simplified by the fact that, since making her southerly turn, *Sibir*'s course and speed had remained constant.

It would be days before U.S. intelligence agencies realized their great error. In fixating on *Atlas* and *Sibir*, they failed to identify the third ship owned by EDG Industries.

Like a stray piece moving on a global chessboard, *Poyarka* set sail from Hambantota under a wave of equatorial heat, a thread of black smoke trailing her main stack. Once clear of the harbor, her bow settled on a westerly course, toward the Laccadive Sea and the Gulf of Aden. Unlike her corporate sisters, her screws turned at a far more leisurely speed. At that point, *Poyarka* was running well ahead of schedule.

Soup at the White House had been served cold that evening, cantaloupe gazpacho, and the follow-on courses arrived in time-honored sequence: harvest salad with red wine vinaigrette, Texas Wagyu beef with sautéed kale, sealed with a soufflé glace celestine. The dinner took place in the President's Dining Room, formerly referred to as The Prince of Wales Room. The space was far more intimate than the larger State Dining Room, and closeness had been the evening's theme.

As the night drew to a close, a distracted President Cleveland thought it a success. She looked around and surveyed the wreckage. White House china and flatware were strewn across the table, and three spent wine bottles stood among it all like mileposts—the stewards had already removed three others. The waitstaff had discreetly taken leave half an hour ago so that delicate state business could be breached. Cleveland was seated between her own national security advisor and the president of Taiwan. Her husband and the First Lady of Taiwan were across the room admiring a photo album documenting the room's previous gatherings—a log of political and monarchical royalty that went back over a hundred years. A handful of other invitees, split between the two governments, had been ushered away so that the two leaders could spend a few private moments together.

Over coffee, Cleveland implored her Taiwanese counterpart, whose English was excellent, to press ahead with a joint military exercise this summer. It was the last item on the president's agenda, having so far covered a new sale of F-35 fighters and a corporate technology sharing initiative. All of it was designed to buttress their common aim: blunting the looming shadow of the Chinese giant.

With the evening winding down, someone had to take the initiative to disengage, and as if on cue, Cleveland's chief of staff appeared. Ed Markowitz crossed the room, leaned down, and whispered into her ear, "We have a crisis. You need to come now."

Cleveland gave her regrets for an abrupt departure, and the ever-graceful Taiwanese president said he understood—which he probably did.

As they made their way to the Situation Room, with a pair of Secret Service men in trail, Markowitz filled the president in. "It's the mission we sent to Wrangel Island. Deputy Director Sorensen's team arrived and joined up with a shore party from *New Mexico*. They'd been at the crash scene for roughly an hour, going over the wreckage, when a squad of Russians showed up—we believe they came from the radar facility on the island. The Russians initiated a firefight, and it didn't end well for them."

"How bad?" the president asked.

"Eight dead, two wounded, two captured. One minor injury on our side. The mission commander made the call to release the survivors, unarmed and without radios, so they could take their wounded back to base."

"Christ!"

They reached the Situation Room, and everyone stood as the president entered. "Seats!" she ordered. "What's the latest? Have we heard anything from the Russians on this?"

"Nothing yet," said the duty officer. "They certainly know about it by now, but it's five in the morning Moscow time."

The president took a seat at the head of the table. "Where is *New Mexico*?"

"She's submerged, but still in the area. Deputy Director Sorensen authorized a search for the sections of wreckage that are submerged."

The president's face screwed into a grimace, an oddly asynchronous countenance for a woman wearing a black Dolce & Gabbana evening gown with pearls.

"This is going to blow up in our faces," Markowitz said. "We haven't even announced the crash of Raven 44."

The president put two fingers to her temple as if expecting a migraine at any moment. "All right, we need to play catch-up. Let's start with a news release on Raven 44. I want our version out there first—Lord knows what the Russians will concoct."

"And *New Mexico*?"

"Tell the Navy to get her the hell out of there. The last thing we need is for torpedoes to start launching!"

New Mexico was hovering near the second site, and again the NRO's position estimate proved stunningly accurate. Seeker quickly found the wreckage, the distinctly unnatural ninety-degree angles of the tail section, bent and battered, standing out from the rocky bottom like an Eiffel Tower on the moon. The image also confirmed a problem.

"The tail fractured," Davis said. "Probably happened when it hit the ice. The right stabilizer is gone, and what we're looking at is most of the vertical tail and half the left stabilizer."

"Do you see the section we need?" Slaton asked.

Davis leaned in to study the screen. "Hard to tell." He put a finger on one edge of the big airfoil. "This is where the vertical tail meets the fuselage. The boxes should be beneath a panel here, but it's taken a hit. Even if the recorders are intact, they might be hard to access due to the damage. Unfortunately, we can't tell from here—the only way to know is to get wet."

"How deep is it?" Tracer asked.

"We're sitting at one hundred and ten feet," said the redhead. "These images are at . . ." he manipulated his display, "one thirty, maybe a little more."

Tracer grimaced.

Slaton understood why. It was a classic case of mission creep—the depth of the dive increasing with each new variable, pressing the limits of safety. On the other side was the pull of getting the mission done—something hardwired into every operator he'd ever met.

"It's at the very limit," Tracer hedged. "We wouldn't have much time."

"I can work fast," Davis said distractedly, his eyes locked on the sonar image. Slaton could almost see him rehearsing how he would attack the panel, plotting what tools to use and from what angle.

All eyes went to the captain. Zimmerman looked like a man in a dentist's chair, the drill poised and spinning. He nodded all the same.

"All right," Tracer said. "Let's suit up and get this done."

TWENTY-SEVEN

Lazarus had greeted Bagdani at the door of room 386 with a phone to his ear. With a series of gestures, he'd brought him inside and instructed him to wait in the main room while he finished his call in what appeared to be the only bedroom.

The place had all the ambiance of his barracks in the Legion. Plaster flaked from the walls, and the only light came from a ceiling-mounted fixture that was missing its globe, two naked bulbs fighting the gloom and losing. It was the latest in a long line of hovels Lazarus used for their meetings. How many had it been now? Eight, nine? Always a different address, although all had been in Almaty.

Bagdani wandered to the kitchen counter, a hip-high expanse of chipped Formica in a terrible watermelon hue. On top were a box of sweet rolls, two missing, and a pot of lukewarm coffee. He helped himself, using a napkin for a plate and pouring the coffee in a paper hot cup.

They'd been working together for a year now, Lazarus serving as the point man with a group he referred to as The Trident. They provided the money and technology, and seemed to have no shortage of either. Bagdani had never been briefed on the greater objectives, and he rarely bothered to hypothesize. As long as his fees arrived on schedule—and they unerringly did—he considered the customer's motives none of his business. He wondered if Lazarus was speaking to them now. Naturally, Bagdani tried to catch a bit of the conversation, but aside from a few random words of English, he deciphered little.

The coffee was bitter, the sweet roll not bad.

He meandered to the only window, pulled back a tattered curtain, and took in the scene. A dreary, mist-enveloped cityscape stared back. He hoped this meeting wouldn't last long—he'd booked a 1:15 flight that would get him home at a reasonable hour. Back to the sun and warmth.

Not to mention, safety.

The question of why he'd been summoned today, on short notice, loomed uncomfortably. He'd received a message on the ride from the airport confirming that *Poyarka* had sailed. With that, his third contract was complete. Bagdani had sought out, vetted, and hired her crew. Now that the mission was under way, whatever it was, he was looking forward to some time off. There had been hints of future initiatives, yet the first three had been so lucrative he could live off the proceeds for years. He was acutely aware that *Atlas* had been involved in the sinking of a U.S. Navy ship in the Black Sea, and while there hadn't been any fallout yet, Bagdani very much wanted to lay low.

He was finishing a second sweet roll when Lazarus ended his call and joined him in the main room. He hobbled to the counter and refilled his own stained paper cup with black coffee.

"Has she sailed?" Lazarus asked. Small talk had never been a hallmark of their relationship.

"Yes, within the last hour."

"Good, I will pass the word. And no issues with the crew?"

"None. A full complement at departure." Bagdani wiped a bit of frosting from his lips with a bent knuckle, and asked, "Is there any news on *Atlas*?"

"She should make port on schedule."

"Is she being tracked?"

"I can't imagine otherwise. The Americans must know of her involvement by now."

Bagdani plucked a third roll from the box. "It's good we chose such a remote location for her next stop."

"It should work, but only once. The same with *Sibir*'s variation. After each mission the playing field will shift gradually. It will be harder to find exit strategies for your recruits in the next phase."

Bagdani nearly expressed his doubts about further work with The Trident, but then thought better of it. "We have always assumed a few will get tracked down and questioned. That is why we took compartmentalization to the extreme. Most have never seen me, and the few that have don't know my name. None of them could know you, or . . ." He let the thought die.

Lazarus didn't pursue the point. Instead, he went over how the three missions would wind down, each to its own inglorious end. Confusion on top of confusion. Bagdani agreed the plans were solid.

At the end, Lazarus said, "The Trident will eventually have more work for us but it won't begin for a few months. Will you take some time off . . . the villa in Saint-Tropez?"

Bagdani's internal Klaxon sounded, yet he showed no outward reaction. He had indeed recently bought a villa and gone to great lengths to leave no trace of the purchase. Or so he'd thought. There was nothing threatening in Lazarus's tone, yet the warning was clear. There would be no hiding from The Trident.

"I'll stay busy," he said weakly.

Lazarus spent ten minutes on administrative matters, after which he gave Bagdani a new phone. "Check it once a day. After things have settled, I'll send a message to arrange our next meeting."

Without comment, Bagdani took the handset.

He was outside minutes later and found the same driver waiting in the same car. He checked his watch and was happy to see that he could easily make his flight. He sat silently in the backseat as the driver retraced the route to the airport, the gray skies overhead finally being cut by the sun. The new phone in his pocket weighed heavy. More than ever, he doubted he would use it. This Trident, whoever they were, were stirring up trouble the likes of which Bagdani had never seen.

Yet he was also struck by a disconnect, the notion that Lazarus, perhaps, had motives of his own that were not in complete alignment with those of their employers. By necessity, Bagdani was a good researcher of persons, and he had been trying for some time to learn more about Lazarus. He'd known him reputationally for years. If Bagdani was a headhunter, Lazarus was a consolidator—a one-stop, logistical marvel who could coordinate diverse purchases of materiel and equipment. The two of them had often crossed paths, swimming parallel lanes in the same dirty pool. More than once they'd supplied opposite sides of the same war, yet neither took it as an affront. Business was business. This, however, was the first time they'd joined forces.

It began early last year, Lazarus approaching him about a lucrative contract for a dozen highly skilled technicians. The payday offered by The Trident seemed a once-in-a-lifetime deal, and a natural off-ramp for two successful but maturing arms merchants. Still, Bagdani didn't completely trust Lazarus. His very name was suspect, a blatant nom de guerre, and he could find no trace of the man's real identity. No history, no nationality, no family ties. No girlfriend or boyfriend or rumors of arrests.

His injuries, obvious as they were, had no clear source—they could be anything from combat wounds to an auto accident. He moved with distinct weariness, yet his mind was sharp and he was clearly motivated. All his clothing was secondhand, and the only passport Bagdani had ever glimpsed was certainly forged. He had never seen the man drink or smoke or show up with a vacation tan. He knew Lazarus spoke three languages, and he suspected there were more. There was an accent on his English, something hard-edged he couldn't quite place.

Yet for all his efforts to identify the man, Bagdani had drawn nothing but blanks.

The sun disappeared again, the Kazakh gloom returning with its leaden vengeance.

Bagdani's mind drifted to the French Riviera, but in a way that surprised him—he had a sudden urge to put the new villa on the market. If Lazarus could find it, others could as well.

More than ever, he felt it was time to go home. It was time to batten down his life until the coming storm passed.

Slaton hadn't put on a dry suit in years, yet the awkwardness was just as he remembered. First came an inner shell for insulation before he stepped into the high-tech outer liner. Most of the garment was one-piece, the only seam being where the neck seal joined the hood. After donning their suits, the three men checked one another's gear, Tracer taking final responsibility that everyone was squared away.

They then backpacked standard twin-80 tanks and regulators. SEALs generally dove with rebreathers, which negated the problem of bubbles—a dead giveaway in most tactical scenarios. The problem today involved the depth they would be diving. There *were* rebreathers designed for deep diving, but those rigs required exotic gas mixtures and extensive training—unrealistic given their breakneck deployment. As it stood, the standard gear would do the job, and bubbles gathering under three feet of polar ice weren't going to give anyone away.

They spent another ten minutes clipping tools to belts, strapping on lights and backups, and coordinating logistics. Slaton held the bulk of the tools, while Tracer would be a floating jumbotron—he was carrying five lights to train on the working area.

"We're not going to have comm on this dive," Tracer said, "so hand signals are vital." He went over the most obvious, then improvised a few that seemed to fit the mission. Davis and Slaton coordinated how they would handle the tools. The wreckage was on the edge of a steep slope, and the last thing they needed was to drop a vital wrench over the submarine cliff.

They lumbered toward the lockout chamber like steamfitters from the apocalypse, tools and lights jangling with every step. They did so under the watchful eye of the captain.

"Understand, I will not put the ship at risk," Zimmerman said. "You have one shot. As soon as you're back on board, we're making for safe waters."

"Understood, Captain," said Tracer.

All three men stepped through the hatch into the chamber. The door clanged shut behind them with the finality of a sealing tomb. Technicians began turning valves, and a churning sound prevailed as water replaced air. The lockout chamber doubled as an escape hatch for the crew in the event of an emergency. In theory it could hold nine divers, but at that moment it looked cramped for three in heavy gear. The techs advised them of progress via a loudspeaker as the compartment flooded.

Slaton had been through the drill before, but always in the balmy Mediterranean. The water rushing in was frigid, yet the cold didn't register until it hit the only exposed part of his body—his face below his mask. When his cheeks got an ice bath it was a bracing reminder of how protected the rest of his body was. And a warning of what he would face if something went wrong. Only then did it dawn on Slaton that diving from a submarine below the ice cap added another risk he'd never faced. On any other dive, when problems were encountered—air supply, communications, navigation—climbing to the surface was always a last-ditch solution. Today it offered nothing but three feet of solid ice.

Once the chamber was completely flooded, and the pressure equalized, Tracer looked at the two other mask-clad faces in turn. Everyone exchanged OK signs with thumb and middle finger, and then turned on their lights.

Tracer opened the outer hatch and led the way into a pitch-black Arctic Ocean.

TWENTY-EIGHT

The water seemed translucent, as if the frigid temperature somehow made the sea more viscous. The exit hatch was lit, but as soon as the team moved away they were enveloped in blackness. The only external lights on *New Mexico* were her standard navigation lights, one red and one green, giving the aura of a pathetic subarctic Christmas display. Their personal lights illuminated the matte-black hull, yet in every other direction the beams faded into nothingness.

The water felt colder than ever on Slaton's face, barely above the freezing point, yet the dry suit was doing its job. He adjusted his buoyancy, adding air to his rig until he had a slight negative dynamic—with each exhale, he sank ever so slowly. Tracer paused long enough to exchange final OK signs, then gave a follow-me signal.

As soon as he started swimming, Slaton noticed a problem: the hacksaw clipped to his hip was snagging on his backup regulator. Most of the tools they were carrying were basic: screwdrivers, pry bars, wire cutters. He felt like a swimming toolbox. It took two adjustments to straighten out, but otherwise things went smoothly—a minor miracle for all the gear he was hauling. They swam forward along the *New Mexico*'s foredeck until reaching the bow. There Tracer hovered above the bow array dome and took a long look back over the length of the boat.

Slaton knew why. He was taking a critical mental snapshot, the orientation of the navigation lights and hull. There was a time in every mission when you had to trust your commander. On this operation there would be no opposing force. Stealth during entry and egress were nonissues. They were simply looking for the remnants of a crashed airplane on the bottom of the sea—a salvage operation that under normal conditions would be simplicity itself. Yet sometimes the simplest of challenges came with daunting complications. In this case, the problem involved navigation: finding the wreckage, and then returning to *New Mexico*.

Back at the shop in Kodiak, Tracer had briefed Slaton on the SEAL Team diving rig, which included a new mask-mounted nav display for diving. A tiny window beneath the left-side lens provided heading information and distance to selected waypoints. Unfortunately, none of that would work here. The system was designed to receive an acoustic locator signal—in essence, using *New Mexico* as a navigation reference. The problem was that *New Mexico* herself was at the mercy of nature. GPS, the wonder of technology that guided people along highways and over city streets, had marginal capability in polar regions, and none at all while submerged. And while *New Mexico* had updated her position while surfaced, she was now relying exclusively on inertial systems, and Zimmerman had warned that one of those units had been acting up. In a body of water with better surveys, *New Mexico* could have updated her position using bottom features, but that wasn't available so close to Wrangel Island. In sum, the world's most advanced technology was below the threshold of accuracy needed, and therefore temporarily out of service.

The standard backup, basic compass navigation, was equally problematic. Magnetic compasses, used regularly by divers around the world, were inaccurate in polar regions: the earth's northern magnetic pole was not geographically north of their position.

Taken together, it meant that the simple act of crossing 150 yards of pitch-black ocean, with no visual cues or directional reference, was an invitation to disaster. Magnifying the danger was the polar ice above. With a limited air supply, if any of them became separated from *New Mexico*, there was no option of surfacing to wait for rescue. They would not survive.

Yet there was a way to get the job done, basic as it was, and Tracer had covered it at length during his predive briefing. Magnetic compasses, while not accurate for finding "north" at this latitude, would show consistent readings. The fact that the magnetic north pole lay in northern Canada—it was actually a moving target, drifting thirty-five miles a year—did not completely negate its utility. Each of the three men wore a wrist-mounted compass. They had compared them inside *New Mexico*, and all gave essentially the same reading: From the bow of the ship, they would swim a 220-degree course to reach the wreckage. The reciprocal, 040 degrees, would bring them back. They would count kicks to measure distance. Zimmerman had put *New Mexico* as close as possible to the wreckage, but some standoff was required due to the sloping, rock-strewn bottom. It left a gap of 150 yards between the sub's bow and the wreckage.

In so many ways, they were going back to basics. Dead reckoning for navigation. Hand tools for the salvage work. Counting kicks for distance. They were improvising to get a mission done—backups to backups, and a validation of so many years of training.

There was one caveat to their dead reckoning method: it required an update of the compass course once in the water and clear of the boat—the sub's metal mass and dense electronics could conceivably induce errors.

Tracer led twenty kicks away from the bow, everyone following and referencing their own compasses. Slaton had his primary light strapped to his arm and trained directly on his compass. He came to a stop, his body easy in the water, and everyone compared readings. Tracer used a small writing slate to scrawl down his estimated course and kick-count. The others used hand signals to convey their own, and he wrote these down as well. The consensus was a 225-degree course, a minor variation from what they'd planned, and 80 kick cycles. With that warm fuzzy, they set out into the blackness.

Beyond the boat they encountered a void of nothingness. The only reference to up and down were streams of exhaust bubbles caught in their beams. Slaton turned to get one last look at *New Mexico,* but she was already gone, her red and green lights swallowed by a pitch-black sea.

The next time Anton Bloch saw his daughter he was not prepared for the sight. Not that any father could be.

In a show of mercy, he'd been warned what was coming by a call from Tel Aviv—Mossad director, Nurin. *"There is a video. It emerged today online. We're attempting to backtrack through social media accounts, but so far we don't know where it originated."*

Sorensen sat beside him as he loaded the footage on her laptop, more crisis counselor than spymaster. Bloch tapped on the arrow and Ayla appeared. Immediately his heart clenched. It *was* his daughter, yet the changes were profound. She looked weary and aged, a twenty-four-year-old girl with bags under her eyes and reddened sclera. Her hair was matted on one side, as if she'd just woken up after a bad night's sleep, and there were abrasions on one cheek and a fat lower lip.

She was seated on a wooden chair, and while only the tops of her arms were visible, they appeared to be wrenched behind her, implying restraints. The background behind her could not have been more neutral, flat drywall in an off-white hue. Like a billion walls around the world. Perhaps more telling was what *wasn't* in the picture. Bloch saw no other people, no flag from a nemesis terrorist group that longed to erase the Jewish state. The clip ran twenty-six seconds, and in the middle his daughter delivered a simple five-second statement.

She spoke in a flat, uncharacteristic monotone. "My name is Ayla Bloch. My father, Anton Bloch, is the former director of Mossad."

And that was all. The recording hit its end with such brute suddenness it caused Bloch to clench the arms of his chair.

He sat trying to make sense of it. A proof of life video with no time-and-date stamp. A few words delivered with painstaking austerity. Bloch never doubted Ayla's abduction was related to his own service, yet here it was . . . proof beyond question.

He felt Sorensen's hand on his shoulder; it seemed to be shaking. It took a moment to realize she wasn't the source.

"I don't get it," she said. "No demands, no deadlines. What's the point?"

Bloch didn't answer—even though one possibility came to mind.

He pushed the thought away, hit the play button again.

It wasn't until the fourth iteration that he began to think it through like the spymaster he was. Scouring the background for clues, analyzing every word, listening for extraneous sounds. Who was holding her? Where? What did they want?

"We'll find her," Sorensen said.

Again, Bloch didn't respond. He recalled, many years ago, saying the same thing to a Shin Bet operative whose brother had been abducted in Lebanon. He also remembered how that had ended. When he finally got his wits about him, he turned to Sorensen, and said, "I am going to return to Israel."

Poyarka battered through heavy swells as an early-season cyclone built in her path. The bow was getting inundated on the backside of each wave, high winds from port sweeping water over the foredeck. Her captain was unconcerned, evidenced by the fact that he was not on the bridge, but rather seated at the tiny desk in his quarters.

His name was Dmitri Constantis. He was a Greek by birth but a privateer by temperament—a man whose voyage through life was as defiant as the sea itself. The weather, he knew, was unusual for this time of year, yet there was nothing to be done about it. The ship's projected course was plotted on a wall-mounted chart above his desk. At that moment, the southern tip of India was to starboard, and soon the Maldives would pass to port. Once *Poyarka* cleared those lanes, putting a day of open water ahead, he could alter course to smooth things out.

There was a tentative knock on his open door, and he looked up to see the chief scientist. This in itself was a first for Constantis—to set sail with a scientist on board. The man was slender, somewhat effeminate, and said his name was Chou. He claimed to be Taiwanese, which Constantis doubted, and also professed to hold a PhD in signals analysis, which the captain could not possibly have an opinion on. Right then he looked unwell, and Constantis recalled what Chou had told him in port: that his only previous time at sea involved a cruise around Hong Kong Harbor. Ten hours after departing the still waters of port, he'd taken on a yellowish hue and his legs wobbled like saplings in a gale.

"What is it?" Constantis asked.

"The dome is taking on water."

The captain's brow arched in concern. "Is that a problem?"

"It could be, yes. My assistant is doing his best, but the water washing on deck has begun seeping beneath the walls—it wasn't properly sealed. We've been stuffing towels in the gaps and using tape on the outside, but it is only getting worse."

Constantis's expression collapsed to full-on worry. Here he was, at sea with the world's mightiest maritime weapon on his foredeck, and they were keeping it dry with duct tape and beach towels.

"Could we possibly slow our speed?" Chou asked.

The captain referenced the weather report. The worst wouldn't be behind them for another twelve hours. Slowing for that long would put them behind schedule. He checked the map again and saw perhaps a bit of open water to the south.

"We can't cut our speed enough to make a difference, but if we steer ten or fifteen degrees to port, that should put the seas on a better angle. Hopefully that will reduce the flooding. I will give the order. Report back in half an hour and give me an update."

Chou looked at him blankly.

"Is there something else?" he prompted.

"No." The scientist disappeared.

On another voyage, in another setting, Constantis might have found the man's discomfort amusing. As it was, all humor escaped him. On his list of things that could go wrong, weather was near the bottom. Yet here he was, altering course for a minor blow. Still, there was nothing to be done. It was vital to avoid compromising the weapon. Probably more important, he needed Chou fit and clearheaded when the moment of truth came.

It was the only way any of them would get out of this alive.

TWENTY-NINE

Seventy-five kick-cycles later the team was nearing its objective.

Tracer paused and began scanning with his most powerful light. It cut the blackness like a lighthouse beam, and halfway through its arc Slaton caught a slight reflection. It wasn't the wreckage, but the next best thing: the sloping bottom, a steep grade of barren seabed. Gray and featureless, the smooth rock was overlaid by a thick blanket of silt, like the surface of some lifeless planet. They swam closer, everyone's lights moving, eyes searching. Slaton checked his compass—their course was dead-on. His depth gauge showed 135 feet, further confirmation that they'd intercepted the upslope at the right spot.

They were nearly touching the bottom when Davis tapped his shoulder, then Tracer's. He pointed to the right, and trapped in his beam was a slab of dull-gray metal. They closed in and the wreckage gained definition. Eerily, on one side, at the edge of a ragged tear in the metal skin, Slaton saw a subdued star-in-a-circle, sided by stripes—the emblem of the United States Air Force. Higher up, close to the tail's crest, a painted American flag seemed to be laying claim to this silt-laden resting place.

Soon the wreckage became clear in its entirety, and it looked remarkably as it had in the images from Seeker: the main vertical tail, and a portion of one horizontal fin. It was lodged on what had to be a thirty-degree slope. Tracer gave a *hold* signal, then swam closer alone. From above, he grabbed the top of the tail and shook it back and forth, then did it again from a different angle. Slaton understood immediately. He was making sure the wreckage was stable, the kind of check one would make before entering a shipwreck. According to sonar, the gradient increased beneath them—if the wreckage started to move, there was nothing to stop it for over a thousand feet. In effect, they were on the edge of a submarine cliff.

Fortunately, nothing moved, and Tracer backed away and began arranging his lights. He waved them in.

As briefed, Davis led the way. He swam straight to the base of the tail, Slaton following. Tracer took up a position behind them, edging to one side. They would coordinate like a surgical team, Davis pointing to the tool he needed, Slaton providing it. Tracer kept his lights on the work area like a stage technician in a theater. He was also in charge of tracking the elapsed time and air supply.

Davis picked out the panel he was after. It was the size of a stovetop, nearly square with rounded edges, the surface contoured to fit the curves of the fuselage. Slaton slapped a standard-blade screwdriver into Davis's right glove.

He immediately went to work.

Of the two ships Langley was tracking, the southernmost became the highlight reel.

Atlas had spent the previous night traversing the Red Sea, and while satellite coverage was excellent in that area, increasing suspicion in command centers across the D.C. metroplex had led to overlapping coverage. A pair of CIA Reaper drones were now tag-teaming, shadowing the ship from medium altitude. Analysts watched *Atlas* ply a straight-and-true course toward the Arabian Sea. They could easily make out crewmen on deck, as one would expect, and noted an oil slick in her wake that suggested a minor mechanical issue.

The standing theory at CIA headquarters was that *Atlas* was heading back to the port where she'd been seen last fall: Hambantota, Sri Lanka. That presumption cratered off the coast of Eritrea.

From the shipping lane, *Atlas* made a sudden right turn. Analysts watched closely as the old trawler began weaving through islands in the Dahlak Archipelago. It soon became clear she was headed for Dahlak Kebir, the largest and most densely populated of the chain's 350 islands. She came to a stop in a notorious bay strewn with wrecks from the Ethiopia-Eritrea War. Countless rusting hulks lay marooned near shore, and the outlines of sunken vessels were clear in the shallow, crystalline water. Under the watchful eye of the Reaper overhead, two inflatable boats were deployed from *Atlas*'s midship boarding platform. Within minutes, twenty-two crewmen split between them and set out toward shore.

The team at the Langley Operations Center didn't know what to make of it. The inflatables beached on a thin crescent of sand near a tiny village. From there, half the crewmen hurried to a cluster of waiting cars and motorcycles, while the rest disappeared into a scattershot collection of buildings. If there was any rule to the scheme, it was that no two crewmen remained together—each seemed to take a different path from the beach. One analyst, renowned for his imaginative reports, compared the debarkation to "roaches scattering when a light gets turned on."

The Reaper operators attempted to track a few of the vehicles but were quickly overwhelmed. Orders were given to settle the optics back on *Atlas*. It was a retired Navy petty officer, double-dipping with a second career at the CIA, who noticed that the ship had never thrown down her anchor. Barely had that comment been uttered when *Atlas* began her next act: With a churn of foam astern, she began to move. The ship performed a graceful pirouette, put her bow toward the channel, and headed back to sea the same way she'd come. An hour later, she was back on her original track, headed southeast toward the open water of the Indian Ocean.

Thousands of miles away, a mystified cadre of intelligence analysts watched in utter consternation.

THIRTY

Davis worked furiously, knowing their dive clock was running. Unfortunately, the access panel he needed to open was damaged, the screws on one side jammed. He switched to a pry bar, and after that a hacksaw. Finally, the panel came free.

Everyone closed in, and Tracer shined his best light inside the cavity. They all saw the boxes—in fact, not black, but life-vest orange, each the size of a large shoe box. Still, there was more to do. The boxes were bolted to the floor of the compartment, four feet below the opening. Even with his long arms, Davis would have to push chest-deep into the cramped bay to reach them.

It was an awkward chore but expected. Each recorder was locked down by four bolts. There was also an electrical cannon plug that, in theory, could be twisted free by hand. Davis pointed to the wrench he needed, and Slaton handed it over. With a cautious look at the others, he pulled himself inside. It was a tight fit—his sheer size, combined with the dry suit and twin tanks, left almost no maneuvering room, and the sharp metal edge where he'd cut away the panel had to be avoided.

Slaton tried to keep light on the work area, and he saw Davis begin with the flight data recorder. He disconnected the electrical plug easily and then went to work on the bolts. The first three came quickly, but then he hit the roadblock any car mechanic would attest to: *there was always one.*

The fastener had likely been bent in the crash. Davis tugged the wrench with increasing force, finally got the bolt to turn, and eventually removed it completely. The recorder should have been free at that point, but as Slaton watched, Davis struggled to pull it off the mounting bracket. He arched and twisted, his hips pressed against the opening for leverage. A final surge seemed to do the trick.

And that was when Slaton noticed it—somewhere in the periphery, a shift.

A terrible grating noise resonated through the water and the entire tail section began to move. Slaton kicked ahead and grabbed one of Davis's ankles. He sensed Tracer doing the same on his right.

Half-buried in the compartment, Davis didn't seem to realize what was happening. They hauled on his legs as the wreckage picked up speed, sliding down the cliff, yet something hung up before his shoulders cleared. Slaton spotted a tank valve hooked on a thin cable and he lurched forward to free it. Davis was pushing with them now, realizing the danger, but that only tightened the jam. The wreckage kept sliding, and the groan of metal over rock became resounding, like the death rattle of some undersea leviathan.

Slaton pulled a pair of wire cutters from his belt, and as the tail section accelerated down the slope, he tried to cut the cable. It took three desperate attempts, but finally it snapped and Davis jerked free into open water. His hands, however, were empty. Slaton's eyes shot inside the compartment and he saw the recorder, free and tumbling to one side as the wreckage began to roll. Without a thought, he hauled himself in and snatched at the box. The device had a handle and he got a solid grip on it. Slaton nearly had it clear when the direction of the slide shifted suddenly. His head hit something hard, but he kept pushing clear. The tail section spun a great half circle; Slaton was completely disoriented and sensed he was tumbling. Something tugged at the belt holding his gear, raking across his back and right side, yet he kept his grip on the recorder. He had the distinct sensation of falling, and knew he was being dragged deeper.

Then, all at once, he was free.

Slaton hovered in the water for a moment, dazed, taking stock. The recorder was in his hand, and he sensed its extra weight pulling him down—his perfect buoyancy had been ruined by what was effectively a twenty pound anchor. The darkness was absolute, yet he instinctively began kicking, his fins countering the new dynamic. The recorder struck something, and an instant later his legs did the same. It could only be the slope. Slaton ended up crouched, bent in an awkward sitting position. At least he wasn't moving. Wasn't going any deeper.

The sound of tearing metal transmitted through the water as the wreckage dropped into the abyss. Slowly the noise faded, and in the end there was nothing but the sound of his own breathing; bubbles venting; the mechanical hiss of his regulator.

The race of his heartbeat thumping in his ears.

Slaton fell completely still, relaxing limb by limb, controlling his breathing. It was the virtual meditative state learned by all snipers. Mastered by the best.

The blackness was absolute, and he sensed a great cloud of silt around him; bits of cold grit brushed his exposed face. He looked to his right arm, saw no trace of the warm beam of his dive light. One gloved hand went to his waist, grasping and searching. His entire belt, including the tools and, more important, his backup light, was gone. He scanned what he thought was up, looking for any source of light, any contour in the blackness. There was nothing. The sliding wreckage had stirred an impenetrable cloud of silt. He reached for his dive computer, felt it hanging by his side. The screen appeared blank, and he brought it up until it was nearly touching the faceplate of his mask. Still nothing. He ran his gloved thumb over the computer's screen and felt broken glass give way.

What else could go wrong?

Tracer and Davis couldn't be far away. Or could they? How much deeper had he been dragged? He sat motionless, weighing what to do. There seemed only one option: move back up the slope. Still holding the recorder, Slaton adjusted his buoyancy to account for the weight, adding air to his rig until he felt weightless relative to the bottom. He carefully began moving higher, but progress was agonizingly slow. Completely blind, he kept his free hand on the rocks—they were his only reference to the earth, to what was up or down. Inch by inch he clawed higher, dragging the heavy box with him.

He continued for what seemed like five minutes, then stopped again. His eyes raked the blackness, searching desperately for some faint orb of light reaching through the gloom. He saw nothing. He moved for another five minutes, stopped once more. The black void held fast. He felt the first sensation of cold water on his back; only a trickle, but enough to tell him he had a tear in his suit.

Had he gone too high? How much air did he have left? He knew his sense of time would be warped, thrown askew by his overstimulated brain. He was sure the others were looking for him. But for how long? Combined with the lack of sensory inputs, Slaton had a great deal to process. And the rest of his life to figure it out.

He cocked his right arm and tried to read his wrist-mounted compass. Finally, a break. He'd had his dive light shining directly over it earlier, and while the compass didn't have backlighting, the rose and needle were photoluminescent. He could see it, but the glow was faint. He instantly recognized a hole in his preparation. He'd left the compass in his gear bag until putting it on for the dive. He should have taken it out sooner, given the luminous material time to absorb the available light. As it was, he had to hold the compass inches from his mask to make out the reading.

045 degrees. 80 kick cycles. He had a way back. *If* he was near where the wreckage had been. *If* the luminescence held up. *If* he could stay level in open water without a depth gauge or the bottom to reference.

Would it be better to stay where he was? Wait for help? There was no right answer. Only odds and variables, all of which were too complex for his cold-soaked brain. His suit was leaking steadily now. In the end, Slaton chose a middle ground. He would wait and watch. Five minutes by the clock in his head—normally reliable, but far less so now. He settled to stillness, a new seat on the sloped bottom. He closed his eyes, but nothing changed. Still blackness all around.

How many times, during his life as a sniper, had he found himself in a similar place? Waiting calmly, with forced tranquility, under conditions of extreme duress. He remembered hiding in shadows on a rooftop in Egypt, the police nearly tripping over him as he waited for the car with his target to appear. He remembered lying in a weed-strewn ditch while a terrorist made love to his mistress, knowing he always took a cigarette on the balcony afterward.

And today?

Today Slaton was a hundred feet beneath the polar ice cap, his only path to safety razor-thin. Perhaps nonexistent.

Curiously, all those situations demanded the same response.

Surreal patience.

Davis burst from the lockout chamber like a man possessed, laden with gear and dripping frozen seawater.

"We have to rig back up! Slaton is still out there!" He shrugged his tanks off and began breaking down his equipment.

"What the hell happened?" the captain asked.

Tracer, emerging right behind him, explained how things had gone wrong. "We pulled Jammer clear, but then Slaton made a grab for the recorder. The wreckage shifted at just the wrong time. Everything went over the ledge and we lost sight of him. We searched as long as we could, but we had to turn back—Jammer was getting low on air."

Davis ordered a petty officer to bring up fresh tanks—an order that, as a civilian, he had no authority to give.

"Stand down!" Zimmerman countered.

The poor seaman froze.

The captain eyed his guests one at a time. "I said you had one shot at this. I don't want to put more divers at risk of—"

"Captain!" A messenger rushed in waving a strip of paper. "Urgent orders from Fleet!"

Zimmerman took the slip of paper and read it. When he finished, his eyes canted up to Davis and Tracer. "We are hereby ordered to leave this area at top speed until reaching international waters."

Davis moved forward until he was all but hovering over Zimmerman. The CO was not a small man, but geared up and wearing the dry suit, Davis looked like Neptune minus his trident. "We are *not* leaving a man out there!"

Zimmerman didn't blink. Yet he saw something in Davis's posture, in his gaze, that told him if he didn't permit a second dive, the man would end up secured in his quarters and under guard for the rest of the cruise . . . and he himself might be in the market for a reconstructive dentist.

He slowly put a hand on Davis's chest, and calmly, but firmly, the skipper pushed him back a step. Then he looked at Tracer. "How long does he have out there?"

Tracer checked his dive computer. "Absolute max—if he's not back in twenty minutes, he's not coming back."

Aside from the divers, Zimmerman felt the eyes of his crewmen. He knew he had no choice. He handed the paper back to the messenger, and said, "Go back to your station. Wait exactly ten minutes, then bring this to me again."

The man smiled, said, "Aye, sir," and disappeared.

Zimmerman looked at Tracer and Davis. "Well don't just stand there—get to work!"

THIRTY-ONE

The vision was that of a dying campfire, Davy dutifully holding a rack of trout filets above a few dying embers. The fire needed fuel, but the dark forest around them seemed empty. No wood, no kindling, nothing but darkness. Cold mountain air crept in . . .

The timer in his head went off, and Slaton left the faraway place.

His eyes flicked open, hope welling, but to no avail—the sea around him remained a blank. Like a blind man, he used his other senses to fill the void. He was still sitting on the ledge, and while the moment with his son had been imagined, the coldness was not. Arctic water continued to flow through a tear in the back of his dry suit. He felt it creeping down his right arm, crawling over his shoulder.

The cold was taking its wicked grip. Seizing his mind. Sapping his strength. It was an additive problem, but at this point the introduction of twenty-nine-degree seawater was nothing but a motivator. Lack of air would kill him before hypothermia. The idea of dying on a mission wasn't foreign, and there was no good way to do it. Most of his tight spots in the past had involved shrapnel or bullets or bladed weapons. But here, today, the thought of suffocating in this hermetic ice-water world, knowing his body would never be found, seemed harsh and inglorious. Slaton forced away the defeatist notion.

Not yet.

He searched 360 degrees for any source of light—a final prayer for a muted beam from the blackness. Still nothing. Slaton brought his compass close to his faceplate. The dial and needle were visible, but only just, the fading luminescence an apt metaphor for his situation. He compared the 045 bearing to the ledge he was sitting on, trying to relate the geometry to what he'd seen when they arrived. He decided it was close.

He took a firm grip on the flight recorder and fine-tuned his buoyancy by feel, referencing the ledge until he was perfectly neutral in the water with its weight; having no reference for depth, it was critical to keep somewhere near level. He set out on his course and began counting kick cycles. *Left, right, one. Left, right, two.* His movement and the change of body angle caused the frigid water in his suit to slosh into new crevices. He ignored the cold, kept scanning, desperate for any trace of light.

Slaton felt like a spaceship launching into an ice-clad universe, cruising weightlessly but without stars for orientation. Unable to see his bubbles, his only sense of up and down became the weight of the recorder. On kick number nine he felt something jab into his ribs, and it jogged his memory:

the big screwdriver Davis had used to loosen the panel was tucked into a pocket of his buoyancy vest. An idea sprang to mind, and without losing his rhythm, without missing count, he reached for the screwdriver with his free hand.

The junior sonar operator monitoring *New Mexico*'s passive array was under strict orders: listen closely for the sound of other ships. Everyone on board knew what had happened shoreside, and it was only a matter of time before the Russians responded. That in mind, the operator had the gain on her system tuned for distant contacts. What she suddenly heard sounded like a church bell.

"Holy crap!" She sat up straight, pulled away one earpiece and toned down the sensitivity.

"What's up?" asked the sonar sup behind her.

She cupped her hand over the remaining earpiece—the way sonar operators had been doing since World War II. "Listen to this."

She put the return on audio, and the E-6 petty officer heard the same thing.

"You thinking what I'm thinking?" the operator asked.

"I don't know what else it could be. We need to tell the captain!"

One minute later, Zimmerman was standing behind them listening to the audio. Kuperman, one of their guest SEALs, was also there to hear it. Every thirty seconds, a metallic clanging noise beat out the same pattern. Three quick clangs, three more widely spaced, then three quick.

"SOS," the captain said.

"Yep," Kuperman agreed. "He's out there, banging a tool on his tanks."

"Can you get a bearing on it?" Zimmerman asked.

"Standby . . ."

Seconds later Kuperman was double-timing toward the lockout trunk. It was halfway flooded when he arrived, Davis and Tracer inside. He picked up the handset for the chamber audio.

Left . . . right . . . seventy-eight.

Left . . . right . . . seventy-nine.

Left . . . right . . .

Slaton went still in the water.

He coasted to a stop, his eyes reaching through the gloom. Still nothing. Once again, he spun a full three-sixty in the water, looking high and low, taking in the entire sphere of his private abyss. No white orb. No red and green nav lights. He kept banging the wrench on his tank, a metronome keeping the rhythm of desperation. *SOS . . . SOS . . .*

He checked his compass; the rose and needle were barely visible, but the reading was solid. He *had* to be close.

Slaton was shivering uncontrollably. His dry suit had become a wet suit—the layer of water inside had been warmed by his body, but it was a losing battle, sapping his energy, lowering his core temperature. Of greater concern was his air supply. He could feel the tanks draining, a slight pull now with each inward breath. Within minutes his lungs would be sucking the last gasps from the twin-80s.

The recorder was getting heavy—he'd had it in his left hand the entire time, and he switched to his right, careful to not let his cold-weakened fingers lose their grip. It was what he'd risked everything for—according to Davis, the best clue available to discover what had brought down Raven 44. And by extension, possibly, who had abducted Ayla Bloch.

He hovered for a moment, every breath like a countdown, and wondered, *What now?*

He was debating whether to keep going, and if so in what direction, when a glimmer caught his eye. His first impression was that of a lone star in a night sky. One o'clock, distance unknowable. His sniper's eyes lasered in, and a second star appeared. He kicked hard in that direction, full strokes with his long fins. Within ten yards he saw more lights beyond the pair, the picture he'd memorized from the bow of *New Mexico*—a great shadow bracketed by one red and one green light. Then he discerned two silhouettes swimming toward him.

One was notably larger than the other. Both were moving as fast as he was.

The increased exertion upped Slaton's air demand, and with half the distance remaining his tanks ran dry. He sprinted through the sea on one last held breath, kicking harder, his lungs straining, demanding relief.

The smaller of his rescuers was in the lead when they merged. Without even trying to find the spare regulator clipped in Tracer's rig, Slaton shot out a hand and seized the one in his mouth.

THIRTY-TWO

They couldn't talk until the lockout chamber drained.

Once it had, Tracer began stripping off his gear, and said, "We stayed on the ledge as long as we could but didn't see you. Eventually we had to come back to the boat because Jammer was running out of air." This was something that always had to be managed: individual divers used air at different rates, and not surprisingly, Davis had the most prodigious "carbon footprint" among them.

"How far did you get dragged downslope?" Davis asked.

Slaton showed them his crushed dive computer. "No idea. I'd guess one fifty, maybe a little more. My belt came off and I lost both lights."

"You were out there in the *dark*?" Tracer remarked.

"In every way."

"Damn—no wonder we had a hard time finding you. How'd you find your way back?"

Slaton gave the abbreviated version.

"Not bad—we heard you banging on your tank. I'm going to put this scenario in the training curriculum."

Slaton didn't respond. A number of his past exploits had found their way into schools in Israel: Mossad basic training, the IDF Sniper Course. He would be perfectly happy to never be a case study again.

The pressure in the chamber began equalizing, and they all saw Zimmerman's face in the porthole window, his expression unreadable.

Slaton hoisted the data recorder, and the skipper gave a thumbs-up.

"Nice job," Davis said, taking it in hand. "Looks like it's in decent shape. We'll get it into a tub of water."

"Why?" Slaton asked.

"It's been in salt water for a few days. A freshwater bath keeps the salt and minerals from drying on the circuitry and causing damage. We'll keep it that way until the engineers take over."

The inner hatch opened, and the captain leaned in. His eyes locked on Slaton, and for the first time since arriving at Wrangel Island, he smiled. "Welcome back, David."

Thirty minutes later, *New Mexico* cleared Russian territorial waters. She made a turn toward the Bering Strait, which would give passage to her home port of Bremerton, Washington. That voyage, however, was one of nearly three thousand miles. The cargo *New Mexico* was carrying required delivery by far more expeditious means, which entailed one interim stop.

Polar Star was one of only two icebreakers in the fleet of the United States Coast Guard. Technically classified as a research vessel, she operated in both Arctic and Antarctic waters. By chance, she was at that moment performing survey work in Goodhope Bay, Alaska. Or at least, she *had* been until her orders were abruptly amended ten minutes earlier. The ship was instructed to make best speed to the west and prepare their Dolphin helicopter for a rendezvous: the submarine *New Mexico* would soon surface in the Chukchi Sea and establish a landing zone on the ice.

Once *Polar Star* was under way, with her bow battering through broken fields of meter-thick ice, her skipper read the orders for a third time. "This is weird," he commented to his exec, who was standing by his side on the bridge. "We're supposed to head toward these coordinates, then launch the Dolphin as soon as we're within round-trip range. Apparently this fast-attack sub will be waiting for us with two passengers and three hundred pounds of cargo."

"A pickup on the ice? Could it be a medical thing—like an ill crewmember?"

"Doubtful—they would have told us so we could send the right staff and equipment. The mission is to deliver these guys and whatever they're carrying stateside ASAP."

"Must be pretty important."

The skipper shook his head in consternation. "Guess so," he relented. "All right. Let's tell the helo crew to gear up for launch."

The directive was sourced from the White House and quickly filtered down to every intelligence agency and major command. American military assets had suffered accidents in multiple theaters, and under suspicious circumstances. All available national resources were to be utilized to get to the bottom of it.

Sorensen didn't hesitate to leverage the crusade on Davis's behalf, laying the groundwork for his investigation into the crash of Raven 44. The RC-135 was originally a product of Boeing, and that company, in spite of decades gone by, retained vital documents and expertise. Company engineers were summoned for the inquiry, and the Air Force put together an accident investigation board. The NTSB was also tasked to help, primarily with analysis of the flight data recorder. Specialists from around the country, and in virtually every discipline—engines, airframes, navigation, software, and operations—gathered in the most practical location, an annex of Boeing's Renton facility north of Seattle.

Davis had forwarded the pictures he'd taken at the crash site using *New Mexico*'s secure communications suite. He included others, taken on board the sub, of the fragments of wreckage he'd salvaged. Those remains, along with the flight data recorder, he would deliver as quickly as possible to the burgeoning team of investigators in Seattle.

Once all that was arranged, Sorensen saw no reason to remain in Kodiak. Her jet was fueled and preflighted for a seven-hour flight back to Langley.

New Mexico broke through the ice a second time 110 miles west of Cape Lisburne, a long-range radar site on Alaska's far northwest coast. Commander Zimmerman mounted the sail with his exec and was struck right away by a breathtaking sight: high in the night sky, the aurora borealis shimmering in ribbons of color.

"Wow—never seen it so bright."

"A sign of good fortune?" Dooley ventured.

"I'm just happy that storm is gone," the captain said. He looked all around and saw nothing but ice, broken chunks surrounding the sail like giant ice cubes.

"Should I give the all clear?"

"Yeah, let's do it. The sooner we set up this LZ and unload our two guests, the sooner we can head for home."

Thirty minutes later Slaton and Davis were standing outside on the ice. The recovered fragments of wreckage were beside them, wrapped in plastic. The flight data recorder was immersed in freshwater in a sealed twenty-gallon container. Both men looked skyward in awe, the palette of colors mesmerizing. Backdropping the aurora, countless stars filled the heavens.

"Don't see that in Virginia," Davis said.

"I wish my son was here," Slaton responded.

"Right, I remember Anna telling me you had a boy. How old is he now?"

"Four."

"Enjoy it, brother. My daughter's twenty-one." He stared up at the sky, and said, "I need to get her up here sometime."

"Here?"

"Well, Alaska would work."

At nearly midnight, the sun remained a faint glow on the southern horizon. It cast the sky above the icescape in pastel shades, and Slaton couldn't help but contrast it to the crushing blackness that had enveloped him on the dive. He drew in a deep breath of fresh Arctic air.

A hundred feet away, a helipad had been scribed on the ice pack using a special chemical dye. Crewmen had swept away most of the snow using brooms, and a circle of lights further defined the LZ. Compared to what the Osprey crews had faced back at Wrangel, the inbound pilots tonight would have it easy.

"I'm not gonna miss this cold," Davis said.

"Me neither."

Tracer arrived to join them. "We just heard from the Coast Guard—the Dolphin is five minutes out."

"Good to hear," Slaton said.

"Wish I could go with you. I'm not looking forward to a week on this sub."

"I dunno—the food's been pretty good." Slaton extended a hand. "Thanks for your help down there."

Tracer shook it. "You'd have done the same for me. And by the way, that was some good shooting on the island."

"We had all the advantages."

Tracer shook Davis's hand as well. "Good luck figuring out what brought that airplane down."

"We'll get the answers. I just hope they don't start World War III."

They all heard the faint sound of a helicopter, and soon landing lights appeared in the clear sky. It came in fast and low, then transitioned to a hover, the signature orange paint job of the U.S. Coast Guard clear. The Dolphin settled on the LZ gingerly, like a kid testing a frozen pond. Snow swirled around the edges of the cleared area, and soon the engines went to idle.

But they didn't shut down.

Within minutes everything was loaded, and with a thumping rhythm the Dolphin clawed its way back into the night sky. On his last look out the window, Slaton saw crewmen already sled-dogging equipment back to *New Mexico*. The chem-circle helipad had disappeared in the aircraft's snowy downwash.

Twenty minutes later, the sub was gone. The only remnant of the entire transaction: one more hundred-foot-long fissure in the polar icecap.

THIRTY-THREE

Bloch was en route to Tel Aviv, having departed Kodiak hours earlier on Mossad Air. Ironically, the shortest flight path turned out to be a polar route, and the jet had flown less than fifty miles north of Wrangel Island. He'd tried to pick it out, but between the low clouds and the ice sheet, the site of the catastrophe remained obscured.

His body clock was a disaster; Bloch had effectively circumnavigated the earth in the last three days. He slept fitfully during the flight yet planned to go directly to Mossad headquarters after landing. A good night's sleep in his own bed sounded wonderful, but the idea was pure fantasy until he had his daughter back safe and sound.

They were somewhere over the Caspian Sea, the shadows of the Caucasus Mountains visible through the window, when the copilot came back and told Bloch he had a call on the secure line. He immediately picked up the handset and heard Nurin's voice.

"Thank you for calling," Bloch said hesitantly. "I know how busy you must be."

"You of all people," Nurin mused. "I suspect neither of us are getting much sleep. How is Moira holding up?"

"I called her before I left Alaska. She's as well as can be expected—which is to say, only miserable."

"I spoke to Miss Sorensen a few minutes ago, and I wanted to give you an update. She's been focusing on getting answers about the crash of their jet."

Bloch tried to be patient, telling himself that if there was news about his daughter, Nurin wouldn't be asking about his wife or conjecturing about air crashes. "Yes. When I last spoke to her she said they were tracking a ship that had been near Wrangel Island when the airplane went down. If the crash is confirmed as a hostile act, I suspect they'll seize it."

"Did she say that?"

"Not in so many words, but it seems the logical response. They are also watching another ship in the Red Sea—one that was in the vicinity of their destroyer, *Ross,* when it sank."

"These events are clearly tied. Does Miss Sorensen have suspicions as to who might be responsible?"

"Russia seems the obvious choice," said Bloch. "Both tragedies happened just outside her borders."

"Which is precisely why it's not Russia," Nurin countered. "It's too obvious, too antagonistic."

"A fair point," Bloch allowed. After a pause, he could take it no longer. "Is there news from Almaty?" He was surprised at how matter-of-factly it came out.

"Unit 8200 has been hitting a wall. A ground team from the embassy was able to track down the car used to abduct Ayla—it was impounded by the police after being abandoned in a parking lot. We'd like to search it, of course, but an official request would raise too many questions."

"What about breaking into the impound yard?"

"We considered it," Nurin replied, "but there were obstacles, and right now manpower is an issue. Anyway, I am doubtful it would produce anything useful—whoever we are dealing with, they seem professional."

"We are professionals as well," Bloch countered, "and still we make stupid mistakes."

Nurin went silent.

"That wasn't meant to be an accusation," Bloch said. "Or if it was, it was self-directed."

Nurin seemed to understand. For all its legendary successes over the years, both men knew Mossad had suffered equally epic failures.

Nurin told Bloch about his deployment of operatives into Almaty.

"Twenty-five . . . a small army."

"Combined with the case officers from the embassy, enough to effect a rescue given virtually any contingency. We simply have to find her."

Nurin was detailing the operation when Bloch heard a chime in the call's background. The director put him on hold for over a minute. He finally came back on the line, and said breathlessly, "A new message from Lazarus has surfaced. He's provided an address where he believes Ayla is being held."

Bloch was hit by a swirl of emotions—not all of them good. "Can we trust it?"

"Who can say? I see no choice but to pursue it."

Bloch was formulating a cautionary response when Nurin cut him off. "I have to deal with this, Anton. Call me as soon as you land."

The connection ended, leaving Bloch staring out the window at a cloudless late afternoon sky. The father in him was ecstatic at the news—a lead to where his daughter was being held.

The spymaster in him felt something else entirely.

The inquisition into the loss of Raven 44 was centered in a minor warehouse near Boeing's Renton, Washington, production facility. More often than not, air crash investigations were based in expansive hangars, providing investigators ample room for laying out wreckage. The case of Raven 44 was different: the sum of the retrievable wreckage, all of which was en route, would easily fit in a standard bathtub.

The most critical information, everyone agreed, would come from the flight data recorder, combined with streamed data taken in the minutes before the airplane went down. Yet the physical evidence would also play a part. The lead Boeing engineer, Dr. Mary Gellar, stood studying a wide-screen monitor. She was getting her first look at the photos Davis had forwarded: most were of the crash site, along with a few of the debris he'd recovered. Next to her was an Air Force colonel, a rated pilot with an engineering background, who'd driven up from McChord Air Force Base in Tacoma.

"Aside from the photos," Gellar said, "this guy included a short report. He says there was damage to the radome that seemed unusual, and he recovered a section to bring back. He also says the right aft cockpit window blew out."

The colonel, who was managing the images, paused on the best shot of the window in question. "Yeah, that one blew out all right."

"Could that cause a crash?" asked Gellar, whose expertise was grounded more in structures than operations.

"By itself? Highly unlikely." He flicked ahead and found pictures of the radome. The concentric circles were evident. "This *is* weird," he said. "You ever see anything like it?"

Her eyes narrowed severely. "Nope."

"Are there any results yet from the mission data that was streaming before she went down?"

"I've got a team going over the sensor outputs. The only thing they've said so far is that there were spikes in some unusual bandwidths. They'll need time to figure it out. There were also anomalies in the airplane's own data suggesting digital flight control problems in the final minutes."

The colonel kept looking at the radome. He finally said, "I've got a friend at AFIT who's done some structures research—how materials react to certain wavelengths." AFIT was the Air Force Institute of Technology at Wright-Patterson Air Force Base, the service's cutting edge research arm.

Gellar looked up and caught his gaze. "Are we talking about what I think we are?" she asked.

The colonel shrugged. "We've been studying this for a long time—sooner or later, it was bound to become real."

She turned back to the image. "It would be a revolution if it is."

"True. And it would mean somebody else got there first. But for now, let's not get carried away. Chances are, it's something way more boring. Metal fatigue or severe turbulence."

"The investigator who went to the scene should be here soon," Gellar said.

"Who is he?"

"Name's Davis."

"*Jammer* Davis?"

"You know him?"

"By reputation," the colonel said. "They say he's a bull in a china shop, but he's got a way of getting answers."

Gellar thought about it, and said, "I'm okay with that. Right now, answers would be very helpful."

Sorensen landed at Andrews Air Force Base at eleven in the morning local time. Ill-rested and information-drunk from the constant updates during her flight, she felt like a general directing a distant military campaign. Her stress level only heightened when she stepped off the jet to find a car waiting, along with an Air Force colonel, who said, "The president wants to see you right away, ma'am."

Weary as she was, they were words that left no room for argument.

Half an hour later Sorensen was in the Oval Office, standing beside the Resolute Desk. President Cleveland was seated behind it, and on the opposite side were National Security Advisor Paul Steiner and Chief of Staff Ed Markowitz.

A large television monitor and camera had been set up to face the president. A smaller screen beneath the camera displayed a live feed of Cleveland—she alone was in the field of view, the others discreetly out of sight. Sorensen had gotten only a thumbnail sketch of what was about to happen.

"One minute," a technician said as he backed away into the anteroom. The room's only other occupant was a State Department interpreter standing statue-like near the president's shoulder.

"When was this put together?" Sorensen asked, trying to get up to speed.

The president said, "The Russian foreign minister put in the request an hour ago. Petrov wants a one-on-one videoconference to discuss what happened on Wrangel Island. I wanted you here in case I need backup on the details."

The monitor remained blank, but a clock in one corner was counting down through thirty seconds—as if a rocket was about to blast off.

"Are you going to bring up *Ross*?" Sorensen asked.

She glanced at Markowitz, who said, "We've decided the best course is to not press that point at the moment—not unless we have to."

"We're still not sure what happened to *Ross*," Steiner amplified. "As you know, we've been tracking a ship that was in the area when she went down, and the statements from *Ross*'s captain and crew raise suspicion. But if there *was* something nefarious, we don't have evidence of it yet."

The monitor flickered to life.

Sorensen saw the president of Russia sitting behind his own desk. Behind him were glittering accoutrements fitting of a czar—not the proletariat-office backdrop he used when addressing the Russian people—along with the white, blue, and red tricolor of the Russian Federation. Petrov was the only person in view, but Sorensen had no doubt that he, too, had advisors and an interpreter within earshot.

"Hello, Mr. President," said Cleveland.

"Hello," said Petrov. His face was cast in a grave expression, although one that Sorensen thought looked contrived.

"I think we should clear up what's been happening in the Arctic," Cleveland began.

"I have a very clear picture," Petrov countered. "You invaded our sovereign territory and killed Russian soldiers." His English was decent, if heavily accented, a product of years spent trying to manipulate world leaders in the most common shared language. Cleveland's interpreter, Sorensen guessed, was here as a precaution, and perhaps to extract underlying meaning from Petrov's word usages.

Cleveland said, "One of our Air Force aircraft went down. It was outside your airspace when it encountered problems . . . the nature of which, we will investigate thoroughly. Some of the wreckage ended up on Wrangel Island, and in the hopes that there might be survivors, I approved a small mission to—"

"Enough of this shit!" Petrov spat. "You sent over a hundred men and instigated a battle in which eight Russians died!"

Sorensen saw Markowitz roll his eyes, then make a fist to prompt the president to push back.

Cleveland bristled openly, and in a measured tone said, "That is *not* the version I heard. The message I will give you is this: America, too, has lost lives. For the time being, I will refrain from making public the details of this engagement, which in various ways do not reflect well on either of us. But rest assured, if I find that Russia is targeting American assets in any way, in any theater, I will not hesitate to bring the full force of our military to bear."

"And if you attack Russia, you will feel a fury you have never known!" Sorensen saw Petrov's eyes flick momentarily offscreen. He then added, "I will not make mention of this incident for now, but I am ordering our forces to high alert. Any further aggression against the Russian Federation will be dealt with severely and without warning!"

The screen went blank, the visual equivalent of a hang up. All that remained was the mirror of their own feed below the camera: Elayne Cleveland's stunned face staring ahead.

She pushed back from the Resolute Desk, and announced, "Well . . . I'd say that went badly."

THIRTY-FOUR

At Sorensen's direction, Slaton's next stop was Tel Aviv. Her reasoning was that it would put him closer to where he might prove operationally useful, and also allow him to act as a liaison with Mossad. For reasons that weren't yet apparent, Israel remained deeply involved in the CIA's multiple unfolding crises.

To get him there, Sorensen went with speed over comfort. She herself had commandeered the CIA's only jet in Alaska, so she put in a request with the Air Force for mission support—the movement of one critical operative halfway around the world. Her request was initially denied, a refusal that came as she was briefing the president over a secure line during her own flight back to Langley. After relaying the details of what had occurred on Wrangel Island, and also under the ice in the nearby sea, Sorensen assured President Cleveland that the Special Operations Group was still hard at work before letting slip that her top operator was stranded at Joint Base Elmendorf in Anchorage.

The commander in chief made one call, and ten minutes later a weary Slaton was being escorted by a full-bird colonel through base operations to his new private jet: sitting on the tarmac, a four-engine, half-million-pound, Air Force C-17 Globemaster. The transport, according to the base commander, was being diverted from a repositioning leg back to Travis Air Force Base in California.

Slaton walked to the forward boarding stairs and was met by the crew. The aircraft commander was a tall, thin-haired major, and his copilot a female captain. They regarded him with a jaundiced eye, and it took a moment for Slaton to realize why. He'd taken a navy shower on *New Mexico* to wash off salt water from the dive, but nothing more. He hadn't shaved in days, his sandy hair was unruly, and he was wearing the only backup set of clothing he'd brought—tactical pants, heavy shirt, Merrell boots, all topped by the outer shell of a mud-encrusted winter jacket that had gone through a microwar on Wrangel. The two pilots stared at him slack-jawed, as if a stray mongrel had just walked into the Westminster Dog Show.

"Your name Slaton?" the major asked.

"It is."

A looked exchanged between them.

"And you need to go to Tel Aviv?"

"That would be great." A pause, before Slaton asked, "Is there a problem?"

The major seemed to lighten up. "No, not at all. It's just that the way these orders came down, highest priority and all . . . we were expecting a general. Three stars, at least."

"Sorry to disappoint."

The captain smiled wryly. "Better this way—flag officers can be a pain in the ass."

Slaton smiled back. "I promise I won't be. Truth is, I could really use some rest."

"You're in luck. It's a long flight, but our jet comes with real bunks. You can rack out the whole time if you want."

The captain led him up the boarding stairs into the aircraft's wide cargo bay, then made a hard left to the flight deck. Against the rear bulkhead were double-stacked bunks.

"Make yourself at home. It's about a thirteen-hour flight, and we'll be refueling once. While the major finalizes the flight plan, I'm going to grab some crew meals."

"I'll take the filet mignon, medium rare, maybe a subtle red with some graphite hues to go with it."

A bigger smile. "You've dined with us before."

"More times than I care to admit."

"I'm on it," she said.

Slaton settled into the lower bunk, rearranging a folded stack of standard-issue blankets and pillows. It wasn't bad, and his outlook began to brighten. Business jets were convenient, but the seating in the cabin rarely went beyond club chairs. This would be noisier, more egalitarian, yet at the moment a real bed seemed far more important than rock-star chic.

By the time the C-17 was airborne, Slaton was fast asleep.

Mossad's focus was laser-like on the new intelligence regarding Ayla Bloch's location. Director Nurin's small army of operatives circled like a noose around the Almaty address provided by Lazarus.

It turned out to be on the east side of town, midway along Pushkin Street. The building was like a hundred others in the city, a charmless vestige of the Soviet era. They were known as Khrushchyovkas, built in the 1960s, the name inspired by former Soviet leader Nikita Khrushchev. In those days, Kazakhstan, like Russia herself, had faced a severe housing shortage, and thousands of apartment buildings were erected, four-and five-story rectangular affairs. They were cheaply built and meant to last no more than twenty-five years. After that, it was promised, the glorious Soviet system would lift everyone to greater prosperity.

When glory came up short, and with housing shortages still widespread, the Khrushchyovkas were patched up and renovated time and again. Residences meant to last a generation were limping along after three. Some of the buildings, however, had aged better than others. Many of the early structures, including the one on Pushkin Street, were built around verdant central courtyards. Decades later, some remained as gardens with mature trees and paths, while others had been repurposed as athletic fields. These surroundings, accidental as they might have been, had become integral to the flow of life. None of which escaped the legion of Mossad case officers surrounding the building in question.

Reconnaissance teams were deployed on both the outer streets and inner courtyard. The source of the intelligence, Lazarus, had gone as far as to provide an apartment number, and it was quickly determined that room 427 was a top-floor, corner unit. The first objective was to confirm that Ayla was indeed inside the building, which required continuous surveillance. By chance, a top-floor apartment in the Khrushchyovka across the street, with an excellent view of both unit 427 and the street-side building entrance, was available on a short-term lease. A female *katsa*, posing as a nurse who'd come to Almaty for temporary work, signed an agreement, paid cash for a month, and had a key within the hour. The flat had been recently patched up, and reeked of fresh plaster and a positive cash flow—real estate investors, apparently, had found their way to Kazakhstan.

High-end surveillance devices, including cameras with telephoto lenses and directional microphones, were brought in and quickly set up. The streets around the targeted building, including the pathways in the courtyard, became thick with Mossad operatives. They watched everyone who entered the building and noted what they were carrying. Cameras were surreptitiously placed near each entrance, outside both stairwells, and in the ceiling of the lone elevator. One operative was even able to place a camera and microphone in the hall outside room 427.

All the captured sounds and images streamed to the apartment across the street, and then were relayed via a secure link to headquarters in Tel Aviv. Within seven hours of getting the tip, teams of analysts at Glilot Junction were barely keeping up with the flood of data. Langley, too, was contributing to the information overload, having volunteered overhead coverage from a passing satellite. The CIA's contribution turned out to be redundant—Mossad had the place effectively surrounded—yet Director Nurin thanked the Americans all the same.

Evidence began mounting quickly.

The targeted apartment had two windows, yet the curtains remained drawn in both. Mossad obtained a floor plan for the unit, which showed one window overlooking the main living area, the other the largest bedroom. Fortunately, while the curtains obstructed a direct look inside, they were not thick enough to defeat a sensitive thermal imaging device that had been brought in.

Three figures could be distinguished inside the apartment. Two moved about freely, while the third sat on a chair in the bedroom. The chair was not near any desk or table, but isolated in the center of the room. The image wasn't precise enough to identify restraints on the person in the chair, yet the occupant's lack of movement, over the course of three hours, suggested that was the case. Further confirmation came when one of the roving occupants could be seen tipping a drinking glass to the lips of the person in the chair. The size and general build of the captive—definitely female—reinforced the idea that they were indeed looking at Ayla Bloch.

The teams outside had more limited success. Over the course of the day, only one person passed through unit 427's front door. A thickset man, fortyish, who could easily pass for a local, departed at three that afternoon, and came back thirty minutes later with take-out food. Pictures taken by a street team, as well as those captured by the elevator camera, were fed into Mossad's comprehensive database, and also forwarded to the Americans. No matches were made using facial recognition.

The deciding bit of information came after a technician made adjustments to a parabolic audio antenna. The sensor had been malfunctioning, but for a time the reception improved and a partial conversation was recorded between the two men. The most consequential lines came across loud and clear.

"How much longer do we wait?"

"Not long. The boss said if there are no new instructions by morning, we end it."

Within twenty minutes Director Nurin was listening to the exchange, but at that point it affected little more than his timing. Based on the evidence they already had, the response was a fait accompli.

Of the contingent he'd sent to Almaty, just over half, along with six embassy personnel, were actively engaged in the surveillance effort. The remainder of the team, ten men and women bunkered up in a large safe house, began planning an armed intervention. Weapons were supplied by the embassy, including equipment for breaching the door. Six vehicles would be available for escape, the goal being to get everyone out of the city before the Kazakhs got wind of the operation. Two fresh safe houses, one along each of the most viable escape corridors, were procured as a contingency—places to hole up if things went south.

The use of deadly force in a foreign country was typically avoided. Sometimes, however, there was simply no other way. A brief debate ran about whether it might be feasible to capture the two guards and spirit them back to Israel, yet any benefits seemed outweighed by countless complications. The two men, whoever they were, knew what they'd gotten into—they would be interrogated briefly if they survived the initial assault, but both were marked for elimination.

At 8:00 p.m. Almaty time, as his predecessor, and the father of the hostage, was touching down at Palmachim Air Base, Nurin called the prime minister to brief him on the operation and request a final green light.

The prime minister gave it.

THIRTY-FIVE

The raid took place at four in the morning in the hopes that everyone nearby—the guards watching Ayla, the neighbors, and the police—would be dulled in their reactions. The plan was for the team to divide and approach from different directions. One group was dressed as though they'd been out clubbing all night; the two women were barefoot and hand-carrying spiked heels, and everyone walked as if they were intoxicated, although an astute observer might have noted a lack of the usual loud, raucous banter. Four men wearing athletic warm-ups and carrying nylon sports equipment bags arrived on a different street; by appearances, they might have been arriving home after a distant soccer tournament.

Altogether, there were eight men and two women in the different cliques, and they arrived at the building on Pushkin Street simultaneously. There were no locks on the main door, so entry was uneventful. One of the women trailed behind the main force, her job being to sweep up the planted cameras one by one. There had been considerable debate on this. One camp felt the cameras might be useful on egress—the feeds were being continuously monitored by headquarters, and all the players were linked with discreet comm units. The other line of thinking, and the one that prevailed, was that egress would be rapid, and it was imperative that as few clues as possible be left behind.

Once inside, the teams converged at the emergency stairwell. Four operatives peeled off at various points to act as lookouts. The rest soon emerged from the fourth-floor fire door brandishing compact assault rifles, all sound-suppressed, extracted from the nylon bags. The number two man in the stack carried a breaching ram. At the door, six men positioned themselves precisely as planned while a piece of tape went over the door's viewing port. When the commander's five-second finger-count reached zero, the ram hit the door.

As it turned out, the sixty-year-old door frame would have given way to a good tennis shoe. Against a ninety-pound breaching device, the door rocked into the apartment like a screen door thrown by a gale. The lead element rushed in and found one of the guards rising from the living room couch. When he didn't immediately put his hands in the air to surrender—his only chance to extend his life another five minutes—the one and only rule of engagement was met. He was cut down instantly by two simultaneous three-round bursts.

The first man into the dark bedroom, the team commander, saw the other guard on the bed. The man had obviously been awoken by the clatter of the door, and when he reached for something on the nightstand, the commander didn't wait to find out what it was. He laced the guard with six rounds, following up with one to the head. The commander quickly cleared the remainder of the room, and within seconds received confirmation the rest of the apartment was clear. He went to the doorway, flicked on the light, and got his first good look at the hostage.

It was indeed Ayla Bloch. Every team member had memorized her face from photos, yet that hadn't been necessary for the commander. He had actually helped train her at the academy—indeed, the reason he'd volunteered to be here.

She was secured to a chair and gagged, and while Ayla had been roughed up, the commander had seen worse. A black eye, bruises on her wrists. Her hair was askew, and her stunningly attractive face was partially hidden behind the gag.

Ayla didn't move for a time but simply sat slumped, her eyes blinking. At first the commander thought it was due to the light being turned on, yet her gaze never quite settled. His next thought was that she'd been drugged, perhaps a sedative to keep her calm. Or maybe a "truth enhancer" to aid interrogation.

He went closer, leaned down to meet her eyes. Finally, she seemed to focus and he saw recognition, his familiar face registering. Then the commander saw something else. Something that made his spine stiffen.

Ever so slowly, in a gesture infused with all the world's sadness, Ayla Bloch shook her head . . .

The explosion could be heard over ten miles away. The quarter of the Khrushchyovka immediately surrounding room 427, twelve apartments in all, collapsed completely in the blast. Windows blew out up and down the street, and a passing car overturned. Two pedestrians on the sidewalk outside, an orchestra musician returning from a long-running after-party, and a garbageman on his way to work the early shift, were crushed by collapsing debris. First responders arrived reasonably quickly, only to find both streets adjoining the building impassable for the rubble. A cloud of dust boiled thousands of feet upward in the muted predawn sky, and by the time the sun rose that morning the upwind quadrant of the city would awake to find itself covered in gray ash.

The death toll, which would not be finalized for nearly a week, would ultimately be put at sixty-two. All ten members of the raiding team were killed, although one woman, assigned as a lookout near the main entrance, survived for two days in intensive care. There was also one Mossad injury across the street—the rented safe house had mostly been vacated for the impending egress, yet one woman, an embassy employee, had been assigned to monitor and record the raid from the window. She arrived at the embassy by taxi, just after daybreak, with a face full of glass and blind in one eye.

Ayla Bloch, of course, was among the dead.

In the hours after the disaster, Mossad descended into crisis mode. Exchanges with government ministries, both foreign and domestic, ranged from limited admissions to outright denials, and obfuscation reigned—anything to deflect Office involvement in what was clearly a terrorist event. The surviving Mossad operatives in Kazakhstan made their way back to Tel Aviv, everyone stunned by the failure.

It would take many months, and an intense internal review, for the agency to learn what had happened. The inquiry would string together evidence from tactical communications, transmissions from body cams worn by the operators, and internal reports from Kazakhstan's State Security Service. The final verdict: For the most part, it had been a textbook operation. The biggest mistake was made by the man who'd cleared the main room—if he'd been thorough, he would have checked the closet built into the central wall of the apartment. Had he done so, he would have noticed the door was locked. So alerted, he might conceivably have recognized a faint tar-like, Plasticine odor coming from behind the door. Yet even in that perfect world, the outcome would not have changed; the bomb had been activated remotely, and the closet door was presumably booby-trapped.

The greater question—that of who had set them up—hung like a shroud over Glilot Junction. Yet even that collective agony, harsh as it proved to be, was inconsequential compared to the devastation that fell upon one particular home overlooking the distant Jezreel Valley.

THIRTY-SIX

Slaton's private C-17 landed shortly after sunrise at Palmachim Air Base south of Tel Aviv. He thanked the crew for their hospitality, descended the stairs, and could not deny a tug of sentiment when his feet touched Israel. He'd long had differences with those who ran the country, but the tawny earth here, with its history and memories, would always be part of him.

He saw a young woman waiting by a generic sedan, a set of keys jangling in her hand. Without introducing herself, she handed him the keys and explained, to the extent of her knowledge, what had happened hours earlier in Almaty.

David Slaton was not prone to shock—no man of his calling could be— yet on learning the fate of Ayla and the team sent to rescue her, his thoughts simply seized. The woman talked a bit more, something about Director Nurin wanting to see him, and how accommodations had been arranged. She pointed toward a gate where he could exit the flight line, then simply walked away.

He might have said "Thank you" as she left, but he couldn't recall.

Slaton drove north from the air base and, immediately ignoring Nurin's instructions, he bypassed Glilot Junction. He continued north, his destination a villa east of Netanya, across the coastal plain where the Samarian Hills spread to the West Bank. He turned onto a long driveway, and soon two men with heavy weapons appeared and ordered him to stop.

Slaton complied and rolled down the window. He gave his name but didn't bother with any identity documents—none that he was carrying would be believed. The guards, curiously, seemed to be expecting him. One of them actually looked familiar, likely from a previous visit. They let him pass, and he parked in front of the house. Slaton got out and stretched, his muscles rigid from the long flight. He stood looking at the front door, or more precisely, the doorbell next to it. On a hunch, he bypassed the front portico and diverted to a path that led around the villa's northern wall. At one point he sensed motion in the trees to his left, but again, nothing unanticipated. Protection was a fact of life for former Office directors.

As hoped, he found Bloch seated at the edge of the travertine terrace, slumped and alone on a wide wicker chair. He was staring blankly into the hills, all the animation of an Easter Island statue. A second chair beside him was empty—last night, when there had still been hope, it had likely been occupied by his wife.

Slaton took a wide arc across the tile, making a bit of noise and putting himself in Bloch's peripheral vision. He never reacted in any way. He only sat there, stone silent, staring at a fading sunrise. Without a greeting or comment of any kind, Slaton settled into the seat next to his former boss.

The air was still and heavy, almost as if in mourning. The hills in the distance were losing their shadows, and a formation of nearby olive trees—remnants of an ancient farm, he'd once been told—shimmered in the early light.

Slaton had sat on this terrace before. Most of those visits related to missions, yet there had been a few social occasions. Office gatherings, minor celebrations. *A birthday party for Ayla.* The patio was expansive, jutting from the house like the prow of a ship. Where the tile ended there was no landscaping or fencing, no border of any kind. Only the beginning of the tawny brushland. Home and earth merging as one.

They sat together in silence, watching the waking hills. A small bird skittered nearby, darting beneath a tough-looking bush. Slaton sensed Bloch had been here for hours. Probably since the news had come. He saw two empty tumblers on a nearby table, an ashtray with a few butts between them. Last night's nightcap, the unsuspecting brink of another era, another lifetime.

After Ayla.

He wondered if Moira knew yet. Was Anton giving his wife a few more hours with their daughter, letting her sleep with the solace of hope? Or had he already imparted the tragedy of their lives?

Slaton hoped it was the former but suspected otherwise.

Finally, Bloch broke the silence. "Thank you for coming."

Slaton nodded but didn't otherwise respond.

"You of all people, David . . . you would understand."

Slaton considered it. He, too, had suffered the ultimate loss, and the manner by which his first wife and child had met their end—or at least how he'd understood it at the time—was on par with what Bloch was dealing with.

"Some things can never be understood," he said.

More silence, and when Bloch spoke again his deep voice was uncharacteristically hollow, as if reaching up from some chasm of despair. "I was thinking about a friend of Ayla's, a lovely girl from school. We knew the family well. The two of them were fifteen years old, as I recall, when she was diagnosed with cancer—took her in less than a year."

Slaton said nothing.

"A terrible thing, yet something like that . . . you understand it. I recall telling Ayla it was 'God's will.'" His fingers worked the wicker arms of his chair like a man reading braille.

"You're not to blame," Slaton said.

"Aren't I? I suppose someone else pulled the levers, made the calculations."

"Yes."

"But the thing is . . . I made those calculations myself many times. Balanced the risks, gave the orders."

"I see differences. Last night a lot of innocent people died. That's something you always weighed. I watched you call off missions for that very reason—because the risk of harm to civilians was too high."

"What happened in Almaty—Nurin could never have seen it coming. I'm sure *I* would have made the same mistake. So much misery and death. Where does it end? So many of the decisions I made . . . they put people in the same place I am this morning. How can I accept that?"

"You don't accept it. You just deal with it, knowing that in the moment, when there were horrible choices to be made, you did your best."

His eyes cast downward. "But did I? Really?"

Slaton mostly let Bloch talk, listening to disjointed thoughts broken by long pauses. He interjected where he could, held back more often than not. He'd come to listen, because that was all he could do. The sun moved higher, the new day taking hold. After some indeterminant length of time, he noticed a light flicker on in the house. Moira was awake.

Slaton stood and said, "I should go."

A nod. Bloch had seen it as well.

He turned toward the path and was a few steps away when he heard, *"David?"* He turned, his gray eyes inquiring.

Bloch looked at him imploringly, words nearing his lips. In the end all that came was a plaintive stare.

Slaton was glad for that. Glad for Bloch's sake. Because he knew what he was about to ask. He turned toward the path and was gone.

Dr. Gellar arrived at the Renton warehouse shortly after midnight, having caught a few hours of sleep at a chain hotel across the street. The place was a swarm of activity, her entire twenty-person team at work.

She had taken part in nearly a dozen accident investigations over the years, but this one felt different. The majority were hectic in the first hours, then digressed into slow, methodical grinds—teams committed to finding answers, but with the luxury of time to get things right. Those inquiries often took months, if not years, of painstaking analysis, report writing, and consensus building. The probe into the crash of Raven 44 was on rocket fuel. The national security implications were clear and immediate, and the overnight directive they'd received only heightened the pressure: no less than the president of the United States wanted answers.

And she wanted them today.

Gellar was booting up her laptop when a door crashed somewhere behind her. She turned and saw a huge man barging in with a plastic container, the size of a twenty-gallon aquarium, cradled in his arms. The other staff were staring as well.

"Who's in charge here?" the man barked.

The worker closest to him, a bespectacled and slack-jawed avionics specialist, pointed to the far end of the room where Gellar was standing. Feeling she had to say something, she called out, "Can I help you?"

He lumbered across the room and dropped the big tub onto an empty table with all the grace of a Scotsman tossing a caber. Based on its weight, Gellar guessed it contained the flight data recorder in a freshwater bath.

He held out an oven-mitt hand, "Jammer Davis."

"Mary Gellar," she replied. "Good to meet you. We were told you'd be arriving soon."

"I've had a busy few days, but there's still work to do."

"I understand you actually traveled to the accident site."

"I did."

"That must have been . . . an adventure."

"Exhilarating," he deadpanned. "I'll tell you all about it later over a couple of beers. Right now, we need progress. I've got more evidence outside, a half dozen avionics boxes along with that section of radome. Did you get the photos I sent?"

"I did."

"Any feedback?"

"We expect some imminently. There's a team from Wright-Patterson going over the photos—they think you might be on to something." She looked across the room and signaled to the colonel from McChord.

He arrived with a printout in hand, and after a quick introduction, said to Davis, "The preliminary just came in." He held out a two-page summary to Gellar and canted it so Davis could read it as well. When they were done, the two exchanged a long look.

"We were right," she said.

Davis nodded, then scanned the room. "Is there somewhere I can make a private phone call?"

Sarah Mizrachi had worked for Mossad for nine years, the last three at headquarters. Never before had she gotten a summons to the director's office.

She took the stairs to the fourth-floor suite, then paused at a hallway mirror. She finger-combed a few wayward strands of hair behind one ear and decided nothing else was askew. Mizrachi tried to imagine why she was being called, ASAP, to see Director Nurin. To the best of her knowledge, she'd done nothing either valiant or criminal in recent weeks, which likely put commendation and termination off the table. Beyond that, she was drawing a blank.

The receptionist was expecting her. "Go right in, the director is waiting."

And so he was. Raymond Nurin looked up immediately.

Mizrachi smiled. "Good morning, sir."

"Is it?"

Having no idea whether he was referring to the time of day or its condition, she said nothing.

"I need your help for the next two days," Nurin said.

"Of course."

"A man is going to arrive at the front gate soon." He pushed a photo across the desk, and Mizrachi saw a rather handsome face with regular features and fair hair. "I want you to meet him, escort him inside, and help him as needed. I set aside a conference room on the third floor."

"Who is he?"

Nurin looked at her severely, and he nearly said something, then checked himself. "He's a researcher. That's all you need to know. You will not mention his presence to anyone unless he asks to meet them directly."

Mizrachi nodded.

"Whatever he wants give it to him."

"What is his security clearance?"

Nurin gave her a pained looked. "If *I* can see it, he can see it."

Another nod, this time a bit more hesitant.

"That's all."

As instructed, Mizrachi was waiting at the main gate when the man arrived in a plain sedan. Through the open driver's-side window, she recognized the face from the photo. The only difference involved his eyes—they were an unusual shade of gray, and at that moment seemed oddly veiled and expressionless.

After directing him to the visitor's parking area, and taking a handshake in which she gave her name but got none in return, she escorted her charge inside. Five minutes and two security stations later, she deposited him in the reserved conference room. A table, a few chairs, and a full-access networked laptop were already in place.

The visitor appraised it all and seemed satisfied.

"What else can I get you?" she asked.

"A coffeepot," he said. "And please, no decaf."

Mizrachi smiled. "What else?"

"Let's start with a whiteboard."

"How big?"

He gestured to the room's longest wall.

"I'll see what I can do."

"I think the operations center has some files for me. I'll also need a secure phone."

"Of course. What about personnel? Would you like help with your research?"

"Right now, I think one smiling face will do. Maybe you could fill me in on the latest information protocols—I haven't worked here in a long time."

"Is that before or after the coffee?"

"After will be fine."

"I can do that." She turned to leave.

"Oh, one more thing."

Mizrachi looked over her shoulder.

"If Documents Section could start working up a couple of good legends—it might prove helpful. I'll need them by tomorrow. I think director Nurin has my photo."

"Do you have any specific requests? Names or nationalities?"

The man with the gray eyes thought about it, then shook his head. "Surprise me."

THIRTY-SEVEN

Anna Sorensen drove back to the White House early the next morning, and on the way in she took the latest in a string of calls from Davis. It lasted fifteen minutes, and afterward she began mentally organizing a briefing based on what he'd told her.

Within the hour she was being guided to the Situation Room. The bulk of the National Security Council had assembled: secretary of state, defense secretary, chairman of the Joint Chiefs, director of national intelligence, along with Chief of Staff Markowitz and National Security Advisor Steiner. Their faces were a collective sea of solemnity.

She made her way to the only open seat, the end of the table opposite the president. Sorensen placed her leather portfolio on the table—she'd brought a few printouts, but there had been no time to build a PowerPoint briefing. Basically, she would be winging it.

"As you all know," Cleveland began, "Anna has been managing things in Alaska for the last two days. I thought we could all use some frontline knowledge. So, Anna . . . any idea what the hell is going on?"

Sorensen took a deep breath, then launched into a detailed description of the mission to Wrangel Island, both the good and the bad. She made sure to mention that a number of her operators had put their lives on the line. At the end, she dove into what Davis had just told her.

"We've had our best engineers going over data from the crash, and also one particular piece of wreckage—my investigator was able to recover it from the scene. It's part of the nose cone of the airplane, and it showed unusual damage. Combined with the signals data, I think we're narrowing in on a possible cause for the crash."

"Quantify 'possible,'" said the president.

Sorensen tried to recall the number. "At this point, investigators don't usually give odds—but I'm guessing it's a better than even chance."

Clearly unimpressed, Cleveland nodded for her to go on.

"This damage stood out because it dovetails with research we ourselves have engaged in." From her portfolio she removed two photos of the damaged radome and passed them around the table. "You're looking at a section of the nose cone from Raven 44. The concentric rings you see are highly unusual. Our technicians believe it's the result of abnormal heating. We also think it's significant that data from certain aircraft components stopped streaming in the moments before the crash. We were able to recover four of the avionics boxes from the wreckage, and two of them showed internal damage. The flight data recorder, fortunately, and some of the other electronics came through unscathed. The difference between the components that were damaged, and those that weren't, involves shielding—certain equipment is hardened against electro-magnetic pulses."

"Are you saying this was some kind of EMP event?" the JCS chairman asked.

"Not exactly. My lead investigator extracted an initial take on the flight data recorder. There were a multitude of problems in the final minutes of the flight, including a depressurization, loss of the flight computers, communications interruptions, and haywire instruments on the flight deck. The critical event appears to be uncommanded flight control inputs to the rudder, a series of full-scale deflections that exceeded the structural limit of the airplane. These were not inputs from the pilots, but from two flight control computers that malfunctioned simultaneously. In essence, a great number of systems on the jet failed all at once, leading to an inflight breakup."

"What could cause so many failures?" the president asked.

"Our engineers see one likely culprit, something we've never seen before outside our own weapons test ranges. We think we're looking at an attack by a directed-energy weapon. More specifically, a pulsed laser."

"A laser?" the president said skeptically. She looked at the JCS chairman, as if for confirmation.

"It's conceivable," the general said. "We've been experimenting with them for a long time. The Air Force tested an airborne laser, and while the program was eventually shut down, it was for funding reasons, not lack of results. The technical problems are gradually being ironed out—focusing the beam, directing it accurately, power generation. The basic science has never been in question."

Chief of Staff Markowitz said, "So can we agree we're talking about the Russians?"

"Not necessarily," Sorensen countered. "Aside from ourselves, a number of countries have been working on DE weapons. Russia is one, but you also have to consider China, India, France, Great Britain, and Israel."

"Russia doesn't make sense," said the secretary of state. "For one thing, it would be incredibly provocative. More practically, if they were the ones who shot this airplane down, they would have beat us to the wreckage."

"A valid point," Cleveland agreed. "Do we have any intel on what the Russians really think of all this?"

The secretary of state responded, "A high-level source tells us there's a good bit of confusion in the Kremlin, which backs the idea that this event wasn't initiated by Petrov. We're told he still hasn't settled on a response to what happened on Wrangel. Militarily, the engagement between our forces was a rout, and that's the kind of thing he'd never want to admit. On the other hand, we violated their territory and Russian soldiers died. There *will* be a response. The question is, will it be overt or covert?"

"I'd concur," seconded Sorensen. "As to finding out who was responsible for downing Raven 44, we do have one lead. We've identified a ship
that was in the area at the time of the crash. Her name is *Sibir,* and if we
really are looking at a DE weapon, she was almost certainly the culprit."

"Where is she now?" asked the president.

"We're doing our best to track her. On the last report, she was entering
the Sea of Japan. Based on her route, we think she might be heading for
North Korea."

"North Korea?" the president repeated.

"That's not a certainty," Sorensen hedged. "But it *would* complicate
matters. If *Sibir* makes port there, it could suggest involvement by the
regime. Or it could mean someone else is trying to hide the ship in a place
they know we can't get at it."

Cleveland, looking pained, said, "All right. Ideas on how to handle all
of this going forward?"

The JCS chairman spoke up, "There's something else to consider. I was
given an update this morning on the investigation into the sinking of *Ross.*
The Navy is convinced the ship's GPS position data was corrupted—in
fact, they suspect it may have been a case of meaconing."

"Meaconing?" the president queried.

"It's a concept that's been around a long time—not jamming a signal,
but replacing it with a false signal. In effect, tricking a navigation system
with a false location. The Soviets did it with air navigation during the
Cold War, and GPS has its vulnerabilities. The data we've acquired from
Ross suggests she was being tracked by a radar. Soon after that began, bad
position data was gradually fed into her nav systems. We think the position
shift was manipulated to bring about the collision."

"So the navigation system was hacked?" the secretary of state asked.

"In rough terms, yes. Other systems might have been compromised as
well to bring about the collision. If this is all true, it would imply a highly
sophisticated attack. Not a lot of countries have that kind of technical
know-how—basically, the ones we've already mentioned."

The room fell silent, thoughts spinning in countless directions.

"It seems increasingly clear," the president finally summed up, "that
we are under attack, and by means that are not unsophisticated. Still, the
question remains—who is responsible?"

The JCS chairman said, "I say we take route one. Right now, we're tracking the two ships that were likely involved. We could seize one or both, go
over their equipment, interrogate the officers and crew."

"Under what authority?" Cleveland asked.

Chief of Staff Markowitz, a lawyer by education, said, "Our proof is
thin, but it will firm up in time. I think we could come up with some kind
of legal justification."

"I don't see waiting as an option," said Sorensen. "We've lost a lot of
lives in what appear to be two complex, well-planned strikes. There's no

telling what's next. A close look at these ships would almost certainly tell us who's running them."

The DNI said, "The one that came from Crimea, *Atlas*—she did something very peculiar yesterday. As we were tracking her, she made a quick port call in Eritrea. We watched her drop off most of her crew near a small village on an island."

"Is she still there?" Sorensen asked.

"No. As soon the crewmen debarked, she headed straight back out to sea. Right now, she's under way in the Indian Ocean. We kept constant eyes on her with Reapers all day yesterday, but now that she's getting farther out to sea, we elected to hand off the shadow to a destroyer that was in the area—*Bainbridge*."

"Is that not a risk?" Markowitz asked. "We know what this ship might be capable of."

"We briefed *Bainbridge*'s skipper on the threat," said the general. "Forewarned of the possibility of meaconing, there are simple countermeasures that minimize the risk. Also, ever since this stop in Eritrea, our surveillance has noted no activity on deck. We suspect *Atlas* is running on a skeleton crew."

"Which makes it even more suspicious," Markowitz added.

Sorensen said, "Going after both ships might not be an option. If *Sibir* is, in fact, on her way to North Korea, she'll reach those territorial waters in less than an hour. We should concentrate on *Atlas*. And for what it's worth, in my view we're past the point of getting bogged down by legalities. We need to go on offense."

President Cleveland looked across the table. There were no signs of dissent. "All right," she said, "we move on *Atlas*. Draw up the plan and we'll reconvene in two hours. If it looks good, I'll issue the order."

THIRTY-EIGHT

The meeting broke, and as everyone began filing out Sorensen noticed the DNI huddled in a private conversation with President Cleveland. Whatever he was saying brought a grimace. After he was done, the president caught her eye. "Anna . . . would you stay for a moment."

"Sure," Sorensen said. As if she had a choice.

The president led the way to a small conference room down the hall, and once they were inside, she ominously closed the door. "I've just received some grim news. Mossad got a tip yesterday regarding Ayla Bloch's location. They were told she was being held in a particular apartment in Almaty. They set up surveillance, decided it was accurate, and sent in a tactical team last night."

"A hostage op in a foreign city? That's risky."

"As it turned, more than they imagined. The raid turned into a disaster. After the team got inside, a massive bomb went off. Half the building collapsed."

"Dear God," Sorensen said, something lurching inside. "Ayla?"

The president shook her head. "She's among the dead. Over fifty, at last count, mostly civilians. The entire Mossad team appears to have been lost, but they're still digging out survivors."

Sorensen pressed her eyes shut, trying to wrap her mind around it. "Poor Anton."

"Yes . . . I know you spent a lot of time with him in recent days."

Sorensen tried to compute what it meant. "The Israelis were targeted."

"Clearly. More alarmingly, the 'source' of this intelligence was the same one who provided the warnings regarding our own recent catastrophes. There can't be any more doubt—this is all related. Someone has been launching strikes against us, and now, apparently, they've gone after Mossad. Who picks battles like that?"

There was a long silence as Sorensen considered it. The only answer that came to mind was fleeting and vague. "The fact that we don't know . . . that might be our best clue."

Cleveland looked at her questioningly, not on the same wavelength. The path of the president's thinking was revealed by her next question. "Where is Corsair now?"

Sorensen was taken aback by the shift, but then realized she shouldn't be. Last year, soon after her election, President Cleveland had signed a document authorizing Sorensen to employ "outside assets" in certain delicate situations. It was called National Security Presidential Memoranda 14, an obscure and highly classified directive that gave Sorensen license to employ Slaton, or other irregular operators like him, on missions on America's behalf. She had used it right away: under the code name Corsair, Slaton had single-handedly spirited a Russian interpreter out of Syria, and then intervened in the rise of a dangerous new dictator in the Middle East. Afterward, Cleveland had wanted to thank Slaton personally. He'd declined respectfully and returned to his family in Idaho. If the president had felt snubbed at the time, Sorensen never sensed it. On the contrary, she seemed more impressed than ever by the priorities of her newest and most lethal operator. Not to mention, his results.

"I sent him to Tel Aviv," Sorensen said. "With Mossad being so involved, it seemed like the logical move."

"I agree," the president said. Then more speculatively, "It also puts him closer to where he might be needed."

Sorensen didn't respond, letting the president lead.

"Anna, our thinking has been too small in scope. I feel like we've been reacting to individual disasters, not viewing the sum of events strategically."

"Maybe so."

"Get in touch with David. I want his opinion of things on that end. And after that . . ." Her voice trailed off.

Sorensen looked at the president questioningly.

"Tell him to be ready."

The most effective way to kill bad news, Director Nurin knew, was to replace it with something worse. Thankfully, the disaster in Almaty had so far been tamped down without his intervention. Outside Kazakhstan, the explosion and collapse of an apartment building was overshadowed by two greater crises: the loss of a U.S. Air Force spy aircraft off the northern coast of Russia, and the sinking of *Ross* in the Black Sea. U.S. relations with Russia were in free fall, and official statements from both sides were low on detail and high on rhetoric. Altogether, it was enough to stretch the bandwidth of the most steadfast spymaster.

Nurin forced himself to focus on Almaty. It helped that the blast was so far being treated as an accident—the latest news reports hinted at a gas explosion in the ancient apartment building. Mossad was doing its best to propagate that theory, Unit 8200 echoing convenient facts and speculation online. That would buy time, but the Kazakh State Security Service weren't idiots. They would find residues from explosive material and discover that a large number of the bodies in the rubble were not residents of the complex, but rather visitors from abroad who'd arrived in the last few days. Nurin's people, both at headquarters and the Almaty station, were doing their best to clean up the mess, yet there would be no escaping some degree of involvement. The Kazakh government would lead the accusatory charge: a gas explosion implied incompetence, which could be laid at their feet, whereas a conspiracy involving foreign spies pointed the finger elsewhere. And for once, it was actually true.

In a month, possibly two, the Israeli ambassador would deliver a statement: something about a terrorist cell and a murky intelligence operation gone wrong. Perhaps even an admission that Israelis, too, had been victimized.

For now, however, Nurin had time. Time to get to the bottom of whatever was going on. More than ever, he was convinced that Lazarus had an agenda. He thought back to the video outside the embassy in Nur-Sultan, the man with a hitch in his gait feeding the gulls. More than ever, he was sure this was their traitor. Two days ago, Nurin had watched that scene play out with detached fascination, thinking it laughably amateurish.

Only now did he realize who the fool was.

THIRTY-NINE

Bainbridge's captain, Commander Richard Coughlin, read the order twice before handing it to the officer of the deck. From near the helm, his gaze reached into the dark night—the moon was obscured by a heavy overcast.

"They want us to board ASAP," the OOD said. "And take the crew into custody for interrogation."

"After what happened to *Ross,* I'm not surprised." They knew *Atlas* had been near *Ross* when she'd gone down, and they themselves had been warned that the ship they were following might be carrying electronic gear that could interfere with navigation. They'd seen no irregularities so far, but the crew were cross-checking position data carefully.

"Is the VBSS team still on alert?"

"They are, Captain."

Bainbridge had been chosen to shadow *Atlas* for a very specific reason: She was the only destroyer in the vicinity with a VBSS team on board. It stood for visit, board, search, and seizure, a unit with special training for just such operations: weapons handling, room-clearing techniques, close-quarters combat, rappelling. Everything necessary to board vessels, with or without permission, and conduct searches at sea.

Coughlin lifted a set of optics from the chart table. "Bearing and range to target?"

"Bearing one-six-zero, range twelve thousand yards."

He trained his low-light optics on the misty marine horizon but saw nothing. That afternoon he'd caught glimpses of *Atlas,* but once the sun had gone down, she'd disappeared. They were quite sure she was running without lights. Her speed was only four knots, which had to be near steerageway—the minimum speed required to still respond to the helm. Everything Coughlin knew about their quarry shouted for caution.

"All right," he said, lowering the optics and addressing the OOD. "Tell the VBSS team to prepare for boarding."

Slaton worked nonstop in his makeshift office at Mossad headquarters. By eight o'clock that night, the files on the table resembled a Jenga game. By ten he needed a bigger table. There had been six briefings over the course of the day, one of them an update on the bombing in Almaty. He had also talked to Sorensen, getting the latest on the American end. Twice he asked for food to be brought in, and later a cot. The farthest he'd been from the room was the bathroom down the hall. Altogether, it was just what he needed—a private space in which to work and think, where he could tune out all extraneous noise. Yet if Slaton's commitment bordered on the devout, what he had in mind was something no man of the cloth would ever countenance.

He closed a file, got up, and stretched. He made his way to the coffeemaker—Mizrachi had set it up on the floor in one corner—and poured the dregs of the evening batch. Slaton sat on the edge of the table and thought back reflectively to that morning. After leaving Bloch's villa, he had stopped briefly at a roadside overlook, watched the shadows of the valley recede. His relationship with Anton Bloch was long and tortured, and more than once the ex-director had sent him into no-win situations. For all that trouble, however, Slaton never doubted Bloch's commitment to Israel. He was tenacious, unrelenting when it came to defending the country. Now his only child was dead as a consequence of that duty. To Slaton, the enduring image in his mind was a stark one: a broken and nearly catatonic man left staring into the hills.

Did absolute commitment always lead to misery? he wondered. Slaton had been able to recenter his own life, yet he'd witnessed more than his share of devastation over the years. Operators lost. Grieving widows and families. Friends and brothers-in-arms sacrificed for the cause. A vague corollary tugged in the recesses of Slaton's mind but misted away without resolving.

He turned toward the big whiteboard on the wall. It was filled with scrawled notes, and in the center was a large circle; bullet points all around were connected by vector arrows and lines. As visual aids went, it resembled a detective's map of a complex murder case. Which, in essence, it was. The center circle, unfortunately, remained maddeningly blank.

He returned to the laptop; Nurin had provided a copy of the video from the embassy in Nur-Sultan. Ignoring the clip's absurd nature—a clownish attempt to deliver a memory stick—Slaton studied the video once more. He concentrated exclusively on the man ambling past the embassy entrance. He had kept his head turned away from the only camera—surely no accident. This *was* Lazarus. A man who somehow had forewarning of impending attacks on American interests, and who routinely disseminated that knowledge at the last moment, when it could no longer be useful. It had all worked perfectly: he'd gained Mossad's confidence, then conducted his own devastating strike.

It spoke to two certainties. The man had insider information—he knew who was attacking the Americans. Yet he also carried a grudge against Israel. Whether he was a party to the strikes, or simply had knowledge of them, remained unclear. Yet the second revelation seemed more telling. And far more likely to provide clues as to his identity.

Slaton hit the play arrow again and again. He studied the man's shape, his clothing, the way he carried himself. He knew he was on camera because he kept his face hidden. Did it therefore follow that the limp was contrived? A preplanned bit of deception, practiced in front of a hotel room mirror? Slaton thought not. It was too obvious, too overtly performed. If anything, the man seemed to be minimizing the hitch in his gait. Slaton also noticed an abnormality in his right hand, the way he held the bag of bread crumbs.

He decided to put in a request to Nurin to have the images studied by specialists. Orthopedic surgeons, physical therapists—Mossad had no shortage of such professionals on call. If the type of injury could be narrowed, it might serve to go back through their records. Check for targets of operations who'd been injured but not killed, or who were documented as having preexisting handicaps. Even bystanders, perhaps, collateral damage of some long-forgotten Mossad mission. It seemed a long shot, yet manpower wasn't an issue. Nor was motivation. Not after what had happened in Almaty.

Right now, the entire agency was laser-focused. Mossad was a relatively small organization, and on the operational side there were few who didn't know someone who'd perished in the blast. For Slaton, it was particularly intimate. He'd watched Ayla Bloch grow up. Seen her follow in her father's footsteps, only to pay the ultimate price. And now—he'd seen the effect it had on him.

There was a fine line between justice and revenge.

In that moment, Slaton was looking straight down at it.

For nearly a day Langley's researchers plumbed the enigma that was EDG Industries. The agency had vast experience unraveling the world's corporate safe havens, yet EDG proved more puzzling than most. Its web of ownership ran through at least six countries and four law firms. Not a single principal officer could be identified through the veiled network of subsidiaries. With those barriers holding fast, a secondary investigative team took the more proven route: they followed the money.

The break actually came from the NSA, and it seemed minor at first: a photocopy of a check sent from EDG Industries to a P.O. Box in Manhattan. The U.S. Postal Service had some years ago instituted a program to photo-scan all mail during sorting, the intent being to make the images available to addressees. What on its face seemed a technological convenience for consumers—a preview of what was coming to your mailbox that day—had proved a bonanza for the NSA.

The agency obtained limited approval to access the files and, using its vast data-crunching resources, was able to highlight a letter bearing EDG's name out of billions of images. They quickly determined that the letter, apparently a check, had been sent from Albania, with the return address listed as a postal box. The receiving party in Manhattan turned out to be a law firm, but that proved a dead end for two reasons: lawyers tended to know their rights when it came to divulging information about clients, and more damningly for the NSA, the firm of Mayer, Steen, and Gondol kept excellent cyber firewalls.

The return address on the Albanian end, however, was another story. The postal box was easily tracked to Tirana. Better yet, NSA had conveniently, over a year ago, accessed cameras in the postal building in question in the course of another operation. Using the postmark date on the letter, they searched the camera's history going back four days. Virtually every face entering the building was captured, and NSA fed 512 profiles into its computational machine. This was viewed as a long shot, since the agency's databases, extensive as they were, contained few ethnic Albanians.

Yet before that search could even run, a second break was realized: another camera in the building sat overwatch on the postal box in question. Shifting among the scenes, they noted a heavily built man depositing a letter, almost certainly the one in question, into the general mail drop one day before the postmark. The man then walked to the postal box, checked it, and walked out empty-handed.

In any number of ways, it was poor tradecraft on the part of the sender: using a postal box to begin, and listing it as a return address on a letter. NSA's success became complete when its recognition software got a hit on the man. The face captured by the camera was one that U.S. intelligence agencies were quite familiar with: a top-tier mercenary recruiter named Zamir Bagdani.

FORTY

Slaton was tipped back in his chair, feet on the cluttered table and hands clasped behind his neck, when Director Nurin appeared at the open door of his workroom. Slaton glanced at him once, then went back to ruminating. Without comment, the director began studying the board.

Slaton had never worked for Nurin—not directly—so he lacked the bond he shared with Anton Bloch. Or for that matter, with Sorensen. The same would be true in the inverse. Nurin knew him largely by reputation, although Slaton *had* aided Israel under his watch. Even so, the trust requisite in such relationships—particularly given their roles as spy chief and assassin—had never been forged. For everyone's sake, they both needed to get past it.

"Any luck?" Nurin finally said.

"It's not a matter of luck. It about effort, putting the loose pieces together."

"As with masonry? Anton mentioned your new sideline."

"Everyone has a calling."

Nurin turned away from the board, waited for Slaton to meet his gaze. "David, I know your history with the Office was not without . . . difficulties."

"That's putting it mildly. But I'm past it. Right now, I'd say we have parallel interests."

"Do we? My duty is to keep Israel safe. I sense your involvement has become more personal."

"As long as our goals are aligned, motives are immaterial." He got up and wandered to the board. "But someone else's motives . . . those matter very much."

Nurin waited as Slaton stood contemplating the board, hands on his hips.

"I learned a good lesson during that op to Wrangel. Something that actually saved my life."

"What was that?"

"It might sound contrived, but it has to do with compasses. Geographic north and the north pole aren't one and the same. Most people know that, in a general way, but I was in a position where it really mattered. I understood that while the needle might not be accurate in the conventional sense, it was always consistent."

He picked up a marker and wrote one word in the center circle.

"Lazarus," said Nurin. "This is where your compass points?"

"He steered Mossad into a disaster, and went to great lengths to do it. I think he's somebody we know." Slaton explained his suspicions about the limp, outlined how they might use it to identify him.

"It's a good thought," Nurin agreed. "I'll put someone on it immediately."

The secure phone Slaton had been given chirped a call. He picked it up and heard Sorensen's voice.

"We've made an ID that should help," she said.

"Lazarus?" Slaton asked hopefully.

"No, but maybe the next best thing."

"Director Nurin is with me—I'm going to put you on speaker."

Slaton did, and she continued. "We've been trying to unravel EDG Industries. We got lucky and were able to identify a letter they sent to a law firm in New York." She explained how NSA had tracked it to a post office in Albania, and then identified the sender. "The name is Zamir Bagdani."

It meant nothing to Slaton, yet he saw a flicker in Nurin's gaze. "The arms merchant," the director ventured.

"That's the one. I'm guessing we both have a file on him." Sorensen paused, a voice in the background interrupting. She said, "Let me call you right back—I'm needed in the operations center. I'll fill you in soon."

It had taken an hour to get the boarding party prepped and briefed. Once they were ready, *Bainbridge* closed the gap quickly. The captain wasn't sure if his counterpart on *Atlas* knew he was being followed—they weren't seeing any sign of radar activity from that direction. Either way, he wanted to give his quarry as little time as possible to react.

Bainbridge closed to within two hundred yards of the smaller ship, which was still wallowing along at four knots. At that point, *Bainbridge* slowed and two rigid-hull inflatables were winched quickly down the port side. Each boat held eleven men. All wore body armor, and they carried an impressive array of weapons: M4 carbines, Mossberg 500 shotguns, and Beretta M9s.

The team spanned the divide to *Atlas* in minutes, and boarding nets were launched upward, snagging firmly on the rails. The lead element began climbing, and after receiving an all clear, the rest of the team followed, save for one man to safeguard each boat.

The unit began leapfrogging ahead, clearing corners and passageways, coordinating with hand signals. As they made their way toward the bridge, they encountered no resistance whatsoever, and in fact saw not a single crewmember. Chances were, at midnight local time, most of the crew would be in their bunks. All the same, the commander of the VBSS team, a lieutenant, felt doubts beginning to encroach.

Fearing the crew might be bunkered up for an ambush, he ordered a pause in their advance. He scoped out the deck ahead, a wash of green-scale hues in his night optic, and still saw no movement anywhere. The team was one deck below the bridge, which was their primary objective. If they could control that high ground, they would control the ship. The ladder leading up to the bridge was thirty yards ahead across mostly open deck.

He keyed his mic to give a sitrep to *Bainbridge*'s command center, knowing full well his words were being transmitted halfway around the world. "We're on board, no resistance, no sign of the crew. I can see the bridge, but there's only one window from this angle and it doesn't give much of a look. This is weird. There's not a soul in sight."

Bainbridge's captain replied, "Copy all. Standby . . ."

Sorensen had returned to the Situation Room to watch the operation in the Indian Ocean play out. The usual duty staff were there, but President Cleveland was not. The only NSC member joining her was the JCS chairman—it was, after all, a Navy operation. The small room was wired for big missions, and two large monitors beamed a pair of images from nine times zones away. One was a night-vision view from the midships deck of *Atlas*, the jittery body cam of the VBSS team commander. Next to that was a God's-eye view of the entire ship fed from a drone *Bainbridge* had launched to support the mission.

The team was presently holding in cover halfway to the bridge. The operation had gone smoothly so far, but caution reigned, and options on how to proceed were being weighed. The Navy was overseeing the mission at Fleet level, and as Sorensen watched it all play out, she arranged for another secure call to Slaton. While that ran its course, she caught snippets of the mission audio—enough to recognize that the lieutenant leading the team seemed spooked.

Slaton answered on the first ring. "What's up?"

"A lot, actually. I'm sitting here watching an op go down. We've been shadowing *Atlas*, the ship we suspect of screwing with *Ross*'s navigation. She's in the Indian Ocean now. The president is getting impatient for answers, and she authorized the Navy to interdict. A team just boarded and I'm watching it all go down in real time."

"Gotta love technology," said Slaton, having himself featured in many such videos.

"Which brings us back to my reason for calling. *Atlas* is owned by EDG Industries, and now that we've tied Bagdani to that company, we'd like to get Mossad's help researching him."

"Agreed. Nurin is already on it—he stepped out a few minutes ago to make it happen."

"Good. If we can find Bagdani, he might lead us to Lazarus. What's new on your end?" Sorensen waited for a response but got only silence.

"David?" she prompted.

"How's the raid going?" he asked out of nowhere.

Doing her best to multitask, she went back to the streaming images. "No change. Our team has been on board roughly five minutes. So far, no resistance. In fact, from the comments I've heard, no sign of the crew whatsoever."

A pause on the Tel Aviv end. "That's strange," Slaton said.

"Is it?"

"How much of the ship have they covered?"

"They're still above deck, working their way toward the bridge. They paused for a conference a couple of minutes ago. The guy leading the unit—"

"Abort!" Slaton shouted.

Sorensen pulled the phone abruptly away from her ear, her full attention back on the call. *"What?* Why?"

"Get that team out! Order them to pull back!"

Before she could ask why a second time, Slaton said, "Almaty!"

And with that, it clicked. Sorensen felt it as well, an icy fear. Impending disaster. She looked at the images, saw the team stalled on a deserted deck. Sometimes you didn't need to be near trouble to smell it. Sometimes you could do that from half a world away.

"Break it off!" Sorensen shouted, dropping the secure handset.

The JCS chairman, who was in direct comm with Fleet headquarters, shot her a look of annoyance.

Sorensen stood and leaned across the table and put herself right in his face. "Order that team back! Pull them out *now!*"

The general, a weathered warrior with an iron-gray crew cut, stammered, "Why would—"

"That's an order, dammit! Just do it!"

FORTY-ONE

Chains of command were a funny thing. The chairman of the Joint Chiefs of Staff was U.S. Army, and he was sitting overwatch of a Navy mission. Sorensen had no military command authority whatsoever. It was an increasingly common dilemma in the era of joint operations: multiple services, different agencies, various pay grades. Competing missions and rules of engagement. Often the principal players had never worked together and were the product of varying cultures. Yet in that moment, in the gone-silent White House Situation Room, one thing was crystal clear: the depth of Sorensen's conviction.

The general didn't understand what was behind it, but it registered loud and clear. He gave the abort order to Fleet headquarters, who quickly forwarded it to *Bainbridge*. When word finally reached the lieutenant on *Atlas*'s deck, the relief in his voice was palpable as he instructed his team to pull back from their incursion of what felt like a ghost ship.

The boarding party descended quickly to their boats, and soon the rigid inflatables were skipping over two-foot seas back to *Bainbridge*. They'd barely covered half the divide when a massive explosion rocked the night.

The lieutenant instinctively ducked as the shock wave hammered the boats, but incredibly neither capsized. Bits of shrapnel punctured both inflatable hulls, yet the manufacturer's promise held: on the same principle as run-flat tires, they remained seaworthy over the final hundred yards. More alarmingly, two of his team were wounded: one took a shard of metal in his neck, barely missing the carotid artery, while another suffered an arm wound. Everyone climbed back on *Bainbridge* with ringing ears, and the ship's medical staff immediately went to work.

On *Bainbridge* herself, the shock wave blew out reinforced windows along the port-side superstructure, and the ship's antenna suite was peppered with damage. It could have been worse. It would ultimately be determined—based on residue taken from various bits of floating wreckage, along with a bill of lading from a port call two months earlier—that *Atlas* had been hauling twenty-one tons of ammonium nitrate in her aft hold.

The smoking shell of the old trawler began listing immediately, and her hull buckled at a mid-station bulkhead. Her back broken, *Atlas* turtled to port amid great geysers of venting air. She disappeared beneath the waves five minutes later, her bent rudder waving a final goodbye to the world.

In the Situation Room, Sorensen watched the scene unfold with surreal detachment. Both monitors had blanked for a time, but a feed from *Bainbridge* was quickly reestablished—the drone camera never came back, the aircraft no doubt vaporized. Amid a cloud of smoke in the infrared image, Sorensen saw an empty sea where *Atlas* had been. All that remained was a churn of bubbles and a feeble oil slick.

She looked down and saw the secure handset she'd been using to talk to Slaton—it was hanging from the table by its cord, twirling like a spent yo-yo. She picked it up, and asked in a hollow voice, "Are you still there?"

"Yeah," Slaton said. "I think I gather what happened."

She took a deep breath. "Right, well . . . that was a good call. Thanks."

Details on Bagdani came thick and fast. Mossad and the CIA scoured their databases independently and both got hits. It was Mossad, however, that kept the thicker file, and for reasons director Nurin was loath to admit—Israel had twice undertaken quiet dealings with him.

Bagdani's origins were obscure. Based on his accent, it was suspected he'd been born in the Balkans. His background became tangible on the day he turned nineteen, when he signed on for a stint in the French Foreign Legion. Mossad actually had copies of his service records, covering an unremarkable four years in Africa. It was after this period that he made his true mark.

Bagdani leveraged contacts made in the service to become a top-tier arms merchant. His customer base was extensive, deals made on every continent. He mostly sourced personnel, and for all manner of buyers: legitimate governments, strongmen, oligarchs, militias. In recent years, he'd specialized in recruiting niche, hard-to-find specialties. EOD teams for land mine removal, mechanics for light attack aircraft, cyber experts who specialized in Bitcoin mining.

Mossad had contracted with Bagdani on two occasions—the reason they'd researched him so thoroughly. Once had been to recruit local help in Mali, a few tactically oriented translators to help free an Israeli diplomat taken hostage by al-Shabab. Later, he had helped hire a South African consultant who was an expert on electrical grids, and who also, by no coincidence, had been the primary architect of Iran's national network.

Aside from those contracts, for which he'd been paid a healthy commission, Bagdani had never been viewed by Mossad as more than a curiosity. Now he was central to everything. On Nurin's orders, sources around the region were canvassed, and it quickly became apparent that Bagdani had made few deals in the last year. At least two regular customers claimed he'd ignored potentially lucrative contracts. For ten months, no one had seen or heard from him.

Which stoked Nurin's suspicions only further.

The sinking of *Atlas*, not to mention the manner in which she'd gone down, put the CIA's interest in the other ship they were tracking into overdrive.

After following *Sibir* through the Bering Sea, across the North Pacific, and into the Sea of Japan, the operations center staff watched intently as she slid behind a breakwater in Kimchaek, North Korea. The port was on North Korea's Pacific shore, and while it was not a major shipping or logistics hub, it was the nearest harbor that could accept a ship of *Sibir*'s size.

The former Kazakhstan icebreaker sided up to the main pier, and mooring lines were thrown into place. Every eye in the ops center was glued to the satellite feed, waiting to see what happened next.

For a time, the answer was nothing. No gangway was set in place, no cranes went into action, and no crew disembarked. The icebreaker simply sat there, silent and still. Like a convict in an orange jumpsuit trying to blend in at a wedding.

And with that, the waiting game began.

FORTY-TWO

The procurement of raw intelligence is a broad church, and Mossad and the CIA held nothing back in their hunt for Zamir Bagdani. They began by lasering in on the last point of contact: the post office in Tirana, Albania.

Personnel from both embassy stations, armed with little more than a photo of Bagdani, spread out to bars and wharves to buy rounds of drinks. Analysts in Langley and Tel Aviv scoured photo-surveillance and signals intelligence, and immersed themselves in chat rooms and social media platforms, looking and listening for any sign of the notorious arms dealer.

Their break came in a dank watering hole on the outskirts of a village called Kodër-Thumanë, and for the most bewildering of reasons—a rivalry between two Italian soccer clubs. A bartender in a waterside pub was approached by a customer he'd never seen, a rough-looking character with dark features, a pitted face, and the most unfathomable of accents. The man ordered a beer and chatted about the weather before holding out a photograph and saying, "I am looking for this man."

The bartender was justifiably cautious. "You are police?"

"Do I look like a policeman?"

The bartender shrugged to concede the point.

"I need a job, and I was told he hires men like me."

The barkeep scratched his brown-stubble chin. "I've seen him, a Juve man. He comes here sometimes for the games."

The Mossad officer nodded as if he understood. When the bartender went to pour a beer for another customer, he pulled out his phone. He quickly looked up "Juve" and learned that the reference was to Juventus, a famous Italian soccer club. He also noticed a red-and-black scarf tacked to the wall behind the bar, and a closer inspection revealed the logo of a different team, AC Milan. A second phone search confirmed his suspicions: AC Milan and Juventus were hardened rivals.

He sensed opportunity.

The Mossad man quickly drained his mug, and when the bartender came to refill it, he said, "A Juve man. He is Italian then?"

A spit of derision. "No, he is an *armb*."

It was a term the Israeli knew well, referring to the local mafia. He nodded understandingly. "Still, I need the job. Maybe he lives nearby?"

The bartender's gaze narrowed, yet his caution seemed overridden by disdain.

"He comes here now and again, I think when the power goes out up on the cliff—as it often does along the coast road. If he can't watch a game at home, he brings a few men, tough ones like you. The boss watches his team play, if you can call it that, and maybe has a drink or two. The others only watch the doors—no game, no drinking. They take up a big table and buy almost nothing. Lightweights, all of them."

"I'll tell you this . . . if he hires me, I'll have them partying like it's the World Cup."

The barkeeper's weathered face broke into a grin.

The Mossad case officer, whose name was Jakob, pulled out a wad of cash, peeled off three bills, and slid them across the bar. One would have covered the price of ten beers. They disappeared under a practiced hand. "He lives at the top of the hill," the barkeep said, pointing up the main street. "The big house with high walls—you cannot miss it."

The barkeeper was right, the house wasn't hard to find. More a fortress than a home, it was set on a peninsula that jutted into the sea like a dagger, roughly a mile from the bar on the edge of Kodër-Thumanë. The house was bigger than those around it, surrounded by a wall that would have done the Ottoman Empire proud. From high on a cliff its broad patio held a commanding view of the azure Adriatic, the sunny shores of Italy just over the horizon. By any measure, the compound was a white stone monument to excess—and a virtual billboard for ill-gotten gains.

Both Mossad and the CIA studied the place, and they agreed on most of what they saw. Ten thousand square feet of living space, stone walls, expansive terraces, and a rooftop full of antennae and observation posts. A study of the local property records uncovered the usual obfuscation of ownership, and while there was no mention of EDG Industries—the mansion had been purchased years before that company's creation—the holding concern listed had once been tied to Bagdani.

Two satellite sweeps were made, and a drone mission was launched from an air base in Italy. Thousands of images streamed in from every possible angle, and in a wide range of spectrums. No vehicle traffic was observed at the compound other than a few deliveries of groceries and small packages. At least five guards were stationed outside at all times, two of them posted on the roof. This surprised no one: a man who recruited mercenaries for a living, a lucrative but risk-laden vocation, would be foolish not to have protection.

Of all the intelligence gathered, none was given as much scrutiny as a handful of photos, captured by a Predator drone on two separate instances, of a man and a young woman sitting on the poolside terrace. The man was big and burly, the woman a lithe blonde wearing a swimsuit beneath her sheer wrap, this despite a temperature in the fifties. Both spent most of their time on their phones, he talking animatedly on extended calls, she flicking casually through what was likely social media fare. The overheads were enhanced using the best available software, and after comparing the images to those on file, the two intelligence agencies were again in agreement. They were looking at Zamir Bagdani.

Having located their man, the question became what to do about it.

The impulse to listen in on Bagdani's phone calls was compelling, yet easier said than done. Encryption was a fast-moving target, and even the NSA, for all its eavesdropping sorcery, hit roadblocks. It *could* be done but might well take time. Simply watching Bagdani, in the hope that he might travel to meet Lazarus, or even host him as a visitor, seemed wishful at best. Neither Tel Aviv nor Washington was in the mood to wait. That being the case, more active methods came to the forefront.

When it came to snatching terrorists, Mossad had a long and storied history. They were the agency that had grabbed Adolf Eichmann off the streets of Argentina and tried him for war crimes, and that had gunned down the terrorists of the Munich Olympics, one by one, across Europe and beyond. The CIA, too, had hunted down terrorists deemed to be threats to U.S. interests. They did so with virtually endless assets at their disposal, yet also onerous legal restrictions.

Logistics was also considered. Israel maintained a small mission in Tirana, with only two Mossad operatives on station. The U.S. embassy in Tirana was larger, although its CIA contingent had been downsized—the Balkans had long ago fallen to a back burner. Not only were boots on the ground limited, but Albania could be a dangerous place to operate, a federated backwater where corruption was pervasive, rule of law aspirational.

Director Nurin and Deputy Director Sorensen held an exhaustive phone conference, debating how best to handle a situation that had vital national security implications for both countries. They needed to find a way to pressure Bagdani into revealing the identity of Lazarus, and to do that they needed to abduct him. It would be no small challenge. Yet while the details remained unsettled, the spymasters quickly came to one point of agreement: David Slaton was going to lead the operation.

FORTY-THREE

The identities Mossad procured for Slaton were first-rate, and even more impressive considering the short notice they'd been given. His passport was Swiss and looked perfectly legitimate. There were also credit cards, a driver's license, and a legend to back it all up: Slaton was posing as a Swiss national working on a church renovation project in south Tirana. The project was real, and he was even given a set of architectural plans to study en route. With his deep knowledge of stonework, he could easily bluff his way past any cursory questioning at the airport.

Using one of two phones he'd been given—one a standard iPhone, the other a seemingly identical device loaded with secure Mossad encryption—he booked a commercial flight to Tirana, Turkish Airlines with a connection in Istanbul. He would have preferred to avoid Turkey, but the schedule was too convenient to bypass.

Time *was* of the essence.

Sarah Mizrachi came through as well, procuring fresh clothing, which fit perfectly, badly needed shaving gear, and a roller bag for hauling it all. Slaton couldn't carry a weapon on the commercial flight, so he arranged for a package with a diplomatic seal to be delivered at speed to the Tirana embassy. Inside were one SIG P226, an Accuracy International AWM chambered in .338 Lapua Magnum and fitted with a suppressor, six flash-bangs, and two Kevlar vests. He had no idea if any of it would be necessary, but as he explained to Director Nurin, "Better to be prepared."

By seven o'clock that evening, he was on a Turkish Airlines Boeing 737 climbing out over the Med with a modest tailwind, a business-class chicken Florentine on his tray table, and a head full of ideas.

While Slaton was en route, the joint operation in Albania began in earnest. The two Mossad case officers in Tirana joined with four peers from the CIA. They quickly identified a rental property that, while not ideal, had decent geometry for surveilling the compound. The deal was consummated in minutes through an online vacation site. Shortly after sunset that night, on the edge of a small enclave of rental properties, two men and a woman keyed the correct combination into a lockbox on the villa's front door. A second car with the remaining team members arrived soon after.

It was a cottage in comparison to Bagdani's castle, yet the place had a nice view of the sea—and a partially restricted overlook of the great mansion three-quarters of a mile north. The team set up an observation post in the second-floor bedroom, positioning a high-power optic in the shadows near the balcony. They fixed a watch schedule, agreed on how to log their observations, and set up communications links with both overseeing agencies.

One man and the woman set out for a leisurely stroll along the street, turning north up the shoreline road. The two held hands as they went, looking very much in love. In fact, their adoring gazes went right past one another to log where cars were parked, which houses had dogs, and they lingered for three minutes near a narrow drainage easement along the south wall of the big compound. While they were gone, the others kept busy at the villa. One man roamed the upper balcony to study their immediate neighbors, searching for anyone who might pose a problem. Another double-checked the villa's physical security.

As the night progressed, the rotations began. Monitoring security, checking messages, keeping a continuous eye on Bagdani's compound, all meshed with periods of rest.

And with that, the waiting and watching began.

FORTY-FOUR

It was nearly midnight when Slaton arrived in Tirana. He passed through customs effortlessly and picked up a rental car that had been reserved in his new name. As requested, it was a Land Rover—more conspicuous than a generic sedan, but not uncommon here. His plan going forward was murky, and the Rover's agility could be only an asset. The premise mirrored that of the weapons cache being delivered—most of it would go unused, but the more options available, the better.

He had no trouble finding the villa, the seaward bookend of a half dozen units lining a small seaside knoll. Even at night it looked like a vacation brochure, all palm trees and string lights and painted shutters. He did a three-point turn in the parking area to give the Rover an easy getaway—probably unnecessary, but a precaution he'd never before regretted.

Slaton guessed he was being tracked via the phone he'd been given, and this was confirmed when the front door opened before he could knock. A tall brunette woman invited him in, and for the sake of a passing stranger walking a dog on the outer street, she gave him a sisterly hug and *la bise* at the threshold.

"Good to see you," she said with an unmistakable Texas drawl. "Nora."

"David, good to meet you." Once inside, he took in the villa and predictably saw bright colors and airbrushed paintings of seashells. "How many with you?" he asked.

"Five others—two Mossad, the rest my ilk. One of my guys is running an errand back at the embassy. Two are standing watch and the other two are sleeping in the back room."

"Just as well. It's going to be a long night."

A pair of men appeared from the main bedroom and introduced themselves—a young CIA kid named Logan, and a grizzled Mossad *katsa* who went by Avram. They regarded him with all the wariness of an EOD team getting its first look at an unexploded bomb. His reputation, apparently, had again preceded him.

"Any sightings of our target?" Slaton asked.

Nora vacillated at his use of the word, then said, "We set up an OP in the bedroom, saw him a couple of times this afternoon. We think we have his bedroom figured out—top floor, seaside. We've been getting regular updates from headquarters as well, both east and west."

"Ok. Show me what you've got."

The main living area had morphed into an operations center. The curtains on the French doors leading to the balcony were drawn tight, and the kitchen table had become a workstation—it was already suffocating under maps and overhead images of the mansion.

"The place is a fortress," Nora said, leading the way to the table and picking out an overhead of the compound. "There are two entrances, both guarded. The doors look solid. There's state-of-the-art surveillance on the perimeter, and a hundred-foot clear area around the main house."

"How long have you been watching?"

"Almost twelve hours now. We spotted him on the balcony with a girl—half his age, nice looking. Since we've been watching, Bagdani hasn't left the compound."

"Anything to suggest he knows he's being watched?"

"No reason to think so. But then, guys like Bagdani always operate like they're being watched. He's got heavy security, at least nine men at any given time. A couple appear to be locals, but we think some are foreign—they all seem competent. We actually identified two, both Slovakian with Spec Ops backgrounds, a history of contract work."

"I guess we shouldn't be surprised. Recruiting soldiers is what he does for a living."

"True. The guards outside have been rotating on four-hour shifts. We've seen one housekeeper and one maintenance guy, probably both permanent party and living on-premises."

Slaton stood straight, glanced at the bedroom where the OP was set up. "Do we have a clear line of sight to the compound?"

Nora gave him a circumspect look. "Decent. There are a couple of palm trees next door that could use some trimming, but we can see most of the place."

"Range?"

"One thousand three hundred twelve meters to his bedroom window," said Avram.

Slaton looked at the Israeli questioningly.

"We brought a laser range finder."

Nora added, "We've been told to expect a shipment from Tel Aviv. A diplo bag, very long and heavy."

Once more, Slaton thought a bit too much of his background might have been forwarded. "I have some weapons en route, but don't jump to conclusions. Our mission is to interrogate Bagdani—I think he can tell us who's behind these recent disasters."

Nora nodded, perhaps with some relief.

With spread fingertips, Slaton drew the overhead photo of the compound closer.

"Do you think there's a way in?" she asked as he studied it.

"There's always a way in," he said distractedly. "The question is, at what cost? On home turf we would have no limits on manpower or tactics. As it is, on foreign soil against heavy fortifications, with seven of us and more of them? Overwhelming force wouldn't be my preferred option."

He stood straighter, then said, "Let's have a look."

Slaton followed the others into the bedroom. Nora showed him a tripod-mounted optic that was set back into the dark room, a chair nearby. The sliding glass door leading to the balcony was partially open, giving an unobstructed line of sight. He leaned down and studied the distant compound, making minor adjustments to the magnification. There were a few lights on in the house, and he saw three guards who looked alert—two on the roof, and one near the gated front entrance. The perimeter wall encompassed three sides, while the edge of the cliff completed the rectangle. The drop-off there was vertical, at least two hundred feet down to a rocky beach. Altogether, not an impenetrable stronghold, but one that presented serious obstacles for an extraction op.

He pulled away from the optic.

"Any ideas?" Nora asked.

Slaton rubbed his chin with a hand and felt another day's stubble forming. He'd slept a bit on the flight—helpful, but not enough for a full recharge. "The problem is, we're in a time crunch. Over the last few days a lot of people have died. Tensions between the U.S. and Russia are ratcheting up fast."

"Langley has been making that point forcefully in their message traffic. If I didn't know better," she mused, "I'd think someone was trying to start a war."

He looked at her thoughtfully, then returned to their tactical problem. "You say he hasn't left since you've been watching the place?"

"Not once. There have been a few deliveries, but that's it."

Slaton went closer to the window, his gaze on the sea. "We need to get him outside."

Avram said, "An emergency? Start a fire?"

Slaton shook his head doubtfully. "No. If the security team is reasonably proficient, and I suspect they are, it would only raise their alert level."

A new voice came from the connecting bedroom, "I say we cut the power."

FORTY-FIVE

Slaton turned to see a burly man whose features were characteristically Mediterranean: black, close-shorn hair, a weathered olive complexion. He introduced himself as Jakob, and said, "I am the one who got the lead on this compound—it came from a bartender down the street. Among other things, he told me that Bagdani is a die-hard fan of Juve."

"Juve?" Slaton repeated. "As in Juventus, the soccer club?"

"Very good. The bartender says the power fails often along the coast road. More than once, Bagdani has gone to the bar to view a live game during an outage."

"Did he mention the size of his entourage?"

"Without my even asking—he said 'a few men.' The bartender was sour that none of them drank or ordered food. They don't even watch the game, and it puts one of his biggest tables out of commission for hours."

Slaton saw where Jakob was heading. It had merit: there would still be security to deal with, but more manageable numbers, and they wouldn't be on particularly high alert. "So, if there was a game, and if we could cut the power to his house at the right time . . ."

"I already checked," Jakob said, having clearly researched the concept. "There is a game tomorrow."

"One problem with that," Nora said. She led back to the kitchen table and pulled two overhead images clear—one was a recent shot with excellent resolution, the other an archived photo that was date-stamped eight months earlier. She tapped her finger on the more recent shot, pointing to a corner of the roof. "He's got a new generator."

Slaton compared the two images and saw she was right: in the more recent shot, the unmistakable boxlike shroud of a high-capacity generator had been added. "Good catch. I can even see construction debris from the installation."

The room fell silent. Then Slaton noticed something else on the roof.

"There might be another way," he said.

"What's that?" Nora asked.

Slaton told her, improvising as he went.

"Seriously?" she asked.

"Humor me."

"It's an ICECRYPT 1.1-meter antenna with a coaxial leading to an internal splitter." Nora was reading the research results from a laptop.

Slaton looked over her shoulder and saw a TV satellite dish exactly like the one on the rooftop. "That's it."

"The carrier's logo is on the dish, so we know which provider he's using. I checked the schedule and Jakob's right. Juventus plays tomorrow at noon, an away league game against a top team."

Jakob said, "If we can knock out the satellite, there's a good chance he'll show up at the bar."

"But how do we disable it?" Nora asked. "There are two guys on that roof at all times—there's no way to reach the antenna without being seen."

Slaton went to the bedroom, parked behind the optic. He scanned the rooftop, found the dish, and studied it at length. Range, angles, environmental variables—the intimate ground he owned. "I could do it from here."

Nora looked at him incredulously. "How? Shoot the antenna full of holes? That would be like banging a hammer on a metal trash can lid—the guards would go nuts."

"The antenna's not the weak point," he said, pulling away. "I could take out the cable."

"Hit a coaxial cable from . . . what, close to a mile?"

"Three-quarters. And I didn't say it would be easy."

There was a sequenced knock at the front door, and it turned out to be right on cue.

Avram went to answer it, and moments later he reappeared in the company of a man carrying a heavy plastic case that appeared shaped for a set of golf clubs. The diplomatic seals were still intact. After setting it carefully on the floor in the corner of the room, he introduced himself as Wilson. Slaton wasn't sure if that was his first or last name, but it worked either way.

Slaton went to the container, broke the seal, and revealed his requested cache. He began by checking that both weapons were clear. The AWM was topped by a Schmidt & Bender high power riflescope, and an ammo box held three full, five-round magazines. The SIG came with a basic Tritium night sight and two full mags. Only after he'd finished his inspection did Slaton realize everyone was watching him.

"You can cut the cable with that?" Nora asked, gesturing to the rifle.

"I don't see why not," Slaton said. "It's not as hard as it sounds. I saw about five feet of cable on the roof, which presents a bigger target. At such a shallow angle the bullet would likely ricochet, and between the round itself and chips of roofing material—it might take a few tries, but we're talking about a pretty lightweight cable. On the other hand, you have a point about the guards. They might hear a round strike the roof. But I think we can minimize that problem."

"We would also need a plan for handling things in the bar," said Jakob.

"True," Slaton agreed. He checked his watch. 1:20 in the morning. "What time does the pub open?"

"Breakfast begins at seven," said Jakob.

"All right. I want two of you to go scout the place early, but not Jakob—you're a familiar face, which could lead to complications. I also want Nora to stay clear until later." A nod from both, even though Slaton's reasoning for Nora's exclusion wasn't clear. Wilson volunteered, and said that Ed, who was racked out, could join him.

Slaton approved it, and added, "Take a lot of pictures, as much of the interior as possible. Also, the surrounding area. Front and back of the pub, streets, parking areas . . . everything. Let's put in a request for overheads as well. How many cars do we have right now?"

"Three, counting yours," said Nora. "But I can get whatever you need."

The plan began to build as such plans did, a loose framework where elements were added, problems defined. Half an hour later they were drawing diagrams and assigning duties.

With everyone on task, Slaton diverted to the bedroom. He paused at the door and scanned wall to wall. A small desk with a wooden chair drew his attention. He pushed the desk nearer the sliding glass door, situating it lengthwise. The chair went behind it. Retrieving the rifle, he sat on the chair and tested his makeshift platform. The height wasn't ideal, but there was no perfect shooting stand—you always had to adapt, find a comfort zone.

He inspected the rifle more closely; it was in excellent condition. Not a new weapon, but limited use. There was a time, a decade ago, when he might have imagined who else had used it, against what targets. He no longer bothered.

For the first time he looked through the rifle's optic, made a few adjustments, and then trained it on the darkened roof nearly a mile away. He easily found the satellite dish, and from there Slaton tracked the cable. It snaked out of the mounting tube and ran toward a knee wall where it disappeared into the house. As Nora had warned, the fronds of a nearby palm tree swayed occasionally into view. A hundred vacationers had probably thought it delightful. *One man's ambiance is another's nuisance,* he thought. Slaton noted an uneven breeze sweeping up the cliff from the sea. The winds would be unpredictable here, and hitting a five-foot-long, quarter-inch-wide target at such a range, barring dumb luck, would likely require more than one shot.

Whatever it takes, he thought.

In the morning, he would survey the cable in daylight and seek out a section where it rested on something solid, hopefully concrete. The harder the surface, the better the odds of skipping the bullet, effectively doubling his chances of success. And chips of flying concrete would be better than soft roofing material for fragging the cable indirectly. Altogether, small advantages, but he would embrace every one.

The suppressor would lessen the sound of the shot, yet the bullet itself would create a supersonic crack owing to its muzzle velocity. Fortunately, at this range the sound of the shock wave would be muted. What *was* a concern was the sound of the bullet actually striking the roof. Depending on where the guards were standing, they might notice it; on the other hand, the sound could easily be lost to the midmorning cacophony of cars and construction. Directly behind the antenna was a solid perimeter knee wall. That was a plus: it would absorb the round, protecting any innocents beyond.

In the end, he deemed the risk manageable. If the crew on the roof were astute—*very* astute—they might put it all together. A sharp, close-in noise, perhaps a few chips of concrete spraying, followed by a distant crack. To mitigate that threat, Slaton would do what all snipers did: keep the number of shots to a minimum.

He set the rifle down and studied the target area with his unaided shooter's eye. The distant compound sat brooding in the night, muted squares of light framing its windows like a backlit dollhouse.

Aim. Timing. Luck.

He would need them all to make the plan work.

FORTY-SIX

The pub was called The Shamrock. There wasn't an Irishman in sight. A pugilistic leprechaun was painted on a sign hanging above the door: fists raised, spoiling for a fight, he looked like a cross between Notre Dame's mascot and a Serbian hit man. Inside were a few neon four-leaf clovers and brass rails, but the beer was local, the music Europop, and the morning bartender would have looked right at home in the morning police lineup.

The two CIA officers arrived and took a table in the middle of the room. Both spoke Albanian, although neither well enough to pass for a local. That being the case, they played the tourist card: casual dress, loud English, expect to be waited on. Wilson wore a polo shirt with the Montreal Canadiens logo, his go-to disinformation attire.

At seven thirty in the morning there were three other patrons: a pair of old men huddled in a corner debating politics over breakfast, and a sullen man at the bar hunched over a beer. The bartender came over and greeted them in English, steamrolling vowels to describe the morning special as "bongers and mush."

Wilson and Ed nodded smilingly, not knowing or caring what they were ordering. As soon as the barkeep disappeared into the kitchen, their phones came out. It had become something of an art form, even a competition, among intelligence officers to manipulate their phones to record images while appearing to perform other tasks. The CIA had conveniently devised an app that allowed the volume keys on a standard iPhone to activate the camera. While the holder scrolled through websites or text messages on his screen, the up button silently activated still shots, while the down button recorded video. It allowed agents to gather intel without the camera screen giving away their intent.

The pair captured every corner of the room from separate angles, and when the bartender disappeared to check on their food, Ed beelined for the restroom in the rear hallway, recording all the way. When the food arrived—the odds-on favorite, sausages and mashed potatoes—both ersatz Canadians put away their phones and dug in. This led to the biggest surprise of the morning: the food was actually good.

Outside The Shamrock, much the same was happening. Jakob and Avram scoured the nearby streets and alleys. They took pictures, drew mental maps, and took note of every person they saw.

By nine o'clock, all four officers were back at the villa on the hill.

In the twenty hours since *Sibir* had docked in Kimchaek, North Korea, the CIA's eyes in the sky had not so much as blinked. The continuous, overlapping coverage was sourced from both air- and space-based surveillance platforms using various bandwidths. In spite of it, the proceedings on the docks had everyone stumped.

"What the hell are they doing?" Anna Sorensen asked.

She was standing behind an analyst in the Langley operations center, watching a feed from an NRO satellite. Sorensen was exhausted and had been avoiding mirrors for the last day. Her ponytail had lost its grip, strands of blond hair flying loose, and her clothes looked like crepe paper from all the wrinkles. She was sure there were serious bags under her eyes. If this whole mess ever got resolved, she imagined going somewhere with Jammer for a long weekend. A little carpe diem.

But then, that was the problem with running SAC/SOG—the days always seized you.

"Whatever it is," the woman at the screen said, "they're trying to hide it. Those tarps set up on deck have some kind of radar-scattering coating. We can't penetrate to image, and electro-optical wavelengths are obviously useless."

Sorensen muttered aloud, "And of all the countries in the world, North Korea is the one where our ground game is nonexistent."

"Maybe that's no accident," the analyst ventured.

It was a valid point. Sorensen speculated, "Cleary they're removing something from the ship."

"That would be my guess."

"And they've been working on it for a day now."

"True."

"Have you seen any sign of where it might be going?"

The analyst used a pen to tap the screen, enlarging a standard shipping container near *Sibir*'s loading platform. "Whatever it is, it's probably being put in these containers. We've seen two get pulled away so far. They leave the pier and disappear into this warehouse." She pointed to the biggest building in the port. "On the other side are loading docks—trucks coming and going constantly, heading throughout the country. Then again, some of the containers are moved to this area." She tapped on rows of containers and crates near a neighboring pier. "Most of those are transferred to outbound ships."

Sorensen caught the analyst's gaze momentarily. "You thinking what I'm thinking?" she asked.

"Probably," the woman replied. "The weapon used to down Raven 44 is being disassembled and shipped out."

Sorensen nodded. "And figuring out where will be like tracking a lone piece of shrapnel from a ten-ton bomb burst."

———————

Timing was everything. That was the consensus opinion of the team at the villa. The game featuring Juventus began at noon, and the nuance of when to "cut the cord" loomed large. If they clipped the signal too soon, someone at the compound might suggest troubleshooting, which could conceivably include a close inspection of the rooftop antenna and cable. Do it after the game began, and a frustrated Bagdani might not consider diverting to the pub. "Especially," Wilson commented astutely, "if Juve falls behind by a goal or two."

In the end they settled on fifteen minutes before kickoff. It left little time to research the problem, yet just enough for a rushed diversion to the pub.

By eleven that morning, everything was in place. Only Slaton's Land Rover remained at the villa. One more car had been procured, which meant three vehicles were positioned around the pub. One was in the back alley, where a handful of parking spots were utilized by the employees of nearby businesses. It would serve as the primary car for the arms merchant's extraction. Jakob remained in that vehicle—having already spoken to the bartender about Bagdani, he couldn't be inside when the arms merchant arrived. Nora, Logan, and Avram were in a second sedan. They would park some distance away, leave the car to serve as a backup, and walk to the pub. The three would split up and enter shortly before Bagdani's expected arrival, with Avram going solo. The third car, with Ed and Wilson, would serve as a floater, ready to run interference in any pursuit and provide reinforcements.

Everyone waited for the *go* signal from Slaton.

Slaton had been concerned about the security team on the roof recognizing the sounds of his bullets striking. As a countermeasure, another employee from the Israeli embassy had been recruited. He was in fact not Mossad, but a foreign ministry employee, no training whatsoever in tradecraft. Slaton decided it didn't matter given his simple chore: a distraction that he hoped would give cover in the critical moments.

By eleven thirty, all was going to plan. Outside the pub things were quiet. There had been no sign of police in the area, and traffic on the sidewalks was sparse. Avram was the first to enter the pub, and he took a seat at the end of the bar nearest the television. He reported via text that all was clear. He explained to the bartender, quite truthfully, that he hoped to see Juve play at noon. The AC Milan supporter grumbled something under his breath, but soon the pregame buildup was running on a wall-mounted screen framed by neon beer signs.

By eleven forty, things were still going smoothly.

Everyone waited.

Alone at the villa, Slaton settled in behind his rifle.

FORTY-SEVEN

The compound looked big and broad, a wash of Adriatic white under the brilliant midday sun. There were multiple tiers of flat rooftop, a schizophrenic wedding cake stepped to various levels. Slaton knew from their reconnaissance that the first level was an expansive garage, graduating upward to the third-floor living areas.

The satellite dish was on the highest rooftop. Fortunately for Slaton, the villa in which he was perched was on higher ground than Bagdani's fortress, giving a slightly downward look angle. A sniper's high ground.

He carefully studied the guards through his optic. There were two, both positioned on segments of the wider second-floor roof. Shifting his reticle between them, he thought they looked alert and engaged—no easy chore, as anyone who'd ever stood guard duty knew. These were professionals, hired by a man who kept perhaps the world's most extensive black book of guns-for-hire. Both were armed with handguns in shoulder holsters, and Slaton had caught a glimpse beneath one jacket lapel of two spare magazines. They had binoculars and earbuds, and while Albanian law precluded the open display of heavy weapons, Slaton noted a cabinet near the stairwell door that was sized perfectly for a few assault rifles.

The two men were separated by a hundred feet, one overlooking the northern perimeter, the other facing south—Slaton's direction. The satellite dish was central, mounted on one of the third-floor tiers. Slaton adjusted his position in the chair, his right elbow and left forearm anchored on the desk. He'd noted a slight wobble in the desk earlier and corrected it using a scrap of wood as a makeshift shim. He was deep enough into the room to be in shadow, and he'd arranged the sliding door and curtains to give him a clear line of sight.

After studying the dish and cable carefully, he settled on severing the coaxial near the point where it disappeared into the wall. A rough hole had been gouged by the installer, and Slaton realized that any rounds striking the junction might make the opening larger but wouldn't change its jagged appearance. He doubted they would penetrate the far side, but if they did, the exterior face couldn't be seen from either guard post.

A slight breeze swept in through the open slider. Slaton estimated the wind to be six knots from his left, with a slight updraft from the cliffs. A festive wind sock on a villa patio downrange, cast in the image of a happy whale, gave a midpoint estimate that matched.

11:44.

He settled his reticle on the cable, applied his calculated wind correction. His finger touched the trigger.

The distraction was set to begin soon.

One palm tree, fifty feet away, remained a problem. The pulsing wind caused a particular frond to rise and fall, sweeping occasionally through his line of fire. He'd considered a round or two to trim the frond at its base, but decided it wasn't worth the risk. It moved in a predictable rhythm, and given that his target was inanimate, he could time the cycle and shoot accordingly.

His breathing slowed. His body fell still, relaxed.

11:45.

Slaton's audible cover came right on cue: Somewhere on the street near Bagdani's compound, a motorcycle began revving an unmuffled engine. The foreign ministry kid gunned the bike repeatedly, even inducing a few backfires.

The palm frond undulated on the breeze, in and out of view. The cable lay dead center in Slaton's wind-corrected sight picture.

The trigger broke and the first round sailed downrange.

It took slightly over two seconds to reach the roof, which was easily enough time for Slaton to reacquire after the recoil. He saw the round strike—a miss, but barely. He had nicked the insulation, an error to the one o'clock position based on where the bullet struck the wall.

After fifteen seconds, the revving motorcycle went to idle. Exactly as planned.

Using the optic, Slaton observed the southern guard. He wasn't looking at the third-floor wall, but rather searching for the motorbike with his binoculars—an unexpected bonus.

Ten seconds later the revving began again. Slaton was ready, his correction already calculated, and he ran through the drill a second time. Noise, palm frond, relax, trigger pressure.

His second round ricocheted off the roof just behind the cable, yet somehow did no damage. Half a minute later, the third shot succeeded; it severed the cable cleanly, a frayed wire jutting up at a ninety-degree angle.

So far, so good.

Slaton quickly sent a group text.

Moments later, on the street in front of Bagdani's compound, an unseen motorcycle could be heard shifting through gears. Its engine noise soon faded.

Less than a mile away, a car with two men parked in front of The Shamrock pub.

Across the street from the car, a couple walked into the pub for lunch, taking a table near the back hall.

While the couple were taking their seats, a dark-featured man at the nearby bar took a sip of his beer. On the television in front of him, the "countdown to kickoff" clock on the pregame show showed sixteen minutes.

Slaton remained still. There was nothing to do but watch.

The entire plan, of course, was no more than a premise—conjecture based on the musings of a local bartender. Slaton had cut the satellite cable, but would the scheme play out as they hoped? Would Bagdani rush off to the pub, as he apparently had in the past, to watch his favorite team? Or was he busy working right then, procuring more hired hands for a terrorist known as Lazarus?

If the ploy failed, they would be back to square one, and against a ticking clock: searching for some other way to get their hands on Bagdani, which could mean storming his heavily guarded fortress. Slaton shifted his reticle back and forth between the guards. After spending the last half hour concentrating on a coaxial cable, their heads filled his scope like melons.

With all the world's patience, he sat back and did what snipers did best. He waited.

While Slaton sat impassively in a sun-splashed Adriatic villa, another man leaned on the rail of a balcony a thousand miles away. The small veranda was one of a hundred siding a sun-beaten building in south Tel Aviv, and while it was nowhere near the sea, if one leaned over the rail, near the far end and at just the right angle, a tiny slice of the distant Mediterranean could be seen.

The owner could have afforded far better, one of the penthouse condos in Netanya with a sweeping beachfront vista. Such trappings, however, had long ago ceased to interest Lazarus. When it came to residences, obscurity was paramount. And the flat in Neve Sha'anan, he was sure, was the last place on earth the traitorous Israelis would be searching for him: a tenement right under their noses.

He lowered himself into a cheap plastic chair, taking the weight off his bad leg. He leaned back and felt the sun on his face, the balmy breeze in his hair. Pleasant smells wafted up from the pizza shop below, which was run, in an ode to globalization, by a Sudanese refugee. The neighborhood was its usual buzzing self. Balconies were packed with bicycles, grills, and terra-cotta-potted palms; he heard his next-door neighbor's laundry snapping in the breeze. Across the divide of the narrow street two women chatted across a rail, their children squealing in the background. Lazarus found it all comforting, a reassuring blanket of humanity.

He got up and went inside. Taking a seat in his best chair, he addressed a laptop and flicked through documents until he found the list of requirements for the "Chapter Two" strikes. That was how The Trident referred to them, as if they were authoring a book that would tell the story of the future.

And perhaps they are, he allowed.

He had already purchased aircraft for two prospective attacks. The first was a tiny trainer, a cast-off Cessna from a North Carolina flight school. Lazarus hadn't been given any details of that mission, only that a basic four-seat aircraft would be required. He decided it could hardly be more ambitious than the second strike.

For that undertaking he'd purchased a Pilatus PC-12, a single-engine turboprop that was also nearing the end of its service life. The aircraft was presently on a small Bahamian island undergoing general maintenance. There were scores of airfields in the Bahamas that went largely ignored, tiny uncontrolled strips, many on privately owned cays, with virtually no oversight. And most of them, conveniently, were within two hours' flying time of Miami Beach.

Bagdani had identified a prospective pilot some weeks ago, a Venezuelan who'd been let go from his oil company job in Caracas, and who was desperate to get back in the air. If the mission ever received the green light, the pilot would be hired to make a delivery to upstate New York. He would be given a detailed route to fly and told nothing about what he was hauling.

The weapon, like the others, was an experimental device. Lazarus was no scientist, but he knew it was designed to emit a strong but localized electromagnetic pulse. Delivered at low altitude, and focused on Wall Street, it had the potential to debilitate Western financial markets for weeks, if not months. Other, less hardened, computers would also go down—insurance companies, banks, retailers, law firms—all sent to digital ruin, and with no damage whatsoever to people or buildings.

Of all the strikes proposed, Lazarus thought this one the most dubious. He'd spoken briefly with the lead engineer—he had needed specs on what kind of aircraft would be required—and the man had offered some backstory. The notion of a small-scale EMP weapon had been around for decades, and the science was solid. This particular program had run into trouble, however, when the government research lab designing it made a damning admission in their midcourse evaluation: any test of the device would be impossible to hide. This meant that subsequent use of a production version could easily be sourced. In effect, outside of a strategic nuclear exchange, the weapon had virtually no functionality. The lone device built was relegated to the R&D dustbin. A never tested, one-off wonder.

Since the program's termination, however, a number of other nations, Russia included, had begun tinkering with similar concepts. This wasn't lost on The Trident—the muddying of accountability if the unique device was to be used. The engineer gave the weapon a fifty-fifty chance of even working, and if it did, he suggested the effects on financial market computers would be scattershot at best. Even so, Lazarus couldn't discount what he'd witnessed so far. Wrangel, Crimea, the Indian Ocean: The Trident's success had been remarkable. Three strikes, all doing significant damage, and still the Americans had no idea who was behind it. His employers were proving masters at shadowboxing; it was asymmetrical warfare on steroids.

No, Lazarus thought, *not steroids. On hyperdrive.*

The strategy was only a progression of what had been brewing for decades. Gone were the days of dueling superpowers, of great land armies engaging in armored battles. That had gone the way of horse-mounted cavalry and sabers. Asymmetrical warfare was where the future lay— moving rent-free into your enemy's head. The Trident's strategy was an evolution following the little green men of Russia's Wagner Group: not just brandless soldiers, secondhand tanks, and the occasional air strike from an unmarked attack jet. The Trident were leapfrogging to the latest technologies. Some of the weapons were unproven, others faced technological hurdles or treaty limitations. To employ them openly would constitute a blatant act of war. To use them clandestinely, however, with the right cutouts, with sufficient deniability, was an entirely new method of warfare. Without sureness of who the enemy was, no law-abiding nation could respond in good conscience. And there lay the American's Achilles' heel—their conscience was forever their guide.

Lazarus worked for an hour, which was typically his limit. He got up slowly, stretched to loosen a few aches, then diverted back to the modest balcony. Leaning over the rail, he saw the Mediterranean in the distance, shining in its clarity. It was a view he wouldn't have for much longer. Soon *Poyarka* would undertake her strike, and with that The Trident's first chapter would end. By then, Lazarus hoped, his own private mission would also be complete—the one he'd been planning for eight agonizing years.

And when it was done? Assuming he survived, he had enough Bitcoin stashed away to disappear. Or at least, as best as one could these days.

Of his three objectives, one was already complete: the ruin of Anton Bloch.

Satisfaction of the others was imminent.

His gaze shifted from the sea to the city, the warrens of Neve Sha'anan vibrant and alive. This was the place of his birth. The city he'd called home until the traitors of Mossad had turned on him. And none more than the *kidon* himself.

Lazarus had lured David Slaton into the open, and now it was time to extract his revenge. That was the only way he could ever sate his demons.

FORTY-EIGHT

It took ten minutes.

Slaton had switched to a pair of binoculars, and the first sign of change was a burst of comm from the guards on the roof. Both began talking, and they exchanged a few purposeful hand signals. One disappeared into the stairwell, leaving the other alone on watch—a first since surveillance had begun.

Slaton shifted his attention to the compound entrance. From where he stood, he could just make out the front portico and a short driveway connecting to the garage. Less than a minute after the guard's departure, a big Audi sedan pulled out of the garage and wheeled to the front door. Slaton trained the binoculars on the entrance and watched a group emerge. He easily picked out Bagdani from the pictures in his file, big and burly with a boss's swagger. More important was what was around him. The driver in the car appeared to be alone, and Slaton saw two men go with Bagdani—one bundled in front, and the other sat in back next to the arms merchant. No other car appeared.

This was the vital detail, and it fell in the midrange of their planning. Bagdani plus two had been the dream. Bagdani plus four the limit. Anything more, given their own manpower, would severely complicate an extraction.

The car snaked up the drive and paused for the gate to open. At the street it turned right, in the direction of The Shamrock. Not a slam dunk, but another positive sign. In five minutes, they would have their answer.

Slaton set down the binoculars and hurried outside, locking the front door behind him. If they were able to abduct Bagdani cleanly, a team of Americans would arrive later to sanitize the villa. And if things didn't go to plan? Then they would reconvene at the villa and try to come up with plan B.

Slaton typed out the critical message on his phone before putting the Rover into gear: Inbound + 3. On my way.

Their luck held: the Audi made a beeline for the pub, pulling in front five minutes after kickoff. Slaton drove as fast as he dared on the steep seaside roads and arrived in time to see Bagdani passing beneath the front awning with his entourage.

Unfortunately, all three bodyguards went inside with him. He'd been hoping one would stay with the car, but either way, the op was a go. He parked two streets away, and then walked briskly to join Jakob in the car near the back entrance.

"I saw him go in," Slaton said, sliding in next to the Israeli. "All three guards are with him."

"There is no word yet on which table they've taken."

Nora and Logan, having arrived early, had taken the table nearest the lone television—effectively holding it. Minutes before Bagdani and his crew arrived, they switched to an empty table directly behind it. They'd reported that the place wasn't full, three other tables occupied by five locals. Avram was still alone at the bar, nursing a beer and pretending to watch the game.

Jakob kept his eyes on the alley while Slaton concentrated on his phone. A message from Avram flashed to the screen. Success, he relayed. They took the big table. A pause, then a follow-up. Better yet, one man went back out to the car. He's sitting overwatch in the Audi.

Jakob pursed his lips. "Not a bad move. The place is not busy, and it gives them eyes outside."

"It makes our job easier," Slaton said.

They assumed all three men were armed. Of Slaton's three operatives inside, two were carrying, as were he and Jakob. Logan had little tactical experience, and Slaton had made the call—the kid seemed tentative, and he didn't want someone packing who might not conceal or use a weapon with discipline. The last thing he needed was a gunfight in a crowded bar.

He checked his watch. The game had reached the twelve minute mark. With all going to plan, he gave the order everyone was waiting for, typing out: Option 1. We wait.

Twenty minutes later nothing had changed.

While Bagdani sat glued to the game, his men stuck to their task, the bulk of their attention on the entrances. There was food on the table, and better yet, drinks—a deviation from what the bartender had told Jakob regarding the previous visits. These bodyguards might have been disciplined, but they weren't above letting the boss buy them a beer. Both men had half-full glasses, while Bagdani was working on his second. Slaton suspected he might soon order a third—Juve was behind two–nil.

"Five minutes to go," Slaton said to Jakob. Halftime, the forty-five-minute mark, was fast approaching.

The timing of their plan was less precise than Slaton would have liked, centered around a referee's watch over a hundred miles away. Soccer, maddeningly, did not run on a public clock—the referee instead added discretionary "injury time" after the forty-five-minute mark. Still, a minute one way or the other shouldn't matter. They were banking on the idea that Bagdani would do what virtually all men did at halftime, especially those who'd just downed two beers: he would use the bathroom. It was their best chance to separate him from his security. If that didn't work out, they would be forced into a direct grab in the main room.

Inside the pub, at precisely forty-four minutes on the game clock, Nora got up and walked to the hallway where the bathrooms were located: one men's, one women's. Nearing the door with the dress-clad figure, she paused and pulled a compact from her purse. She dabbed at her lips while using the mirror to glance over her shoulder. She could see the shoulder of one of the seated guards, but he wasn't watching her. She edged toward the door at the end of the hall. It led outside, and the team this morning had reported seeing the cook pass through twice to dump garbage into the bins in the alley. Her job was to make sure it hadn't been locked in the interim. The handle turned freely. She cracked the door open slightly, then disappeared into the ladies' room.

Slaton saw the door shift ever so slightly, and a gap appeared at the frame. "Good girl," he said rhetorically. "Time to move."

He and Jakob got out and walked to the door. Slaton paused to listen, then edged it open slightly and double-checked there was no one in the hall. With a nod to Jakob, they both hurried inside. Passing the door with the *W,* Slaton gave it a single rap with his knuckles. He and Jakob disappeared into the men's room.

The bathroom matched the pictures from this morning's reconnaissance: one wash basin, one urinal, and a toilet with a privacy stall. The fixtures were dated and yellow, and Slaton saw an uneven water stain around the baseboard from some ancient plumbing disaster.

A text buzzed from Avram at the bar: Halftime whistle. Standby.

Things would happen quickly now.

Slaton had briefed a number of variations on how they would proceed. If Bagdani declared an urge to use the toilet, it was possible one of his guards might inspect it first. Then again, they might clear only the hallway. In a perfect world, the security men would do nothing at all, remaining at the table while Bagdani addressed his call of nature. If a guard did come to clear the room, they would hopefully have a few seconds' notice: Jakob would stand on the back of the toilet while Slaton took the seat, only his legs visible beneath the closed door of the stall. On appearances, he would appear to be a cook on break—notwithstanding the SIG that would be poised in his hand.

For a time, nothing happened. Bagdani took out his phone and made a call. The guards kept their focus. Everyone waited. Slaton hoped none of the other patrons, only two of whom seemed to be watching the game, needed to use the toilet. Nora remained in the ladies' room next door.

Finally, with minutes to go before the second half, Avram reported: Bagdani talking to guards. Pointing to hall.

Seconds later, success, and it turned out to be the middle ground. One of Bagdani's men got up and checked the hallway. Nora had emerged at the far end. She was primping in front of the ladies' room, her back turned but the mirror again canted down the hall behind her. The guard nodded that the coast was clear.

Bagdani got up.

Slaton read the incoming text: Coming now.

He pocketed his phone and put his back to the wall near the door. Jakob mirrored him on the opposite side. Slaton looked across and held a finger to his lips. He wasn't pleading for silence—that was a given—but rather giving a reminder to honor a curious order he had not yet explained. There was to be no speaking in Bagdani's presence, and if they did have to coordinate they would use Hebrew.

Outside in the hall, Nora headed toward the bar. She passed Bagdani in the narrow corridor, and they bladed past one another. Once she was clear, she glanced at the guard ahead. Nora was not an unattractive woman, and she held his gaze just a bit longer than necessary. Interest, perhaps.

The man smiled and backed up slightly to let her pass.

Bagdani pushed through the bathroom door. It was halfway closed when Slaton rushed him from the right. The Albanian was big, so Slaton didn't hold back. He got the man off-balance, then redirected his momentum. With one hand seizing his jacket and the other a handful of hair, he propelled Bagdani cranium-first across the room. His head struck the chipped plaster wall, and he dropped like a sack of wet gravel. Jakob was on him immediately, stifling a barely audible groan with a rag and a roll of duct tape.

The noise had been minimal, Bagdani so taken by surprise it never occurred to him to shout for help. All the same, Slaton moved to the door and listened. He heard no signs of a reaction outside.

He gave Jakob a thumbs-up. The Mossad man rolled Bagdani facedown and began securing his hands with heavy-gauge zip ties. He didn't tie the wrists together, but rather attached each to his belt on the respective hip—it wasn't a very secure method but would give a more natural appearance for the short crossing to the car. Once they were in the back seat, they could make it more permanent.

Next came the needle.

Jakob sank a hypodermic with 5ccs of a fast-acting tranquillizer into Bagdani's thigh. It would take two minutes to kick in, or so they'd been told, sedating him for the car ride. Jakob rolled the Albanian on his back and he blinked once. He looked dazed, a bloody welt growing on his forehead. Slaton saw a spiderweb crater of plaster on the wall near the wash basin and thought he might have overdone it. *Better that than the other*, he allowed.

There were no text updates. Still no sound other than the distant TV. A whistle blew to start the second half. The next thing Slaton heard flipped the op entirely: Nora shouting for help.

FORTY-NINE

Slaton gave Jakob a closed-fist *hold* signal as he quickly drew his Sig. He burst through the door with the gun level. Nora was at the top of the hall, grappling with the guard, a tall, muscular man with ponytailed hair. Having no clear shot, Slaton rushed him. In the background he saw Avram leap toward the table where the other guard had to be, followed by a massive crash of furniture.

The guard in front of Slaton put Nora in a choke hold. She was fighting back gamely, but clearly fading. When ponytail spotted Slaton bearing down, gun in hand, he recognized the higher threat. He tried to twist Nora between them, turn her into a shield, but Slaton bladed between them like a flying wedge. The man lost his grip on Nora, and both he and Slaton crashed toward the bar. Slaton whirled around with the SIG in a close-quarters, bent-arm grip—he didn't intend to shoot, but ponytail had no way of knowing it. Then, just as the man saw the gun and fell still, Slaton got whacked on the arm from behind with what felt like a club. The SIG went flying, tumbling toward the melee across the room.

His arm stinging in pain, Slaton half turned and saw the bartender leaning over the bar. He was cocking back a cricket bat for a second swing. With threats in front and behind, Slaton made his choice instantly. He beat the barkeep to the punch, jabbing a full-force palm-strike into his face that sent him bowling into the pit behind the bar. Slaton crouched low as he turned back, not sure what was coming. Ponytail was two steps away, drawing a weapon from his shoulder holster.

Slaton lunged for his gun hand and locked it down tight. The big man shifted his weight, and they tumbled together through a battered pair of saloon doors into the kitchen. Slaton kept a relentless grip on the gun, and they grappled and stumbled across the worn tile floor. He caught a glimpse of a skinny young kid in a white apron planted against the far wall—there was a look of abject fear on his face, an iron skillet in his hand. For a moment Slaton thought he might follow the bartender's lead and swing the skillet. Instead he dropped it clanging to the floor and ran out.

Ponytail planted a leg behind Slaton, trying to put him on the floor. Slaton sensed it and countered by lowering his base. He saw improvised weapons everywhere: knives, heavy pots, hot surfaces. With better leverage, Slaton twisted left and forced the man's gun hand onto a grill full of sizzling bacon. He screamed and pulled away, yet somehow kept his grip on the gun.

Ponytail pushed away desperately from the grill, and Slaton capital-ized, rotating ninety degrees and planting a knee in his groin. The instant he doubled over, Slaton released one hand from his arm, grabbed the base of his ponytail, and plunged his face into a deep fryer.

The gun clattered to the floor as ponytail rocketed back from the fryer and crumpled, rolling on the greasy tile and screaming. Slaton left the man where he was, writhing and yelling, clutching his ruined face. His own left arm stung, having been splattered by boiling grease, and he tried to wipe it off on the side of his pants.

The saloon doors parted and Nora appeared. She spotted the dropped weapon by her feet and picked it up. Slaton recognized it as a Glock 19. He held out a hand, and without hesitation she handed it over. No sooner had she done so than Slaton saw alarm in her eyes as they snagged on something behind him. He whipped right and brought the Glock to bear. Behind the dead-level, Tritium-enhanced sight he saw the bartender. He was frozen at the connecter to the bar with the cricket bat still in his hand.

Without a word, Slaton flicked the barrel once toward the exit. The bartender didn't hesitate, disappearing in a clatter of heavy footsteps.

Slaton rushed back to the hall, Nora right behind. The place had emp-tied and the front door was wide open. The table near the television lay splintered on the floor, shattered wood and flatware all around. Avram and Logan had the second guard facedown on the floor. He wasn't mov-ing, and there was blood on the back of his head. Slaton guessed he was alive, since the green CIA kid was planted on his back. Nora went to the front window, checked the situation outside, and gave a thumbs-up to say the coast was clear.

Avram nodded. The situation was back under control.

It's about damned time, Slaton thought.

He quickly accounted for all the weapons, then spun a finger in the air, the international signal for *Let's get the hell out of here.*

The scene in the North Korean port of Kimchaek seemed more and more like the old shell game. Only instead of three cups and a ball, it was two hundred containers, a dozen roads, six ships, and four warehouses, all of which, it was suspected, concealed the transfer of one disassembled directed-energy weapon.

Sorensen conceded that trying to track it was futile, and even felt a trace of admiration for whoever had concocted the scheme. Not only had they managed to shoot down a reconnaissance jet, but they were now very effectively hiding the evidence. And *Atlas*, the other ship that had attacked an American military asset, was on the bottom of the Indian Ocean.

She stared at the feed from the harbor in Kimchaek. It was tempt-ing to blame North Korea for what was going on, yet while she reckoned they might be complicit, laying it all at their feet felt wrong. On principle she didn't doubt the North Koreans might attempt such strikes, yet she couldn't cross the hurdle that the technology seemed beyond them.

Frustration was getting the better of her, her mood sinking, when a bit of good news finally arrived. She was handed a message from the team in Tirana: *Bagdani in custody. No major complications. Heading to Bravo.*

Sorensen blew out a long sigh of relief. Bravo was a prearranged safe house outside town. Slaton had come through.

"It's about time we got a damn break," she said under her breath.

FIFTY

Slaton took the wheel while Jakob sat in back with a drugged and bound Bagdani. The others dispersed to the remaining vehicles, two of which would return to the embassy. As Slaton pulled out of the alley, he saw Bagdani's Audi still parked in the main street. The only difference now: the driver's-side door lay detached and crumpled in the road twenty feet away.

He got on his phone, and Wilson, who'd been stationed out front, explained what had happened. Bagdani's third man realized something was wrong only when the barkeeper had bolted frantically from the pub with a cricket bat in his hand. Ed had wheeled out from his parking spot, three slots behind the Audi, and clipped the driver's door as it opened. As the stunned guard recoiled into the Audi, Ed and Wilson stopped, got out, and leveled their weapons at Bagdani's man from behind their own car. There was no hesitation from the guard: He bailed out the passenger side and disappeared down the street. It was conceivable he'd called for reinforcements from the compound, but even if he had, they would never reach the pub in time. More likely, the guard was halfway to the airport and the first outbound flight.

In Slaton's experience, that was the trouble with rent-a-soldiers—no matter how impressive their training and background, their commitment to the cause never went further than the next paycheck.

For a mile he drove quickly to separate from the pub, but then slowed so as to not draw attention. Their prearranged safe house was a farm in the nearby countryside, and within ten minutes Slaton was navigating a rural road with light traffic and no cameras—always a plus these days. The deeply pitted lane curved into the hills, and a final left transitioned to a rutted dirt path. Vegetation pressed in from both sides, and he veered left and right to avoid rain-swollen potholes. Slaton did his best to keep the speed up, and every time the car bottomed out he heard a moan from the back.

"How's he doing?" he asked in Hebrew. Heavy sedatives could backfire, he knew, if the subject had complicating medical conditions, and Bagdani didn't appear to be the model of a healthy lifestyle.

"He is still with us," Jakob replied.

Soon the safe house came into view, a weather-beaten farm cottage. The main house was square with loose clapboard siding and a gabled roof that sagged with age. Having studied pictures of the place, Slaton knew the garage was in back. He pulled up to find Nora standing near the open door of what was once probably a barn. It was in worse shape than the house, but he cared only that it was big enough to conceal two vehicles. Nora's embassy sedan was already inside, along with Logan and Avram.

Slaton pulled inside, and as soon as he got out, Nora said, "Sorry for the trouble back there. The guy reached inside his jacket and I thought he might be going for a gun. I figured I had to do something."

"You did fine," he said. "It all worked out."

"Not as clean a grab as we'd hoped."

"Trust me, it's never as clean as you hope. The police will show up, but the situation is contained. No shots fired, a few minor injuries. It'll all be written up as a barroom brawl with a minor hit-and-run accident out front."

"Not an abduction?"

"The only ones who know that Bagdani is missing are his crew, and I'm guessing they won't bring it up with the police. That would raise questions, like who he is and what he does. All the same, the car that clipped that Audi—I'd tell the embassy to keep it out of sight for a few weeks."

"Already done."

"Good." He gestured to Avram and Logan. "Let's move our guest inside."

Poyarka had found calmer waters, the protected narrows of the northern Red Sea. Her captain saw Hurghada to port, Sharm al-Sheikh in the distance to starboard. They were entering the Gulf of Suez, which funneled to even smoother seas.

A sailor dressed in greasy coveralls—the ceaseless uniform of the day on *Poyarka*—appeared with a message from the new Deck 3 control room. Constantis took the printout and read: *Objective running four hours behind schedule. Make speed accordingly.*

The captain grinned humorlessly, and muttered, "Of course she is."

The sailor looked at him expectantly. Constantis was sure he'd looked at the message, but he could never decipher its meaning. He dismissed the man and he disappeared down a companionway. The captain looked out over the Sinai, its tawny undulations of sand carrying as far as the eye could see. There was nothing to be done about the schedule now. Once they were in the Mediterranean, he could adjust their speed and course as necessary.

"How far to the staging point?" he called across the bridge.

His second-in-command, a swarthy Pakistani who'd been booted from his country's navy for insubordination, replied, "One hundred and forty miles. We will easily arrive in time."

Constantis's gaze shifted to the foredeck and the half dome near the bow. The chief scientist, Chou, assured him that the water had been kept at bay, no damage done to the vital wiring and circuitry. He pinched the bridge of his nose. On past voyages, his worries had never gone beyond containers washing overboard or seawater seeping into grain shipments. *How different this voyage would be.* His luck was so far holding, yet like a hundred generations of captains before him, Constantis made his living as a pessimist. Sooner or later, something *would* go wrong.

He only hoped he would respond well enough to complete the mission and keep his crew alive. Most of them, anyway.

Barring that . . . he fully intended to save himself.

The house was "safe" in the clandestine sense, a decent place to hide. That said, Slaton decided he would never want to weather a heavy storm inside. Paint peeled from the walls like bark from a shedding tree, and brown water stains painted the ceiling in a kind of sewer-based fresco. The floorboards creaked with every step, and the slightest gust of wind brought groans from the rafters. Slaton had actually checked the weather during his planning, and thankfully no storms were forecast in the next forty-eight hours.

They put Bagdani in the least insecure of the three bedrooms. It was the only one without a window, and the door seemed solid. They chained him to an iron bed frame that had to weigh two hundred pounds. All the room's other furniture had been removed, save for a chair near the door where a full-time guard was stationed.

Once their man was secure, Slaton checked his phone. Not surprisingly, he had no cellular signal. He powered down his handset and borrowed Nora's CIA-issued sat-phone. He stepped outside to give the antenna the best look at the sky and placed a call. It took thirty seconds for the connection to go through.

FIFTY-ONE

"We're going to go with drugs," Sorensen said.

Slaton nearly pulled the phone away from his ear. "For interrogating Bagdani?"

"Director Nurin and I have discussed it at length. We've developed a new cocktail that's particularly effective, and I think it's our best chance. By the way, is he awake yet?"

"Stirring. How long until this truth serum of yours gets here?"

"A doctor is en route with an interrogation team. They'll bring everything they need and should arrive early tomorrow."

"Tomorrow. And how long does this process take?"

"You know interrogations. The new meds work fast, but breakdown isn't always immediate. I'd say two days, minimum."

"I don't think we have that much time."

"David, nobody understands the urgency better than I do. That's why I'm bringing the team to you versus a rendition somewhere more secure—there's more risk, but it's quicker. Lives may be at stake."

Slaton scanned the perimeter of the property. The surrounding tree line was impenetrable, and at various points it came near the house and garage. It would be extremely difficult to defend, even *if* he had more manpower. "Maybe there's a better way," he said.

"Let me guess—you want a crack at him? No, David, I want Bagdani intact."

"You don't give me enough credit. I think there's a way to break him faster, probably without laying a hand on him—at least, not any more than we've already done. But we'd have to recruit some help." The idea had been brewing in his head since yesterday. Slaton explained it in detail, and there was a long pause on Sorensen's end.

"Consider where we are, Anna. Remember what these people went through."

"It could work," she allowed. "But getting somebody like that on board—I'm not sure it's possible."

"Trust me, I know guys like him. He'll do it—you just have to offer the right incentives. For what it's worth, we have Bagdani locked down. So far, he's seen a couple of faces, but he hasn't heard any of us speak."

"You've been planning this all along."

"As a contingency. In my line of work, you seek every advantage."

"David, in your line of work . . ." A long hesitation, then a sigh. "All right, let me look into it. I'll get back to you."

For two hours Slaton and the others waited. Bagdani largely recovered from his sedation, yet he remained restrained and a hood was put over his head. He was kept under continuous watch by Avram, who was the most natural Albanian speaker. Even then, he'd been instructed to say nothing. Bagdani rattled lamely against his restraints and called out a few times with grievances about his injuries. It took one fist by Avram, square to the prisoner's jaw, to demonstrate how the complaint department worked. The arms merchant slumped to the bed in resigned silence, leaving little for him to contemplate but the one question Slaton wanted in his head: *Who is holding me?*

Bagdani could have no way of knowing who'd abducted him. It could be related to his work with Lazarus, yet men in his field made more than their share of enemies. Unhappy customers, contracts gone unpaid. Yet if Slaton's scheme was approved, the pressure would ratchet up immeasurably. Bagdani would be presented a fate worse than anything he might have imagined. A devastating bit of shock and awe that would hopefully get them what they needed.

When the return call from Langley came, Slaton again went outside with the sat-phone. A chill was building in the air as the sun fell behind the western hills.

"It's a go," Sorensen said.

Slaton was impressed she'd put it together so quickly. Even surprised. "Okay, well done."

"We'll see. I'm still not sure about this. You need to monitor the situation. If it's not going well, cut it off and we'll go with the pharmaceuticals."

"When can we expect him?"

"Roughly two hours. It's not a big country, and speed was part of the bargain. Oh, and he did have one demand," she added.

"Let me guess—we're supposed to be unarmed."

"I guess you *do* know guys like him."

"More than anyone should. What's in this for him?"

"I'd rather not talk about it."

"I'm in charge here, Anna. I need to know."

A hesitation. She knew he was right—notwithstanding the classification level, Slaton was boots on the ground, directing the op. She said, "There was some money involved. And if he gets us what we need . . . a *possibility* of having the war crimes charges lessened."

"Seriously?"

"The United States doesn't have the final say, and he won't be off the hook entirely."

Slaton, too, began to wonder if they were doing the right thing.

"Look, David, I think this might work. We both know Xhaka is an animal, but—"

"So does Bagdani," he finished.

"Exactly."

"Okay. I'll start getting things ready."

An hour later Slaton and Jakob were in the barn working up a sweat despite the cool evening air. Slaton had a pry bar in hand, and he was pulling rot-infused planks from the back wall.

"Would you like to tell me what we're doing?" Jakob asked, wrenching an ancient oak timber free and throwing it into a growing pile.

"We're getting ready for some company."

"Company? Someone being brought in by your friends at the CIA?"

Slaton levered off another board. "Yeah, but the guy coming doesn't work for them. And I should warn you—when he gets here, he's going to have heavy protection."

Jakob paused and looked at Slaton. Curious, maybe a hint of concern. "Does he have a name?"

"Dragun Xhaka."

Jakob lowered the board he was holding. "Xhaka, here? Tonight?"

"In the flesh." Slaton watched the Mossad case officer work it out. "This is why you insisted we not talk in front of Bagdani."

A nod.

He turned back to the wall. "All right. But I hope you know what you are doing, my friend."

Slaton ripped off another board, and thought, *So do I.*

FIFTY-TWO

The motorcade arrived shortly after dark. That was what it looked like, anyway—a convoy of heavy sedans, big German engines purring, headlights juttering up the dirt path in something near a formation. On any real road it would have suggested a politician heading for a rally, a dignitary on his way to a meeting. *Or a funeral procession,* Slaton mused.

There were four cars, which seemed overkill—including their captive, there were only six of them at the farmhouse. Still, Dragun Xhaka would not be alive today were he not an exceedingly cautious man. Xhaka had made a bargain on short notice with a distant adversary, one who professed a need for time-critical help. He would be rightly suspicious. He would be acutely on edge. Thankfully, like so many of his ilk, his caution was outweighed by greed: a chunk of money, along with the possibility of a get-out-of-jail-free card from the international community. The fact that he'd come at all told Slaton that Sorensen, on some level, had a method of communication pre-established with the man. It wasn't surprising—intelligence agencies often kept contact with the world's most notorious rogues.

Xhaka, however, was more toxic than most.

He had risen to infamy as a mid-grade officer in the Serbian Army. During the war in Kosovo, he'd been linked to some of the worst atrocities against ethnic Albanians. The challenge in the aftermath, of course, was proving it. The International Criminal Court had for twenty years tried to bring Xhaka to justice, yet so far had little to show for it. Witnesses disappeared, politicians got paid off. Xhaka, in the meantime, had not been idle. His repute for brutality was the perfect résumé for an aspiring crime boss. Many former officers of the Serbian Army had gone that route, and Xhaka rose quickly, taking over large swathes of territory along the Kosovo-Albania border. Drugs, women, protection—the usual rackets, all of which thrived under weak national governments and corrupt municipal leaders. The war might have ended on paper, yet the underlying rot was festering as always.

The cars drew to a stop near the house, yet their engines were left running, trails of vapor steaming from silver tailpipes. Slaton stood in front of the house with his team, the only exception being Avram, who was guarding their captive.

Nothing happened for a time as the clock in Slaton's head ran. Still nothing.

Finally, on some unseen command, the cars emptied. Slaton counted twelve men, all armed, carrying everything from machine pistols to handguns. A few wore body armor. Their builds were solid, their expressions surly. Grooming was clearly optional, and their union hadn't negotiated a dental plan. *Add a few bandoliers and some donkeys,* Slaton thought, *and we could start a revolution.*

Yet if the thugs were straight from central casting, they seemed reasonably alert. A few focused on the house, but most stood watching the perimeter with all the wariness of a herd of spooked elk. Two moved closer and took up positions on either side of Slaton's entourage.

Xhaka finally emerged from the second car, instantly recognizable. Sorensen had sent a photo, but it didn't do him justice. With the swagger of Mussolini and the belly of Buddha, he looked like a past-his-prime strip club bouncer—the kind of guy who wore his menace like a neon sign. His eyes settled on Slaton, who was front and center in the welcoming party. The mob boss scoped out the house and the barn, seemed satisfied, and strode closer with all the grace of an arthritic ox.

He stopped a few paces away.

Slaton had complied with Sorensen's instructions—their weapons were in the cars. Xhaka's men didn't search them, but their eyes were busy, sizing up everyone, looking for telltale bulges.

"Very well," Xhaka said, holding his hands at his side, palms outstretched. "You need Xhaka's help, so here I am." His English was barely decipherable under a thick accent.

Slaton said, "You'll be glad you came."

"This man you have, Bagdani—I have never done business with him, but I know people who have. A few guns here, a guard there."

"He won't be selling you anything tonight."

Xhaka chuckled under his breath, a gurgle rising deep in his chest. Slaton was close enough to smell cheap antiperspirant that was losing the battle.

"You have talked to him?" the Serb asked.

"No, we were careful. Our accents would have given us away."

A slow nod. Something close to professional appreciation. "So . . . you planned this? Me coming to help you?"

"You . . . or someone like you."

His gaze diverted to the great pyramid of wood, centered in a dirt-clear area, that Slaton and Jakob had built. "And this?"

Slaton explained.

The crime boss thought about it for a long time, then he smiled a viper's smile. Slaton thought it might signify relief. His suspicions were subsiding, things starting to make sense. "You know our history," he said.

"If that's what you want to call it."

The Serb's face hardened.

Slaton's gaze never wavered, his gray eyes a blank.

Xhaka regarded the others, then settled back on Slaton. "I see Americans here. But you . . . I think not. What is your interest?"

"I'm on a personal mission."

"Which is?"

"To kill someone."

The gangster's eyes narrowed, then a jowly grin. He raised an index finger, a detective who'd figured out a murder. "I think maybe you will. But thankfully it will not be me. You need Xhaka."

Slaton said nothing.

"Where is he?"

"In the house."

"Very well. Since I will be talking, tell me exactly what you wish to know . . ."

FIFTY-THREE

Slaton finalized his stagecraft with a can of gasoline. He'd siphoned it earlier from one of the cars with a length of garden hose, and now he doused the pyramid of old lumber. Harsh fumes filled the air, a pungent additive to the visual deception.

Nora and Logan had been banished to the house—Xhaka wanted them out of sight, saying they didn't look Albanian enough. Nora being a woman was a second strike—in this scenario, given the fiction they were building, a woman had no place. Slaton himself was questionable, with his muted Scandinavian features, yet his presence was nonnegotiable. He would remain at the back of the crowd. The illusion they were creating to keep Bagdani off-balance was a delicate one, and distractions had to be minimized.

With everything in place, Slaton stood back and took in the scene. It was much as he'd envisioned, yet for the first time he felt reservations. The idea had been his, yet the only way to carry it out was to relinquish control of the situation to a soulless killer. *As long we get answers,* he told himself, *it's all good.*

Slaton went inside to retrieve the prisoner.

Bagdani's head hurt terribly. He desperately wanted to rub the lump on his forehead, but the restraints on his hands prevented it. He knew he'd been unconscious, and suspected he'd been drugged—his mouth was fuzzy and he felt tingling in his hands. He'd heard a bit of shifting nearby, probably a guard, but the only response to his questions had been a stone-fisted punch in the jaw.

The matter of who had abducted him loomed large. The most logical answer was the Americans. The Trident had dealt them two terrible blows. Yet therein lay his second problem. In truth, Bagdani didn't know who his employers were. His only contact was Lazarus, a cutout who was in place, he was sure, to keep the real principals insulated. He'd speculated, naturally, as to who was behind the greater scheme, yet it had never gone beyond that—pure conjecture. The technologies they were using were beyond anything he'd ever seen, and the specialists he'd recruited had stretched even his extensive connections. Still, they paid him handsomely, and he guessed it was a state actor, or something very near it. As Bagdani knew better than anyone, in today's world the distinctions between government and criminal entities was increasingly ill-defined.

His headache was intensifying. Bagdani squeezed his eyes shut beneath the hood. Even before today he'd been getting nervous, knowing the next strike would be the most sensational of the three. He'd been laying the groundwork to disappear only last night. He had put the villa in Saint-Tropez on the market and was beginning to explore how best to go off-grid. According to one friend, property records in Chile were virtually untraceable.

But what good was any of that now? He'd waited too long and someone had intervened.

The Americans? The Trident itself?

These were the thoughts spinning in Bagdani's head when he heard the first voices outside. He'd noted the sound of vehicles not long ago; the low rumble of engines, tires on gravel. Now he heard what sounded like orders being given, and in the last language he would have expected: Serbo-Croatian.

This sent an electric jolt down his spine—as it would any ethnic Albanian. The Yugoslav Wars of the '90s, indirectly, were the reason he'd run to France. From the relative safety of Gallic training grounds, and later Sub-Saharan Africa, Bagdani had watched the devastation here unfold. Two of his best friends had joined the KLA, only to be captured by the Serbs. The accounts of what was done to them, prior to execution, were all but unspeakable. One of his cousins had been raped and tortured, surviving as but a shell of the young girl he'd once known. They were the kinds of wounds that never healed, even if Bagdani himself hadn't been a combatant.

The Serbs? he wondered. *What would they want with me?*

He had done a few deals here after leaving the Legion: some ammunition and night vision gear to Montenegro, a few crates of rifles to the Albanian mafia. Yet even that had been years ago.

Approaching footsteps shattered his rambling thoughts. Two sets of heavy boots, then a jingling of keys. His arms were seized in an iron grip while his restraints were unlocked, then reconnected behind his back. His ankle chains were removed.

"What is happening?" he asked.

They stood him up, one on each side hauling him by the armpits.

"Where are we—" Again, his question was cut off by what felt like a brick striking his cheek. Bagdani buckled at the knees, groaning in pain. Only the hands under his arms kept him upright. He felt something loose on his tongue, probably a piece of a tooth, and his mouth filled with blood.

He asked no more questions.

They dragged him across a wooden floor, his feet swimming to keep up. Then through a door and down a short set of steps onto what felt like dirt, the toes of his loafers digging in. Even beneath the hood he could smell the outside air, feel the night chill. His journey stopped abruptly, and he was struck by another smell—one that caused his heart to race.

Gasoline.

The hood was ripped off.

Bagdani blinked against bright lights. They slowly resolved to become headlights, three cars on his right. His eyes adjusted further, and a semi-circle of men materialized. The one who was front and center he recognized instantly. A face any Albanian would know—Dragan Xhaka.

FIFTY-FOUR

Slaton remained in the rear echelon, standing near the house as the performance played out. Jakob was next to him, and when Xhaka began speaking in Albanian he streamed a hushed translation into Slaton's ear.

"You know who I am?" Xhaka asked, regarding Bagdani as if he was something he'd just scraped off his shoe.

A weak nod—Bagdani seemed physically shrunken, a shell of the bruiser they'd taken from the pub.

"Yes, you would. That is good, it will expedite our business."

"Business?" Bagdani croaked, the word emerging like mush from his swollen mouth.

"You and I have never met, not professionally. Yet I have learned you are now working for a certain man, someone I very much want to find. He calls himself Lazarus, although that is not his true name. He has a limp, a man who travels so much he seems to have no home. As it turns out, he owes me a great deal of money."

"I don't know anybody like that."

Xhaka heaved a woeful sigh. He went closer, his face inches from Bagdani's. "I am not a patient man, Zamir. You must understand this. And you know how I feel about . . . your kind."

Bagdani said nothing.

"But the war . . . that is past us now. Like you, I am no more than a businessman. I will find this person I am seeking, yet your assistance might save me considerable trouble. Help me now, and you can go back to your little castle. Perhaps there could even be some business between us in the future."

Bagdani averted his eyes, and Slaton tried to imagine his thought process. He would be rightly suspicious of Xhaka's motives, and that was driving hesitation—a calculus of the threat before him compared to that of Lazarus and his employers. The direness of his immediate situation, however, had not yet been demonstrated in full. Fear *would* prevail. The sort of fear that was endemic in these hills, that went back to the days when Yugoslavia was a country. Capitulation was coming—it was only a matter of when.

Xhaka shook his head, feigning regret. "So be it."

The Serb stepped aside, and for the first time Bagdani focused on what was beyond. Fifty feet distant, centered in the open field, the pyramid of timber Slaton and Jakob had built. It was fifteen feet tall, nearly as wide, a great spire of wood. One of Xhaka's men casually lit a match and tossed it on the bonfire. Under the accelerant of the gasoline, it lit off like a Roman candle, engulfing the entire stack in a flash of combustion.

Bagdani's response was predictable—his face collapsed into a mask of sheer terror. Like any Albanian, he knew the horrific stories from the war. Serb soldiers had a reputation for building such fires, not for the warmth they provided, but for the sport of throwing prisoners onto the pyres and watching them burn alive. All wars had their archives of terror, yet Kosovo had more than its share.

Flames shot skyward, licking into the black sky. Bagdani was frog-marched toward the inferno, his heels digging in to no effect.

Up to this point, everything had gone as Slaton expected. Had he interrogated Bagdani himself, he could have inflicted pain. Alternately, Sorensen could have used her drugs. In either case, however, Bagdani would realize he was being held by Americans, and so he would know there were boundaries; waterboarding, trauma without leaving marks, mock execution, nonlethal injections. All had their grim uses, but in the end the Americans were constrained: They were a nation that played by the rules. They honored laws and kept to a code of decency.

Men like Xhaka were not so bound.

Now as Bagdani was hauled toward the dancing flames, the Serb's barbaric reputation displaced all other thoughts in his mind.

"All right!" Bagdani shouted. "Lazarus . . . yes!"

The men dragged him onward, stopping a few paces short of the flames. The heat had to be intense. Xhaka's men turned and looked at their boss, who gave them a nod.

Slaton expected them to drag Bagdani away, but instead they thrust him forward, quite literally putting his feet to the fire. Slaton surged ahead, but two of Xhaka's men blocked his path, machine pistols pointed at his chest.

Bagdani's legs were thrust farther into the base of the blaze. His screams shattered the still night.

Xhaka turned and glanced at Slaton, then gave his men a second signal. They pulled Bagdani clear and dragged him back toward the mafioso, dropping him unceremoniously at his feet. He writhed in the dirt, unable to stand. Slaton could see Bagdani's shoes melted to his feet, and his pants were black and singed to the knee.

Xhaka gave Bagdani a few moments to gather himself, then asked, "You were about to say something?"

His voice cracking, Bagdani blurted, "Yes . . . Lazarus. I hire people for him. He tells me the specialties he needs, I fill the positions. Some are technicians and engineers, very specific skills. Others are more typical recruits—crewmen for ships, others for security. He recently asked for an expert marksman."

"A marksman?"

"Yes, a sniper. I put him in touch with a Libyan."

Xhaka seemed unimpressed. "This Lazarus, what is his real name?"

"I don't know . . . *I swear it!*" A whimper of pain. "That is the only name I have heard. I tried to learn more about him myself. For the last five years he has been busy—he sells equipment, everything from bullets to aircraft, and sometimes manages small operations. Before that, there was nothing. He appeared out of nowhere like a ghost."

"How many times have you met him in person?"

"Eight, I think . . . maybe nine."

"Where?"

"Always in Almaty. Most of our work is by phone, and he sends me emails . . . requirements for the people I must recruit."

Xhaka pressed for specifics on the meetings, where and when they'd taken place. Bagdani tried to answer, but his replies were increasingly stunted and confused. More from pain, Slaton guessed, than evasion.

"What is his nationality?"

Bagdani reached down with his bound hands to touch one leg, then pulled away in agony. "What?"

"Where is he from?"

A shake of the head. "I don't know. He speaks English, Farsi, French—I think maybe some Arabic. I could never place his accent. He once said something that made me think he had spent time in Syria."

Slaton exchanged a look with Jakob as he translated those words.

Xhaka pressed on, covering all the ground Slaton had requested. Bagdani admitted that another strike was imminent. He'd procured the crew for a ship that had sailed days earlier from a port in Sri Lanka. He claimed not to know its destination or mission. Xhaka asked the name of the ship.

Bagdani didn't respond.

On Xhaka's command, one of his men kicked Bagdani's half-melted shoes.

The shriek was piercing.

It was here that the shortcomings of torture became apparent. Bagdani knew the ship's name and had a rough understanding of its mission. Yet the pain had become so excruciating, his thoughts so delirious, that he simply curled into a fetal position, broken and mumbling.

Xhaka turned away and walked toward Slaton, leaving Bagdani in the dirt. As the Serb approached, Slaton caught traces of a hauntingly familiar scent, one that he'd experienced in the aftermath of terrorist attacks, in the wary moments after firefights: the putrid odor of burnt flesh.

Xhaka stopped in front of him and stood arrogantly, a boxer posturing before a fight.

Slaton held his gaze unswervingly.

"There you are," the Serb said. "You have the information you wanted. Are you satisfied, or is there something more?"

With the prisoner crumpled in the dirt and babbling, there could be only one answer. Slaton would follow up with Bagdani later, after Xhaka was gone and the Albanian was coherent. The psychology would be easy—he would tell Bagdani he'd bargained for his freedom, but that the agreement was contingent on further cooperation. "That's enough," he said.

"I think you are right. Our arrangement is complete then?"

Slaton nodded. "It is."

"Good." The Serb gave a hand signal, and his men began moving— but not toward their cars.

Machine pistol barrels lifted all around, causing Slaton to glance at the car where their own weapons were stored. Starting a war wasn't in anyone's best interest, and even Xhaka wouldn't be so bold as to massacre a contingent of CIA officers. The guards began shoving him and Jakob toward the house.

"Wait!" Slaton shouted. The response was an elbow from behind. Once they were inside, three of Xhaka's men remained at the door, their weapons poised.

"What is happening?" Jakob whispered.

Slaton thought he knew, and before he could answer he was proved right. The tortured screams of Zamir Bagdani began echoing through the hills.

FIFTY-FIVE

Captain Constantis looked out into the night, and under a full moon he saw a curious sight for a sea captain—both port and starboard, endless tracts of desert reaching to the horizon. The Gulf of Suez was dead calm, a light breeze directionless. Ten other vessels were moored in the darkness around *Poyarka*, everything from bulk freighters to oil tankers, hulking shadows waiting patiently.

Transiting the Suez Canal was always a gauntlet, but for Constantis it had never been more fraught than tonight. The ships were queuing up for transit, and soon they would line up in a single-file convoy. The northbound "elephant walk" left at daybreak each morning, a passage that would take twelve hours. If all went to plan, they would break out into the Mediterranean before dark.

Constantis watched a disinterested Egyptian customs inspector meander *Poyarka*'s foredeck. The sickly yellow beam of his weak flashlight swept across the deck and rigging. He scanned the hull of a lifeboat and tugged on a few ladders, going through the motions. Twice the captain had watched him stop and reply to text messages on his phone. There was little to inspect. She wasn't a big vessel to begin with, her holds were empty, and her crew complement was minimal. The office in Port Suez had already approved *Poyarka*'s paperwork: The aging hydrographic survey ship was supposedly en route to a dry dock in Marseille. All transit fees had been paid in advance and the ship's papers had been filed electronically. Everything was in order.

Still, Constantis found himself holding his breath when the inspector neared the dome. Other than the control room on Deck 2—little more than two computer workstations—it was the only equipment on board that might draw attention. *Poyarka*'s paperwork claimed she was carrying an "advanced sonar array mapping vehicle." What lay under the golf ball could easily pass as such: The dome was topped by an access door large enough to extract such a device, and a deck crane hovered nearby. The weapon itself was shrouded by a tarp, and the lines of its muted silhouette loosely resembled those of an underwater research vehicle—at least to the untrained eye. The high-tech control room below deck further backed the idea. Altogether, nothing to raise the suspicions of any typical port inspector. Before leaving Hambantota, Constantis had expressed concern that the Egyptians might bring aboard a bomb-sniffing dog. The man who'd hired him, whose name he didn't even know, assured him it wouldn't matter. The explosive charge in the weapon, he explained, was not particularly large and was contained in a vessel so well machined there could be no chance of detection. The captain thought this odd but took him at his word.

The flashlight beam finally reached the dome. The inspector walked closer and actually rapped it with his knuckles. Constantis heard the hollow clang from the bridge, and it seemed to satisfy the man—he continued on, finished at the bow, and minutes later was back on the bridge.

"Everything is in order," the Egyptian said. He signed a form on a clipboard, separated two carbon duplicates, and handed one copy to *Poyarka*'s master. There might be computers in the office, but the onboard inspectors did things as they always had—in triplicate with a good black pen. "Transit begins at 0400 Zulu."

"Yes, thank you," Constantis replied.

Minutes later, the Suez Canal Authority boat was churning away toward the next ship in line.

"It's my fault," Slaton said, his voice weighted. "It was my idea to bring Xhaka into this."

Sorensen's voice came with a delay over the secure satellite connection. "David, you had no way of knowing he would do something like that. And don't forget, it's not like Bagdani was a saint. He spent his life selling arms, headhunting mercenaries. American airmen and sailors are dead thanks to him, and more would have been if you hadn't seen the threat coming on *Atlas*. I hate to be callous, but the world is a better place without Zamir Bagdani."

"Maybe so," Slaton allowed. "But what Xhaka did to him . . . nobody deserves that, Anna. Nobody."

Sorensen excused herself to check another call, and the link fell silent for a time. Slaton's thoughts were less quiet.

Jakob had already spent thirty minutes on a conference call briefing Sorensen and Nurin on the details of the interrogation—Slaton wanted Jakob to do it since he had been translating and could better answer their questions. He explained that another attack was imminent, although the only real clue—that the ship had recently departed a port in Sri Lanka— seemed of limited value. While Jakob was filling in the spymasters, Slaton had recruited Avram to help him recover Bagdani's charred body, or what was left of it, and place it in a hastily dug grave on the edge of the woods. At the end they'd both stood silent for a minute, lost in their private thoughts.

Slaton had long lived on the front lines, in those conflicted corners of the world where good and evil mingled in endless shades of gray. As a sniper, he was no stranger to death. Yet for the second time in days, he was looking at pointless cruelty. First Ayla Bloch and a Mossad team, along with so many innocents, had perished in a bombing in Almaty. Now on a bonfire he'd built as nothing more than a stage prop, the most senseless of brutalities had been imparted. Combined with the downing of Raven 44, the sinking of *Ross,* and the explosion on *Atlas* . . . the carnage just kept coming.

Slaton had looked into the abyss before, more than any sane man should have to. He was convinced there was no bottom to depravity, no cure for hatred. He also knew that no one man could ever put an end to either. Yet if every man did their part . . .

"David?" Sorensen's voice back on line. It kept him from falling further. "Are you okay?" she asked, sensing his edge.

"Yeah, sure."

"Look, I know what happened to Bagdani sucks, but we have to think forward. Other lives are at stake, and I need you with a clear head."

Slaton had never been more appreciative of Sorensen than in that moment. From halfway around the world, she'd sensed his darkness and was trying to pull him through. "Okay," he said.

"Our priority has to be figuring out this next attack. We'll chase down what we can in Sri Lanka, but I'm not hopeful. Whoever is running these attacks, they're covering their tracks well. Our best chance still is to find Lazarus, and Bagdani's information might help. We'll begin with the meetings. We know he works out of Almaty, and now we have dates. Maybe we can nail down a few places where they met. I'll get NSA digging. We can go through Bagdani's phone records, bank accounts, credit card transactions. We might get lucky and make connections."

"He said Lazarus spoke some Arabic, and that he might have spent time in Syria. If he was in Syria, that's Mossad's ground. I should head back to Tel Aviv."

"I'd concur. Do you need transport?"

"That would be helpful."

"Chances are, it'll be another military transport."

"Whatever gets me there quickest."

FIFTY-SIX

"There has been an incident," said the spokesman for The Trident.

Lazarus switched the phone to his better ear. The call had woken him from a deep sleep—a rarity these days—and after seeing who it was, he'd moved to the window. From there the darkened building across the street blocked out the sky, the only signs of life being squares of yellow light in a few windows and a sure-footed cat prowling a second-floor balcony. "What kind of incident?"

"Our people in Albania have been keeping an eye on your recruiter. It seems he has disappeared."

"Disappeared?" Lazarus considered it. "That might not be a problem. I assumed he would run at some point. Bagdani is not a fool, he can see the implications of these strikes as well as anyone. I expect he will lay low for a time and—"

"He hasn't run! He was abducted from a bar by a team of professionals."

Lazarus straightened. He stepped out onto the balcony, and from the rail he saw Tel Aviv sleeping soundly. A cool night breeze lifted malodorous scents from the dumpster below. "The Americans?" he theorized.

"Who else? The question is, how much can he give them?"

"Very little. I did precisely as you asked—Bagdani knew only what was necessary to fulfill our requirements. The exact kind of specialist, how long they would be needed. He knows nothing of your identity."

"What about yours?"

It was nothing short of an accusation, but Lazarus answered confidently, "I never gave him my name."

"Yet he knows about our recruitment efforts, the types of technicians sought. It could give away the next strike."

"That would take time to piece together—more than what exists. *Poyarka* is nearing her target."

"The target has been delayed."

"For how long?"

"Right now, only a matter of hours, but who can say? The Russians are grossly incompetent in this field."

"Even if the Americans deduce the type of weapon involved, they could never guess the target. By this time tomorrow, the strike will be behind us. You can sit back and watch a war of attrition that will decimate both sides. The next chapter may not even be necessary."

"But if it is?"

"Then I will have plenty of time to find a new recruiter."

A long silence from the East, then, "Very well. Call me if you hear anything more."

The line went dead.

Lazarus dropped the phone to his side and leaned against the rail. His right hip was always stiff when he got out of bed, but lately it seemed worse than usual.

His relationship with his employers was becoming problematic. Bagdani's abduction could hardly be a surprise to them. Their arms-length strategy, the way they outsourced talent, was both a strength and a weakness. Carefully governed, it absolved them of attribution, yet it also lessened their control and guaranteed a limited sense of commitment from those on the front lines. Most precariously positioned were middlemen like Bagdani . . . and, of course, Lazarus himself.

He knew what The Trident, collectively, had to be thinking: that he was fast becoming a liability. And they were right. Fortunately, his personal mission would soon be complete, and after that, he had loose plans to disappear. It wouldn't be easy, requiring a second complete erasure of his existence. Not only would the Americans and Israelis be looking for him, but also the Russians—and, he never doubted, The Trident as well. He'd never given much thought to his escape, but he might come up with something. And if he didn't?

Then I will at least die with some satisfaction. With payback extracted.

From the railing he looked up appreciatively at the stars. It was the simplest of sights, yet one he'd long thought he would never see again. He felt a deep weariness setting in, as if his bones were filling with lead. In the five years since he'd become human again, Lazarus had not had an uninterrupted night's sleep. Between the pain and the nightmares, he'd given up hope. The doctors were amazed he'd lived as long as he had, his ruined kidneys a marvel of adaptation. Yet the medications he'd been given weren't working as well, and he desperately wanted to raise the dosage. Too much, however, would make him foggy. And right now, more than ever, he needed to keep his wits about him. *Lest I end up like poor Bagdani.*

He pushed back from the rail and went inside. If *Poyarka*'s mission succeeded, one of two things would happen: America and Russia would be at war, or cooler heads would prevail. Even in the latter case, mistrust would run so deep it was only a matter of time. The Trident would keep stirring chaos until a red line was crossed. They were playing the long game, as they historically did. They had the financing, technology, everything necessary. The fate of Zamir Bagdani and those he'd recruited? They would be all but footnotes.

As I will be, Lazarus thought.

It was no revelation. He knew what he'd gotten into.

His own life had effectively ended twelve years ago, on a windswept night in Lebanon. Thoughts of marriage or children had long ago been discarded. His life expectancy had been halved, or so the doctors told him. He had plenty of money, but what good was that to a man with no future?

He hoped Anton Bloch was suffering, feeling some fraction of what he had endured. There were still two others to deal with: one he had located easily, and the other, the one that proved so elusive, had finally appeared. He'd been seen at Mossad headquarters, and also at Bloch's residence. Lazarus had been searching for the *kidon* for years, yet Israel's legendary assassin seemed to have vanished without a trace. There were rumors of his demise, yet Lazarus never bought into them. The man was simply an apparition, fading in and out of the ether—one of the reasons he was so good at what he did.

Altogether, it had left Lazarus but one option.

He had to make David Slaton come to him.

The C-130 Hercules clawed through thin air high above the Balkans. The big transport, call sign Tanner 21, had departed Aviano Air Base in Italy five hours ago. Its original destination had been Riyadh, Saudi Arabia, a load of two jet engines to be delivered to the Royal Saudi Air Force. The Herc had been at twenty-five thousand feet, churning above the Adriatic, when orders were received for a diversion: drop into Tirana, Albania, pick up one passenger, and deliver him at best speed to Tel Aviv. It was a highly unusual change but sourced from such a high level that the crew couldn't argue. Now having made the touch-and-go, Tanner 21 was back under way.

Slaton had been seated in back for takeoff with the female loadmaster, a master sergeant named Melanie Cooper. They occupied fold-down seats on opposite sides of the cabin, and between them two GE F110 engines, encased in plastic for shipping, were chained to the cargo deck. Cooper was an amiable Nebraskan, and she'd chatted Slaton up for a time. Pleasant as she was, he soon professed a need for sleep. Understandingly, Cooper unbuckled and led him up front. Like the C-17 that had delivered him from Alaska, the newer Hercules had crew rest bunks aft of the flight deck. The pilots were equally accommodating, telling him to make himself at home for the three-hour flight.

Slaton appreciated that none of the crew had so far asked the obvious question: What kind of vital mission was he on that necessitated diverting a scheduled logistics flight? He supposed they knew what the answer would be—none of them had a "need to know."

He lay down and closed his eyes, the hum of the engines hypnotic as they churned eastward toward the Aegean Sea. The bunk rocked gently in light turbulence, and Slaton did his best to force away Bagdani's wretched fate and focus on what he'd said. Lazarus spoke multiple languages, including some Arabic; he had a hard-to-place accent; he'd possibly spent time in Syria. In his head, Slaton replayed the video from the embassy in Kazakhstan, a lone figure limping past the gate.

His thoughts then shifted to the most obvious clue of all: the name *Lazarus*. The biblical figure raised from death by Jesus. Was it a message? A calling card of some kind? Certainly, there was meaning behind it.

The airplane rocked gently, the drone of the turboprops relentless. Slaton's thoughts grew ponderous and his body relaxed. He had nearly drifted to sleep, restful and still beneath a drab-olive blanket, when the answer came.

Slaton's eyes snapped open.

FIFTY-SEVEN

"Lazarus is one of us," Slaton said.

He was back on Anton Bloch's familiar terrace, the enduring hills spread before them. The rows of ancient olives tress, witness to so much joy and torment over the centuries, stood impassive as ever. Like the last time, Slaton had arrived in the early morning, yet today's sky was different, brooding clouds sweeping in from the north, the scent of rain on the air.

He'd been planning on going straight to Mossad headquarters after arriving, but his revelation had brought him here. He began by telling Bloch what they'd learned from Bagdani, and finished with how the Albanian had met his end. After a long career as a spymaster, Bloch's threshold for atrocity was high, and he listened without comment. After all that, Slaton dropped his accusation like a bomb. Lazarus was not a former Mossad target, not a bystander who'd been collateral damage. He was one of their own.

"Your reasoning?" Bloch inquired. Not doubting. Verifying.

"Ayla. The fact that the rescue team was lured in with her. If Lazarus had wanted to hit back at Israel, there would have been easier ways. Almaty was a strike against the heart and soul of Mossad. It was personal."

He watched his old boss's expression, but as usual it gave nothing away. Much like the last visit, Bloch looked drawn and weary. Yet there was life in his eyes now. An alertness, and . . . yes . . . a sense of purpose. The initial shock had subsided, and the former director was dealing with his daughter's loss in the only way he knew how. In the way Israel had been fighting since 1948. He was contemplating retribution. An eye for an eye.

"It makes sense," Bloch agreed.

"You saw the video from the embassy in Kazakhstan?"

"Nurin shared it with me, yes."

"The way Lazarus was limping—I think it was legitimate."

"Someone injured in the line of duty perhaps?"

"That's what I was thinking," Slaton said. "The very name—Lazarus."

"Risen from the dead. Perhaps a Christian as well?"

"That strikes me as misdirection. I think he's screwing with us."

"We could go back over Mossad records. Serious injuries resulting from operations are exhaustively documented, especially if the individual takes a medical retirement."

"That's a long list—we've spilled our share of blood over the years."

"As you would know better than anyone."

Slaton said nothing.

"I think it's possible. Someone who was injured on a mission during my tenure. It could be a legitimate complaint, a mission with bad intel, or one that never should have happened from the outset. We all make our share of bad calls. Even on the good calls, there are often those who disagree with tactics and decision-making. You see it in virtually every after-action report."

"I've written my share of those dissenting opinions."

"Don't remind me."

After a pause, Slaton asked, "How is Moira holding up?"

"She's eating a bit. Otherwise . . . despondent."

"Would she approve if you went to the Office?"

A heavy sigh. "If I presented it with enough caution . . . perhaps."

A gust of wind snapped at the furled porch umbrella between them. "Come with me, then. We need all the help we can get."

"I am in mourning, David, not feebleminded. My daughter was killed, yet I was the one being targeted. No one would have a better chance of identifying the kind of malcontent you're suggesting than me."

"Do any names come to mind?"

"Far too many, I'm afraid. Perhaps another look at that video would jog my addled brain." Bloch stood abruptly. "I'll go have a word with Moira. We're wasting time."

Slaton returned to the small room at headquarters he'd occupied days earlier, this time with a former director at his side and a new objective: identify a former Mossad officer who had been injured on a mission. The time frame was straightforward—they would go back twenty-one years, to the beginning of Bloch's tenure.

It proved overwhelming.

Clandestine missions were opaque by design, yet Israel was in a league of its own. No nation on earth put more emphasis on intelligence operations, because no nation on earth was surrounded by such a sprawling cast of enemies. Mossad often teamed with Shin Bet and AMAN, as well as subsidiaries like Caesarea and Unit 8200—the secret services of Israel were a Byzantine web of overlapping fiefdoms and competing priorities. Missions ranged from large-scale, cross-border military operations to solo arrests on home soil. Literally thousands of operations had been planned, scrapped, run, and aborted. Some were great victories, others abject failures.

This last group seemed most likely to give them what they were looking for: an injured and disillusioned operative. Unfortunately, with no way to sort missions on that basis, things quickly went old-school, sifting through the summary file of every Mossad mission since Bloch had become director. That, combined with one man's phenomenal memory.

By early afternoon their shirt backs were wrinkled, sleeves rolled up, and collars tugged down. The room took on the aura of a foxhole, stale smelling, and littered with spent Styrofoam coffee cups and crumpled sandwich wrappers.

"June 2006," Slaton said. "Operation Aurora, six operatives into Jordan to assassinate Abu Ammar. The Jordanian police were tipped off and the mission fell apart. Three made it back across the border, three were arrested outside Amman. One of those who made it back was injured when his motorcycle crashed in the desert—broken leg."

"Name?" Bloch inquired.

"Yitzhak Abrams."

The directorial mind churned. "No, I remember him. He worked long thereafter and became a unit commander. What came of those who ended up in Jordan?"

Slaton scrolled through the electronic file. "We made a deal after three days, traded them quietly for an Egyptian banker we'd locked up."

Bloch shook his head. "Next."

Slaton dictated five more condensed mission reports. None seemed promising. At that point, he stood and stretched, checked the clock on the wall. Four thirty in the afternoon. "We've been at it for seven hours. Dinner?"

"Put in an order to the cafeteria—I recommend the chicken sandwich. Order two, and a great deal of coffee."

Slaton picked up the internal phone and put in the request. After hanging up, he drew a hand over his chin. Bloch, seated at the table, had closed his eyes. A casual observer might have thought him resting. Slaton knew better—he'd never seen the former director so energized.

"Six years to go," Slaton said.

"Then we should get started."

"And if nothing clicks?"

"Then we do it all again."

Slaton settled back behind the laptop, not arguing the point. He knew how motivating death could be. His hand was hovering over the mouse when he froze, seized by that thought.

. . . *how motivating death could be.*

Bloch was watching him now. "What is it?"

Slaton took a moment to respond. "We're not taking him literally enough."

"Who?"

"*Lazarus* . . . the name. We've been looking for a man who's crippled, someone whose career with Mossad ended due to an injury on a mission gone bad. But it wasn't an injury. The answer has been right in front of us all along . . . the name he gave us. We should be looking for a dead man."

Anna Sorensen listened patiently, and with rising discomfort. She was again in the White House Situation Room, and a Navy admiral was wrapping up his briefing to the National Security Council. The president was in attendance, and the subject of the admiral's talk was vulnerabilities. The smell of coffee was thick as morning light broke in the world above.

In the last twenty-four hours, evidence had only hardened that America was under attack. Further engineering analysis of the wreckage and flight data recovered from Raven 44 all but confirmed that the aircraft was downed by a directed-energy weapon—most likely some kind of pulsed laser. The investigation into the sinking of *Ross* was equally damning— new signals intelligence sourced from a British ship that had been in the area, and also a nearby CIA listening post, backed the idea that *Ross* had been lured into a collision by faulty guidance. Then there was the fate of the two ships suspected in the attacks: one out of reach in a North Korean port, the other at the bottom of the Indian Ocean.

"We've doubled down on our surveillance along Russian borders," the admiral said. "Those missions are being backed by fighter escorts, tanker support, and a number of space assets have been refocused on the Arctic. We've got five Navy ships in the Black Sea, six more en route. The Russians are responding in kind. They're swarming all over Wrangel Island, and every available ship in the Black Sea Fleet is either at sea or will be soon. The Northern Fleet was already en route to Tartus, Syria, with their carrier *Admiral Kuznetsov* acting as flagship. We're also seeing ground forces moving on the borders of Ukraine and the Baltic states. Needless to say, tensions are running high. In light of intelligence suggesting a third attack, we're going to issue an all-service warning to be on high alert."

Sorensen had the first question. "Will this warning mention Russia specifically?"

"It will."

"I think that's a mistake."

President Cleveland eyed her. "Why is that?"

"Two reasons. First, I think it puts too much emphasis on Russian-flagged military assets. Both the attacks we've seen have come from what appear to be civilian vessels. Second, if we put out a global alert like that, word is going to leak out. The press will catch wind and make the connection to the two recent incidents. Suspicions are already falling on Russia, but this would put them firmly in the crosshairs—and increase the pressure on us to respond."

"At some point we *do* have to respond," the admiral argued.

"We have reason to watch Russia closely," Sorensen countered, "but there's still no hard evidence linking them to these attacks. Hybrid warfare is the new norm, and the very fact that we can't figure out who was operating these ships—I find that highly suspicious."

They both looked at the president.

She said, "Anna has valid points. We need to be cautious, and we need to watch non-flagged vessels. Let's put out the warning, but tell everyone to keep a broad outlook. We can focus on regions where the Russian military is active, but let's not name them as a suspect . . . not yet." Cleveland locked her eyes on the secretary of defense. "Having said that, I want a full range of options for response by noon today. Everything from limited strikes to full-up deployments."

The SecDef told the president she would have it.

Cleveland then shifted to Sorensen. "We *really* could use some timely intel. If there *is* another threat, we need to get out ahead of it—maybe even figure out who's responsible."

Having thrown down that gauntlet, the president got up and left.

FIFTY-EIGHT

The list of Mossad operatives killed in action was far less lengthy. For Slaton, some of the names were familiar, although only a few came with faces. Bloch knew every one, a commander's burden.

The sorting proved far easier than their earlier quest. Right away, Slaton excluded every case in which the body had been recovered and identified. It left a short stack of summary files: twenty-one special operators, case officers, and agents who were listed as killed in action, yet whose remains had never been recovered.

In four cases, Slaton recognized the names of men and women lost on missions he'd been involved in—typically, as the primary shooter or sitting overwatch. For Bloch it had to be like reliving his nightmares—sleepless nights agonizing over missions gone wrong. Some were likely disasters from the get-go, others perfectly good ops cursed by perfectly bad luck. Of the twenty-one names, however, one leapt out at Slaton.

He dug that file from the stack. "Operation Starlight."

"I remember," Bloch said, looking at him questioningly. "As would you."

Slaton's thoughts were already in overdrive, going back to the video from the embassy in Nur-Sultan. The disastrously bent figure on the sidewalk. *Was it possible? The one man who never came back that night . . .*

Slaton knew the details of Operation Starlight better than anyone on earth, every sight and sound and smell. And for the most damning of reasons: he had been the mission commander.

Poyarka broke into the Mediterranean right on schedule after spending the day funneling through the Suez Canal with the morning flotilla. Captain Constantis was looking appreciatively at the broad expanse of open water ahead when he felt a buzz in his pocket. He pulled out the special mobile handset Chou had given him—a low-power, local network connecting him to the control room downstairs.

He saw a relayed message from their employers. After reading it through once, the captain dropped the device back in his pocket. There were no additional delays. Their target had cleared Malta and was heading east at a surprisingly steady speed. Also notable were the ships around her, a small fleet buzzing in support, with one outlier on the fringe—this perfectly predictable, and critical to the mission. Elemental to the fog of war that *Poyarka* would create.

"Set course two-eight-zero," Constantis said.

As soon as the order was acknowledged by the helmsman, Constantis departed the bridge.

He exited to the catwalk and descended a rust-flecked ladder to the main deck. As he made his way forward, his captain's eye noted countless corroded fittings. On any other voyage he would have set idle crewmen to scraping and painting. As it was, he had no one idle. Ten men, counting himself, had gotten the ship this far. Two of those were the technicians, their only duty being to maintain and operate the weapon. He reached the dome and found the access door open. Constantis stepped inside to find Chou fiddling with a circuit board. More surprisingly, the weapon was exposed, its tarp gone and the rectangular launch tube hinged open.

"Is everything all right?" the captain asked in English, the default language they shared with marginal fluency.

The Asian, who was built like a preschooler's stick figure, glanced over his shoulder. "Yes, is good. I am running minor test."

"Did you get the message?"

A befuddled expression confirmed he hadn't.

"No more delays are expected."

"Good. Finish soon." Chou went back to work.

Constantis took a step back and regarded the weapon. He had never before seen it in full. Nearly twenty feet long, it rested on a telescoping rail that would extend for launch. To say the design was sleek was an understatement, but he supposed that was a given.

He checked his watch. They were eight hours, more or less, from the engagement zone. At that point, assuming their target didn't slow, it was simply a matter of finding the right opportunity. Waiting for convincing geometry. Press one button, and their mission would reach its inglorious end.

At that point, Constantis would give an order he had never before given—one that most captains gave only in their nightmares.

He would instruct his crew to abandon ship.

FIFTY-NINE

Operation Starlight had been born, like so many clandestine ventures over the ages, from an affair of the heart. The target of the operation was Hassan Duba, the operations chief of Syrian Military Intelligence—the Syrian *mukhabarat*. Duba had long been a facilitator of terrorist groups infiltrating Israel, which put his name at the top of Mossad's "kill list" in permanent red ink. Carrying out that judgment was another matter altogether: Duba rarely left the country, and Israel had a strong aversion, for reasons both practical and political, to operating on Syrian soil.

The opening arrived during a low point in the abyss of Syria's civil war. Duba took a mistress, a strikingly beautiful young woman he'd met at a Damascus club he frequented. He was anything but a lothario: balding, rotund, and long married, he was probably surprised to find such a vivacious young woman receptive to his advances. He showered her with gifts, and assumed she was impressed by his powerful position in the *mukhabarat*, which he made no effort to hide.

In fact, it was true, although not in the way he imagined.

The girl's name was Reena, and what Duba didn't know, and what his pride did not allow him to research, was that he was not her first lover. A year before they met, she had been madly in love with a dashing young student, a boy from a solid family who was pursuing a college degree. It was a whirlwind romance, and they were engaged within a month. Those plans, however, like so many others in those days, fell victim to the war. Two weeks after their engagement, Reena's lover received a letter conscripting him into the Syrian Army. He went to a recruitment office and confessed his pacifist leanings. The recruiter confessed, in reply, that he didn't give a damn about his leanings. The next day they threw him in the back of a truck and sent him to basic training. Reena's future husband fled the first night of boot camp. Within a week he'd been hunted down by the *mukhabarat*, literally torn from her arms, and executed for desertion on the street in front of her apartment.

As wars went, the conflict in Syria had more than its share of such tragedies. And consequently, more than its share of disconsolate widows. Reena mourned for months, but it did little to soften her pain. The only thing that brought relief was a recurring fantasy: the idea of extracting payback.

In a fit of anger, she sent a letter to a Christian friend in Beirut, confessing the fire in her heart for exacting revenge. The Christian knew a Druze, who in turn knew a Jew. Within a week the letter had made its way to Glilot Junction where Mossad did its best to verify its authenticity. They were buoyed more than ever after seeing a picture of Reena, an exquisite, raven-haired beauty. Quiet contact was made, and they asked her if there were limits to what she might do to exact her revenge. Her response was more than they could have hoped for: *"I will take Hassan Duba as far as his lust permits."*

And with that, Mossad had their agent. A rare opportunity had fallen into their laps.

For six months the Office planned. Reena was given instructions on how to meet Duba, how to entrap and manage him. She succeeded spectacularly, and the affair commenced. With the snare in place, and the war in Syria raging, Reena announced that she would depart to live with an aunt in Beirut, confessing to her lover that she no longer felt safe in Damascus. Of course, he understood. Everyone understood in those dark days. Duba responded by telling her that, by chance, he traveled regularly to Lebanon to take meetings with his counterparts in the Lebanese secret police and Hezbollah.

Reena feigned surprise.

Duba not only aided her departure, but actually procured for her a pied-à-terre, a small flat in a nine-story building in one of the better quarters of Beirut.

And with that, the stage was set.

Mossad waited for a green light, and it came in late October. Duba messaged Reena that he was coming to Beirut for meetings, giving her two days' advance notice. Mossad was ready.

Slaton had been put in charge of a complex mission. They would insert nine commandos by sea, delivered to a point twelve miles off the Lebanese coast by a fishing boat, and the remaining gap covered using inflatable boats. Every inch of the neighborhood surrounding the pied-à-terre was studied using overhead images, as well as footage taken from ground level by a trusted Lebanese agent.

Reena, playing host to a *mukhabarat* lover she reviled, was to provide two updates: she would notify the team when Duba arrived, and give any possible information regarding his security arrangements.

Even now, so many years later, Slaton remembered the insertion that night, a shimmering view of Beirut from the sea. It was precisely as he'd memorized from photographs, the city's lights as familiar as a constellation of stars guiding them to a remote stretch of beach.

The ingress went faultlessly, and after dropping nine commandos in the surf, dressed in civilian clothes and wearing waders, the boat captains retreated offshore to wait for the extraction. Three cars were prepositioned, and in teams of three they drove to the flat by separate routes. They had nearly arrived when Reena sent word: Duba was with her, and she'd seen the usual security contingent, two men at the building's main entrance and two in a car out front.

Slaton's group was the first to arrive and deploy. They accessed a building across the street, an office complex under renovation, and set up an observation point on the roof beneath a wood-and-metal scaffold. The overwatch had a commanding view of Reena's flat, the front entrance of her building, and a side entrance where the strike team would enter. Slaton set up with his weapon, an IWI Dan bolt action rifle, and began scoping the area.

He easily picked out Duba's security teams, a pair by the street-level door and twin shadows in a Mercedes out front. The curtains on Reena's flat were closed, but the lights behind them were on, giving an occasional silhouette from within. It would be an easy shot from where Slaton lay, but the chance of misidentification was too high. Unfortunately, Reena had reported early on that Duba was paranoid about standing near uncovered windows—and with good reason.

Slaton gave the go order, and the teams began to advance. He watched all six men use the side entrance to access the emergency stairwell—Reena had blocked the door open hours earlier. Two of the men took up defensive positions while the strike team of four climbed quickly.

At that point, things began to unravel, and for the most basic of mistakes: the strike team in the stairwell never bothered to count floors. The source of the trouble wasn't determined until days later. The fire doors in the stairwell had recently been replaced, and whatever moron had done the work had accidentally switched the doors—on which large numbers were painted—of the seventh and eighth floors. The team later admitted to confusion, but there was never any hesitation. They entered the hallway one floor below their target and found the first door on the left locked— Reena had been instructed to leave it unlocked.

The team had come prepared for this contingency. They quickly breached the lightweight door using a small explosive charge, only to burst inside to find a family of four having dinner. Knowing this wasn't right, the leader improvised quickly, hoping to salvage the mission. He claimed loudly, and in excellent Arabic, that they were a Lebanese police unit searching for a terrorist named Reena Hadad. He watched the family intently, and it was a girl of no more than ten, sitting behind a plate of lamb and couscous, who reacted. Her trembling finger pointed directly overhead.

The team backed out with the leader apologizing profusely and telling the family to remain quiet, which, by all accounts, they did. Unfortunately, critical time had been lost. Worse yet, Duba's security team had been alerted by the detonation of the breaching charge.

Not aware of the specific problem, but knowing something had gone wrong, Slaton saw the two guards at the door suddenly pull their weapons.

It was all he needed. Already prone, he sighted on the most exposed man and put him down with a single round. The second man disappeared into the building before Slaton could re-sight. He shifted his scope to the car and sent one man flying to the pavement as he exited. The other dove low behind the car, sensing where the fire was coming from. In his low-light optic, Slaton couldn't see the man directly, but he noted the glow of a mobile phone in use. He got on the comm network and called out, "Hyper!"

It was one of a half-dozen prearranged code words: *Secrecy blown. Proceed with all speed and egress as planned.*

Sixty seconds late, the strike team flew through Reena's front door, turned left, and found Duba. He hadn't reacted to the breaching charge going off, or to his mobile phone, which was vibrating madly on the counter. The obvious reason was that he was being ridden by a naked Reena, his head thrust back in ecstasy. As soon as Reena saw the team, she threw herself to the floor. Seconds later, the operational chief of Syrian Military Intelligence was pinned to the mussed bed by twenty-two nine-millimeter rounds.

For her part, Reena stood calmly, in all her naked glory, and said, "What took you so damned long?"

The team paused only long enough to take pictures of Duba, excise a DNA sample, and for Reena to put on an abaya and shoes. They ran for the door to the sound of sporadic gunfire—their defensive element downstairs engaging Duba's remaining door guard.

The moment Slaton received the report that Duba had been eliminated, he and his own group began racing to ground level. The next minutes revealed Mossad's second mistake. It had been noted in planning that the district police station was a mere three blocks away. In order to delay the response, Unit 8200 had been tasked to provide cover. Their plan was to call in a terrorist attack on the opposite side of the district's territory minutes before the strike, demanding an all-hands response in the wrong direction. The problem was that the police district map Mossad had used was out of date, and a recent change caused the response to come from a sister district. Thus, when an urgent call for assistance arrived from the Lebanese General Security Directorate, who'd been alerted by Duba's guard, police flooded the area.

The consequences were damning. Before any of the teams could reach their vehicles, five police cars had arrived, backed by four officers who'd been patrolling nearby streets on foot. The melee that ensued was nothing less than a running firefight encompassing an entire city block. Because Slaton's handpicked team were solid operators, it wasn't a fair fight. Still, two men in the strike team were hit. One of them was helped to a car by his partner, and a second car departed full, including Reena. Both vehicles shot off toward the beach. Slaton took the wheel of the third car, waiting for his last two men. He'd heard on the comm net that one of them had been hit inside the building. Police were swarming, but they hadn't yet locked on to his vehicle. Finally, a lone figure came running from the side entrance, tumbled into the passenger seat, and shouted, *"Go!"*

"Where's Zev?"

"He didn't make it."

Slaton had felt a turn in his gut. *"Where is he?* We're not leaving anyone behind!" He reached for the door handle as a pair of policemen came into view.

"He's dead, I tell you! I saw it myself, a straight headshot. Go!"

The two policemen had their weapons drawn, their heads swiveling, searching.

To that point in his career, it was the most difficult operational decision Slaton had faced. You never left a man behind. Yet the man sitting next to him, whose name was Gideon Kalman, had no doubts—his partner was dead. If Slaton tried to go inside, the odds were high that they would both be killed or captured.

Sensing his doubts, Kalman said it again, "He's dead, David!"

There seemed only one choice. Slaton put the car in gear and sped away.

The remainder of the extraction was harried, but largely went to plan. The inflatables picked them up on the beach, spun seaward, and with a Lebanese Navy patrol boat bearing down, they rendezvoused with an Israeli Navy corvette.

In the aftermath, the mission was rated a qualified success. Duba had been eliminated at the cost of one man lost, another injured. The post-mission debriefings were consistent. Kalman verified that his partner had been hit twice, including a round to the head, and was dead before he hit the floor. Mossad spent months trying to confirm the account through Lebanese sources but drew only blanks.

The name of the man killed had since been engraved in stone, one of nearly a thousand fallen intelligence warriors commemorated in the national memorial labyrinth. It etched far more deeply in Slaton's mind—he was the first man to die under his command.

His name was Zev Eitan.

SIXTY

They split the file as they read, all others pushed aside. Sitting in the quiet room with Bloch, who had ultimately approved Operation Starlight, Slaton found himself reliving the mission as he hadn't in years.

Zev Eitan had come to Mossad after a tour in the Israeli Defense Forces. He'd been a solid performer for three years, with a talent for logistics. On Starlight, Slaton had put him in charge of acquiring weapons, equipment, and transportation for the raid. He'd done a flawless job—until the unpredictability of battle intervened.

Slaton remembered visiting Eitan's grieving parents, telling them how bravely their son had fought and died. He also recalled being thankful, but also conflicted, that there hadn't been a widow and children. Fewer family members to console, but also fewer to remember a good man. Zev Eitan had been twenty-six years old.

The mission bothered Slaton for a time, a commander's second-guessing of what he might have done differently. Those doubts, however, were scrubbed away quickly by the usual agent—the ceaseless operational tempo.

He pushed away from the table, looked squarely at Bloch. "This is the one—it feels right. Eitan had a knack for logistics. He survived Starlight, and now he's become Lazarus."

A circumspect nod. "Perhaps. But how to pursue it?"

Slaton tapped a finger on the wooden table, then said, "To begin, we talk to the last man to see him that night—Gideon Kalman."

Bloch's thick features pursed, an exercise in concentration. "He was still working for the Office when I left," he said, his tone a shrug. "But that was a few years ago."

Slaton got up and headed for the door. "I'm going to see Nurin."

Nurin thought Slaton was chasing ghosts but backed him all the same. Slaton learned that Gideon Kalman was not only still employed by Mossad but in fact serving as an instructor at its training academy. The facility, referred to as the Midrasha, was a sprawling campus in Herzliya, on the northern edge of Tel Aviv.

Slaton himself was a graduate of the school; he'd run its gauntlet of Krav Maga, honed his proficiency in tradecraft and weapons employment. Tel Aviv itself was incorporated into the curriculum, an unsuspecting proving ground where prospective spies applied their lessons in real-world conditions.

He made the drive alone, leaving Bloch to continue researching Zev Eitan. Security at the Midrasha was predictably tight, and Slaton was greeted at the gate by a personal escort—the director's weight having its orbital effect. The young man gave him a wary look and led the way without comment into the complex. The place was marginally changed from what Slaton remembered—he'd been here on a few occasions after initial training, mostly to impart operational techniques in a "graduate-level" course with the informal, and decidedly uncollegiate, name Liquidation 101.

The office he was guided to was familiar: that of the academy's director.

Slaton entered to find a leanly built, serious man behind the desk. While the man wasn't familiar, the desk was—Slaton had stood before it more than once during initial training. The Midrasha director, whose name was Cohen, stood. After a cordial handshake, he regarded Slaton in a way that confirmed he knew who he was and what he did. "I understand you've come to see Gideon Kalman."

"That's right."

A hesitation, although nothing ominous. Merely a supervisor wondering why an assassin had come looking for one of his people—and with the blessing of Mossad's director.

"Can I ask why you want to see him?"

"No."

A nod of acceptance. "Gideon was here earlier, but he went home unexpectedly about an hour ago."

"Did he say why?"

"No."

The director held out a slip of paper. Slaton took it and saw an address. Cohen had been ready. "Thanks."

"Let me know if there's anything I can do to help."

"Actually, there is one thing . . ."

Ten minutes later, Slaton was walking back to his car, a SIG P226 holstered beneath his jacket and the guarded eyes of the academy director tracking him from a distant window.

Kalman lived twenty minutes from the training academy, a tony community of upscale villas. His home, on the edge of the development, was a narrow two-story affair bordering an ocean of red tile. The front yard was manicured xeriscape, and through the narrow gaps between neighboring houses Slaton saw hardpan wilderness behind.

A car in the short driveway implied Kalman was home. According to his file, he was divorced, no children, and lived alone—it was Mossad's business to know such things about its employees.

Slaton parked in the street, and moments later he was knocking on the door of a man he hadn't seen in twelve years. Kalman answered promptly and stood staring for a moment. He clearly recognized Slaton, yet there was something else in his expression. Surprise was a given, but also . . . caution?

"It's been a long time," Kalman finally said.

"It has," Slaton agreed, offering a handshake that was met.

His memory of a once-lean commando shifted slightly. Back in the day, Kalman had been Slaton's own height and build. He was softer now, heavier around the waist, jowls coming in. His gaze, however, was clear, and his IDF bearing remained.

"Come in," Kalman said, stepping back. Slaton followed him into a simple living area that joined to a kitchen. Everything was neat and squared away, and through panes of glass in a pair of French doors Slaton saw a sitting area out back with a small table and umbrella.

"I know why you're here," Kalman said.

"Do you?"

"Something to do with Zev Eitan."

Slaton didn't reply.

"Is it true?" Kalman asked. "Is he alive?"

"Where did you hear that?"

A pause, then, "Have you come to second-guess me? About that night? I said it then, and I'll say it now—I *saw* him go down. It was a headshot!"

Slaton visualized the after-action report. "As I recall, he was hit here," he said, touching his right temple with two fingers.

"Exactly."

"Headshots cause a lot of bleeding, but they're not always fatal."

A shake of the head.

"Did you check for a pulse?"

"I was under fire, dammit, and Zev wasn't moving! He was also hit in the hip." Kalman's face warped in agony, the scene playing in his head—as it probably had a thousand nights since. He shook his head sharply. "No! I had to get out fast, and there was no way I could have stopped to . . ." His words trailed off.

Slaton backed off a step, studied the room. He saw a wedding picture on the wall, a much younger Kalman in his IDF uniform, a pretty, raven-haired woman gazing up at him starry-eyed. How long had it lasted? he wondered. Had mission-induced stress contributed to the failure of the marriage? No way to tell, but such outcomes were legion in the intelligence services.

Kalman walked across the small room and sank into a chair near the French doors. His military posture broke and he hunched forward, his hands clasping his knees. His voice fell to a mere whisper. "Not a day has gone by that I haven't thought about that night. I remember seeing Zev, how bad it looked. I kept telling myself I made the right call, but it wouldn't go away. And then today . . ."

"Look at me, Gideon."

The defeated eyes rose slowly.

"I know what you're feeling. Every time you lose a brother, you second-guess yourself. You wonder what you could have done differently. Sometimes you come up with answers that don't sit well. We've all made mistakes, probably me more than anyone. All you can do is accept them and move on. You'll go back to work tomorrow. You're an instructor, and this is why—you can teach the recruits *everything* you've learned."

A blank stare in return, then a somber nod.

Slaton took a seat on the nearby couch and weighed how to proceed. He could grill Kalman, go back over the mission in detail, but at this point it hardly mattered. Yet there was one thing he needed to know. "You asked me earlier if it was true, if Zev was alive. How did you know?"

Kalman seemed to refocus. "I got a call today from an unknown number. I didn't pick up, but there was a message afterward. I recognized the voice right away—it was Zev."

Slaton's attention ratcheted higher. "What did he say?"

"He wanted me to meet him later today."

"Did he say why?"

"He just said we needed to talk. I was stunned. When I saw you at my door—I knew it had to be connected. I thought maybe you could tell me what was going on."

Slaton replied carefully. "We've been looking into the bombing in Almaty, and we think a former Office employee might be involved."

"*Zev?* The bombing in Almaty?"

"We don't know, but that's how his name came up. We began looking at operators who'd been declared KIA, but whose deaths were never verified."

"Where could he have been all this time?"

"That's the question, isn't it?" He watched Kalman process it all. "Where did he want you to meet him?"

"It was strange." He got up and retrieved his phone from the dining room table, called up a text, and showed it to Slaton. "Right after he left the message, he texted this coordinate set. I plotted it out as a spot down in the Negev, open desert outside Dimona." Kalman's suspicion was palpable. "Is that not shady as hell? It would mean he's here, in Israel."

"Were you going to go?"

He shrugged. "I don't know. I couldn't decide what to do—that's why I took the day off. On one hand, I wanted to tell my boss, Cohen. On the other . . . I realized what a terrible mistake I made twelve years ago. I figure I owed something to—"

Kalman's words cut off like a cable had been cut, and in the next instant the reason became clear. His body lurched forward in an explosion of blood and tissue.

SIXTY-ONE

Slaton threw himself behind the nearest wall, a stunted hallway leading to a bedroom. He pressed against the drywall, getting low and small, expecting more incoming fire. When none came, his burst of adrenaline ebbed. He pulled the SIG all the same.

He glanced at Kalman, saw a massive wound dead center in his chest. He quaked once, then stopped moving, and likely never would again. When no shots rang in after a minute, Slaton ventured a look to the far side of the room. As expected, he saw a hole in the top left windowpane of the cream-colored French doors. Based on Kalman's wound, the round was large caliber, confirmed by a three-finger hole in the opposite wall where the round had carried through.

Slaton knew where Kalman had been standing, so it was simple enough to connect the dots and draw a line outside to estimate where the shot had come from. He crawled closer to the window for a better perspective, ventured an instantaneous glance outside, then pulled back into cover. With that snapshot in mind, he guessed the likely perch was a hill two hundred yards distant.

That's where I'd have set up.

The question: How to respond?

There was clearly nothing to do for Kalman. He cast a second quick look into the desert, saw no movement whatsoever. Only still earth under a hard sun. Was the shooter still there, waiting? He suspected not, but either way, Slaton needed to move. He would be vulnerable on the way to his car, but a bit of weaving and staying low would better his odds—being a sniper himself, he knew precisely the kind of movement that made tracking difficult.

He holstered the SIG and edged toward the front door. Halfway there, he paused. Slaton diverted to retrieve Kalman's phone. It was still unlocked, and he called up the message with the rendezvous coordinates. He took a picture with his own phone, then ran low toward the door.

Slaton called Nurin as he drove. He began by explaining what Kalman had confessed, then finished with the tragic news. "I'll leave it to you to clean things up," he added.

"Did you get a look at the shooter?" Nurin asked.

"No."

"Clearly you've stumbled on to something, David."

"Clearly. The question is, what?"

"Kalman actually spoke to Eitan today?"

"He got a voice message—said it was definitely him."

"Very well. I'll stand up a search for Eitan. I take it you are on your way back to headquarters?"

"Of course."

After a bit more coordination, Slaton ended the call.

He tossed his phone on the empty right seat. He'd made one omission in his report, a spur-of-the-moment call. Now that he had time to think about it, it still felt like the right decision: He hadn't told Nurin about the meeting set for tonight between Kalman and Eitan. He had no idea if it would still happen. Could Eitan have been the shooter? It was plausible, yet other possibilities loomed. He trusted Anton Bloch, and for the most part Director Nurin, yet Mossad itself was a large and tangled organization. After what had happened to Ayla, and now a long-serving operator, Slaton couldn't discount the chance of a leak at the agency. And there was simply no time to dig into it.

Which was why he wasn't actually going back to headquarters. He didn't like lying to Nurin, yet more compelling was an urge to not telegraph his every move. Slaton's next stop would be the training academy. With Cohen's approval, which he knew he would get, he wanted to requisition some more equipment. After that, he was looking at a long drive south to the Negev.

"The pumps aren't keeping up," said *Poyarka*'s chief mechanic.

Captain Constantis looked at the wretched Indonesian—he'd arrived on the bridge moments ago as if spit from the bowels of some greasy volcano. Barely five feet tall, a hundred pounds wet, he looked thoroughly defeated. His overalls were sodden and covered in oil, and black smudges creased his face like war paint.

"How many are running?" the captain asked.

"Two at full speed. One other is clogged but working. The rest are down. I could remove the unit that is clogged, take it apart and clean the impeller and screens, but that would make the problem worse for a time."

Constantis frowned. It had been an ongoing problem since leaving Hambantota. There were numerous leaks in the hull—all ships had them, although *Poyarka* was overly blessed—yet the heavy seas on the first day had caused the ship to take on an inordinate amount of water. The stressed pump system had begun failing on day two, and now it was so degraded they had taken on tons of water. The ship was actually listing measurably to port. On any normal voyage it would have necessitated making for the nearest port for repairs. Today Constantis had no such option. It was hard to shake the irony of it all: here he was, carrying one of the world's most advanced weapons on a ship that was slowly sinking.

"I would recommend a port call, Captain," said the mechanic, who knew nothing of the greater mission. "We will have trouble reaching Marseille as things are."

"I will take it under consideration," Constantis said. "Don't take the struggling pump off-line. I will give you an update after I've conferred with the owners."

The Indonesian looked doubtful, but nodded and went back below, a tattered black rag trailing from his back pocket.

Chou, the weapon system engineer, had been listening from the nearby nav table. "Is this a problem?" he asked.

Constantis shook his head. Casting a glance at the two crewmen near the helm, he said in a low voice, "Not as long as our target keeps close to schedule. We will reach the staging area in six hours, and from there the attack can commence at any time. After it does, I plan to disable the pumps anyway."

"You will do that yourself?"

"I'm the captain—I do what I please." He knew what Chou was thinking. The two of them, along with the other technician, Wu, were the only ones on board who understood that *Poyarka* would never get anywhere near Marseille. It was a necessary deception, yet one that came with complications. Constantis tried to look on the bright side: If they'd lost control of the pumps a day sooner, the entire mission would have been lost. As it was, the old tub was holding together just long enough.

Barring catastrophe in the coming hours, they would soon have the one chance they needed.

Across the globe, United States military and intelligence forces watched Russia with a raptor's eye. Satellites monitored troop movements, naval vessels, and even other satellites. Listening outposts vacuumed signals and messages faster than they could be interpreted.

Forewarned by the previous strikes, civilian vessels loitering near U.S. Navy ships were given a particularly hard electronic stare. This was no simple undertaking, and it proved overwhelming in the vicinity of high-volume shipping lanes. The Mediterranean was a case in point. Among the busiest maritime corridors on earth, its east-west channels were plied by thousands of vessels each day. The bulk of the traffic kept to the central and northern routes, and the U.S. Navy's presence was concentrated in the eastern waters near the Saudi Peninsula.

Which was why, amid all the nautical commotion, little attention was given to a five-thousand-ton hydrographic survey ship plodding slowly westward thirty miles off the coast of Egypt. Her course kept her tight to shore, a hundred miles clear of the primary sea-lanes, and farther than that from the nearest U.S. Navy capital ship. That geometry would alter, albeit slightly, by the end of the day as *Poyarka*'s target came within range.

A target that the Americans, for all their intelligence acumen, would never think to protect. At least, not until it was too late.

SIXTY-TWO

The sun was menacing the horizon as Slaton neared his destination. The last trace of civilization stood miles behind him: the city of Dimona, gateway to the Negev Desert, and home to the Negev Nuclear Research Center, Israel's tightly guarded and secretive nuclear facility.

The road twisted into a valley between rain-carved hills. The topography reminded him of southern Utah, a camping trip taken the previous summer with Christine and Davy. They'd spent two weeks wandering through mesas, skipping rocks into creek beds, searching for fossils; days as carefree as the last few had been perilous. The notion of bringing his family here someday came to mind, but it dissipated quickly: after tonight, he feared, his memories of the Negev might forever be ruined.

He hadn't seen another car for miles, and he expected more of the same as darkness fell. It was a secondary road that eventually connected to the main highway leading to the resort town of Eilat. He'd requisitioned a handheld GPS navigation device from the training center, and it showed twelve miles to go to the rendezvous point.

With Dimona fading in the mirror, Slaton pulled to the side of the road, the milquetoast sedan provided by the Office stirring a cloud of red-brown dust. The western sky was ablaze, and all around him were plots of red-hued rock, crumbling at the edges, interspersed with feathered islands of straw-brown grass. He got out, popped the trunk, and removed the remainder of the gear he'd requisitioned. He took off his dark jacket and shrugged on a lightweight plate carrier; the vest wouldn't stop anything heavy, but could prove useful against small arms.

The carrier also had an integral holster, into which he sheathed a new SIG—he'd upgraded to a red dot sight. Slaton recalled the armory clerk's take on the weapon. "We're in the red dot revolution. It will turn you into the marksman you always thought you were." Slaton, possibly the most accomplished shooter Israel had ever produced, had smiled appreciatively.

Truth of it was, he would never give up any advantage for the sake of ego. All his training and operational experience aside, he had no qualms whatsoever about putting a red dot on a target if it would increase the chances of a hit. He shrugged his jacket back on, looked at himself in the reflection of the car's window. The vest was hardly discreet, but on the other hand, it added a bit of heft, which put his silhouette more in line with that of Kalman—a thought that turned discomforting when Slaton remembered what had happened to him.

In fact, he had no idea if Eitan would even show up this evening. It was possible he'd been the shooter that afternoon. If so, combined with the death of Ayla Bloch, it meant he was a man bent on revenge. And since Slaton had been the mission commander of Operation Starlight, he himself was likely next on the list. Might Eitan have sent the meeting spot to Kalman's phone simply to draw Slaton into his killing ground? That, too, was possible. Conversely, if Eitan *did* show up for the meeting, it suggested he had no idea Kalman was dead. The implications of that scenario seemed incalculable. Slaton's only choice was to make the meeting and be ready. To that end, he pulled from the trunk the last item he'd signed for at the armory: an IWI Dan bolt-action precision rifle. The same rifle, barring a few upgrades, he'd carried that fateful night. He gave it one final check, then placed it securely in the floor well of the passenger seat.

Slaton got behind the wheel and set out into the shadowed hills. The daylight was fading, burnt-orange hues painting the sky behind. He ran down the window and sweet desert air swirled in, cool and bracing. The nav unit plotted the rendezvous point as being a quarter mile past the terminus of an unimproved side road that lay ahead. The road accessed a network of hiking trails, all of which would be deserted this time of day.

Twenty minutes later he took the final turn, and where the road ended, he encountered a small patch of earth that had been bulldozed into a parking apron. There was room for ten cars, but right then he was alone. He wondered if another would come. Having studied the map at length, he knew that the rendezvous point could be reached by at least three other combinations of access roads and trails.

He moved the rifle beneath the front seat, out of sight but situated for quick access from the driver's-side door. He had debated taking it with him, but when he considered the possible scenarios, a discreetly carried SIG seemed more conducive to a positive outcome than a shouldered sniper rifle. Still, he was glad to have it available—one more option if things went to hell.

Which, he thought regrettably, was highly likely.

Slaton locked the doors and set out into a fast-falling dusk.

The air cooled quickly as the sun faded. Slaton was wearing a jacket, partially zipped to give access to the SIG, and a baseball cap with Mossad's blue-and-white logo—they'd been selling them as a fundraiser at the training center entrance. He never asked what the cause was, although it was probably worthy. He simply wanted the hat for cover: from a distance, especially in the fading light, he could conceivably pass for Kalman.

The trail was rough, the downhill grade weaving into the basin of a *makhtesh*. The terrain around him, Makhtesh Katan, was one of the Negev's geological wonders. He'd hiked here as a teen and remembered learning the Christian legends. These were the hills scouted by Moses's twelve spies, a barren landscape that had never been settled, discounting occasional encampments by nomadic Bedouin. A number of *makhtesh* were scattered through the region, extending to the Sinai and beyond. Roughly circular, they resembled craters from meteor strikes, only miles wide, formed by eons of erosion and the collapse of the hard limestone floors at the bases of the ridgelines.

Slaton's eyes kept sweeping that high ground. To the left, five hundred meters distant, one particular ridge loomed large. The higher elevations to the right were more distant, less vertical. Other than a distant cluster of lights in the north, the scene had to be little changed from biblical times. Slaton regretted not having an infrared optic for scanning the surrounding terrain, but the training center's armory hadn't been so equipped.

His comfort level sank a notch lower.

The final turn carved a gap between two gentle hills. Then, all at once, the horizon opened up before him. Backed by high clouds still reflecting the set sun, it was a glorious view. And one that Slaton took no time to appreciate.

He referenced the GPS.

He was nearing the rendezvous point.

SIXTY-THREE

Every sense was on high alert over the final hundred yards. Slaton took in the scents of the desert, the soft sound of the breeze brushing over scrub. He did so without any sense of fulfilment or pleasure, but simply to establish a baseline. He had to recognize the slightest deviation.

The outlier he noticed was a visual disturbance: choppy movement in the tranquil desert ahead. The motion resolved into a figure approaching from the opposite direction. Slaton froze on the trail, his eyes taking in everything. He saw no secondary threat, and after getting a better look at the man, Slaton quickly made associations; the same awkward gait, the same crooked posture he'd seen in a looped video. The only difference now: instead of a sidewalk in Nur-Sultan, it was a path on the edge of the Negev.

Zev Eitan had come.

He appeared to be alone, and was dressed much like Slaton: dark jacket and pants, a watch cap in lieu of a fundraiser baseball cap. His hands, notably, were empty. It struck Slaton that the last time he'd seen Eitan, in the flesh, had been from a prone position beneath a lattice of scaffolding on a dark night in Beirut. Operation Starlight. Eitan had been part of the element watching the raiding team's back, and Slaton recalled catching glimpses of him and Kalman as they engaged Duba's men and moved into cover. Moments later, somewhere out of Slaton's view, Eitan was hit, leaving Kalman to fight for his life.

And since that night? For twelve years Zev Eitan had fallen off the face of the earth.

Eitan spotted him and came to a stop, creating a standoff from the Old West. He stood crookedly but alert in a minor clearing, his eyes penetrating, longing for recognition. Slaton held his ground, still less concerned with Eitan than the panorama around him. Seeking threats; looking for possible concealment; gauging distances and angles.

Slaton began moving again, and as he neared Eitan he saw a perceptible cock of the head—a dog trying to make sense of something curious. He'd been expecting to see Kalman. Instead, he recognized the assassin who'd given him his last orders before . . . *what?* Slaton wondered. *Where have you been all these years?*

He drew to a stop with twenty-five yards between them. A distance at which Slaton could employ the SIG with dead-on accuracy. A distance at which most other men would miss in a stressful situation. The two studied each other with mutual suspicion. Searching for traces of intent, hints of weapons or backup. Yet as he stood there, looking at a man he'd left for dead so many years ago, Slaton was struck by something he'd never felt so purely: a commander's remorse. A sense that he'd made a terrible mistake. That he had failed one of his own.

Thinking it best to de-escalate, Slaton held his hands outward, turned both palms forward. A gunslinger's truce.

"I wasn't expecting to see you," Eitan said. If it was a lie, it was a convincing one.

"I could say the same thing. I honestly never expected to see you again." A flash of something in Eitan's gaze, a tensing in his neck. Anger? No . . . more likely hatred. "But I'm glad you came."

"Where is Kalman?"

"I'll get to that," Slaton promised. "But first, I'd like to hear your story. Where have you been all these years?"

Eitan took a long breath, as if bracing himself. "I've wanted to tell you about it for a long time. You, Kalman, Bloch. I've dreamed of telling you."

"All right," Slaton said cautiously, "so now's your chance."

Six hundred meters south, and one hundred meters up, hidden expertly near the crest of the ridgeline, a shadowed figure lay still behind his weapon.

He'd been settled for nearly an hour, this after investing another hour in scouting out the ideal hide. Beneath a minor outcropping of rock, he'd identified a low ledge, a crevice just long enough to conceal his entire body. He'd swept the niche first, during daylight, and was glad he'd done so—a large scorpion had been curled in one corner. After taking care of that, he had backed into a coffin-like hide that seemed almost custom-built, and then pulled loose strands of brush across the opening. He would be invisible from virtually every angle, every wavelength of electronically aided search. He doubted the job would require such measures. He'd been hired to kill one man, and given the modest range, that was simplicity itself. Then again, he'd never walked away from a mission thinking, *I was too prepared.*

He settled the optic of his bullpup rifle on the scene below. Conveniently, from the angle he was watching, he could see both men simultaneously in his high-power optic. They were talking calmly, although both appeared wary. In the background he noted a small acacia tree, its branches perfectly still. The wind was calm. He had already calculated the range and elevation drop using a laser device, illuminating a nearby rock. It would be accurate to within a few meters—he hadn't known *exactly* where his target would end up standing.

As he regarded the two men, he was struck by the humor of the scene—one of them he was viewing through his scope for the second time that day, over a hundred miles removed. *It's just not his day.*

The sniper's finger settled on the trigger, his breathing went calm.

And then his entire plan shattered.

A poisonous barb pierced his right testicle.

It was all he could do to stifle a scream.

The sniper threw his gun into the dirt and leapt out of his hide like . . . like a man who'd been stung in the balls by a scorpion.

SIXTY-FOUR

"You left me!" Eitan said in a venomous hiss. "You left me behind!"

"I know," Slaton found himself saying. "Kalman told me you were dead—he said it was a headshot. Going back for you would have meant walking into the teeth of the response. But if I'd believed there was any chance you were alive, I would have done it. I think you know that."

Eitan reached up and pulled off his watch cap. Even in the dim light, Slaton could see a jagged scar on one temple, raking along the scalp line. "This is from the bullet that night." He then reached a hand to the front of his jacket. Slaton shifted to a ready stance, prepared to pull the SIG. Eitan pulled down the zipper of his jacket and shrugged it off, then unbuttoned his shirt. He pulled it off to reveal a bare chest etched in scar tissue from top to bottom, a virtual tapestry of pain. It didn't stop there. In a surreal display he took off his pants and boots, leaving him standing in the cool evening air in nothing but a pair of boxers. His right leg was misshapen, his left foot gnarled. He reached for his boxers, then hesitated, and said, "I'll spare you that. Suffice to say, I will never have children, never be a husband."

Slaton stood silently, no idea how to respond.

"Yes," Eitan said, "I *was* unconscious from that headshot. I came to in a hospital in Beirut, guards all around me. The Lebanese had no use for me, so they handed me straight to the Syrians. By the next morning I was in Sednaya."

Sednaya. With that, the clarity began. It was the most infamous prison in the Middle East, which was akin to being the hottest fire in hell. Tens of thousands had died there in extrajudicial killings. They were the lucky ones.

"They beat me mercilessly, demanded information about the mission. As far as I can remember, I gave them little. A few details, a few names, most of them fictional. I remained true to my country, true to Mossad. True to you and Anton Bloch. I was confident the Office would find a way to get me out. The beatings went on and on. At some point, probably weeks after I arrived, they came in and showed me a news report from Tel Aviv. I had been honored as having sacrificed my life in the service of Israel. There was even a quote from my 'unnamed commander' saying I had 'died a hero's death.'"

Slaton remembered it like it was yesterday, giving the quote and meaning every word.

"After that, the beatings only worsened." He pointed to his leg. "They broke it with a bat. Then again a few days later. Six times in all, although my memories are hazy. To the interrogators, I became something of an amusement. I was dead to Israel, dead to the world. Over seven years I endured a century of pain, chained to the same iron bar in the same cell. Beating after beating until my tormentors were exhausted. Still, I survived"—he looked down at his fractured body—"if that's what you can call this."

In the half-light, Eitan stood with forced rigidity, straining for dignity. Slaton imagined he had envisioned this moment a thousand times: doing his best to stand tall, to face the commander who'd abandoned him, who had doomed him to rot in a Syrian torture chamber.

"Seven years," he repeated.

"How did you escape?"

"Compassion rears its head in the most unlikely of places . . . even Syrian dungeons, apparently. One of my chief jailors, a major, took pity on me, wretched as I was. He said he was astounded I'd survived as long as I had, and that some of the senior officers believed I was no longer of any use. Late one night, he and another guard came to my cell, dressed me, and tossed me into the street outside Sednaya with a hundred U.S. dollars in my pocket. He told me he would report that I'd died that night, and say he'd ordered my body disposed of—Sednaya, as you know, has its own crematorium. No one would doubt my death, given the condition I was in." Eitan laughed humorlessly. "So there you are. I died once in Beirut, then again in Syria. And still"—he spread his crooked arms awkwardly— "here I am."

"What happened then?" Slaton asked. "You didn't return to Israel."

"Israel? The homeland I nearly gave my life for? The country that abandoned me to a fate worse than death?"

"If we had known you were alive, we *would* have gotten you out. Bloch would have made a swap, anything."

Eitan shook his head. "I could never go back."

"Why not?"

"Endure what I did . . . then perhaps you would understand. My country betrayed me, so I turned away. After seven years of agony, the sudden arrival of freedom was like staring at the sun. I was stunned, and for days did nothing but eat and sleep. When the money ran out, I stole a car, an old Lada, and made my way to the coast. I lived in that car for weeks, begging and thieving, getting my strength back. I eventually took a ferry to Cyprus, looked up a man who ran logistics for a Russian arms syndicate—I had dealt with him once on Mossad's behalf. He took pity on seeing my condition and brought me on. Within a year I was running his operation. Shortly thereafter, he died unexpectedly and I took over."

"Unexpectedly?"

"As a nine-millimeter hollow point tends to be. No one mourned him. It allowed me a new identity, a new business. My incarceration had infused me with a new temperament, one that was ideal for trafficking weapons—after seven years in Sednaya, any sense of morality is wiped from one's soul. The business became quite successful, leading me eventually to the group I work with today."

This was the juncture Slaton had been aiming for. "Who are they?"

A shake of the head. "No, *kidon*," he said, using the Mossad term for assassin. "It's your turn. Where is Kalman?"

"Dead."

Eitan seemed to consider it. "Your work?"

"I had no reason to harm him. I suspected you might be involved in the Almaty bombing, so I went to see him this afternoon at his house. I asked him about Operation Starlight, whether there was any chance you'd survived."

"And?"

"He admitted it was something that had long bothered him. I took that as a yes—there was a chance you'd been left behind. I'm guessing it was no coincidence that you confirmed it yourself today—he told me you called him, asked for this meeting. That was the last thing he said before he was taken out by a sniper."

And with that, Slaton saw the first crack in Eitan's graveyard demeanor. He seemed suddenly disoriented, enveloped by uncertainty. Still, Slaton needed confirmation. "Almaty was your doing, wasn't it?" he prodded. "Anton's daughter? Payback against him, against Mossad?"

No response.

"Who are you working for, Zev? Who's running these attacks against America?"

His tortured face canted left, roving over the hills to the south. "I honestly can't give you names. But then, that's how things work these days—and the reason men like Bagdani, like me, are increasingly in demand. I've been dealing with three men who refer to themselves as The Trident. For a man in my business, it's best to know your clients; however, these three proved difficult to trace. I'm sure they are all wealthy, and they confessed that two of them had once headed large corporations—one that built electronics, the other weapons. The third had a more academic background, research and development tied to the defense industry. All three left behind lucrative, high-level positions to somehow arrive in my shadowed world. There were rumors they'd fallen out of favor with their government, but I'm not convinced. What I *can* tell you is this: three men who spent their lives developing and manufacturing cutting edge military technology very suddenly left their institutions. They hired me, I hired Bagdani, who in turn recruited the foot soldiers. The Trident has deep funding, but I could never determine where it came from. The wider strategy, however, is clear. They supply advanced hardware and mission objectives, then pay others to throw the spears."

"Outsourcing war?"

"It's hardly new. There have been mercenaries since our ancestors were living in caves. In recent years it has become increasingly common. Russia exports its little green men across the globe. Proxy wars have been decimating Africa for generations. Even the Americans do it, although they would never admit it. Private security contractors in the Afghanistan campaign, protection details in Iraq, pilots flying signals intelligence aircraft from Saudi Arabia. The Trident is only taking things to the next level, leveraging the latest technology. The next attack is a case in point. It will employ a weapon against which there is no known defense."

"When?"

"The timing is situational . . . for all I know, it may already have happened. If not, then a strike is imminent."

"What kind of weapon are we talking about?"

"A hypersonic missile."

Slaton should have been stunned. It was a technology that had been on the drawing board for years, yet one that faced great technical hurdles. The idea that such a weapon could be used by a nonstate actor, a guns-for-hire offshoot seemed stunning. But no less stunning, he supposed, than directed-energy weapons or GPS meaconing—the already-wreaked havoc of recent days.

He studied Eitan closely. Standing nearly naked in the chill half-light, backed by the rugged terrain, he looked frail and insubstantial, a porcelain figure of a man. Then he noticed Eitan's right hand brush his ear. That, along with his drifting gaze, brought Slaton's thoughts back to the present. To his immediate situation. He considered what had happened to Kalman. Considered a veiled group with access to advanced weapons. Considered Eitan's mild surprise that he was here instead of Kalman. Slaton put it all together, ran a calculation. The answer he came up with seemed implausible. If he was wrong, his life was at imminent risk. Yet if he was right . . .

"He's not Bagdani's recruit," Slaton ventured.

"Who?"

"The sniper on the ridgeline. You requested a shooter, and Bagdani passed along the name of a Libyan gun-for-hire. But I don't think that's who's up there."

Eitan's eyes flicked between Slaton and the hills.

"Did you ever meet the shooter in person, or was it all remote? Messaged instructions and electronic payments? Was that the signal you just gave, a hand to the ear?"

Silence.

"I wish I'd gone back for you that night in Beirut, Zev. I made a call in a fast-moving situation, based on what I knew—and I got it wrong. No man should ever endure what you did in Sednaya, but that doesn't excuse the bloodshed you've brought in return. Innocent people died."

Eitan still said nothing.

"There is a lot more at stake here than you getting revenge against me, Bloch, and Kalman. One more strike by The Trident could lead to war between the United States and Russia. I'm guessing you don't give a damn about these people or what their objectives are—for you, it was simply a means toward payback. A way to get Mossad to let its guard down. But you can still stop it! Tell me where the next attack is coming!"

Slaton now had Eitan's attention. He was shaking his head, wondering why the shot hadn't come.

It was time to go all-in. "Think about it, Zev. You were surprised when I showed up tonight. You were expecting Kalman. Which tells me you knew nothing about him being eliminated hours ago. Don't you see? The *Trident* gave that order. They sent their own man here, and somehow learned that you reached out to a Mossad officer. They had to intervene . . ."

The headshaking stopped.

"You signaled and nothing happened. Think it through . . . killing me means nothing to them." Slaton pinned his gaze on Eitan, then placed his bet. "If there *is* a sniper on that ridge right now . . . he's not aiming at me."

High above, the black-clad figure had gathered himself. His crotch was on fire, aching from the scorpion sting. It wouldn't be fatal, but the pain was excruciating. He hadn't bothered to put his pants and boots back on after scrambling out of his clothes in desperation. He had at least killed the damned thing, and even found another in his boot. He must have put himself in a nest of the horrid creatures. He looked miserably at the abandoned hide, then out across a lunar landscape that was fading into the night. He couldn't wait to leave this godforsaken place.

He settled onto open ground behind his gun, taking up a prone shooting position. Needless to say, he wasn't crawling back under the damned ledge. He sighted his optic a second time and saw the scene unchanged. At least that was in his favor. Then, however, he did a double take. The smaller of the two men was nearly naked, having stripped off his clothes. *Crazy Israelis.*

He had no idea what it meant, but at this point it hardly mattered.

He'd broken cover.

His balls were throbbing.

It was time to finish things.

The reticle fell still over his target.

Eitan was staring at Slaton, and in the waning light his expression couldn't have been more clear: the sudden realization that he'd become the architect of his own demise.

A different man, a less damaged man, might have been quicker. In the last instant Eitan moved, a spin to his right just before the bullet struck.

Slaton dove for the cover of a nearby depression; not thinking, just re-acting. He'd caught a glimpse of a distant muzzle flash, more or less where he'd predicted the shooter would be. The distant crack of the shot sounded through the otherwise silent valley.

He low-crawled, dragging himself behind a rock outcropping, and waited for the follow-up. When none came right away, he peered out and saw Eitan on the ground. He'd been hit on the right side of his chest, a massive wound from a high-caliber round. Unlike that afternoon, how-ever, Slaton saw the rise and fall of breathing. A second shot rang in, and Eitan screamed as it struck him in the left thigh. Lying on the ground he was a smaller target—but a target all the same.

Slaton had no choice. Having left Zev Eitan for dead once, he wouldn't do it again.

He scrambled low and fast, seized both of Eitan's legs, and began drag-ging him toward cover. A third shot came up short, sending chips of stone flying through the air. Before the fourth could arrive, Slaton got them both behind the low pile of stone.

He immediately checked the wound on Eitan's chest—it was bleeding profusely, blood pulsing. His eyes were open wide, yet he seemed oddly calm. A man accustomed to unimaginable suffering.

"I'll get you out of here," Slaton said.

A gurgling cough. Eitan blinked a few times, then looked at Slaton. "You didn't leave me this time . . ."

"Don't worry, I'll take care of you." Slaton stole a momentary glance at the ridgeline.

A rattle from somewhere deep within as Eitan looked at him with new desperation. He rasped, "Admiral . . ." He was fading fast, his hand drooping to one side.

"*What?*" Slaton prompted.

Eitan blinked again, and with the last breath of his life, he said, "Kuz . . . netsov."

SIXTY-FIVE

The great behemoth plowed through cobalt seas like an island cutting a current.

At over a thousand feet in length, *Admiral Kuznetsov* was the largest ship in the Russian navy, and while she was considerably less in tonnage than her American counterparts, she was Russia's only operational aircraft carrier.

She had sailed three weeks earlier from her home port in Severomorsk, a pass-in-review parade across the doorstep of Western Europe. Like most of *Kuznetsov*'s voyages, it was part mission-oriented cruise, part publicity stunt. As flagship of the fleet, she was to Russia what *Bismarck* had been to the Third Reich: a titanic symbol of power projection. This was mostly derived from the strike aircraft—SU-33s and MiG-29Ks—which had been modified for carrier operations from her ski-jump bow.

Kuznetsov was the only vessel of her class to have survived the budget cuts of the '90s. Two sister ships had originally been commissioned, but for lack of funding both were sold to China. One had been transformed into that country's first operational aircraft carrier, while the other was destined for humiliation: Its partially completed hull was to be repurposed as a floating casino. In time, however, an increasingly expansionist Chinese government converted that shell into a second, slightly larger carrier.

In spite of being held as the pride of the Russian Navy, *Kuznetsov*'s dismal operational record had been exhaustively documented. Because she was not a nuclear-powered ship, her massive engines ran on heavy fuel oil, resulting in a giveaway trail of black smoke that, on a clear day, could be seen for fifty miles. Her boilers and steam turbines were so unreliable that *Kuznetsov* was accompanied at all times by an ocean-going tug. Her pipes froze in the winter, faulty evaporators caused water shortages in the summer, and half the latrines were out of service year-round.

Her few deployments were a running chain of calamities. During a fleet exercise in 2005, one of her SU-33 fighters rolled into the ocean, and countless fires have broken out below deck. *Kuznetsov* was responsible for one of the biggest oil spills ever off the coast of Ireland, and problems with the aircraft arresting gear have resulted in multiple crashes. In 2018, while in retrofit, the drydock cradling the carrier sank, causing a seven-ton crane to collapse and tear a massive hole in her midship deck. This was followed by yet another fire.

Kuznetsov was, if nothing else, a symbol of Russian perseverance. Three months earlier, after extensive repairs, refits, and sea trials, she once again returned to action. The deployment to Syria had been ordered by President Petrov, a high-visibility cruise to the most embattled region on earth. And a place where Russia kept a heavy hand.

From the bridge overseeing an acre of flight deck, Captain 1st Rank Nikolai Stepanov lifted his binoculars and trained them to starboard. In the scant light of dusk, he easily picked out a ship on the distant horizon. "She is still with us," he commented to his executive officer.

"Yes, Captain. Range now nineteen kilometers. I doubt we will be rid of her until we reach Tartus."

The captain gave a Slavic shrug. He'd been hoping to arrive off the coast of Syria early tomorrow, close to the original schedule. The plan was to drop anchor just outside the port of Tartus—the harbor could not accommodate a ship of her class—and pause there for a week, longer if necessary, to make boiler repairs. Then the official mission would begin: ply the Eastern Med to conduct air operations.

Or at least make an honest effort.

Even after the ship's most recent overhaul, the aircraft arresting gear remained an issue. Fortunately, they would be operating close enough to the coast that if the arresting system failed, or the deck became fouled, the jets could easily divert to landside airfields. One way or another, Stepanov was determined to start flying. *Kuznetsov* was the crown jewel of Russia's navy, and while three years had passed since her last disastrous cruise, so far things were going smoothly. The boilers had broken down only once, and they'd repaired them on the fly. By *Kuznetsov*'s standards, the voyage was going well, and for that her captain was grateful.

He again lifted the binoculars and studied the American ship, a mere silhouette beyond the protective ring of his own battle group. It had peculiar lines, sharp and angular, like a knife blading through the sea. He knew it was a modern Zumwalt-class destroyer, with the latest technology. He'd had detailed briefings on the weapons the ship carried: ranges, weaknesses, available countermeasures. On previous voyages such trivia had seemed little more than academic, yet today it was front and center in Stepanov's mind.

In light of the recent tensions between the nations, the captain would be watchful.

Twelve miles from *Kuznetsov*'s starboard beam, a better pair of binoculars was being lowered by the commanding officer of USS *Michael Monsoor*. Standing on the bridge, Captain Eric Lagarde checked the display linked to the Combat Information Center and saw their position holding steady. They'd been shadowing *Admiral Kuznetsov* since the Straits of Gibraltar, which wasn't particularly difficult. Sixty thousand tons, crawling along at twelve knots, surrounded by a dozen escort ships—tracking *Kuznetsov* was about as challenging as tracking the Big Dipper across a clear night sky.

This would typically be a routine mission for *Monsoor*—the Navy always shadowed *Kuznetsov* on the rare occasions when she left port. The recent warning issued by Fleet command, however, fueled by the sinking of *Ross,* had everyone on edge. If that wasn't enough, Lagarde knew the British and French were also in the area, and that a CIA SIGINT boat was somewhere to the north. Combined with *Kuznetsov* and her own flotilla, it was a virtual three-ring nautical circus rolling across the Med.

As per the new order, *Monsoor*'s tactical radar was tracking not only surrounding naval vessels but also shipping traffic. Right then, twelve such targets were being painted: bulk carriers, container ships, a pair of tankers. All were plowing laboriously through crowded sea-lanes. The only return that had not yet been identified was forty-eight miles south. The raw signal was marginal at that range, owing to the curvature of the earth, but enhancing software smoothed things out. The target was lying still on the sea and appeared to be relatively small—likely a coastal freighter, which were common in this part of the world. The electronic warfare specialists were keeping an eye on it, but so far there had been no sign of suspicious signals or interference.

Lagarde very much hoped it stayed that way.

On the periphery of a very busy plot of sea, Captain Constantis had *Poyarka* right where she needed to be. It hadn't been easy. She lay dead in the water sixty miles north of Tobruk, Libya. The ship's list to port had grown more pronounced, but wasn't yet critical. Constantis explained to the crew that the owners had ordered the ship to pause in her present position. It was perfectly true, although the reason he gave over the loudspeaker—that they were considering a diversion to work on the dodgy pumps—was a blatant lie.

The helmsman manipulated the thrusters to keep the bow pointed north. He was probably wondering why this was necessary—it put them abeam to a light wind and served no nautical purpose—yet he never questioned the order.

Constantis knew that their target, *Admiral Kuznetsov,* was roughly sixty miles over the horizon. More precise location data was streaming constantly to the control room downstairs, relayed, he guessed, from a satellite overhead. At that range, even a ship of her size would not be visible, nor would *Poyarka*'s standard marine radar have any chance of picking her up. The same was true of the second vessel they were tracking, now fifty miles away. He scanned with his binoculars and saw a few shadows on the horizon, but none drew his interest. He wondered if the U.S. Navy ship, *Monsoor,* was watching *Poyarka*. He supposed they were, but it wasn't a concern. The Americans would have little interest in a rust-bucket survey ship lying still at such a range. Just to be sure, Constantis had ordered electronic silence: the sat-comm was receiving downloads, but *Poyarka*'s radar and radios were turned off, emanating no signals.

No, he thought with satisfaction. *All eyes on* Monsoor's *bridge will be pointed in the other direction.*

He felt the small local device buzz in his pocket. Pulling it out, he saw a call from the control room downstairs.

"Go ahead."

"We still wait for the desired geometry," said Chou, "but expect to have it soon. How long can you keep us in position?"

Constantis looked, in turn, at the helmsman, the clear sky, and the most recent estimate of how much water they were taking on. He guessed the latter would be the limiting factor. "Until we sink, which gives us the rest of the day."

Chou, clearly put off, promised to give another update soon, and then hung up without another word.

Constantis shook his head derisively. *No sense of humor, these people.*

SIXTY-SIX

Slaton ran as fast as the terrain allowed.

Behind him was a dead man he'd once failed.

Ahead was a killer.

He veered off the trail he'd arrived on and scrambled over fields of sand, rock, and brush. The GPS device was in his pocket, but for the moment he didn't need it—speed was all important, and by using the high terrain as a reference he could focus on the rough ground ahead. He would fine-tune things once he neared his objective.

He hadn't been able to save Eitan, but his final words rang in Slaton's head: *Admiral Kuznetsov.* He knew what it was—Russia's only aircraft carrier. He would forward that to Sorensen when he could. The Americans would know where the ship was, and they would understand the threat of a hypersonic missile. Right now, however, there was another source of intelligence nearby.

One that would soon disappear.

The incoming fire had stopped after he pulled Eitan into cover. Slaton couldn't discount the chance that the shooter was still on the ridgeline, or that he might be trying to stalk him. Yet he'd been on the other side of that equation. Snipers didn't kill wantonly. They had a mission, and after a solid hit on Eitan, this one was likely complete. Slaton doubted he himself was a target. In addition, the sniper had no way of knowing what communications he might have or what backup he might be calling in. Taken together, he guessed the shooter would call his mission complete and egress. As he weaved through stands of brush in the fading light, it occurred to Slaton that he was betting his life on a lot of assumptions.

He was at least thankful for his preparation. He'd studied the topo map thoroughly, and that picture remained fixed in his head: the layout of the primary terrain features, every road and trail leading into Makhtesh Katan. The most practical ingress and egress for a shooter on the ridgeline was a road to the east. It would not only take him away from the scene of the crime, but also connect conveniently to the main highway where he could fade into anonymity. If Slaton was right, it gave him a window of favorable geometry: the shooter would have to negotiate the steep backside of the ridgeline, forcing slow progress over rocky terrain and switchbacks. If Slaton moved fast enough, he could reach the access road first—where he expected to find a car waiting. Once again, conjecture. But conjecture based on years of experience.

Nearing the base of the hill, Slaton stopped to reference his GPS device.

It showed less than a mile to go to the point where the road ended. By the terrain contour lines, a slight downward grade from his position. He hoped the map was accurate. Even more, he hoped he was right about the shooter not getting there first, and that he wasn't stopping on the backside of the ridge to scan for threats. More assumptions.

Slaton set out again on a dead run.

He found the car right where he expected it to be, a generic rental sedan locked up tight. Slaton saw no sign of the shooter but was cautious all the same, his SIG poised.

The car was parked on a tiny apron at the end of the unimproved road, much like the one he himself had used a few miles away. All around he saw flat scrubland with little concealment. There were a few low stands of vegetation, the odd pile of rocks, but nothing that would prevent the shooter from seeing him, especially if he was using an optic. Sometimes the best plan was the most simple. He ducked behind the car on the driver's side, which was situated away from the high ground.

Slaton waited and listened, still catching his breath after the mile-and-a-half dash. Chill night air swept over his face, and he used a sleeve to wipe perspiration from his brow. Once again, he instinctively began logging the background, every sight and sound and smell—the buzz of insects, the deepening shadows, the motion of nearby grass.

He considered how his adversary might be armed. It was conceivable the shooter had left his rifle on top of the ridge. Discarding it would make getting down the hill easier, and at some point the weapon would have to be ditched anyway to catch a flight or cross a border. On the other hand, Slaton doubted the shooter would be packing much else for such a simple mission. Optic, bipod, suppressor, comm gear, maybe some water and a few energy bars. With such a light load to begin, there seemed little reason to part with a perfectly good weapon. On balance, he decided the rifle would be retained. And a backup handgun was a virtual lock.

His plan was to let the shooter get close before making his move. The nearer he got to the car, the more confident he would be. The more his guard would be down. If he went for his rifle, close quarters gave Slaton an advantage. Big guns weren't built for tight spaces—it was like using a jousting lance in a knife fight.

Slaton didn't know if the shooter would be wearing body armor. If there was any doubt, he would aim accordingly. His objectives, in a perfect world, were to disarm the man, ask a few questions, and then call Sorensen and Nurin to tell them what he'd learned. All in that order.

Unfortunately, Slaton's world was rarely perfect. A concept made painfully clear when the first bullet struck him in the stomach.

SIXTY-SEVEN

Slaton flew back, launching himself behind the trunk of the car as two more rounds clanked into the fender. He looked down and saw a tear over the bottom plate of his vest. It had to be small caliber—the round hadn't penetrated.

He hadn't heard a sound, hadn't seen any movement. Most likely, the shooter had made a careful approach, probably circling the car from a distance and using an optic to his advantage. Which meant he was trained as well. Whatever the method, the shooter knew his exact position.

Slaton, however, had an approximation of his: somewhere off the left front quarter of the car, probably inside fifty yards.

He cast a lightning glance around the left taillight. No movement, little concealment available. The man could never close in without being seen, so he was probably laying low, waiting for a follow-up. Snipers were inordinately patient.

Yes, we are, Slaton thought.

He did nothing.

He waited and listened. His eyes searched left and right, but otherwise Slaton remained motionless. Five minutes passed. Ten. The man probably guessed he'd scored at least one hit. At some point he would become curious, wonder if the job was done.

Five more minutes. Still nothing. A contest of nerves.

And then . . . *something.*

A boot treading softly, pressure on sand and gravel. Then, ever so cautiously, another. Passenger side. Fifty feet away? No, less. A long, wary hesitation.

Soundlessly, Slaton eased himself lower until he could see beneath the car's chassis. There, ten paces in front of the right front tire, he saw a pair of boots. Twin size-8 targets, frozen in place.

Ever so slowly, in total silence, Slaton rotated his shoulders and lowered the SIG. He contorted to bring the gun to bear. In that moment—twisted like a pretzel, his weapon beneath a gas tank, and with one hole already in his vest—he was perfectly happy to join the red dot revolution.

He lined up the SIG with a steady hand and unleashed three tightly spaced shots. Slaton scrambled up and transitioned to a kneeling stance behind the rear quarter-panel. He saw the man down, his right boot shredded and bloody. To his credit, and to Slaton's surprise, he returned fire immediately. Flat on the ground, four shots came at a steady interval. Nothing aimed, only suppressive fire. The man would have crawled for cover, but there was nowhere to go. Slaton held behind the fender for a beat, the back right wheel and tire giving marginal protection—he, too, was vulnerable beneath the car.

When the incoming fire paused, Slaton swung out far enough to group three sighted shots. The sniper jerked sideways, and the hand with the gun—always the most important—dropped to the dirt. Slaton waited, his sight settled squarely. The man didn't move. The gun remained near his hand but was no longer in his grasp.

Slaton stood and went closer, the red dot never wavering. He saw blood on the man's hip and beltline. From the angle Slaton had been shooting, those hits would have traveled upward into his abdomen and chest cavity. Finally, he saw the man's eyes. In the faint light they were reflective, twin mirrors cast skyward in a forever stare. Slaton kicked the gun clear, ensured his other hand was empty. He saw no sign of breathing. He kneeled down, checked for a pulse—nothing.

It was a failure of sorts. He'd wanted the man alive, wanted to ask him who he was working for. On the other hand, some manner of justice had been served. This sniper had killed two men today. Likely many more.

Slaton stood tall, secured his weapon.

He pulled out his phone and called Anna Sorensen.

As the satellite connection ran, he studied the body at his feet. Slaton would soon go over it thoroughly, check every pocket, and then the car, searching for any kind of identity documents. He didn't expect to find much. Or at least, nothing that was truthful. Yet as he stood over the sniper, he did notice two things.

First were the man's features—he was undeniably Asian. Second was the weapon slung on his back. It was a NORINCO KBU-97a, an export version of the QBU-88 bullpup rifle. Slaton didn't like jumping to conclusions, but the connection was inescapable: the shooter could well be of the same provenance as the gun.

Which would make him Chinese.

SIXTY-EIGHT

Admiral Kuznetsov was plowing ahead at minimum speed. Boilers two and six had been acting up, and the associated turbines were struggling. Stepanov's chief engineer, who'd been battling the problem for days, had given him tentative assurances she could limp all the way to Tartus. That hopeful plan died somewhere south of Crete.

The captain felt the trouble before anyone told him about it: a low frequency shudder reverberating through the deck as some vital component went through its death throes. The coffee in his cup on the chart table developed concentric rings.

"Damn it!" Stepanov muttered.

Moments later, the call came from the engine room. "Sir, boiler two has suffered an uncontained failure!"

"All engines stop!" Stepanov ordered. More vibrations as the four great propellers spun down and fell still. At that point, *Kuznetsov* was coasting eastward, her speed bleeding off slowly. A leviathan by any measure, she would travel another four miles on momentum alone.

Stepanov was livid, cursing the operational delay report he would have to send. What he didn't realize then—but would appreciate days later—was that for the first time ever, *Kuznetsov*'s failings would work in her favor.

Captain Constantis was in the control room, watching over the shoulders of Wu and Chou. The technicians didn't seem thrilled to have him there, but he assured them he wasn't required on the bridge. They were too busy to argue.

All eyes were glued to the satellite feed that displayed the near-real-time position of three ships: *Poyarka*, *Admiral Kuznetsov*, and the American destroyer *Monsoor*. Constantis didn't know exactly where the data was coming from, but the involvement of Chou and Wu was proof enough: at some level, the mission was being aided by China. Of the three symbols, only *Poyarka* was stationary. The other two ships were running more or less in formation. *Monsoor* was fifty miles north, *Kuznetsov* twelve beyond that. At this point, it was all a matter of geometry. When the three dots neared a straight line, the missile would be launched.

"How long?" Constantis asked.

"Fifteen minutes. Perhaps a bit more," said Chou.

"Target is slowing," Wu said, pointing to a speed readout on *Kuznetsov*'s data tag. "Eight knots now, four less than before. Why would an aircraft carrier slow here?" he asked, addressing Constantis.

The captain shook his head. "I have no idea. Maybe a mechanical problem. Or perhaps her captain is toying with *Monsoor*."

The technicians both looked at him, clearly not comprehending the turn of phrase. Constantis was about to explain when the phone from the bridge rang. He answered, spoke briefly to his second-in-command, then hung up.

"I am needed above," Constantis said.

"Is there a problem?"

"No, nothing critical." He was about to leave when it occurred to him that he would not see these two again until after the attack. "You remember the rendezvous point?"

Both nodded. Constantis turned toward the companionway and disappeared.

As he made his way above, Constantis passed the companionway that led to the engine room. He put a hand in his pocket and felt three reassuring shapes: a small but powerful Maglite, a pair of wire cutters, and an adjustable wrench. He had no illusions regarding what was about to happen: he and his shipmates were undertaking a military strike. They were doing so, however, not as uniformed soldiers or sailors, but as mercenaries. A few cast-off hirelings on a tramp vessel attacking one of the most powerful military ships on earth. Only he and the two Chinese were privy to the scheme, and by no coincidence, their escape was carefully arranged. The rest of the crew were little more than cannon fodder, yet if they were competent, they would find their way to the lifeboats and survive. And if they weren't? *Then they should never have gone to sea.*

The moment the missile launched, Constantis would have one final chore. He would immediately go below and perform a sequence he'd been rehearsing for days. The first task was to disable the operating bilge pumps, cutting premarked wires at two separate electrical junctions. Next, he would manually open six seacock valves with the wrench. Three were easily reached, yet the others necessitated crawling through cramped, grimy spaces in the deepest bowels of the hull. Hence the flashlight.

He estimated he could do it all in no more than fifteen minutes. After that, he and the two technicians would meet at the fantail and lower the fiberglass runabout. With calm seas forecast all night, the crossing to Tobruk should take no more than a few hours. There they would be met at the pier and transferred immediately to a waiting turboprop at the airport. A quick flight to Tunis, then Constantis would part with the others, the three of them scattering like leaves in a gale.

He reached the bridge, checked *Poyarka*'s heading, and found it well within the desired range. He looked forward and saw the launch door opening on the golf ball. The rest of the dome remained in place, and because the missile would lift off over the bow, it was not visible from the bridge. Constantis was glad for that—it saved him explaining to the crew why a research ship was carrying what was obviously a weapon. He'd heard a few rumors—all good captains knew their ship's scuttlebutt—but the dome had remained strictly off-limits aside from Wu and Chou, and the rest of the crew seemed oblivious to the danger.

Constantis thought back to his one look at the missile. It was a futuristic device, twenty feet long with a thin wedge shape. The exterior surface was odd, something between metal and ceramic. He wondered how it actually worked. He'd seen the map display below, so he knew there were dozens of ships in the target area. How would it discern which one to strike? Could it pick out *Kuznetsov* by her mere size? Her exact position? He'd wanted to ask Chou but decided against it. His employer, Bagdani, had been cagey when it came to details. Or perhaps he was equally in the dark. Constantis had been given just enough to fulfill his part of the mission, and he guessed Chou and Wu were equally compartmentalized.

He saw movement on the foredeck—the rail telescoping out from the opening in the dome. Constantis had put *Poyarka* in position, and now everything relied on the men in the control room. They were sixty miles from *Kuznetsov*, which seemed excessive, yet according to Chou that was far closer to the missile's *minimum* range than its maximum—it took that long to reach top speed.

A call on the special handset from below. Constantis answered and heard Chou.

"The target is nearly in alignment. We expect to launch in twelve minutes. Keep us stable until then."

The line went dead. Constantis put the device back in his pocket, thinking, *The next time I remove it will be to throw it into the sea.*

He looked at the helmsman and saw him busy on the thruster, holding *Poyarka* steady.

After so much preparation, it was time.

SIXTY-NINE

"Where the hell have you been?" Sorensen asked. "I've been trying to reach you at Mossad."

"I've been otherwise engaged," Slaton said. "Long story, but I found Lazarus."

"Who is he?"

"Actually, it's a matter of who he *was*."

"David—"

"Not now, Anna. He gave me something you need to act on right away. Another ship is being targeted, and the strike is imminent." He gave her Eitan's dying words.

"*Admiral Kuznetsov?*" she repeated incredulously. "The Russian carrier?"

"The one and only."

"Hang on!"

In the background he heard her giving orders to locate the ship. It didn't take long. "All right," she said. "*Kuznetsov* is in the Med, apparently on her way to Tartus."

"I'm guessing you have ships shadowing her?"

More questions, more waiting, then, "Yeah. At the moment she's being followed by *Monsoor*, a guided missile destroyer, and one of our own CIA SIGINT boats. Any idea what kind of attack we're talking about?"

"Hypersonic missile."

"*What?* How could—"

"There's no time to explain, Anna! This attack is about to happen. By my understanding, if it really is a hypersonic missile, there is no defense. Your only chance is to interdict, find the boat carrying this missile before it launches."

"Any clues on that?"

"Nothing new. It has to be the ship Bagdani mentioned, the one that sailed from Sri Lanka. I'd look for what we've already seen twice. Not a flagged naval vessel, but a civilian ship somewhere in the area."

"Okay, I'm on it."

"There's one other thing to consider. If it's true, this is a reversal. Not an attack on America that might have come from Russia . . ."

"But an attack on the flagship of the Russian Navy. And with an American missile boat in the area."

"Exactly, which means the fallout could be catastrophic. But there is one way to lessen the risk."

"What's that?"

Slaton told her.

Sorensen didn't hesitate. "I think you're right—I'm on that too."

Sorensen cut the call with Slaton and immediately placed a series of others. Speed of communications was a prime function of command centers, and in that moment Sorensen was thankful for it. Her first call was to the president.

She explained the situation to Cleveland, and relayed Slaton's suggestion: that the intelligence regarding an attack on *Admiral Kuznetsov* be immediately shared with the Russians. The president agreed and placed a hotline call to Moscow.

Sorensen next dialed the chief of naval operations. The Navy relayed the details of the impending attack to *Monsoor,* whose captain immediately called the ship to general quarters. *Monsoor*'s formidable suite of scanned array radars, both X-band and S-band, began searching the sea and sky in an electronic storm.

Her antennae covered a full 360 degrees, and data links with satellite assets both filled in blank spots and corroborated the ship's own returns. For a time, nothing showed up that hadn't already been seen. *Kuznetsov,* which was inexplicably slowing, had come to a virtual standstill thirteen miles north. *Monsoor* herself had slowed accordingly, barely making headway. The sensor specialists were told to give special emphasis to unidentified vessels—an ominous sign given what had befallen *Ross* days earlier.

It was a link to an overhead satellite that provided the first warning: an infrared bloom at the bow of a mystery target far to the south. The suddenness and intensity of the signature could have only one meaning.

"Missile launch!" said the petty officer monitoring the screen.

Hypersonic missiles, by design, are inherently destabilizing weapons. They breach the gap between tactical and strategic, between first strike and retaliatory, and are capable of delivering both conventional and nuclear payloads. They travel at speeds that give adversaries little time in which to make tectonic decisions, and less yet to react. Even if a response were to be ordered, no effective countermeasures have yet been fielded: antimissile systems existed to engage ballistic missiles, and anti-aircraft systems were effective against aircraft and cruise missiles. The gap between the two, however, the domain of hypersonic weapons, remained an unsolved problem.

The missile surging off *Poyarka*'s foredeck was a Lingyun-2. For years China had been performing research on hypersonic technologies, and the Lingyun-2 demonstrator was a stepping-stone on that path. Built by Chengdu Research Corporation, a state-owned defense conglomerate, the missile had spent five years in development, two more in testing. At that point, two years earlier, the program had been scrapped in favor of more promising variants. This was typical of research and development across the globe. Weapons were conceived, designed, tested, and often discarded in favor of the next bright shiny object. The lessons learned were often applied to the next generation. Designers and engineers were repurposed in the same way, as were laboratories and equipment. Left in the wake of this technological churn were a handful of test vehicles that transitioned, virtually overnight, from cutting edge to obsolete. Some were simply scrapped, while others endured destructive testing. A few found their way into museums.

The last prototype of the Lingyun-2 program had, for over a year, sat in cold storage in a quiet warehouse on the outskirts of Nanchong. It might have been forgotten had the former head of Chengdu Research not formed an organization known as The Trident. The missile was quietly resurrected, as was an experimental pulsed laser built by another conglomerate, and an electronic warfare suite designed to impair the navigation of enemy ships.

And just like that, under a new umbrella organization, the "arsenal the unproven" was given its shot at glory.

SEVENTY

The missile flew off the rail in a maelstrom of smoke and fire. Much of the dome that had been its home for months melted in its wake. It rose on a near-vertical trajectory, the sleek form clawing skyward initially under rocket propulsion. A trail of white smoke was clear in the fading light, a catch-me-if-you-can taunt as it climbed straight up for nearly six miles.

At that point the aft-mounted elevons adjusted the flight path ever so slightly, and the wedge-shaped nose settled northward as speed continued to build. Passing Mach 3.4, over 2,500 miles per hour, the rocket shut down and the high-Mach engine took over. It was called a scramjet, a method of propulsion in which a shaped duct compressed air, added fuel, and maintained combustion in the supersonic airflow.

The Lingyun-2 kept accelerating, and its altitude peaked in the thin air seventy-two thousand feet above the sea, twice the height generally flown by commercial airliners. This put the scramjet in its optimum envelope. The speed passed Mach 4. Then Mach 5.

Had the airframe and propulsion engineers who'd designed the Lingyun-2 ever seen the data—and they never would—they would have been proud of its performance. Also working flawlessly was its navigation system, an onboard inertial platform, backed by BeiDou, China's copycat version of GPS. Most impressive of all were the coatings on the missile's outer skin that endured the scalding heat generated by such extreme speeds.

With everything working perfectly, the Lingyun-2 tracked toward its target and nosed over right on schedule. At that point, the missile was little more than a rocket-powered roller coaster poised for the big drop.

With the ship already at general quarters, the announcement of a missile launch in *Monsoor*'s combat information center was met with steely determination.

"Say position!" barked Lagarde.

"Due south, range forty-nine miles. One of the distant civilian targets."

The X-band radar immediately backed up the satellite warning, locking on to a fast-rising return. Passing sixty thousand feet, the trajectory began to flatten. The target's speed readout was spinning up like a slot machine paying out a jackpot.

In an observation of great significance, but one that didn't register in the moment, the CIC watch officer said, "It's coming our way, but I think it's going to fly right over our heads."

"We have to try to take it down. Prepare to launch Sparrows," Lagarde said, referring to the Mk.57 quad-launcher loaded with four Evolved Sea-Sparrow missiles.

The order was acknowledged, and a battery of surface-to-air missiles were spun up for launch.

Radar said, "I have a good lock on the target but . . . holy crap!"

"What?" asked Lagarde.

"You won't believe how fast this thing is moving! And high . . . *really high*! It's way outside the envelope for our missiles."

The captain thought about it for only an instant. "Doesn't matter—we do what we can. Fire Control, launch when you have the best geometry!"

Eleven miles north, *Admiral Kuznetsov* lay dead in the water. Her pro-pellers were still as engineers dealt with the blown boiler, and her escort group had slowed to a crawl, steaming lazy circles to wait the situation out. Two miles distant, her dedicated tug was steaming closer as a precaution.

Captain Stepanov stood on the bridge sipping coffee. He was in no hurry. He'd been through this drill before, all too often, really, and was confident his engineers could solve the problem. An hour, maybe two, and they would once again be limping along.

He drained his mug and was weighing a refill when a sharp voice said, "Captain! I have an urgent message from Fleet command . . ."

The four missiles launched from *Monsoor* amounted to little more than a fireworks display. The geometry was straightforward, yet what the mis-siles were being asked to do was simply outside their aerodynamic enve-lope. Far, far outside. It wasn't like hitting a bullet with a bullet—more like hitting a meteorite with one.

Of the four Evolved SeaSparrows launched, three lost lock on their tar-get and simply went ballistic, six-hundred-pound explosive darts setting sail into the Mediterranean twilight. The fourth held on, only just, and ended up in a hopeless tail-chase with a target flying five times its own speed—a Model T chasing a Ferrari that was running flat out. In the end, the Sparrow's motor ran out of propellant, sputtered once, and a million-dollar projectile fell sizzling into the sea.

The Lingyun-2 was by then traveling more than a mile each second. It had so far been guided purely by position data: the missile was flying to a preprogrammed coordinate set, updated moments before launch, that would put it in the neighborhood of *Admiral Kuznetsov*. From that point, which was fast approaching, terminal guidance would kick in for the final twenty-mile run. This was obtained through sensors, one radar and one optical, that looked "over the nose" of the missile to seek out the target.

Once verified by software, commands to the steering surfaces would guide the missile to a strike in the final seconds.

And this was where everything began to go wrong.

The missile's radar software, adapted from another program, came with a feature that filtered out ground clutter. It did this by assuming that any returns displaying zero speed could be eliminated as terrain. The result was that *Admiral Kuznetsov,* now a great stationary blip on the sea, was written off by the software as being an island. It was the kind of error that would have been sorted out in operational testing, yet the Lingyun-2 had never gone past the experimental stage.

Things only got worse from there. The targeting system reverted to backup algorithms and locked on to the nearest moving object: two miles away, a far smaller return moving at twelve knots. This was the ocean-going tug hurrying to assist *Kuznetsov.*

The missile's steering did its best to guide toward a target barely a hundred feet in length. The tug had a stout build, yet the Lingyun-2 was meant to strike targets ten times her size. The missile did its best in the terminal moments of its blazing life, its elevons working furiously to correct the glide path.

The 250-pound warhead, a kinetic energy penetrator, was designed to pierce the armor plating of capital ships. Milliseconds before impact the warhead detonated, creating thousands of shards of metal that converted into molten jets. Had it struck a target like *Admiral Kuznetsov,* the super-heated matter would have cut through deck after deck in an expanding fireball of destruction.

What happened was far less dramatic.

The missile struck the tugboat's forward windlass at over four thousand miles an hour. Instead of a domino-like transfer of energy and deck-by-deck annihilation, however, the warhead flew through the tug's foredeck like a flaming arrow through paper. After that came one bulkhead and the thin hull, before its massive shock wave was absorbed by the sea. For the tug the impact was predictably fatal, the forward twenty feet of its bow simply disappearing, much of the wood and metal vaporized. Beneath a cascade of thrown water, the remains of the crippled boat plowed ahead another hundred feet before nosing headlong into the sea like a diving duck.

The tug's crew consisted of six Russians, and by sheer good fortune all were either aft or in the protected wheelhouse. Three men were blown clear into the water. The stunned captain, who had no idea what hit him, was slammed to the deck behind the helm as the windows around him imploded. When he managed to stand, covered in shards of glass and debris, he had the distinct sensation he was leaning forward, like a surfer going down the face of a wave. After one look through the empty frame where the forward windscreen had been, and seeing nothing but blue water, he shouted the order to abandon what remained of his ship.

Most of the evidence was claimed by the sea.

Monsoor closed in on *Admiral Kuznetsov,* and quickly established that no damage had been done to Russia's flagship. The same could not be said for her remora-like tugboat, which had disappeared from radar after taking what appeared to be a direct hit from the missile. A frigate from *Kuznetsov*'s battle group could be seen plucking crewmen out of the water, and a minor oil slick reflected moonlight on the table-flat sea.

Once *Kuznetsov*'s survival was confirmed, *Monsoor* received follow-on orders to pursue the ship that had launched the missile. Proceeding at top speed, she arrived ninety minutes later to find the aft ten meters of what looked like a small freighter jackknifing from the water, her barnacle-encrusted stern lifted high amid burbles of venting air. Captain Lagarde studied the ship in the beams of *Monsoor*'s powerful spotlights, and as she scythed down in her dying moments amid a minor field of flotsam, the name on her fantail became clear: *Poyarka.*

The name would soon undergo intense scrutiny in the halls of Langley and the Pentagon, yet in that moment it meant nothing to anyone on *Monsoor.* When Lagarde noticed two lifeboats bobbing nearby, it almost came as a relief: finally, a problem he could handle. As demanded by maritime custom and international law, if not common decency, he immediately ordered his crew to rescue seven cold, wet, and disoriented sailors from the unrelenting sea.

SEVENTY-ONE

Slaton had never been to Camp David before, and it was smaller than he imagined.

He sat on the wooden deck of Dogwood Cabin, the unit he'd been assigned yesterday evening. After arriving at Dulles on a commercial flight, he was collected by a car arranged by Sorensen. The mostly silent driver had delivered him here.

Slaton had done nothing since but sleep, recharging from a blur of travel and time zones and punishing operations. His abdomen was bruised where his vest had taken a bullet, and there was a minor gash on his back from the encounter with shifting aircraft wreckage under the Arctic ice cap. A dozen other aches and bruises were a virtual catalogue of recent hardships, yet for Slaton one stood out above the others: the calluses on one palm he'd gotten from digging a grave in Albania. He did his best to ignore it, to recalibrate to the civilized world. That was always the challenge after missions, yet this one had been particularly troubling.

The Adirondack chair was comfortable, the mug of black coffee strong. He'd come across a guest log in the cabin, complete with historical photographs, and so he knew countless world leaders had occupied this unit. Presidents and kings, foreign ministers and diplomats, all mingling and plotting in the arboreal stillness. Slaton never considered making his own entry. Others could seek their spotlights, live in the world of the overt, but for all the risks and scars, he was content where he was—quietly making a difference on the opposite end of the spectrum.

Spring had come early to Maryland, new foliage budding on trees, perennials bursting from perfectly tended beds. He'd been told the compound's hiking trails were open, and while they were probably spectacular, he wasn't so inclined. Slaton pinged between two worlds, one predictable and bucolic, the other haphazard and perilous. It had become his ritual— perhaps even a superstition, for a man who held few—to separate his two lives, to put clear lines between them. He would save hiking for the Bitterroots. For Davy and Christine.

And with that in mind, he made one allowance.

Slaton reached for his phone.

Christine tapped her phone on the second ring, the length of time it took her to stir awake, roll over, and recognize the incoming number.

"Hey," she said, a red-sky dawn stirring in the transom window.

"Hey," he replied.

No two words between them had ever been simpler. Or more complete. She felt as if she'd been holding her breath for a week.

"How are you?" she asked, knowing it was a loaded question.

"I'm good. You?"

"Never better."

"Davy?"

"I can barely keep up."

"Hope I didn't wake you."

"Of course you did, but I'll give you a pass . . . just this once."

They talked for ten minutes about everything and nothing. Less to exchange information than to hear each other's voices. Christine covered Davy's adventures at preschool, her volunteer work as a physician at the senior's clinic. She told him a guy was coming next week to give an estimate on the barn roof. It was all boring and delicious, baby steps back to normalcy.

He concentrated on the future tense, as if the last week hadn't happened. He was explaining his plans for a camping excursion to explore the ridgeline behind their house when Christine heard a *whumping* sound in the call's background.

He broke off what he was saying. "Sorry, babe . . . I've got to go. There's somebody I need to see."

"What's her name?"

"Elayne."

"Is she better looking than me?"

A pause. "Uh . . . no."

"You took a long time to answer."

"It's complicated, but trust me—she's not in your league."

Christine smiled behind her handset.

He said, "I can tell you she's a woman who doesn't like to be kept waiting."

"Neither am I."

"Point taken." Then, after a few beats, "God I've missed you."

"Yeah . . . you too."

"I'll be home soon," he said, not giving a day or time.

She didn't ask for one. "We're looking forward to seeing you—both of us." She almost added something else but decided against it.

The sound in the background grew intense as the call ended.

Christine sat up in bed, swiveled her feet to the floor, and set the phone back on the nightstand. The red LEDs on the bedside clock read 7:10. Davy would be awake soon. Her eyes shifted from the clock to what was next to it. She picked it up and smiled, thinking, *Not over the phone—I want to watch you when I say it.*

Twirling in her fingertips was a cheap plastic stick. It was mostly white, but one end was cut by a solid blue chemical line.

Marine One swept in low and fast, thundering to a landing in a nearby clearing. Through a break in the trees, Slaton watched as the stairs lowered and two familiar figures emerged: President Elayne Cleveland flanked by Anna Sorensen.

Slaton's valet—a first for him—had explained he was to remain at his cabin. Sure enough, he watched them advance up a connecting path trailed by a half dozen Secret Service agents. As they neared, the agents dispersed. The president of the United States and a deputy director of the CIA climbed the stairs to the deck looking like a pair of Airbnb hosts.

"You look comfortable," the president said.

"Life is looking up," he said, standing to shake hands with them both.

Cleveland and Sorensen settled into sloped-back chairs of their own.

"You look better than I envisioned, given what you went through," Sorensen commented.

"Thanks . . . I think."

"Director Nurin's version of what happened in the Negev was pretty dramatic."

"Body armor is a wonderful thing, but it does leave a mark."

Cleveland asked, "How are the Israelis handling things on their end?"

"Mossad sent a cleanup team down to the Negev. I debriefed them afterward. I'm sure there will be some soul-searching at Mossad, but the threat is behind them now."

"And Anton?" Sorensen asked. "How is he holding up?"

Slaton's reply was measured. "How can anyone hold up to something like that? His only child was killed because of mistakes made years ago. Operation Starlight came back to haunt us. We mistakenly left a man behind, and the Syrians broke him in every sense. There was plenty of blame to go around, some of it mine—I led that mission."

Sorensen said, "Trust me when I say, I know how it is—sometimes there are no good options. Based on what Nurin told me, if you'd gone back for Eitan that night it could have turned into a disaster."

"We'll never know."

"But the larger question remains," the president said.

"Who was Eitan working for?" Slaton said, finishing the thought.

Sorensen provided the latest. "We still don't know. It seems almost certain this Trident group is linked to China. We have physical evidence from Raven 44, the sinking of *Ross,* and now the failed attack on *Admiral Kuznetsov.* Unfortunately, none of that is a slam dunk, just bits and pieces: signals intelligence, projected capability reports, interviews with a few of the crewmen we tracked down from *Atlas.*"

"About that," Slaton said. "Did you ever figure out if anyone was on board when she blew up and sank?"

"Our standing theory is that the entire crew got off in Eritrea. From there, we think the ship went autonomous and sailed a preprogrammed course, although there's a chance it was being controlled remotely."

"Is that a thing? Drone ships?"

"This day and age, very much so. We'll probably never know exactly how it worked, but in essence, *Atlas* ended up as a fifty-ton IED. We think it was detonated remotely—they were probably watching the boarding team using either onboard cameras or a satellite. We're not the only ones with eyes in the sky. It put our sailors at risk and sent the evidence to the bottom of the sea."

"Pretty clever, in a sick way."

"On another angle, we've been working with Mossad to identify the sniper you killed. So far, it's a dead end. His DNA confirms Chinese ethnicity, but beyond that the trail goes cold."

"Can't say I'm surprised," he said. "This all reminds me of Russia's Wagner Group." He was referring to the private company that did President Petrov's dirty work: military operations outside the normal chain of command.

"But with far more advanced weapons," Sorensen agreed. "We're doing our best to source the devices used. If we could figure out where they were designed and built, it might tell us who had access. So far, there's nothing firm."

"Whoever is behind it, I doubt they're finished. The last mission failed, but I'm guessing they view the other two as successes."

"We can only assume The Trident will remain active. The crewmen we recovered after *Poyarka* went down were no more than contract labor. The only ones who knew what the ship was up to, apparently, were the captain and two engineers, and they somehow disappeared."

"More degrees of separation."

"No doubt. I suspect the only ones who ever had direct contact with this Trident organization were Eitan and possibly Bagdani. Now they've become the ultimate cutouts."

Slaton diverted his gaze to the forest and seemed to study it for a time. "How do things stand with the Russians?" he finally asked.

Cleveland answered, "Not great, but war is off the table. Petrov is still simmering about what happened on Wrangel Island. Thankfully, you got word to us just in time about the attack on *Kuznetsov*. It was set up to have the missile fly directly over *Monsoor*."

"Trying to make it look like an American strike," Slaton suggested.

"The Russians might still be wondering if we hadn't taken your advice and warned them. For the time being, Petrov is wary. But he's not going to declare war over a sunken tugboat. Basically, we've settled into an uneasy status quo, everyone treading carefully. In the meantime, we need to learn more about The Trident and cut it off at the source."

"And we watch China like a hawk," Sorensen added.

"If that's who's funding it, I wouldn't be surprised to see The Trident go dormant. China is good at the long game. It could be six months, maybe a year before you hear from them again."

"Very possible," Sorensen agreed.

"And Jammer?" he asked. "How is he holding up?"

"Jammer is Jammer."

"Did he mention his new call sign . . . Ahab?"

Sorensen's curious look implied he hadn't.

Slaton grinned. "He's a keeper, Anna."

"Maybe so."

One of the president's aides appeared on the path and twirled a finger in the air. Cleveland stood. "I've got a meeting with the Japanese foreign minister." She held out her hand a second time, and said, "I came to thank you, David. You saved our ass, and not for the first time."

He shook her hand. "I had a personal interest in this one."

"If you'd like to stay for a day or two, I can arrange it."

"Thanks, but I've got plans."

"Fair enough. Enjoy your time off." Cleveland was soon walking away down the tree-lined path, her security falling in like a string of train cars. It left Slaton and Sorensen alone on the deck.

"I'd like a debriefing this morning," she said, "but we can make it short. I know you want to get home."

"I do . . . but there's one thing I need to take care of first."

"What's that?" Sorensen asked.

Slaton was silent for a time, then gave a slow shake of his head, and said, "It's something I want to handle on my own."

SEVENTY-TWO

As a general rule, habits in life are healthy. Volumes of empirical data shore the idea, medical studies that prove consistent hours of sleep, regular meals, and routine exercise are conducive to longevity. The concept is virtually universal, no exceptions made for age, gender, or socioeconomic status, and are uniform across all surveyed professions. There is, however, one outlier. For all their expertise and rigorous methodology, the researchers who authored the studies never thought to include crime bosses in their modeling.

Dragan Xhaka had long survived by avoiding habits. He traveled at irregular intervals, and rarely abroad. He made random forays to nightclubs, never with forewarning, and always in the company of heavy security. At no point in his life had he kept an office, preferring to meet with lawyers and accountants in random safe houses. Yet for all that unpredictability, Xhaka did have one ritual. Each morning, immediately after waking and drinking a single cup of coffee, he undertook a routine that never varied.

He had loved to swim since he was a child, and because of it he'd had a lap pool installed at his residence. It was an outdoor pool, tightly confined between the house and a courtyard wall. This was the only space the builder could find to install what Xhaka wanted: one twenty-five-meter lanc of blue-aqua coolness with a line of black tile down the center. There was another pool in the rear courtyard, a more artful, free-form variety with waterfalls and grottos and a bikini-detaching waterslide. This was the site of the legendary parties—girls, booze, and drugs in an overchlorinated bacchanalia—that Xhaka never personally attended.

The lap pool, however, was his and his alone.

Every morning, rain or shine, even in the depths of winter—the temperature was regulated to a constant seventy-five degrees—Xhaka dropped in and swam fifty laps. He had long ago timed his workouts but relented when the numbers began to rise. He'd been gaining weight in recent years, and became short of breath during exertion. Shoulder surgery restricted him to a few modified strokes, and his buoyancy had increased with his weight. Still, the swim was the anchor of his day. The same exercise, in the same place, every morning.

His security chief had warned him of the risk, yet Xhaka was not put off. "They're going to get me one day," he said, referring to his enemies, of whom there were many.

So it was, when the shot came one calm morning, it wasn't a surprise. Not really.

The bullet froze Xhaka in the middle of his breaststroke sequence, dead center in the pool. There was no splash or shout, no sound of any kind. The Serb simply stopped swimming, ending up in a dead man's float at the ten-meter mark, the crystalline water around him going red.

His security detail was caught off guard, but they responded as best they could. The man in charge called for an ambulance, although everyone could see it was no use. The rest drew their weapons, called in reinforcements, and within minutes teams were scouring the nearby hills.

When they came up empty-handed, the chief of security decided to call the police. The ambulance took half an hour to arrive, in part because the compound was remote, and in part because the four EMTs on duty had taken the time to draw straws: the locals rarely went near the boss's compound. The police were even slower to respond, but they showed up in the end.

Owing to Xhaka's ignoble past, few in the community shed tears at his passing, and talk in the pubs that afternoon ran closer to gossip than mourning. In the next days, however, official interest began to rise. The reasons were varied, but always bred of self-interest. The local police commissioner, who'd long been in Xhaka's pocket, had suddenly lost a prime source of income. Even more concerningly, he recognized that a rival mob would surely make a move on Xhaka's territory, and getting to the bottom of his murder might foretell which way the winds were blowing.

The Albanian State Police, an arm of the Ministry of Internal Affairs, had also had quiet dealings with Xhaka. Authorities in Macedonia and Kosovo, where Xhaka's territory overlapped, expressed concerns as well, leading to the involvement of those foreign ministries. There was even a plea from the Albanian prime minister, who took particular interest in any videos that might have been left behind in the safe at the newly departed's residence.

The upshot of it all was that the national police began a monumental effort to get to the bottom of Dragan Xhaka's murder. The nation's top detectives were brought in to solve the crime, and all national resources were put at their disposal.

The direction from which the single shot had come was easily determined, and legions of police officers were dispatched to scour the nearby hills. They covered every inch of terrain for nearly two miles in line abreast formation. At that point, the crest of a hill sank away to the neighboring valley.

The only discovery of note, half a mile from Xhaka's villa, was a matted down area of pine needles beside a trail. Experts went over the spot to test for gunpowder residue or any other evidence they could harvest. Their main discovery turned out to be traces of reproductive DNA—by testing, of Albanian ethnicity—that suggested an amorous encounter. Things clarified further when a detective uncovered a discarded thong beneath a nearby bush.

The ballistics specialists seemed the best hope for a break. Precise calculations were made to nail down the range, angle, and type of propellant used to send one .338 Lapua Magnum round through Dragan Xhaka's heart. The Albanian Army's best snipers were even brought in to give advice. They surveyed the scene and gave their opinions on how and where a shooter might have set up. These spots were given intense scrutiny, but still nothing was found.

Every person who lived within two miles of the search area was interviewed, asked if they'd seen anything or anyone unusual in the hours leading up to the shooting. All professed ignorance, although to be fair, in those traumatized hills it was rare to find a witness who would admit to the rising of the sun.

The inquest continued for a full month. At that point, certain politicians in Tirana began questioning why so much time and money were being spent to track down the killer of a known crime boss and probable war criminal. Once again, rumors began circulating of a video that might have been in Xhaka's possession, something involving the prime minister in a highly compromising group setting. The prime minister emphatically denied the speculation, and soon after the investigation ended abruptly.

In the end, the inquiry proved no more than an exercise in frustration. In the matter of Dragan Xhaka's death, there were a thousand suspects with a thousand motives, yet not a shred of physical evidence to suggest which of them was responsible. No casing, no sign of powder residue. No shooter's hide pressed into the forest floor. No sightings of strangers by neighbors or suspect arrivals at airports. No suspicious cars or weapon purchases. No unresolved thefts of motor scooters or bicycles.

The police, the army, the investigators of two nearby countries, not to mention five neighboring and very concerned crime families, threw up their hands in collective surrender.

It was as if Dragan Xhaka had been killed by a ghost.

ACKNOWLEDGMENTS

Every writer begins as a reader. With that in mind, I'd like to give a long overdue thanks those who came before me. To Robert Ludlum, Tom Clancy, and Vince Flynn, the giants of their day, and Frederick Forsyth and Ken Follet who remain, quite justifiably, at the top of so many bedside TBR piles. To Daniel Silva whose elegant prose seems so effortless (trust me, it's not), and Lee Child who proved that less can be more.

From that foundation, others are ably carrying military and spy thrillers forward. Brad Thor and Kyle Mills have set a new standard. To Mark Greaney, Jack Carr, Marc Cameron, Brad Taylor, Tony Tata, Simon Gervais, Tim Tigner, Jeff Wilson, and Brian Andrews: it's been a pleasure getting to know you all at ThrillerFest, Bouchercon, and beyond.

Thanks as well to Best Thriller Books, *The Crew Reviews* podcast, and *The Real Book Spy* for helping spread the word. To James Abt, the architect of BTB, and his team of "super-readers" who put so much time and effort into making it a success. Chris, Derek, Kashif, Sarah, Steve, Stuart, Todd, David, Ankit: your enthusiasm is uplifting.

Much appreciation to my agent, Susan Gleason, for her patience and enthusiasm. We've been working together a long time, and it's always been a pleasure.

Tor/Forge publishing is simply the best. Much gratitude to Robert Davis, Eileen Lawrence, Libby Collins, and Jennifer McClelland-Smith— your work has been, and will remain, essential. A special thanks to Debbie Friedman for putting up with my stylistic incompetence.

I'm blessed to have worked for many years with Bob Gleason—there is no better editor in the business. Thanks also to Robert Allen and Katy Robitzski at Macmillan Audio, and of course to the incomparable P.J. Ochlan for bringing David Slaton to life with his spot-on narration.

Brian Andrews (again) and Louis Rudbart were especially helpful in advancing my understanding of submarines, destroyers, and the nuances of naval operations. Any errors remaining are on me.

I'd also like to thank the professionals at Southwest Airlines who make my "day job" so enjoyable. The pilots and flight attendants I work with there are second to none, as are the flight operations instructors who resurrected my sorry skills after a year of COVID-19–induced dormancy, and who got me up to speed on the MAX-8.

Finally, thanks as ever to my family. Rose, Kara, Lance, and Jack— you've been there for me all along, and I know you always will be.